celg

THE CRYSTAL CAVE
TRILOGY

THE CRYSTAL CAVE
TRILOGY

SUSAN WITTIG ALBERT

THORNDIKE PRESS
A part of Gale, a Cengage Company

GALE
A Cengage Company

Thorndike Press® Large Print Mystery.
The text of this Large Print edition is unabridged.
Other aspects of the book may vary from the original edition.
Set in 16 pt. Plantin.

LIBRARY OF CONGRESS CIP DATA ON FILE.
CATALOGUING IN PUBLICATION FOR THIS BOOK
IS AVAILABLE FROM THE LIBRARY OF CONGRESS

ISBN-13: 978-1-4328-8224-2 (hardcover alk. paper)

Published in 2020 by arrangement with Levine/Greenberg Literary Agency, Inc

Printed in Mexico
Print Number: 01   Print Year: 2020

CONTENTS

■ ■ ■ ■

NoBODY

BOOK 1

■ ■ ■ ■

The great advantage about telling the
truth is that nobody ever believes it.
                                    Dorothy L. Sayers

Nobody gets justice. People only get
good luck or bad luck.
                                    Orson Wells

PROLOGUE

The dream came to Ruby Wilcox for the first time on Saturday night.

It had been a busy week at the Crystal Cave — Ruby's wonderful little shop, still the only metaphysical shop in Pecan Springs, Texas. It was August, when she always did the late-summer inventory, getting ready to stock up for the coming fall and winter. On Wednesday and Thursday evenings, she had led workshops for the local Wiccan group on using divination tools — tarot, runestones, crystals, pendulums, and scrying. On Saturday, she had taken her daughter Amy and Amy's beautiful toddler, Grace, out for lunch. And on Saturday evening, she had spent a couple of hours working out at her new gym, Body Matters. So she was tired enough to fall asleep right away, even with Pagan (the black cat who had shown up at her kitchen door a few months before) snuggled up tight against the warm curve of her body.

But she hadn't slept well. Her muscles were already a little sore from her workout at the gym, and she spent several restless hours tossing through a series of uneasy dreams. But they were only previews for the horror-movie nightmare that jerked her awake with a stifled shriek an hour before dawn.

In her dream, she was standing concealed in a thicket under a live oak tree beside the hike-and-bike trail that ran along the river north of Pecan Park. But she wasn't herself. She was . . . somebody else, a man, she couldn't tell who. She was inside his mind, witnessing his dark, ugly thoughts as he watched a woman in a pink shirt and white shorts running along the trail. This wasn't the first time he had watched this woman, or the first place. And as he watched, he was consumed by a fiercely brutal pleasure, lingering over each ugly detail, seeing, tasting, fantasizing.

And then Ruby woke. She was drenched in sweat, her mouth paper-dry, her pulse racing, her heart banging like a drum in her chest. She had been inside the mind of the man who was thinking — no, *planning* — something unthinkable. She had been trapped in his thoughts like a frantic animal

14

in a cage, a cage that she couldn't escape.

She pulled the covers over her head and huddled in her bed, while the images in his mind smashed into her like brutal blows.

And that was only the first night.

CHAPTER ONE

It is Wednesday morning. Ruby Wilcox closes her cash register and steps out from behind the counter at the Crystal Cave.

"I probably won't be gone very long," she says. "But in case I'm held up, don't forget that the Friends of the Library have reserved the tea room for lunch. I don't have any classes scheduled and I'm not expecting any special problems. But if you —"

"Ruby," China says patiently, "you are driving across town, not trekking to India to visit your guru. Cass and Laurel and I can handle the shops and the tea room for a few hours." She gestures at the shelves where Ruby displays her magical wares — healing crystals, I Ching coins and yarrow sticks, Ouija boards, rune stones, pendulums, magic wands, Tarot cards, incense, and scented candles.

"If a customer wants a crystal ball or a Tibetan prayer flag and we can't locate what

17

she's looking for, we'll just tell her to come back when the swami is here." She frowns. "No, wait. 'Swami' is masculine. What do we call a female swami? A swama?"

Ruby wrinkles her freckled nose. "Please don't be snarky, China. I really don't want to talk to Sheila about this . . . this *thing,* you know. I'm mostly doing it because you think it's a good idea."

In spite of their occasional differences, Ruby and China Bayles are as close as sisters. They are partners in a multilayered enterprise that includes the Crystal Cave, China's Thyme and Seasons herb shop, a tea room, and a gourmet food and catering service called Party Thyme that they share with their friend and gourmet chef, Cass Wilde. Like all women who manage their own small businesses, they have faced a great many challenges together, some of them pretty hair-raising. But that has only drawn them closer.

This morning, Ruby has dressed to cheer herself up. Her orange tunic is off-the-shoulder and floaty, fun to wear over lime-colored leggings and open-toed sandals. Feeling the need for extra brightness, she has added an orange chiffon scarf and a half-dozen orange plastic bangle bracelets. It hasn't helped a lot. She still feels apprehensive and draggy, as if she's not getting enough sleep. Which is true. It's those dreams, those awful dreams.

China, on the other hand, is dressed in her usual shop uniform: jeans, sneakers, and a green Thyme and Seasons T-shirt. In her former life, she was a criminal defense attorney, and she still views the world from that skeptical, *uber*-rational point of view. When she has questions, she wants answers. When she doesn't get answers, she gets frustrated. She is frustrated now — not a surprise, given the weird dreams Ruby has told her about — and trying not to show it.

"I'm sorry," China says contritely. "I know you're uncomfortable about discussing your dreams with Sheila, but you'll feel better after you've got this off your chest. Maybe you can even talk her into doing something. Like putting a couple of patrol officers on the hike-and-bike trail?"

Ruby understands that China doesn't always believe her when she comes up with something out of left field, like the dreams she has just told her about. But she also knows that China always believes *in* her, which is much more important. She has never not given Ruby the benefit of the doubt.

Talking to Sheila Dawson, Pecan Springs'

chief of police, is China's idea, and Ruby has reluctantly agreed. She can think of a dozen things she would rather do at the Cave this morning, like sweep the floor and dust the crystal display and restock the bookshelves. Sheila and Ruby are longtime friends, but Sheila is even more left-brained than China. She lives in a cop's universe, where time is always linear, facts matter, and two and two can only make four: nothing more, nothing less, ever.

Still, Ruby has to admit that China, however skeptical, is right. If what she has seen in these dreams bears any relationship to the real world, it is definitely a police matter. A young woman is going to be kidnapped by a man who is stalking her. It's not the first time she has dreamed something and the dream has come true. But it's the first time in years that a dream has recurred over so many nights with such a frightening emphasis. If she doesn't report this and then reads the story in the *Enterprise* or sees it on the KXAN-TV news, she will be swallowed by guilt.

But Ruby also knows that prediction is fluid, untrustworthy. Events can be influenced by hundreds of factors, and outcomes are never cast in stone. If Sheila can be persuaded to put an extra patrol on the hike-and-bike trail, what Ruby has seen in those dreams might not happen. *If* Sheila can be persuaded. That *if* is as big as the *Titanic*. And what might happen after that is totally unpredictable.

"Once you've got that off your mind," China goes on, "why don't you take the rest of the day off? Even better, the rest of the week." She slides Ruby a concerned glance. "You've been working hard. You deserve a vacation."

For privacy's sake, Ruby usually hangs a Do Not Disturb sign on the door to her best friend's thoughts. But she doesn't need to be psychic to know that China is worried about her. Ruby had a mastectomy several years ago, and the threat of a recurrence of the cancer is always there, like a resentful has-been actress hanging out in the wings, hoping for one more chance at a starring role.

"I'm fine." Ruby holds up three fingers. "Girl Scout's honor. Cancer free."

It's true. She passed her recent checkup with flying colors and a congratulatory high five from her doctor. But this thing she's dealing with, this frightening dream — while it isn't cancer, it is terribly, maliciously malignant. Like the threat of cancer, it lurks on her inner horizon, an ugly, menacing cloud.

"And I really don't need a vacation," she adds defensively.

China gives an exaggerated eye-roll. "I didn't say you needed it, silly. I said you *deserved* it. Anyway, now is a good time to give yourself a little break. The last week of August is hardly our busiest time of year. We don't have any catering gigs, our workshops don't start for a few weeks, and there's nothing on the calendar that requires your urgent attention. Plus, I'm not sure that you've fully recovered from that bike crash a couple of weeks ago."

"That little accident?" Ruby says. She had ridden her bike into a tree and ended up with a mild concussion. The only trace of it was a healing scar just under her hairline. "That was nothing. Just a few headaches, that's all."

"Several massive headaches, some dizziness, and a blackout or two," China corrects her. "A few days' rest will do you good."

Ruby thinks about this for a moment. The concussion has given her more problems than she likes to admit, and it is certainly true that she's had a lot on her mind. In fact, the whole summer has been unsettled, what with one thing and another. She hasn't been getting enough sleep. Her appetite is flagging. And on top of that, the dreams.

"Well, I suppose I could take a few days off," she concedes reluctantly. "Maybe just until after Labor Day." Today is Wednesday, so that means she'll be back at work in less than a week.

"Terrific!" China says brightly, then remembers something and frowns. "Oh, I nearly forgot. Ramona called before you came in this morning. She wants to talk to you. She sounded . . . excited."

"Uh-oh," Ruby mutters. When her sister Ramona gets excited, things happen. Crazy things. Unpredictable things. "Did she say what she wanted to talk about?"

"You know Ramona." China waves her hand dismissively. "She has another great idea — something only the two of you can do together." Dryly, she adds, "She wouldn't tell *me,* of course."

"Of course," Ruby murmurs. Ramona is jealous of China. In the past, she has tried every trick in the book to come between her sister and her sister's best friend. This happens so often that China calls her Ruby's "evil twin," which sounds like a joke but isn't.

"If she calls you again," Ruby adds, "tell

her to phone my cell and stop bothering you."

"She likes to bother me. It gives meaning to her life." China makes a shooing motion with her hands. "Now, go and talk to Sheila. You'll feel better when you've got that thing off your mind."

Ruby seriously doubts that talking to Sheila will get "that thing" off her mind. It seems to be an endless loop in her brain, programmed to turn itself on ten minutes after she falls asleep and keep on playing all night. But whatever.

"Okay, China, it's all yours." Ruby picks up her handbag and slings it over her shoulder. "Hold the fort until after Labor Day. If you or Cass need me for anything —"

"We won't," China says, adding reassuringly, "Don't worry about the Cave or the tea room or anything else. Just open a bottle of wine, take off your clothes, and lie in the sun. Spend time at the gym. Go country dancing with your cowboy. Do whatever soothes your soul."

"Yes, ma'am," Ruby says dutifully, although lying naked in the Texas sun on a hot August day doesn't strike her as terribly smart. Also, it's been over a month since she's heard from her latest cowboy — Pete, who manages an olive ranch in the Hill Country west of Pecan Springs. She'd been on the brink of falling in love with him, but distance proved to be a powerful divider. Their attraction to one another wasn't strong enough to bridge it, and Ruby still hasn't gotten over the disappointment.

But she likes China's suggestion of the gym, definitely. The Pecan Springs Fitness Club, where she has been a member for ten years, closed a few months ago — financial troubles, she'd heard. She has a new membership at another fitness club. But she's been there only a couple of times since she joined, and she's eager to get back to her regular workout program.

Actually, the more she thinks about taking time off, the better she likes it. A few days away from the shop may restore her energies, give her a better perspective. And maybe even unplug that dream.

She leans forward and brushes her lips across China's cheek. "And please don't worry about me, sweetie. I'm fine."

"Really? *Are* you?" China holds her out at arm's length, eyes searching her face intently.

"Yes," Ruby says. "Really." She manages a bright smile. "Of course I am. I'm fine."

CHAPTER TWO

I'm fine.

Of course she isn't, and Ruby understands that saying it doesn't make it so. All her life, she has had to cope with being . . . well, different, which isn't fine at all. She inherited this aptitude (if that's what you wanted to call it) from her grandmother, who inherited it from her mother, who brought it from Ireland along with the red curls and freckles that run in the family. Her sister Ramona got a strong dose of the family gift, too, although she missed out on the discipline required to manage it. The gift seems to be somehow coded into her family's DNA.

But even though Ruby prefers not to think of herself as "psychic," she has to admit that she has remarkably strong intuition. Early in her life, she knew which team was going to win the softball game on the other side of town, or who was on the other end of the phone when it rang, or what her best friend would be wearing that day. She could even hear people's thoughts and feel their feelings. But no child wants to be different, so she was always struggling to pretend that this spooky stuff wasn't happening. She longed to be just like everybody else.

Ruby's friend Sophia D'Angelo (who teaches classes on intuition at the Cave and is very wise about such things) says that the same thing happens to a great many psychics when they are children. "People don't understand us," Sophia says. "We don't fit in. We're different. Which means that we try very hard to suppress who we are and what we can do, just so we can be like everybody else. And that's a shame, don't you think?"

As a teacher and coach, Sophia urges Ruby to learn to *use* her psychic abilities, rather than disavow them. "You won't be a whole person until you integrate all the parts of yourself," she often says. "You're a strong woman now, Ruby — imagine who you could be if you deliberately channeled your intuitive power."

But Ruby is still reluctant. She learned long ago the importance of avoiding situations where she might be tempted to use her abilities. Trespassing in another person's mind feels like an unpardonable invasion of privacy. When she's inadvertently drawn in, she gets out as fast as she can. She's uncomfortable when it comes to making predictions. What if she tells so-and-so that this-and-that may come about, and the person counts on it, and it doesn't happen? What gives her the right to tinker with other people's futures?

What's more, there are dark places in the human mind — in some minds, anyway — where she doesn't want to go. Hate is there, and fury and lust and revenge. Terrifying fantasies, primitive instincts, irresistible urges, obsessions. Once she's swimming inside somebody's head, she runs the risk of drowning in whatever's in there, no matter how ugly and hateful it is.

So she stays on shore. The Crystal Cave is safe for her. It's a sheltering haven where she can flirt with the fun of being psychic without being swallowed up by it. She's okay (she's *fine*) with little parlor tricks, like the readings she does for friends with her Ouija board or the I Ching or the tarot. But even those can be risky when something serious shows up and she feels duty-bound to plunge into it. So she sets limits. She's careful not to get sucked into somebody's stuff, unless it's so compelling she can't help herself.

When that happens — and it does, sometimes — it's a huge drain on her emotional and physical energies. It's like being suddenly charged by an enormous power surge or jolted by a mini-lightning bolt. She's plugged in, turned on, energized, manic, even. When the power goes off, the energy ebbs swiftly and she's drained, exhausted, limp. It takes a while to become herself again.

She's afraid, sometimes, that she won't.

Pecan Springs is halfway between Austin and San Antonio, on the eastern rim of the ruggedly beautiful Texas Hill Country. Ruby was raised here (unlike China, who is a refugee from Houston), and she's watched the town grow and change — for the better, some say; others, for the worse.

About growth, Ruby is ambivalent. She loves having lots of customer traffic in her shop; she doesn't love getting stuck in traffic when she goes shopping. Tourists are terrific when they're browsing the shelves in the Cave. They're terrible when she's standing in a long line of them in the mall.

But most residents agree with the Chamber of Commerce, which brags that Pecan Springs is a small town with big dreams and an even bigger heart. The big dreams are on brazen display along the east side of I-35, where the chain retailers and the hotels and the outlet shops keep popping up like so many toadstools after a warm spring rain. The big-hearted part of Pecan Springs is tucked away in the cedar-covered hills to the west of the interstate, where the original German settlers built the old town around a courthouse square, just a stone's throw from the spring-fed Pecan River.

That's where tourists go if they're looking for a taste of small-town Texas. They admire the old Adams County Courthouse, which looks like a wedding cake carved out of pink granite. They enjoy a plate of nachos and a salt-rimmed margarita at Bean's Bar and Grill. They visit the Sophie Briggs Historical Museum, which features (among other irresistible enticements) a dollhouse that belonged to Miss Pecan Springs of 1936, Sophie Briggs' famous collection of ceramic frogs, and a pair of scuffed cowboy boots worn by Burt Reynolds during the filming of *The Best Little Whorehouse in Texas*. They also visit the old brick building that houses the Tourist and Information Center on the main floor and used to house the Pecan Springs Police Department in the basement and an impressive colony of Mexican free-tailed bats in the attic. The tourist center is still there. But the bats migrated to the I-35 bridge over the Pecan River, and the police department now shares a modern office building on West San Marcos Street with City Hall and the municipal court, where you go to pay your traffic tickets.

The police department. That's where Ruby is going this morning. She parks her yellow Chevy Cobalt in a lot filled with pickups with gun racks, rifles, and various Second Amendment stickers in the back windows. *Keep honking, I'm reloading. Fight crime: shoot back. My other auto is a 9mm.* This is open-carry Texas, after all, and guns are as ubiquitous as armadillos and rattle-snakes.

Ruby is getting out of her car when her cellphone rings — the *Exorcist* theme, which she likes because it's mildly creepy. When it rings at the shop, people smile. She doesn't need to look at the screen to know that it's her sister.

"Hey, Ramona," she says. "What's up?"

There is a brief burst of static. Ruby winces and holds the phone away from her ear. Ramona makes a special point of displaying the family gift on all possible occasions. When she gets excited, she discharges startling jolts of electrical energy. Now she is speaking in all caps, italics, and exclamation points.

"WHAT'S UP is this UTTERLY *FABU-LOUS* idea I have for us, Ruby! Let's do lunch today. I am *DYING* to tell you!!!"

Ruby isn't dying to hear Ramona's latest "utterly fabulous" idea, but she doesn't let on. "I don't think lunch will work," she says mildly. "I'm doing something this morning that may take a while. This afternoon, maybe? My house?"

Another burst of static. Ramona isn't pleased. But she only says, "Sure. How about one o'clock? That'll give me time to do a little more research. See you then." She clicks off without waiting for Ruby's reply.

"Grrr," Ruby mutters. The last time Ramona had an idea that involved the two of them, she was *dying* to buy a half interest in the Crystal Cave and the tea room. Being Ramona's sister is a challenge all by itself. Being her partner is out of the question.

Ruby uses the back entrance to City Hall, where the fluorescent lights ping and hum, washing all colors out to a neutral gray. The uniformed young lady at the police department's information desk signs her in, then directs her down a long corridor to the chief's office. There, she finds Sheila Dawson's assistant peering into the computer monitor on her desk.

"Good morning, Connie," Ruby says.

"Oh, hi, Ruby." Connie Page is a civilian employee, a recently divorced forty-something, neat and attractive in a no-nonsense white blouse and dark skirt. "Hang on a sec and I'll see if the boss is ready for you."

She reaches for the phone, buzzes the chief, and says, rather formally, "Ms. Wilcox is here." Putting the receiver down, she eyes Ruby's outfit with a sigh. "You are always so *colorful*, Ruby. I wish I could wear clothes the way you do. I'm more meat-and-potatoes. Besides, I'd feel conspicuous, especially around here."

With a little laugh, Ruby looks down at herself. "If you were six feet in your sandals, with frizzy carrot-colored hair, you'd feel conspicuous no matter what you wore, anywhere."

Maybe she shouldn't be laughing. Her off-one-shoulder orange tunic and lime leggings fit right in with the crystal balls and tarot cards at the Cave. But this is the police department and she is here on serious business. Maybe looking like a carnival fortune-teller will make her seem less credible. Maybe she'd better go home and change.

Or better yet, just go home. Her mouth feels dry and there are butterflies in her stomach. Maybe —

Sheila opens her door. "Hey, Ruby!" she says warmly. "Good to see you. Come on in." To Connie, she adds, "When Ruby and I are done, I need to see Detective Connors about the report on the Montgomery incident. I have a couple of questions."

"I'll tell him to stand by," Connie says, and reaches for the phone.

Sheila Dawson is that rare thing, a female police chief in a small Texas town. She has bucked the good old boys to make a place for herself and she is holding onto it, in spite of the odds. She is also blonde and highly attractive, even in her uniform — although as China says, you have to wonder about somebody who thinks like the regional director of the FBI and looks like a beauty pageant winner. What's more, Chief Dawson (who is married to the former sheriff of Adams County) is displaying a conspicuous baby bump under her maternity uniform.

The windowless, all-business office is just big enough for the chief's desk and chair, some shelves, a neon-green plastic philodendron, and a pair of visitor's chairs. There are no feminine fripperies because in Texas, as elsewhere, policing is still a man's world. To minimize her femaleness, the chief doesn't put pretty things on her shelves. She also wears very little makeup and skins her hair into a tight golden wad at the back of her head, efforts that are belied by the baby bump.

Ruby sits in one of the visitor's chairs, shifting uncomfortably. "You're looking terrific," she says. "Feeling better, I hope." Sheila has been plagued by morning sickness well into her second trimester.

"Oh, lots better," Sheila declares, but Ruby can hear her thoughts, which are a very loud whine. Sheila isn't feeling better. She is sick of being sick. She is especially sick of the guys she has to work with, who view a pregnant cop as suffering from a gender-based preventable disability. She is tired of feeling like an elephant. She is worried about an incident that was reported that morning. And now here is Ruby, who —

Abruptly, Sheila puts up her walls, closing off Ruby's access to her thoughts. "I was talking to China a few minutes ago. She says you're taking some vacation time?"

Around the planet, the rule might be six degrees of separation, but in Pecan Springs, it's closer to one or two, three at the most. Sheila and China have been good friends for years. China's husband Mike McQuaid and Sheila's husband Blackie Blackwell — both former law enforcement officers — are partners in a private investigation firm. Sheila and Blackie live down the block from Ruby, and Sheila and her Rottweiler Rambo run past Ruby's front porch every morning just at dawn — or they did, until Sheila decided to take running out of her exercise regimen until after the baby's arrival. It's no surprise that China and Sheila talked a few minutes ago.

But if China happened to mention *why* Ruby has come to see her, Sheila doesn't give any sign. She gestures to the stacks of paper on her desk. "I envy you, Ruby, taking a few days off. If I don't keep after this paperwork every day, it piles up to the ceiling."

"Are you taking a leave when the baby comes?" Ruby asks.

"Sort of." Sheila sighs. "I'll work at home for a couple of weeks, anyway. Maybe I can figure out a way to sign requisition forms while I'm breastfeeding." She puts her elbows on her desk and gives Ruby a straight look. "So what's on your mind?"

Ruby is suddenly conscious of her bangles and floaty gauze top and shiny orange toenails. She starts to speak, clears her throat, and wishes she'd had the sense to prepare a script, at least an opening sentence or two.

36

She clears her throat again and tries to make her voice firm. "A woman is going to be kidnapped," she says. "And worse."

And there it is.

CHAPTER THREE

A long moment's silence. Sheila is looking at Ruby intently, pulling her brows together.

"Oh," she says. "Kidnapped, huh? So, like how do you know? Did somebody tell you?"

Know. Ruby twists her fingers together, understanding that her "know" and Sheila's "know" are two quite different things.

"Nobody told me," she says uncomfortably. "I've been seeing it in a dream, the same dream, over and over again. I talked to China this morning, and she suggested . . . that is, we both thought . . . well, you seemed like the logical person for me to talk to." She is aware that this sounds pretty lame. Totally wacko, actually.

Sheila frowns. "I would have thought a psychologist might be a more logical choice." With a reflective look, she puts a hand on her bump and Ruby knows she can feel the baby moving.

"I can see why you say that," Ruby says.

"Dreams may not seem . . . reliable." She wants to appear reasonable. But she also feels an obligation to the woman — the *victim* — in her dream. She straightens her shoulders. "What I'm seeing is a crime, Sheila. Or it will be, if he does what he intends to do. And you're the chief of police."

Sheila is about to say *And right now I wish I weren't.* But she settles for "So you're giving me a tip?"

Is that what she's doing? "Yes, I guess," Ruby says. "Yes. A tip, yes." She wishes Sheila would smile, even a little bit. But she doesn't.

"A tip about something that hasn't happened yet?"

"I . . . guess." Ruby frowns. "Yes." What she sees doesn't have a time-date stamp, although she judges from the urgency of the dream that it's a current event.

"And your tip is based on . . ."

Ruby hears her disbelief, muted by politeness but clear enough. "Based on what happens in my dream." She takes a breath. "Here's the thing, Sheila. I'm in this guy's head. I'm seeing through his eyes and feeling with his feelings. He is watching a woman jogging on the hike-and-bike trail, and he wants her. He's thinking about what

39

he's going to do when he . . . when he has her." She knots her fingers, trying to keep her voice from trembling.

But now the urgency is bleeding through, and Ruby wants the chief to hear it. She blurts it out. "He's planning to kidnap and *kill* her, Sheila."

Sheila leans back in her chair, making a tent of her fingers. "I suppose you'd better tell me about it, then." With a ghost of a smile, she adds, "You're probably aware that it's difficult for a police officer to deal with . . . intuition — as opposed to facts, that is. But don't let that bother you. Just tell me."

Yes. Ruby is aware that Sheila believes in things she can weigh and measure and evidence that will stand up in court. But what Ruby is about to tell her is nothing like that. She closes her eyes and sees it again, the same scene she has been seeing for the last several nights, in her dreams. She opens her eyes.

"I don't know who she is," she says. "She's in her late twenties, pretty, dark-haired, athletic. She's wearing a white ponytail cap and her ponytail — sort of long, not very neat — is sticking out of it. She's got one of those armband holders for her cellphone, and she's wearing earbuds. She's jogging.

He's hiding in some bushes, watching her. He's been watching her for a while." Ruby pauses, correcting herself, trying to be precise. "I mean, this isn't the first time he's done this. Watched her when she's running. He's stalking her. Figuring out the best place to grab her."

Sheila frowns, shifting in her chair. "Who is he?"

"I don't have a clue." Ruby feels apologetic. "I can't actually see him, you know. I'm seeing her *through* him, through his eyes. He's not thinking about himself — he knows who he is, so the subject of identity doesn't come up for him. And he doesn't look at himself, or at his shoes or his watch or anything. That's why I can't actually see *him.* Just her."

She wraps her arms around herself, suddenly struck by the futility of this. Even if Sheila believes her story, she doesn't know enough to be of any real help. But she's started down this path, so she has to go on, stumbling a little over the words.

"And all I know is that he *wants* her — physically, I mean. He's half out of his mind with anticipation. He intends to snatch her and take her to this place where he's going to keep her captive for a while. A long while. He has . . . he has plans for her. Intentions."

Ruby's head is starting to hurt, seriously. She doesn't want to crawl into this man's dark places. She shudders. "After he's done . . . all that, he means to kill her. He's looking forward to it."

Sheila blows out her breath. "Jogging." She is leaning forward now, elbows on the desk, eyes narrowed, all attention. "Where? Where does this happen?"

"The hike-and-bike trail, north of the park. I run there sometimes, so I recognize it."

Ruby loves that trail. Nearly seven miles long, it parallels the Pecan River from Artesian Lake to the interstate bridge. There's always more traffic — joggers and bicyclists — on the longer southern section, from Pecan Park to the bridge. The northern section, from the park to the lake, is only about two miles. It is less frequented and (in Ruby's opinion, anyway) much prettier. Big pecan trees and live oaks overhang the gravel path so that the sunlight is dappled. It's cool there on a hot summer day, and the air is scented with fresh leaves and the damp earth along the river's edge.

"Okay," Sheila says in an odd tone. "When does this happen? Daytime? Night? When?"

"I'm not sure," Ruby says. The man through whose eyes she is seeing this scene isn't paying attention to the time. "It's almost dark, either just after sunset or just before sunrise. It feels like evening, but I suppose it could be very early morning. Some people like to run before they go to work."

"How about the season? Month? Day of the week?"

Ruby closes her eyes, seeing it again. "Summer. The trees are covered with green leaves, and I can hear cicadas. The dream feels so urgent, I think it's got to be happening now, right now. But as far as the day of the week —" She shakes her head. "Sorry."

But she is pleased and a little surprised that Sheila actually seems to be listening. The chief is watching her, too. Intently.

"The victim," she says. "What's she wearing?"

This is a question Ruby can answer without hesitation. "White shorts with a pink band around the legs. Pink running shoes. Pink T-shirt. On the front, it says 'Be Bold, Be Fearless, Be More.' On the back, it says 'Race for the Cure.' "

Ruby recognizes the shirt because she has one just like it. It's the special signature pink T-shirt that breast cancer survivors received when they registered for last year's Race for the Cure. She will be wearing hers when Amy and Grace join her for the race in Austin next month. Grace will ride along in her stroller, wearing her own pink T-shirt and with pink balloons and her sweet pink teddy bear. She'll think they're having a party, just for her.

"Stay put," Sheila says, and reaches for the phone. "Connie, tell Detective Connors I need to see him. Now, not later. Pronto."

She puts the phone down. Her eyes are narrowed, intent. "Okay, Ruby. Let's say I'm willing to consider this. Tell me again how you got this information." She gives Ruby a tight smile and adds, "I remember being at China's house once when you used a Ouija board. But that's not how you did this?"

She's right, Ruby thinks. Sheila was there several years ago when China's son Brian went missing. The Ouija board had told them to look for the boy at the Star Trek convention, and that's where he was found.[*]

"I remember that, too," Ruby says, with her own small smile. "But this didn't come through the Ouija board or the cards. I must have brushed against this man somewhere, or held something he touched." She pauses.

[*] *Rosemary Remembered*

44

"Sometimes, like when I take money from a customer at the shop, I get plugged into the person's mind. I back out as quick as I can," she adds earnestly. "I don't like to hang out in people's heads. It feels like I'm eavesdropping."

Sheila seizes on the obvious. "So this man — he might be one of your customers?"

Ruby frowns. "I don't think he's the kind of person who'd be shopping at the Cave. And he's a big man, muscular, heavyset, so I'm sure I would have noticed him. I probably encountered him at the grocery store or the mall. It could even be that I touched something he'd had his hands on — a cart or something. If he'd been remembering what he had seen along the path or thinking about his intentions, I could have picked it up."

"Like a radio broadcast?" Sheila is obviously searching for a way to deal with this rationally, even though she doesn't believe it. "You're saying that you sort of, like, tune into it?"

"Something like that, I guess." Put into words, the whole thing sounds pretty ridiculous. But Sheila seems to be expecting an explanation. "Sometimes a message comes through loud and clear. Other times it's just a whisper. Or it's garbled, or there's static."

45

Sheila is studying her face intently. "You've never . . ." She searches for a word and comes up with one. "You've never tuned into somebody who was planning a murder? Or somebody who committed one?"

"Not exactly. But I have tuned into . . ." Ruby stops, remembering. It's painful and she winces.

"Go on," Sheila says, pushing for detail. "Who was it? How did you make the connection?"

Ruby looks down. "Her name was Ellen Holt. She was staying in the cottage behind our shops, working on a writing project. You probably don't remember this, because it happened over in Indigo, quite a while back. China and I found her body in the basement of an abandoned school."*

"You're saying you tuned into a *dead* person?" Sheila sounds skeptical.

"No. I'm not a medium." Ruby takes a deep breath. "And in this case, I made the connection through Ellen's car. China teases me about that — about getting an urgent message through a Honda Civic." She made a rueful face. "I know it sounds funny — funny ha-ha, I mean. But it wasn't,

* *Indigo Dying*

really. We were too late. When we found Ellen's body, she was still warm. If only I had
made the connection a few minutes earlier,
we might have been able to save her. If only
—" She stops. And there was Sarah, of
course. Another if-only. Another too-late.

There's a sharp, quick rap at the door and
Sheila looks up as it opens.

"Ah, Connors," she says. "Come in."

47

In his mid-forties, Connors is slim-hipped and broad-shouldered. His face is craggy, his dark hair regulation short. He is dressed in conservative street clothes — neatly pressed chinos and a navy blazer with a light blue dress shirt and a blue-on-blue checked tie. The blazer is unbuttoned, and Ruby can see that he is wearing a shoulder holster under his left arm and a badge clip and handcuffs on his belt. She has a quick awareness of strong intelligence, controlled energy, and arrogance. When his gaze falls on her, there is an undisguised curiosity in his ice-blue eyes. He is measuring her. She squirms.

He looks from Ruby to Sheila. "You wanted to see me, Chief?"

"Sit down, Connors." As he moves the other chair so he can see Ruby, Sheila adds, "Ms. Wilcox, this is Detective Ethan Connors. He came to us a few months ago from the Bexar County Criminal Investigations Division. Detective, this is Ruby Wilcox. She has a shop over on Crockett Street. The Crystal Cave."

"The Crystal Cave." He narrows his eyes. There is something hard and unyielding in him, Ruby thinks, and wary. Too much experience, maybe. "What do you sell there, Ms. Wilcox?"

"Books," she says, knowing that whatever she tells him will provoke some inner amusement. "Candles. Jewelry." Like Sheila's, his walls are up, but she can almost hear the judgments he is making on the Cave, on the clothes she is wearing, on her.

She gives him a deliberate smile and something more to chew on. "Horoscopes, tarot cards, crystal balls. A little light palm-reading on the side." The minute the words are out, she knows they are too flip for the occasion and regrets them, for the same reason she regrets her outfit.

He stifles a snort and Sheila hastily interrupts. "Ms. Wilcox has something to tell us, Detective. Ruby, let's hear it again, just the way you told me. Everything, and from the top, please."

The detective's mistrust is a cold December wind, freezing her. But Ruby takes a deep breath, summons as much focus as she can, and tells the story one more time, trying not to be defensive or defiant, just urgent. The dream, the repeated, persistent, inescapable dream. The river trail, the running woman, the watching man, his malevolent intention. The need to do something to keep this from happening. The need to do it *now.*

The detective is watching her face, his arms folded. As she talks, he sits straighter, and she can see a growing tension in his shoulders. She is sure that he has decided that she is a total dingbat, but he is wearing his cop face and his walls are up, firm and high. She couldn't hear his thoughts even if she wanted to, which she definitely does *not.*

There is a silence when she's finished, as Connors processes what she's said. He is skeptical and distrustful, with a what-kind-of-freak-show-have-I-wandered-into attitude. But she has the somewhat comforting sense that this is more a habit of mind than his assessment of her as a person. He simply doesn't want to believe what he is hearing. It will take dramatic evidence — strong, serious evidence — to convince him. And he won't be pleased if that evidence presents itself. It will knock him off balance. He will be pretty pissed off.

Finally, he breaks the silence. "Pink cancer

shirt, pink shorts, white cap. You're trying to tell me you got all this stuff from a damned *dream*?"

Evenly, Sheila says, "I think we should treat this the same way we would treat any other tip, Detective. Evaluate it against what we already know." She pauses. "How much of it squares with the details in the Montgomery case?"

Ruby is jolted. This . . . this situation has actually happened? It's a *case,* with somebody's name on it? But when? Where? Heart thumping, she starts to ask, but Connors is speaking, his voice hard and flat.

"The physical description is a match."

"How much of it?"

"All of it. Clothes, cap, hair, the cellphone armband. According to Montgomery's housemate." Connors is looking at Ruby. "The earbuds. Color?"

"Pink." Ruby doesn't hesitate. "The cellphone is pink, too. She's a survivor. A breast cancer survivor, I mean."

"Maybe she just likes the color," Sheila says in an offhand tone. "Or maybe she has a friend with breast cancer and she's a supporter."

Ruby closes her eyes and sees the woman again, running, her body graceful, her stride athletic. She opens her eyes. "No," she says

51

positively. "She's a survivor."

"Connors?" Sheila asks.

"Correct," the detective replies, and now there's an odd inflection in his voice. "I talked to the housemate on the phone when she made the report. Montgomery is active in one of the local survivors' groups. She volunteers on the hotline, the housemate said. That's where she was supposed to go after her run last night. She never showed up."

She never showed up.

Ruby's stomach muscles tighten and she sucks in a breath. She's been describing a dream. Now it is suddenly real.

Shockingly, horrifyingly real.

"This . . . this has already *happened*?" she blurts out, feeling sick. Too late. She'd been too late with Sarah, too late with Ellen Holt. Now, once again, too late.

"Tell her," Sheila says.

Connors is curt. "A woman named Allison Montgomery was reported missing by her housemate — Emily — this morning. She left in her car about seven-thirty yesterday evening, to go for a run." He pins his gaze on Ruby, narrowing his icy blue eyes. "You know this woman, Ms. Wilcox?"

Ruby shakes her head. Allison Montgomery isn't in her survivors' group. Still,

52

they are both breast cancer survivors, which is a kind of bond. It makes her wonder about other possible links between them. The volunteer hotline, maybe? Ruby works there several evenings a month, and she doesn't know all of the other volunteers by name. Is Allison one of them?

"Or maybe you know the housemate and the two of you are collaborating on the description." Connors is ratcheting up his suspicions. "Or maybe you witnessed the snatch and you figure to get some gold-plated attention. So you show up here with this ludicrous woo-woo and try to sell —"

"That's enough, Connors," Sheila says firmly. "You don't have to believe that Ms. Wilcox is psychic. But her description of Montgomery matches what you heard from the housemate. We have to deal — straight up, this morning — with Ms. Wilcox's information, just as we would with any other witness. Got that?"

"Got it," Connors says gruffly, not pleased.

Sheila turns to Ruby. "We're going to need a statement — the same thing you've told us here, but for the record. Connors will take care of that. Then I want the two of you to go over to the park and walk the trail. Keep your eyes open, see if anything catches your attention." She looks at the detective. "Montgomery's car?"

"A blue Chevy Trax," Connors says, and reads the tag number. "She apparently runs in different areas around town, usually late in the evening. She drives, parks, jogs, drives home — or like last night, to her volunteer work. The housemate didn't know where she might have been running last night, and it's too early to begin a needle-in-a-haystack search. But I went ahead and put out a BOLO on the Chevy."

"That means be on the look-out," Sheila says to Ruby. "You have any suggestions?"

"Check out the lot at the north end of Pecan Park," Ruby replies, and then qualifies her suggestion, because this wasn't a part of her dream. "I'm guessing. That's where I leave my car when I'm running upriver."

Sheila glances at Connors. "Check the north lot before you walk the trail." She looks back at Ruby, hesitating. "I think you're aware of just how *weird* this is, Ruby." The detective's eyebrows go up when she uses Ruby's first name. "If it weren't for the fact that you've nailed Montgomery's description, I'd probably blow you off. Even so, it's hard for me to accept what you're saying. Probably even harder for Connors."

54

Dryly, she adds, "But he's an experienced detective. I'm confident that he'll follow this lead as patiently and thoroughly as he's following all the other leads in this case. Right, Connors?"

"Whatever you say, Chief," he replies, with an edge of irony.

Sheila purses her lips. "I don't suppose we have any other leads to check out right now."

He rolls his eyes with a give-me-a-break look. "This is a missing person report. A missing *adult*. It's only a few hours old. All we have so far is the housemate's story — and this."

He scowls at Ruby. He doesn't say *this crap*, but he wants her to hear him thinking it, so she does.

He adds, "Of course, as soon as the story hits the TV news and the newspaper, the tips will roll in. There'll be plenty of other weirdos."

"I don't doubt it," Sheila says. "So while we're waiting, let's get this tip checked out. Seriously. No matter what you think of it."

She turns to Ruby, her eyes narrowed. "One other thing, Ruby. Stay away from Jessica Nelson. If Montgomery doesn't turn up by the time the missing person call appears on our daily crime log, she'll be on this story like a duck on a June bug. I'm sure she would love to know that you have a theory of the case. But we don't need to feed the media circus. Let's keep a lid on it."

"Of course." Jessica Nelson is a reporter for the *Enterprise* and a friend who is always willing to arrange a little free publicity for the Cave. But Ruby knows that Sheila is right. Jessica would pounce on this story. And the last thing in the world Ruby wants — the *very* last thing — is her name in the paper.

Connors doesn't buy it. "You're going to miss out on an opportunity to get your photo on the front page?" His question has a strong hint of snark.

Sheila pushes her chair back and stands. "We're done here, Detective," she says firmly.

"Yes, ma'am." Connors stands, too. "Let's get your statement, Ms. Wilcox." With an exaggerated politeness, he ushers her out of the chief's office.

CHAPTER FIVE

Ethan Connors is exasperated.

He is accustomed to having his days interrupted by the strange and unexpected. In fact, that's one of the things he likes about police work. He has a short attention span. He needs something new and challenging on the radar every so often. But this morning's woo-woo nonsense is just that. Nonsense. Baloney. Bunkum. Bullpucky.

But Wilcox is obviously a friend of the chief, who (for whatever reason) finds it useful to give her some air time. And an order — even a manifestly ridiculous one — is an order. Doing his job, Connors seats the woman in front of a microphone logged into the computer's dictation software. Her story is well organized, she tells it competently, and there are only a few corrections to be made when she's finished. She signs it, he saves it, and they're done with that.

"Now the park," Connors growls, making

no effort to mask his displeasure. Jeez, it's almost ninety out there already.

She replies, "Yes, sir," in a snippy tone. With a scowl, she adds, "A walk in the park isn't *my* friggin' idea. I know you don't like this psychic stuff, and you don't like me. And if it's any consolation, I'm not crazy about you, either. I wouldn't be doing this if the chief hadn't told me to."

Her blue eyes are snapping, her red curls are dancing, and she's so vehement — and cute — that Connors is tempted to smile. But he doesn't.

"Come on, then," he says, moderating his tone. "We've both got better things to do. So let's get it over with before the day gets any hotter."

Connors' unmarked Crown Victoria is at the back of the lot behind the police station. As they walk, he can't help noticing that she is half-a-foot taller than most of the women he knows. At six foot three, he still tops her, but not by much. Plus, she is long-legged and easily matches his stride, so he doesn't have to slow down. She's wearing an off-one-shoulder top that is gauzy and floaty and colorful, and her graceful movements give it a fluid motion. With that red hair and ivory skin, she is a very attractive woman. If this were a different situation —

But it isn't, and Connors breaks off the thought. It is a typical cloudless late-August day, and the temperature is still climbing. The shards of sun are brutally bright, and he puts on his sunglasses. When they get to the car, he opens the doors to let the interior cool off, takes off his blazer, and stashes his shoulder holster and Sig Sauer P226 in the gun safe in the trunk. He loosens his tie and rolls up the sleeves of his light-blue shirt. It's not going to get any cooler, so he might as well get comfortable.

The Vic is parked under a spindly ash tree that provides almost no shade at all. It is as hot and steamy as a sauna, and he lowers the window while the car's air conditioner, always cranky, struggles to pick up the load. Wilcox gets in, and as he turns the key in the ignition, he catches a whiff of her subtle summery perfume. It's the same citrusy scent Carole liked to wear, or close to it, and he feels the jab of an unbidden desire, sharp as a switchblade but swallowed swiftly by the usual unwelcome guilt. He had stayed with Carole, hating it but still loving her, until long after he should have left. If he hadn't held on, she might have found the strength to pull out of her opioid dependence on her own. He was her crutch, but they were both casualties.

But he hadn't known that then — how could he? He barely knows it now, is only guessing, really, after the marriage fell to pieces and the damage was done. Inevitably, Carole got the worst of it. But he wears her scars, and they're deep ones.

Beside him, Ms. Wilcox repositions the fins of the AC vent to get a little more air, and he sees that she has long, delicate fingers. She turns toward him as he pulls out of the lot.

"You said that Allison lives with a housemate. She's not a student, is she?"

"Your crystal ball isn't working?"

"Left it at the shop," she replies lightly. "It's kind of a nuisance to carry around. I might drop it and then where would we be?"

"Allison isn't a student," he says, checking for traffic before he makes a left turn onto Cedar Avenue. "She worked at the Texas Economic Development Office in Austin. But she quit last week, according to Emily, the housemate. She's supposedly looking for a new job."

"Her parents," Wilcox says. "Do they live in town? Does she have a boyfriend?

"Don't know. The investigation isn't officially open yet."

She frowns. "But I thought —"

"Here's how this works." He has been

waiting to tell her, so she will understand just how much of a stretch this is — this thing she's started with her so-called dream. "If a child goes missing, or an adult with dementia, state law says we have to open the investigation immediately. In all other cases, we use due diligence in deciding when to investigate. It depends on the department's workload and priorities. And resources — of which there's never enough."

He makes a right turn at Blanco Street, slowly, to let a gray-haired woman and her leashed Lab puppy clear the crosswalk. "You've got to understand that it's not a crime for an adult to disappear. People do it all the time, for all sorts of reasons. On the surface, they may look like your ordinary Joe or Jolene, but they have hidden lives. Secret debts, money embezzled from an employer, a love affair. In a case I worked a couple of years ago, a husband reported his wife missing. He'd convinced himself that she'd committed suicide. But I located her living with her girlfriend in Florida — and not happy about being found. I pissed her husband off, too, because I wouldn't tell him where she was. Which is the law, by the way. She has a legal right to her privacy."

Wilcox starts to say something, but Connors is just getting wound up.

"Allison Montgomery hasn't been gone twenty-four hours yet. She's a grownup. She's entitled to do whatever the hell she wants. She didn't have a job to get up for this morning, so maybe she went out for a night on the town and she's sleeping it off somewhere. Maybe she ran into an old friend and decided to spend the night with him. Or her." His voice becomes harder, flatter. "Dead bodies get our attention, Ms. Wilcox. When we have a no-body incident, we tend to take things slower. If the chief hadn't given me an order, I wouldn't be opening this investigation until —"

"Until there's a body," she says. She turns the words over slowly, as if they are pieces of a jigsaw puzzle she is fitting together. "She's a no-body until she's a dead body."

Well, good. She gets what he's saying. No-body incidents don't merit consideration because there's nothing worth considering. Allison Montgomery is receiving his attention right now because he's following orders. Because this weirdo friend of the chief has come in with a cockamamie story about seeing a kidnapping-in-progress, in a dream. In a *dream,* for the love of Mike. He puffs out an irritated breath.

"Or until there's a ransom demand," he says. "That gets our attention, if it's cred-

62

ible. But maybe it isn't. Maybe it's a phony. Maybe there's a conspiracy." He slides her a glance and waits.

"A conspiracy?"

"Here's an example," he says, promptly, so she'll know he's been waiting to tell her this. "A couple of years ago, there was this porn star out in LA who faked her own kidnapping. She and her accomplice — her lover, who was pretending to be her kidnapper — demanded a twenty-five-thousand-dollar ransom. The husband paid. They grabbed the money and ran. They were caught in Mexico, extradited, and charged with extortion. The 'kidnap victim' got fifteen years. Her coconspirator got ten. The husband got some of his money back, and a divorce."

She moves uneasily, and he figures she's heard his threat.

For good measure, he adds, "Conspirators who waste cops' time by staging fake crimes can go to jail."

But she only says, "In this case, there won't be a ransom demand."

"Oh, yeah?" He isn't looking at her, but he hears something in her voice — a confidence, an assurance — that catches his attention. "Why not?"

"Because he didn't take her for money

and he doesn't plan to let her go. She's his prize. He plans to keep her as long as he can." She takes a breath. "And then he means to kill her."

They drive the rest of the way in silence.

CHAPTER SIX

A few weeks ago, Ruby read a book by an archaeologist who studied ancient cave paintings in the Lower Pecos Canyonlands, along the Rio Grande, two hundred miles to the south of Pecan Springs. The paintings suggest that the artesian springs that feed the Pecan River were the spiritual destination of pilgrimages by early indigenous peoples, and that the area around Pecan Springs and the nearby town of San Marcos may be the oldest continually inhabited site in North America.

Ruby thinks of this often as she runs along the river trail, wondering what those ancient pilgrims would make of the asphalt and concrete that now covers their land and the glass and stone and metal buildings erected on it. It often seems to her that every square foot of land has been remade in the service of humans.

But the river itself is still its own creature,

wild and beautiful. It flows along the base of a cedar-covered ridge on the west side of town, fed by a cluster of bubbling springs that early settlers welcomed as an inexhaustible source of pure water. The trail runs along the east side of the river, an unkempt green thread of live oak woodland and underbrush, interspersed with mini-pockets of grassland. It's the last refuge of wildness between the river, the town, and the interstate.

Connors turns left off Blanco onto Artesian Drive and follows it to the parking lot at the north end of the park, where a tube rental concession is crowded with river rats all summer long. But the kids are already back in school, so there are only a couple of dozen cars and pickups in the lot. One of them, parked in the far northwest corner, is a small, dark-blue SUV.

Ruby doesn't have to be psychic to recognize the Chevy Trax. "There." She points. "That's hers."

"Huh," Connors grunts.

He doesn't say *How did you know?* or *What makes you so sure?* But Ruby can hear him thinking it, and she knows he's annoyed that she was right about the car, that they would find it in this parking lot. He pulls out a small notebook and checks the license plate against a handwritten note.

"Yep, this is it," he says in a careless tone, barely disguising his impatience, and takes out his cellphone. "Could be she parked it here and went off with a friend," he adds, and calls his dispatcher to cancel the BOLO.

Now that she is actually here, Ruby is feeling reluctant again. But it's too late to back out now, and she approaches Allison's Chevy cautiously. The windows of the SUV are only lightly tinted. On the floor of the front seat, she sees a handbag, half-covered with a sweatshirt. In the back is a blue nylon gear bag, a tennis racket and can of tennis balls, and a six-pack-size cooler — everyday equipment for an athletic woman. When she puts the flat of her hand on the hood and stands very still, all she can hear is a dull metallic silence. No whisper of fear, of violence, of pain. She guesses that when Allison locked her car and left it, she had no reason to believe that she wouldn't be back after she finished her run.

Connors pockets his cell and looks at her irritably. "Getting some sort of psychic signal, are you? Like thought waves, maybe? A little ESP?"

"No," she says, dropping her hand. "There's nothing."

It's the truth. Whatever happened to Allison had nothing to do with the Chevy, and the car has nothing to tell her about what happened here. She isn't sure whether to be disappointed or relieved.

"Come on," Connors says impatiently, with a jerk of his head toward the path. "Let's get this over with. I've got things to do back at the station."

Important things, he means. Investigations that matter, unlike this missing person investigation his boss has ordered him to open.

"Lots of bodies to detect, I suppose," Ruby says. "Dead ones." But at least they're bodies, she thinks. He's already said he doesn't do no-bodies.

He gives her a withering look and they set off in silence. Heading north into the greenbelt along the river, they walk for ten or twelve minutes. The breeze has dropped and the air is heavy and motionless. Branches sag from the trunks of trees, burdened by the weight of dust and green leaves. To the left, through the thick green underbrush, Ruby sees the silver glint of the river and catches the bright streak of a cardinal, a brushstroke of brilliant crimson. The rich, musky scent of river mud fills the air, flavored with the sharp tang of wild mint. Their feet crunch on the gravel of the path, red-winged blackbirds launch musical sorties from patches of cattails along the river's edge, and a car alarm blares in the parking lot. They walk without speaking.

Ruby is increasingly uncomfortable. She has started this thing, and she knows she has to finish it. But she is irritated by the way the detective is brushing this off and — more than that — apprehensive about what lies ahead. As they walk down the trail, her mouth begins to feel sandpaper dry. But her face and neck are wet with sweat and she is short of breath.

Connors is moving along at a brisk pace, and she wishes he would slow down. He is keeping his eyes on the path, which is covered with caliche, a rocky material that is as hard as a cement sidewalk when it's dry. Ruby knows he won't see any foot-prints, but he won't want her to tell him this. She is watching the dense clumps of bushes to the right of the trail, where — in her dream — the man was standing. He was watching Allison run north, expecting her to run the full two miles to the point where the trail ends, then turn and head back south again, but slower, cooling down, maybe even walking. He was electrified by a greedy eagerness, knowing that she had to come back, past him. He could hardly wait to step out onto the trail and take her by surprise.

The greenbelt is fairly narrow here, and twenty yards off to the right, on the other side of the wedge of trees and thick underbrush, there is a residential street. Harper Lane. Ruby suddenly sees a quick mental flash of an image and knows, with dead-on certainty, that the man who was waiting for Allison had parked his vehicle — a nondescript gray panel van — on Harper Lane. When he had her, that's where he intended to take her.

And then she stumbles and has to slow her pace. She is feeling an increasing pressure in her chest, and the air is so oppressive that she can scarcely catch her breath. The sky seems to have darkened perceptibly, and the birds have fallen silent. Her skin is stretched drum-tight, and static electricity seems to be lifting her hair from her scalp. She is tingling all over and there is a persistent staticky crackle in her ears. It's as if she has just stepped into a highly charged energy field.

"Here," she gasps. "Right here." She puts out a hand and stops. "Please."

The detective turns and backtracks. "Here *what*?"

She points. "There. That live oak." Her

hand is shaking and there's a sharply metallic taste in her mouth. She's light-headed, her ears are ringing, her vision is blurred. Her skin is tingling, as if she has just walked into an electrostatic field.

"He was standing behind that big tree, waiting for her to come back south along the trail." Her tongue feels thick. She's finding it hard to speak. "He knew she'd be walking, cooling down. He stepped out behind her and grabbed her and —"

His hot, sweaty hand is over her nose and mouth and she is paralyzed with terror. His powerful fingers are pressing against her neck, just under the point of her jaw. Their pressure is constant and hard, harder, harder. She can't breathe. Her vision darkens, star-spangled, then goes to black. Her blood is ice, her bones are plastic, her muscles jelly. She is falling, swamped by a roaring, swirling blackness that pulls her down and down . . .

CHAPTER SEVEN

"Hey, Ms. Wilcox," Connors says. He grabs both her upper arms, steadying her when she seems about to fall. "What's going on with you?" He shakes her. "Hey, you okay, Ruby? *Ruby?*"

Trembling violently, she opens her eyes and tries to focus on his face. "He caught her here," she whispers. "Right here. He's a big man, incredibly strong. He grabbed her from behind and pressed his fingers against her neck until she passed out. Then he picked her up and carried her —" Her face is paper-white and every freckle stands out. "He carried her through the woods to Harper Lane. That's where he was parked."

"His van?" Connors is pissed off. More of that psychic bullshit again. He doesn't believe her. Nobody would believe a wild story like this. She's making it up.

"An older model panel van. Gray, no windows in the back. Inside, it smells

72

like . . . like sweaty workout clothes. Dirty socks." Her voice falters, her eyelids flutter. "Please. I can't . . ." She wavers, beginning to crumple.

He circles her waist with one arm. She sags against him, warm and limp, and once more he's aware of her summery perfume and the disturbing jumble of images and emotions it triggers — emotions he doesn't want to feel again. There is a large oak log at the edge of the trail, and he lowers her onto it. Her breathing is fast and shallow and she's unresisting and pliant, as if she has no strength of her own. While he doesn't have a lot of experience with half-fainting women, she is so pale that it seems to him that this has to be genuine, probably because she herself believes what she's told him. This vision or whatever-it-was — she seems to have worked herself into quite a state.

He kneels beside her, watching her face, holding her hand. Her fingers are trembling, icy. "Ruby?" he says, concerned in spite of himself. "You okay?"

After a moment, she takes a deep breath, puts her free hand to her neck, and raises her head. "I'm sorry," she says.

"No problem." Feeling awkward, Connors drops her hand and stands up. "You stay here. I'm going over there for a minute or two." He jerks his head in the direction she has pointed.

"Please," she whispers. Her blue-green eyes are wide and she is clearly frightened. "Please don't, Ethan. He might —"

"Might what?"

She shudders and covers her face. He can barely make out her next words. "I can still feel his hands. Around my throat."

"Stay here," he says again. He stands and puts a hand on her shoulder. "You're okay, Ruby. Nobody's here. Nobody's going to bother you. I'm not going far."

He leaves her and walks toward the tree, carefully watching where he puts his feet. He is looking for places where the grass is bent, where a weed has been broken off or something has been dropped. He's not expecting to find anything, but a half-dozen paces off the trail, he stops and stands very still, looking down.

What the hell? What the bloody hell?

He's jolted, disbelieving, then angry. He bends over, picks up a stick, and uses it to nudge a few leaves aside. He takes out his cellphone, crouches, and snaps a picture, then another. He pulls a plastic bag out of his jacket pocket and carefully bags the object. A moment later, he's standing in

74

front of her.

"Okay, Ms. Wilcox. I want the truth." His tone is flat and accusing. He is trying not to let her see how angry he is — and bewildered. "Just what the hell is going on here? What kind of a scam are you trying to pull?"

"No scam," she whispers. She rubs the side of her neck, wincing a little. "I'm not pulling anything. I —"

"Hey, wait." Frowning, Connors bends over and yanks her fingers away. "Where did you get those bruises?"

"Bruises?" she says faintly. "What bruises?" She looks up at him, eyes wide and frightened, and he notices that the irises are dark-rimmed and electric blue. A redhead with blue eyes — a rare genetic combination, he remembers, that has something to do with recessive genes. If the hair color is real, which it probably isn't.

There is a silence. "Crap," he says finally. "Hold still." He pushes her hair back, not at all gently, and snaps a couple of photos of her neck.

She puts her hand on his wrist and pulls his cell toward her, and they both stare at the image. It clearly shows finger marks, already the color of overripe plums, on the ivory skin of her neck. He knows those bruises weren't there earlier, and from the angle, he's sure she couldn't have put them there herself — physically, that is. But he's read about psychosomatic bruising. Is that what's going on here?

She closes her eyes and pushes the phone away. "He has her," she whispers. "He can do this to her — put his fingers on her neck and knock her out — anytime he feels like it. He likes doing it. He does it over and over." She wraps her arms around herself and rocks back and forth, as if she is in pain. "And worse. Oh, my God." Her voice is thin and brittle.

His jaw muscles knot. "You said this guy was driving a gray van. Sure about that, are you?"

She nods. "He parked in a spot where he could get her into it without anybody seeing him." She stops rocking, drops her arms, takes a breath and holds it, lets it go, takes another. "When you were poking around in the underbrush a minute ago, I saw you put something in a bag. What was it?"

He wasn't going to show her, but he changes his mind. He holds up the plastic bag. In it is a pink iPhone.

"It's Allison's." She doesn't sound surprised. She doesn't say *I told you so,* either, for which he is inexplicably grateful.

"Maybe, maybe not." He pockets the bag–

gie. "We won't know for sure until we get into it." He gives her a narrow-eyed, calculating look. "Maybe it's a plant."

She looks confused. "A . . . plant? But that's a cellphone. Plants are green and —"

"A throw-down." He's annoyed at her, disgusted, almost. "Something you — or your friend, this so-called 'missing person' — planted to make this look like an abduction."

She pulls in her breath sharply, as if he has slapped her. She closes her eyes and drops her forehead to her knees. "Earbuds," she says, after a moment. Her voice is muffled.

"What?" He scowls at her.

She lifts her head. "Over on Harper. In the grass beside the curb, where he parked. They're pink. They match her phone."

"You planted the earbuds, too, huh?" He takes out his cellphone and turns and walks a dozen paces away, calling for his crime scene team to do a full search of the area. Then he returns and holds out his hand. "Can you make it back to the lot under your own steam, or do you want me to phone for EMS?"

"No. No EMS, please." She grasps his hand and he pulls her to her feet. Watching, he sees her close her eyes briefly, as if she is dizzy, and he puts out a hand to steady her. But her color is coming back, her eyes are more focused, and she manages a fleeting, defiant smile.

"I'm fine, Detective. Really. I can manage." She squares her shoulders. "You don't have to worry about me."

So it's Detective *again, not* Ethan. Disturbingly, there's something about that rebellious glance that reminds him of Carole, who would tell him she was fine even when she was down for the count. *Women. Always think they can take care of themselves, when they can't.*

"Well, come on, then," he says, and they start down the path toward the parking lot. He is perplexed and stewing and a storm of thoughts are swirling through his head. Whatever happened here and however Ruby Wilcox is connected to the crime (if there was one), he now has to go through the usual things he does to secure a crime scene (even if it isn't one).

He's got to get somebody from Parks to close the trail at both ends. Put the crime scene team to work at the spot where he found the cellphone. Call for a tow of Montgomery's vehicle and get it processed. Look for the damned earbuds, which he will no doubt find right where she has told him to look. Which means he'll have to assign several uniforms to canvass the houses on Harper Lane and find out if anybody claims to have seen the gray van or the driver. Also update the chief. Oh, and keep the whole damned mess away from the media. If anybody gets the idea that some so-called psychic is calling the shots in a no-body case, they will have a media circus on their hands.

He shudders, imagining the headlines.

"Well, you're not going to get any argument from me about that," she says. "The last thing I want is for people to see my name in the paper."

He jerks toward her. "*What? What* did you say?"

"Sorry," she replies apologetically. "Most of the time, I make an effort to stay out of people's heads. You're thinking so loudly, I can't help overhearing. You could turn the volume down. Or put your walls up. You did that earlier, you know, and it shut me out."

"Walls?"

"What you do. When you need to feel closed in. When you don't want anybody knowing what you're thinking or how you're feeling. You raise your walls. You block."

"Sweet baby Jesus," he mutters. Carole had always said the same damned thing. *You*

don't want anybody knowing how you're feel-
ing. You put up your walls. You block me out.

There's a half-amused glint in her eye.
"Who's Carole?"

It's as if she has just socked him, savagely,
in the belly. "None of your damned business," he growls. His jaw tightens. Making a
massive effort, he shuts her out.

"I understand," she says quietly. "I hope
you know that I don't *want* to hear what
you're thinking."

At the parking lot, he turns to face her,
pulling down his mouth. "Ms. Wilcox. I
don't pretend to understand what happened
back there — whether it was for real or
some kind of elaborate play-acting that you
and Allison Montgomery cooked up together. But just so you know, I'm thinking
that this whole thing has got to be a fraud."

"I can't imagine why in the world you'd
think that," she says wryly.

He hardens his voice. "I'm putting you on
notice. Until I get an explanation that satis-
fies me, you are *not* in the clear. You got
that?" He pauses for emphasis. "There is
way too much woo-woo going on here. Stay
the hell out of my investigation."

He hears his voice rising. "No. More. Woo-
woo. You got that?"

She meets his eyes. "You're welcome,

Detective Connors," she says, and manages a crooked smile. "I'm glad you found Allison's phone. I hope you find her earbuds, too. And somebody who saw the van. And the kidnapper." She pauses. "And Allison. I hope you find Allison."

Holding himself stiffly, he takes out his cell. "Give me your number. I might have some questions for you later."

"I can't wait," she murmurs.

CHAPTER EIGHT

The little Cobalt is as hot as an oven and the small air conditioner can't do more than recycle the rubber-scented air. Driving home from the police station, Ruby sags in the seat. The episode on the hike-and-bike trail was physically and emotionally exhausting, and she is still stinging from Connors' accusation. But it's no surprise. It's why she's been concealing her gift for most of her life.

She peers at herself in the rearview mirror, pushing back her hair so she can catch a glimpse of her bruised neck. It looks even uglier than it did when Detective Connors — Ethan — showed her the photo. She can still feel the pressure of the attacker's fingers. He has massive hands, powerful hands. He could easily have killed Allison instead of just knocking her out.

Ruby shudders, knowing that she should try to put it out of her mind. But she can't

82

let it go. She can't forget the paralyzing, bone-softening terror Allison felt when the man grabbed her, and the dark, cold slide into unconsciousness as he pressed his fingers against her neck. Where is Allison now? She has been her abductor's prisoner for more than fifteen hours. What has he done to her? Is there any way to stop him? To find her?

Damn it. Ruby's fingers grip the steering wheel so hard they feel frozen. She doesn't know what she can do to help, going forward. The idea that she has plugged into the powerfully negative energy of Allison's capture is simply impossible for the detective to comprehend. Well, she can't blame him for not understanding when she doesn't understand it herself.

But he would have to come up with some rational explanation for finding that pink cellphone. And for the earbuds he'll discover when he follows the trail through the trees to Harper Lane, where the van was parked.

And that has to be the end of it, as far as she's concerned. She has done her civic duty. She has reported a crime, and it's up to the detective to believe her report and act on it — or not. She had liked Ethan Connors and felt that, in different circumstances, they might be friends. She hadn't intentionally eavesdropped on his thoughts, but she is aware that her perfume reminds him of someone named Carole, whom he loved — loves still? — and whose loss left him painfully scarred. She could feel his angry determination when he warned her to stay the hell out of his investigation, and she knows that anything else can get her into serious trouble.

But she also knows with a sense of unsettling apprehension — the kind of stomach-churning dread you feel when a Category Five hurricane is barreling toward you and all the evacuation routes are closed — that this isn't the end of it. There is more coming, and worse. She can't escape, and she can't even talk about it to anybody, because *nobody* will believe her. If she could just . . .

And then she thinks of Sophia D'Angelo. They have both been busy this summer, Sophia has been traveling, and there hasn't been time to get together. But always, Sophia is a calm, centering presence. She will have some insight to share, some wisdom, perhaps even some answers. She will understand — and she *will* believe.

Still thinking about Sophia, Ruby pulls into her driveway and parks. Hers is a quiet street in an older neighborhood, lined with two-story Victorians built in the early part of the last century. The houses, surrounded by well-kept lawns and mature live oaks and pecan trees, remind her of dignified dowagers dressed in pastel gray and brown and ivory, sitting with gloved hands sedately folded and ankles primly crossed, smugly displaying their Historic Home badges like trophies won in the Home and Garden show.

But Ruby's Painted Lady is made of different stuff. The Lady's walls are purple, her shutters are fuchsia, and her gingerbread trim is spring green, smoke gray, and passionate plum. The wicker rockers on her front porch are daffodil yellow, the cushions are covered in a bright red-and-green tropical print, and green-painted buckets of red geraniums march up her steps. The glorious color scheme gives the neighbors heartburn, and Ruby knows why. It's as if your grandmother has dabbed on orange lipstick and mauve eye shadow, slipped into a flouncy fire-engine-red dress and fishnet stockings, and is dancing the tango with a handsome hunk half her age. The other houses are all jealous, and their owners are resentful. Although nothing has come of it yet, there have been whispers that the homeowners' association may try to force Ruby to repaint.

Inside, the Lady is even more gaudy. Ruby

restored the old golden oak woodwork and floors to their former glory but painted the walls bright orange, golden yellow, lime green, and dark red. A brightly patterned Guatemalan rug runs down the length of the hall, and the hallway walls are hung with framed photos of Ruby's family: daughters Shannon, who is teaching physical education in Fort Worth, and Amy, who lives just blocks away with her partner Kate and their little girl, Grace. Ruby loves Mexican furniture, and the gaily painted chairs, tables, cabinets, and benches look like they're all dressed up and ready to go dancing. She's a quilter and weaver, and she hangs her quilts and rugs on the walls and displays her collection of handcrafted baskets and sculpture and bowls on the shelves and in the cabinets.

And the kitchen — well, a couple of years ago, Ruby fell passionately in love with watermelons. She put up red-and-white striped kitchen wallpaper, added a watermelon border, and painted the table red and the four chairs green and red, with little black seeds on the seats. There's a watermelon rug under the table, watermelon placemats, and red and green dishes. Even in the dead of winter, the kitchen feels like a picnic in July.

In the kitchen, Ruby is greeted by Pagan, the black cat who appeared one stormy night a few months before and took possession of her and the house. Sophia (who knows about such things) says that all black cats — the familiars of witches and symbols of instinctual energy, mystery, and magic — are psychic, but that this one got an extra dose. Ruby doesn't doubt it. She has seen him staring at the phone just before it rings and going to the door a few moments before a visitor arrives. And she catches him watching her with a tilt of his head and a look in his amber eyes that leads her to suspect that he is tuned into her mind.

With a polite meow, Pagan reminds her that neither of them has had lunch yet. Ruby runs upstairs and changes quickly into white capris, a yellow sleeveless blouse, and yellow sandals, then goes back to the kitchen to remedy the matter. Pagan settles down to a bowl of kitty food while Ruby rounds up cottage cheese, a sliced tomato from the garden, lettuce, a spoonful of leftover tuna salad, a handful of crackers, and a glass of hibiscus iced tea from the pitcher in the fridge.

As she sits down to eat, she wonders how China is making out with the Friends of the Library lunch and hopes things are going okay at the Cave. It feels strange not to be there in the middle of a work day, and she is revisited by the nagging guilt she used to feel when she skipped school or didn't get her homework done on time.

But worries about Allison push all that out of her mind, and the questions come back. *Where is she? What has he done to her? What does he intend to do?*

Ruby can't answer these questions, and China, while she's supportive, wouldn't be much help. Hoping that Sophia won't be away on one of her trips, she takes out her cell to call and find out when they can get together. Sophia will understand what's going on.

Ruby is relieved when her friend picks up the call. "Okay if I drive out for an hour or so?" she asks. Sophia lives just outside of Wimberley, a village in the hills northwest of Pecan Springs. The drive will be pretty, and it will do her good to get out. She adds, "I need to talk with you about something — something important."

"Of course," Sophia says warmly. "I'll be here — and I'll be glad to see you. Someone is here now, though. Maybe an hour, hour and a half?"

"Thanks. I'll be there."

Ruby glances up at the slice-of-watermelon clock over the fridge. She is still feeling beaten and battered by the incident on the river trail and is glad to see that there is time for a nap before she starts for Wimberley. With that in mind, she is taking her luncheon dishes to the sink when Pagan fixes his gaze on the kitchen door and hisses malevolently.

"What's up, guy?" she asks.

Pagan hisses again, and a moment later, she gets her answer. Three quick, light raps, and then two more. Ruby's heart sinks. She won't be getting that nap, after all. It's her sister's knock — Ramona.

In all the excitement of the morning, she'd forgotten that she and Mona were supposed to be getting together this afternoon.

CHAPTER NINE

Ruby's sister obviously has something on her mind. Her freckles are popping, her red hair looks like it's full of static, and she is bouncing excitedly from one foot to another. In her orange shorts and purple-and-gold striped top, she looks like a firecracker about to go off. Ruby knows when she sees her that Ramona's poltergeisty spirit is in charge today.

"I went to the shop and China told me that you're taking some time off," Ramona says, "so I figured you'd be here. I can't wait to tell you about my fab idea. Really, Ruby, it is just totally *awesome*. I know you'll love it!"

Pagan puffs up his black tail to twice its size, hisses again, and withdraws to his basket beside the pantry door. He doesn't trust Ramona. When she comes for a visit, he stations himself in a spot where he can keep an eye on her and make sure that whatever weirdness she gets up to, she doesn't harm Ruby.

Ramona frowns at Pagan's hiss, and the microwave gives a short, loud *ping!* "I don't understand why you keep that ugly creature," she says. "Black cats are bad luck."

Pagan growls.

"Calm down, Mona," Ruby says, in her big-sister voice. She points to a chair. "Sit, and I'll get you some iced tea."

The microwave turns on, then off, then on again. Pagan gives an exasperated *meow.*

"Ramona," Ruby says sternly. "Stop."

"Stop what?" Ramona has taken a chair at the table. Her eyes are round and innocent. "I'm not doing anything, Ruby. Honest."

The coffee maker begins to beep irregularly, like an arrhythmic heart beating out of synch.

"Stop showing off." Ruby pulls the plug on the coffee maker. It gives two plaintive beeps and lapses into silence. "Stop doing your childish poltergeist thing."

"I'm not doing *anything.*" Ramona throws up her hands. "Really, Ruby. Sometimes electronic equipment just goes wacky — for absolutely no reason at all."

As she takes the pitcher of iced tea out of the fridge, Ruby glances up at the watermelon clock and sees that its hands are merrily spinning backward. "Weird that it only goes wacky when *you're* around," she remarks. "The rest of the time, everything in this kitchen is very well behaved." She stares at the clock until it stops, spins forward, and stops again, at the correct time.

Ruby loves her sister, but she has to admit that Ramona tries everyone's patience. The family aptitudes came to her primarily in the form of psychokinesis — and not a very controllable psychokinesis, at that. Ruby herself has some of that ability (just about enough to reset that silly clock). But Ramona has a great deal more. When they were girls, whenever she was excited or stressed or annoyed, weirdness happened. Toys went berserk, books flung themselves out of the bookcase, chairs tipped over, milk spilled, grownups were annoyed.

It's not a lot different now that Ramona is a grownup herself. Ruby has tried to help her learn to control her abilities. But Mona isn't very cooperative, maybe because she's still competing with her older sister, the way she used to do when they were kids. Plus, she simply enjoys acting out. She still gets a big kick out of annoying people.

So when Ramona is around, ordinarily sensible objects turn themselves off and on, fly around the room, fall off shelves, or just all over. China (who has seen her in action several times) jokes about Ramona being Ruby's evil twin and stays out of her way as much as she can.

But Ramona is not Ruby's twin, not at all. They have the same curly red hair and freckles, but Ramona is short and roundish while Ruby is tall (*very* tall) and thin. Ramona is almost four years younger — young enough, when they were kids, to make her a tagalong nuisance. The quintessential little sister, she always wanted what Ruby had and whined until she got it. When she was in a bad mood, she could make bad things happen, sometimes just by thinking of them, at other times, by more direct means. A bottle of red nail polish tipped over on Ruby's pillow. Bath powder dusted on Ruby's best blue dress. The heat in Ruby's electric curlers turned up hot enough to fry her hair. And so on.

Ruby pours two glasses of hibiscus tea and sits down at the table. With a big-sister smile, she says, "So tell me, Mona. What's all the excitement about?"

Ramona leans forward eagerly. "We — you and I, Ruby — are going to open a psychic consulting service."

Ruby is startled. "A psychic . . . *what?*"

"Consulting service," Ramona repeats.

"You and me. Together. We'll call ourselves the Psychic Sisters. We'll advertise ourselves as professional psychics, helping people use their intuition, develop their psychic energies, get in touch with their spirit guides. We'll do clairvoyant readings and online tarot card interpretations and offer phone consultations — all that sort of thing!" She claps her hands happily, and the salt shaker falls over. "Don't you think it's brilliant, Ruby? We'll make a ton of money!"

We can do that? Ruby thinks. *We* can be professional psychics? It is the most ridiculous scheme Ramona has ever come up with. The very idea of letting the world know about the family gift makes Ruby want to throw up. She is staring at her sister, speechless, which Ramona seems to take for encouragement. Meanwhile, out in the hallway, the old grandmother clock — which hasn't run in years — begins to chime.

"You already do a lot of this, I know," Ramona goes on. "All your crystal ball stuff, and tarot, and Ouija and the I Ching and astrology. You can just keep on doing whatever you like, and I'll do on-site readings with clients." She picks up her glass and takes a sip of iced tea. "We'll have a website, of course — I have some terrific ideas for

94

setting it up. Plus, we can do podcasts and webinars. And we can Skype my consultations. I don't know why I didn't think of this earlier, Ruby. We'll be a perfect team!" The grandmother clock chimes ten times and stops, as if too astonished to continue.

Ruby takes a deep breath. "It all sounds very . . . interesting," she says. Why hadn't she seen this coming? "But you and I feel differently about using our psychic abilities. I would rather —"

"You would rather hide your light under a bushel," Ramona says scornfully. "You downplay it all the time, even at the shop. You've got to stop selling yourself short, Ruby. You could do so much more if you would only let go and let it happen. You're afraid to have fun with your psychic abilities."

Let go and let it happen? Ruby shudders, thinking of the experience on the river trail. Using her psychic abilities hadn't been fun this morning, for God's sake. It had been unspeakably *awful.*

Pagan understands Ruby's feeling, for he growls again, low in his throat. Ramona gives him an irritated glance. "How can you tolerate such a bad-tempered animal?"

"To each her own." Ruby makes an effort at cheerfulness. "Here's the thing, Mona. I already have my shop and the tea room and the catering service — which is just about all I can handle and still keep my head above water. Of course, if you want to open a psychic service by yourself, you should feel perfectly free . . ."

Her voice trails off. Ruby doesn't need a crystal ball to see that this is not going to end well. Her sister will get herself into situations she can't handle, with people who don't understand the limits within which real psychics have to operate. Or who understand too much or too well — yes, there are those — and who would use Ramona to create some seriously upsetting psychic havoc. It's possible. It is certainly possible.

Ramona thrusts out her lower lip in the childish pout that Ruby knows all too well. "You don't want me to do this, do you?" Her chin trembles. "Not only will you refuse to be a partner, you won't support me in what *I* want to do."

Overhead, the ceiling fan starts to whir. A couple of paper napkins blow out of a holder on the counter and flutter around the room like a pair of seagulls. Ramona sounds genuinely injured, and Ruby is sorry she can't do what her sister wants her to do.

Not sorry enough to change her mind, however.

"That's not it at all, Mona." Ruby gets up and flips the wall switch. The fan begins to slow. One of the paper napkins flutters onto the floor like a wounded bird, the other into the sink. "But maybe you ought to think about it for a few days. This isn't the sort of thing you want to just jump into. You'll want to take things slowly, show people they can trust you, build your reputation."

"But don't you see? That's exactly why it would be so good if you were involved!" Ramona reaches across the table and puts her hand over Ruby's. "You have a *fabulous* reputation here in Pecan Springs. People love the shop and admire what you do. They know you and trust you. You're regarded as a wise woman, and any time you give a card reading, people believe what you tell them. By myself, I'd have to start from scratch. From *nothing.*" Her voice rises plaintively. "Don't say no right away. Say you'll think about it. Pretty please?"

Ruby sees that the clock on the wall has whirled ahead again. But instead of correcting it, she gasps and points. "Oh, gosh, just look at the time! It's nearly two! I had no idea it was so late. I promised Sophia D'Angelo that I'd drive out to Wimberley and see her this afternoon."

Ramona sighs and withdraws her hand. "I'll go with you," she offers. She and Sophia have met at the shop several times, and once at Ruby's house, when Sophia was talking to Ruby's Wicca group about ways to strengthen intuition. "We could tell her about the business we're planning. I'm sure she'd be enthusiastic."

"Today would not be a good day for you to visit," Ruby says firmly, wincing at the thought of Ramona's finding out about Allison. She would probably want to saddle up and launch her own psychic investigation into the kidnapping, which would cause all kinds of trouble. Ethan Connors had a problem with psychics. Ramona would give him nightmares.

"Too bad." Ramona sighs. "Well, another day." She pauses, tilts her head, and gives Ruby a long, considering look. "You seem a little . . . wrought up this afternoon, Ruby. Is something going on with you? Something —"

She stops. Her eyes widen, and Ruby knows what's coming next. "What happened to Allison?" she asks breathlessly. "And that man you were with this morning. He's a *cop*?"

That does it. Not only is her ditzy sister

pestering her with this idiotic psychic consulting thing, now she is poking around in Ruby's head. She hasn't done that for a very long time, and Ruby definitely doesn't want her doing it now.

Pointedly evicting her sister from her thoughts, Ruby gets up from the table. "I hope you don't think I'm trying to get rid of you, Mona. But I promised Sophia I'd be there. I hate to keep her waiting."

"Okay." Reluctantly, Ramona drains her iced tea glass. "Once you've had a chance to think about the possibilities of Psychic Sisters, I know you'll see just how brilliant it is." She pushes her chair back from the table and stands. "Tell you what. I'll draw up a business plan that we can go over together, including marketing and the website. You'll be impressed."

"Have a good afternoon, dear," Ruby says, and steers her toward the door.

Ramona keeps right on talking. "I'll get the plan done as soon as I can. There are all kinds of amazing promotion possibilities here. The sky's the limit, Ruby. Why, we could —"

"Bye, Mona," Ruby says, and pushes her out the door.

When Ramona has gone, Ruby turns to look at the clock. Obediently, it resets itself to the correct time.

She won't be so terribly late to Sophia', after all.

CHAPTER TEN

Wimberley is a village of about three thousand people, twenty-some miles northwest of Pecan Springs on Route 12. It began as a trading post and gristmill back in the 1850s, when the area around Cypress Creek was home to Native Americans and a host of whitetail deer, buffalo, Rio Grande turkeys, cougars, and coyotes. Now, it is known especially for the scenic beauty of the cedar-covered hills that surround the little town, and for the clear Blanco River that flows through it. And — sadly — for the flood that caused such terrible destruction just a couple of years before.

Fed by springs that rise out of the limestone hills of the Edwards Plateau, the Blanco River is usually clear, cool, and ankle-deep. But one recent Memorial Day weekend, there was a sudden cloudburst upstream. In less than three horrible midnight hours, the shallow river rose to thirty feet above flood stage, a roaring torrent laden with trees, vehicles, and the debris of wrecked houses and barns. Almost a dozen lives were lost, hundreds of homes and businesses destroyed, and bridges and roads swept away. Wreckage was strewn for miles in the wake of the flood.

But Wimberley — home to a dozen art galleries and many more artists — is a village of indomitable spirit. After the catastrophic flood, the members of the Wimberley Valley Arts and Cultural Alliance put their heads together and came up with a unique public sculpture project: thirty-six-foot-tall fiberglass cowboy boots, each one painted with an original design by a Wimberley artist and installed at thirty locations around town. You can see one at the Taste Buds Market, another at the Wimberley Pie Company, a third at Brewster's Pizza, others almost everywhere you look. One is painted with local birds, another with cactus and bluebonnets, another with flowers and butterflies, and so on. There's nothing that says "Texas" better than a cowboy boot, and each of these boots tells a chapter of Wimberley's unique story. They were just what Wimberley needed to reboot its optimism after the flood.

The kids have already gone back to school.

but as Ruby drives through the village, she sees squadrons of vacationers wandering the streets. Most are briefly clad in halter tops and shorts and sandals, appropriate to the sultry heat. Seeking shade, they sip iced lattes on the tree-shaded deck of the Leaning Pear, or linger under the awnings on the Square, where the shops and galleries and antique stores are displaying festive flags and red-white-and-blue bunting in anticipation of the upcoming Labor Day holiday. The Old Mill Store and the Wimberley Café are both crowded with customers, and tourists are clustered around a couple of fiber artists — a spinner with her wheel and a gray-haired man with a wooden lap loom — in front of Ply, which sells fiber, fleece and yarns of all kinds. Ruby is tempted to park and drop in, but she doesn't want to be late.

The morning's bright blue sky has clouded over, and a thick stratum of darker clouds is settling just above the western horizon. Visitors are likely to find themselves seeking shelter from a thunderstorm before the afternoon is out, and townspeople will be keeping a wary eye on the Blanco. It's been a dry summer and the river is probably too low to flood. But there's no telling with a gully-washer. It can take you by surprise.

All Texans know (or should know) the phrase "Turn around, don't drown."

Sophia D'Angelo lives in a rustic log house with a forest-green roof on the bank of Cypress Creek. She was widowed years ago, has never remarried, and has no children — except for the students and clients and friends who are her extended family. She is generous with her time and attention, although there is a private part of her that seems to remain remote and just out of reach. Whatever her story, she keeps it to herself, and not even those who are closest to her know who she was before she moved to Cypress Creek about ten years ago.

Sophia's log house has the same feeling of remoteness and mystery. It is located a quarter-mile off the highway, at the end of a narrow lane that twists between dense, dark-green cedar brakes and open meadows laced with goldenrod and snow-on-the-prairie. The front porch looks out across a sweep of late-summer wildflowers to a stand of cypress trees along the creek, where, in the evening, the whitetail deer gather to drink, does with their tawny fawns and bucks showing off their racks of antlers. The house — a cabin, really — is compact, just right for one person. But Sophia has built an addition at the back: a screened-in porch, a room for her classes, and a smaller, more intimate room for readings and consultations.

In her mid-sixties, Sophia has a mane of long, silvery-gray hair that she usually wears in a single braid down her back or coiled up on top of her head. Today, when she meets Ruby at the door, it is loose and wildly curly, a gray cloud around her face. She is wearing a gauzy ankle-length green cotton dress, and she's barefoot. She's not conventionally pretty and she spurns makeup. But her bright, fearless eyes are deeply set under dark brows in a finely boned, unlined face. It's not a face you forget easily.

Sophia has always been straightforward about her abilities. She is clairvoyant and has the telepathic ability to pick up thoughts from those around her and — in the right circumstances and with the right person — at a distance. But in her classes, she often reminds her students that there's nothing at all remarkable about being psychic. In fact, she says, *everyone* is innately, inherently, naturally intuitive.

"All of us possess truly psychic abilities," she says. "Your sudden hunches, those flashes of insight and moments of inspiration — they're all coming from your three-pound universe, your brain."

The problem is, she explains, that Western society rewards us for using the logical, rational, thinking mind — the brain's left hemisphere. We're taught to discount anything that comes from the perceptive, creative, feeling part of the brain, the *right* hemisphere. But that's the part of our minds we need to encourage, she says. Cutting off that part of ourselves is like cutting off an arm and a leg.

"Listen to the voice of your own inner wisdom," she urges. "Trust yourself. *Trust* yourself. You know more than you think you know. You are more than you *are*."

When Ruby phoned to arrange the visit, she didn't say what was on her mind, but Sophia has obviously tuned in. Now, as they walk down the hall toward the back of the house, the older woman says, "You've been having quite an experience."

"The morning was . . . difficult," Ruby replies ruefully. "Nothing like that has ever happened to me. That's what I'd like to talk about."

The house is cool and pleasantly shadowy. To the right, the living room is uncluttered and sparely furnished, with a handsome handwoven Indian rug on the polished wood floor and a few hassocks and benches and seating cushions scattered around. To the left is the kitchen, where Sophia conjures up the delicious food she often serves to students and clients. The hallway is lined with the work of psychic artists, most of it gifts from students and friends. A George Winston piano album is playing in another room, its ethereal melodies just audible.

Two glasses and a frosty pitcher of iced tea, garnished with mint leaves and fresh orange slices, are waiting on a low table on the screened-in back porch. Sophia chuckles as she sits in one of the white wicker chairs and gestures to Ruby to take the other.

"I imagine that nothing like that had ever happened to your policeman, either." Her voice is soft, husky, melodic. "It must have been a major challenge to his belief system."

Sophia's psychic ability can be unnerving for people who don't know her well, but those who know and trust her find it intimate and somehow comforting. You don't have to tell her what's been going on. She already knows.

"Detective Connors isn't ready to admit that something has happened that he doesn't understand," Ruby says, pulling down her mouth. "Not that *I* do, of course. I don't have a clue."

Sophia picks up the pitcher and fills their glasses with tea, but she frowns a little as she hands Ruby her glass. "Are you really all right, my dear? An experience like the one you've had can be exhausting — especially after that bike accident. I hope your headache is better."

"I'm fine, although I intended to lie down for a half hour," Ruby says, taking the glass. "Ramona came over. Which is a whole other story."

"I'm afraid it is," Sophia replies ruefully. "Psychokinesis is a skill that's easy to flaunt but requires a great deal of discipline to master. Not everyone who possesses it is able to use it wisely. Too often, it's just annoying. And disruptive." Her voice is calm and uncritical.

"Do you think I should try to talk Mona out of this psychic business idea?" Ruby asks seriously. "Most of what she does is meant to be playful and entertaining, not intentionally troublesome. But she's capable of causing serious chaos when she's in one of her moods. I worry about the damage she might do if she actually tried to work with clients."

Sophia tucks her bare feet under her. "I don't think you can talk her out of it. Ramona is following her own path." Her eyes are dark, and Ruby has the feeling that she sees where Ramona is going and is troubled.

"If your sister has never listened to you in the past, is she likely to start now?"

Ruby sighs, knowing that Sophia is right. "I just wish I could keep her from being hurt."

"But you can't. There are things in the future that you can change, and things that are going to happen, whatever you do. It's not within your power to keep Ramona from being hurt — or hurting herself."

Sophia pauses, deliberately allowing Ruby to hear what she's thinking. *Much as I might wish, it's not within my power to keep you from being hurt, either, my dear.* After a moment, she adds, aloud, "And Ramona's issues aren't as urgent as the other thing you're concerned about. That's where you should place your attention."

Ruby nods, agreeing. The iced tea is refreshingly tangy with fresh mint and orange, and both of them are silent for a moment, savoring it. The porch looks out on a small, neatly mown square of grass surrounded by dense green woods — live oak, Ashe juniper, hackberry, redbud. A bird feeder hangs from a low limb, and a bright red cardinal and two black-capped chickadees are feasting on sunflower seeds. A mourning dove calls plaintively, and the air is rich with the scent of honeysuckle. The sky is growing dark, though, and it looks like the threatened storm is almost on them. In the distance, thunder growls.

A Siamese cat appears at the door with an inquisitive meow. "Come, Pyewacket," Sophia says, and the cat leaps effortlessly onto her lap. Stroking his charcoal ears, she says, "I have the general gist of this morning's events, Ruby. But why don't you fill in the details for me? I might have missed something."

So while they sip their tea and watch the birds come and go — a pair of neatly coiffed tufted titmice and a male painted bunting, splendid in blue, orange, and chartreuse — Ruby tells Sophia the story from start to finish, beginning with the malignant dream and ending with the incident on the trail.

She adds, "I hope that finding Allison's car and her cellphone and earbuds were enough to convince the detective that she was truly abducted. Which would mean that he will open a full-scale investigation." She makes a face. "But I'm afraid he still believes that she just went off somewhere without telling anyone, or that the two of us are collaborating on some sort of scam. He's all too eager to drop her into his no-body file."

"His *nobody* file?" Sophia is stroking Pyewacket, whose purr is a throaty rumble.

"No body," Ruby says, separating the two words. "Unless it's a child or an elderly person, the police don't open an immediate investigation when somebody disappears. When there's no dead body." Her mouth tightens. "The cops need something to prove there's been an abduction — a witness or a ransom note or *something.* Otherwise, it goes into the no-body file."

"Ah," Sophia says. One eyebrow goes up. "It must have come as a surprise when your detective understood that you witnessed the kidnapping — psychically. When you led him to the car and the cellphone."

"He's not *my* detective," Ruby says, and adds, almost automatically, "and I'm not a real psychic. I just have a few strong intuitions —"

"Stop." Sophia breaks in with unusual abruptness. "You *are* psychic, Ruby, and it's high time you stopped denying it." She regards Ruby intently. "I've told you before that I think the mild concussion you suffered in that bike accident may have sharpened your psychic abilities."

Reluctantly, Ruby nods. Sophia has mentioned this several times, pointing out that some researchers believe that psychic experiences may be more common after brain injuries, especially to the right temporal lobe

— and especially for people who have previously shown psychic aptitudes.

"You were already exceptionally empathic," she has said. "You had a high degree of telepathic awareness. Even a slight brain injury could have boosted that power in substantial ways, making you even more sensitive to all kinds of energies, positive and negative."

Ruby isn't sure she believes this, or that she *wants* to believe it. But she has to admit that she's noticed changes. Since the accident, the visual auras that used to be dim and diffuse have grown stronger and more luminescent. Her hearing seems to be more finely tuned, and her sense of smell . . . well, odors that to others seem faint can sometimes be quite distinct.

"I also have the sense," Sophia continues, "that this situation with Allison Montgomery can be an important turning point for you. That from now on, you'll be able to focus your psychic skills, to use them with greater awareness and a more powerful effect. And that you *will* find new ways to use them."

"A turning point?" Ruby asks uncertainly. "But things are already difficult enough. I don't think I want to —"

Sophia waves her hand impatiently, dismissing Ruby's objection. "This can be a point from which you can begin to grow into the potential your abilities and aptitudes offer. Begin using them to solve a problem, to help someone." Her smile doesn't quite reach her eyes. "The Ouija board is an amusing and clever tool, my dear. But it won't take you where you need to go."

Ruby bites her lip, feeling hurt. "I hope you're not suggesting that I buy into Ramona's psychic consulting scheme."

Sophia shook her head. "That's *her* version of 'helping,' which is mainly about helping herself. That's as far as your sister can see. You already see further and you can do more — as you did this morning. You went to the police because you wanted to prevent a crime."

"But I was too late," Ruby reminds her. Her stomach knots painfully. Too late. Too late to help Sarah, all those years ago. And Ellen Hunt, in Indigo. And now, too late again.

Sophia smiles, a real smile now. "I know it hurts, Ruby. But when you learned that you were too late, you stuck with it. You *chose* to help, even though you were afraid. Am I right?"

Ruby thinks that it wasn't exactly a matter

of choosing. But she nods, slowly.

"And choosing took courage. It also took courage to go out on that trail with the detective this morning. He's a self-assured man who doesn't believe he can learn anything from you." She pauses, thinks for a moment, then adds, "But he *will.* More than he can begin to guess."

"I'm glad you think so," Ruby says wryly, wishing but not believing that Sophia could be right. Ethan Connors considers her a fraud. And he isn't the kind of man who is likely to change his mind.

Sophia hears her skepticism. "Be patient, Ruby. The detective is capable of more than you imagine. And you are, too. What happened on the trail today was a new experience for you. It signals a sharpening and strengthening of your abilities. Watch for evidences of that — some of them will be frightening, but you'll learn to handle them. And each time you choose to use your psychic gift deliberately, for an important purpose, you'll find yourself stronger. You will able to go further, go deeper, do more." She is emphatic. "Much, much more. It will happen quickly. And soon." She smiles slightly. "Sooner than you expect."

Ruby shakes her head. *Go deeper? Do more?* She feels a touch of vertigo. *But*

114

don't want this, she thinks, almost in desperation. *I am so not ready for it.*

So not ready.

don't want this, she thinks, almost in desperation. I am so not ready for it.

So not ready.

CHAPTER ELEVEN

In Pecan Springs, it's past three and Detective Ethan Connors is heading back to the police station after a quick Rueben bagel (pastrami, sauerkraut, and melted Swiss cheese) at the Bagel Connection on West Cedar. Lunch was late because he's spent the past several hours coordinating the Montgomery investigation. Now, as he drives, he is mentally reviewing what needs to be done next — but without his usual enthusiasm. He's too strung out.

After he found the pink earbuds lying beside a concrete curb on Harper Lane, Connors knew he had to pursue this nobody investigation, whether or not he liked it, whether or not he believed it. As a matter of fact, he does *not* believe any of this psychic crap Ruby Wilcox is handing out, not for one minute, not for even a fraction of a second — although he has to admit that whatever happened with her out there on the trail seemed pretty convincing at the time.

And it's not just that he feels personally uncomfortable with all that psychic woo-woo, although he certainly has a right. Over the years he's been in law enforcement, he has seen far too many screwballs who come forward to "help" the police, each one spouting a favorite brand of psychic mumbo-jumbo — clairvoyance, divination, channeling, ESP, astral projection, precognition, telepathy. For some mysterious reason, psychics are especially drawn to no-body cases, which seem to attract them the way road-kill attracts hungry vultures.

But in Connors' experience (and he's had plenty), these weirdos have two things in common.

One, they waste the time of hard-working, already stressed-out detectives, diverting resources that could be directed to more credible leads. There's only so much time and money available for an investigation, and chasing down psychic leads is a waste of both.

Two, without exception, they have been friggin' flat-out full-bore, one-hundred-percent *frauds.* Not one psychic has ever come up with anything even remotely helpful in the cases they claimed to "assist."

What they are really after is attention — from the cops but even more from the media. Which makes things worse, of course, because the public can never get enough of this crackpot stuff. They gobble up any kind of ridiculous psychic nonsense like it's candy, so newspapers and the television just keep on dishing it out, the more the better. Bottom line, psychics are money in the bank.

This is the mindset Connors has brought with him into this particular no-body case, which wouldn't be a case at all, at least for another seventy-two hours, if it weren't for Ruby Wilcox. The trouble is (and it's *big* trouble, the kind you would stay away from if you could) that Wilcox is not only a close friend of the chief, but an unusually attractive, intelligent, and sympathetic woman who gives every appearance of telling the truth. If he'd had less experience with psychic nutcases, he might be tempted to give her the benefit of the doubt. If they had met in different circumstances, they might even have become friends — or more, maybe, although the odds against that happening with any woman seem pretty damned high these days.

And it isn't that he still loves Carole, either, although it's possible that maybe he does, at least a little. He's often lonely and misses having someone to come home to, even though home hadn't been all that comfortable and welcoming, at least toward the end. He would like to get back into dating, but trolling in singles bars isn't his style and he's never gotten the hang of connecting online.

It's a problem that other guys didn't seem to have. Take Dylan Miller, for instance, one of the PSPD detectives. He got divorced and now practices what he calls "serial monogamy," seeing one woman for a couple of months, then switching off to another, then to someone else. "The secret is always keeping a queue," he says. Currently, he's dating one of the women in Dispatch while he's got his eye on Jessica Nelson, that cute blonde crime reporter.

But keeping a queue isn't Connors' style, either. Maybe, if he hadn't cared so much for Carole, it might be easier to find somebody else. But he had, and she was gone, and that was that. Over and done with. He's smart enough to know that what happened would have happened whatever he did, and that there's nothing he can do now to change things. At least they hadn't had any kids, which would have compounded the heartbreak.

And anyway, he couldn't be interested in anybody like Ruby Wilcox, no matter how attractive he might find her. Somebody who could conspire to fabricate a kidnapping, waste police time and resources, and make a damn fool of herself in the process — that's not a woman he wants to get close to. Because he is now convinced that she and the so-called kidnap victim — Allison Montgomery — *did* fabricate it, although he doesn't yet know why.

But he's working on it. He's had a phone conversation with Allison's housemate, Emily. Prodded, she admits that Allison has been acting restless and discontented for quite some time. According to Emily, she had split up with her boyfriend of a couple of years, had quit a good job, and was talking about moving to Montana or Idaho so she could live "close to nature" — all of which leads Connors to suspect that she had been planning for some time to stage a dramatic disappearance.

He has also connected briefly with Allison's ex-boyfriend, a good-looking, self-assured guy named Kevin who manages the Tres Hermanos Cantina on Gruene Road. Kevin claims not to have seen Allison for several weeks and to know nothing about a disappearance, let alone a kidnapping. Staff at the restaurant confirm that he had been on the job from five until past midnight the night before. Connors will get somebody to double-check the alibi, of course, but in his judgment, the boyfriend is out.

And there's more. Allison's sister Nadine lives in Austin and works in the governor's office. After a couple of tries, he finally managed to connect with her by phone. No, Nadine hadn't seen Allison in a month or more. No, Allison doesn't have a key to her apartment.

The sister had sighed and added, "To tell the truth, I might be a little more concerned if she hadn't disappeared for two weeks last year without letting anybody know where she was. I keep telling her she needs counseling, but she doesn't listen. Not to me, anyway."

As far as Connors is concerned, Nadine's remark is the last straw, and he's ready to blow the damned thing off. But the crime scene team has reported that an investigation of the area where he found the pink cell phone reveals that somebody recently hung out under that live oak tree for a period of time *after* yesterday morning's rain. The damp earth has revealed an indistinguishable welter of shoe prints, a torn corner of a Jolt energy chewing gum pack

("Each piece contains as much caffeine as a cup of coffee"), and a chewed wad of gum. The fragment of Jolt packaging yields only smudged fingerprints, but the wad will undoubtedly yield DNA. Also, on the path to Harper Lane, they've found (and taken a cast of) a print of an Adidas shoe sole in a man's size twelve.

And there is the pink iPhone, which Connors is now having searched — legally, since police have a right to look at what's on a phone in an attempt to locate the rightful owner. And the pink earbuds. And the gray van, which one of the Harper Lane neighbors claims to have seen the evening before, just at dusk. Unfortunately, she didn't see the driver (male? female?) or notice a license plate or any other distinguishing features about the vehicle, so the report is virtually a dead end. There must be hundreds of gray panel vans running up and down I-35 every day.

And anyway, the confirmation of the van only *seems* like a corroboration of Ruby Wilcox's tale of a kidnapping. Connors' view is far different. In his reconstruction of this case, Allison drives her Trax to the park and leaves it. Wilcox drives the gray van to Harper Lane, where she waits for Allison to plant the gum wrapper under the tree, the pink iPhone beside the path, pink earbuds next to the curb, and at least one clear print of the men's size-twelve Adidas she is wearing. The two women meet on Harper Lane and Wilcox drives them both away. Leaving her car in the lot to be found, Allison goes off wherever, and the next morning, Ruby brings her cock-and-bull story to her friend, the chief of police.

That's Connors' scenario, and the more he thinks about it, the more he's convinced that it had to go down that way. There isn't a body, or a kidnapping, or a crime. This is a made-up case with a fake crime scene, fabricated by a couple of women, one of whom needs counseling and the other of whom wants some media attention, probably to give a boost to the astrology and tarot and divination classes she teaches in her shop. He knows about these, because he's taken a few minutes to check out the Crystal Cave website, which is full of New Age claptrap.

And before the day is much older, he's putting an end to this nonsense. His next stop is police headquarters, where he's going to lay the whole thing out for Chief Dawson, start to finish. She might be Ruby Wilcox's friend, but she'll have to agree that there's plenty of reason to bring the woman in for another round of questioning.

And charge her with making false statements to the police.

CHAPTER TWELVE

At Sophia's house, it's beginning to storm. Lightning flickers through the bruised-looking clouds, accompanied by a continuing rumble of thunder. The trees toss in the wind, and rain drums noisily on the porch roof. The air is filled with the warm scent of fresh leaves and damp earth.

With a dark fear in the pit of her stomach, Ruby hears the echoes of Sophia's words. "Each time you choose to use your psychic gift deliberately, you'll find yourself stronger. You will able to go further, go deeper, do more."

It's not what Ruby wants to hear. Go deeper? Do more? I am so not ready for that.

So not ready.

Sophia regards Ruby with a deep interest. "Yes, you are," she says, in answer to Ruby's unspoken protest. "You are more than ready. But you are also right to feel afraid.

There are risks and threats in any psychic journey, and dangers, too. You can't escape them. But if you know why this has happened — especially why *now* — you may be better able to meet the challenge. Shall we try to figure it out?"

Feeling Sophia's question as a command, Ruby nods wordlessly.

Sophia smiles a little. "Since you saw Allison's kidnapping through the attacker's eyes, the experience may have begun when you came into personal contact with him or with something he was touching, perhaps at the same time that he was thinking about his plans. You tapped into a persistent and highly charged energy field created by his thoughts. I wonder if this might have happened at your shop."

"I don't think so." Ruby repeats what she said when Sheila asked her that question. "The guy who abducted Allison is muscular, with broad shoulders and a big torso. If he came into the Cave or Thyme and Seasons, I'm sure I would have noticed. I would remember him."

"Are there other places where your paths might have crossed?"

Ruby frowns, concentrating. "The vet clinic, maybe? I took Pagan to get his shots last week. I've also been to the supermarket and the gym and the library." She brightens. "Or it could have been at Gino's. Amy and Kate and I took Grace there for pizza on Saturday — and I had the first dream on Saturday night. I didn't notice him, but he might have been sitting at a table near our booth."

Sophia raises her eyebrows. "Or perhaps you sat in the booth he'd just left. Strong feelings — anger, fear, or a dark, illicit desire — can create an intensely negative energy. The more potent the feeling, the more powerful the negative energy. And if it's powerful enough, the energy can be transferred to things the person has touched or held."

Ruby shivers. "But why didn't I connect with it at the time?"

"Maybe because you were busy with your family and other things. It registered, but you weren't aware of it until you went to sleep and your unconscious allowed the energy to script your dreams. Not just once, but again and again — that night and the next. And the next."

Ruby shivers. Again and again — that night and the next. That's what happened.

Pyewacket yawns and stretches and Sophia puts the cat on the floor. "As your abilities grow stronger, you'll likely experience this kind of thing more often. Instinctively, you reach out, even through your own walls. Born psychics do that, you know, without intending to. It's an urgency that's native to us. We simply don't operate within the same restraints that most people impose on themselves." She gave Ruby a sympathetic look. "You may find yourself becoming a magnet for other people's feelings and desires."

A magnet? "That doesn't exactly thrill me, you know," Ruby says bleakly. "I'll have to learn how to protect myself better."

"That's true, of course." Sophia sighs. "People might be surprised at how often this kind of energy transfer can occur, even for those who aren't especially telepathic. It might explain some pretty bizarre dreams." Her expression is serious. "But you'll learn how to defend yourself against unwanted intrusions. We all do. We psychics, I mean. We have to."

The rain is coming down harder now, pounding on the grass, bending the flower stalks. The birds have disappeared from the feeder and the wind is whipping the wet leaves on the trees. The rain-washed air smells fresh and sweet, like new-mown grass.

Ruby frowns. "What you're saying might

explain my connection to the guy who attacked Allison. But how was I able to get in touch with *her*? Out there on the trail this morning, I *was* her. I could feel his hands, attacking her. He choked her until she passed out, and his fingers bruised my neck." She lifts her hair and turns her head.

"Oh, dear," Sophia said softly. "Yes, I see. And then he took her to his van. And then what?"

"He drove her to wherever he's keeping her, I guess," Ruby says, her frown deepening. "I'm hoping the police will find the van. That's probably their best chance of finding her."

Sophia watches Pyewacket as he goes to sit at the door, looking out into the rainy garden. "Shouldn't you be helping?" Her voice is disarmingly gentle.

"How can I help?" Ruby laughs shortly. "Ethan Connors told me to stay out of his investigation, and he means it. There's no way on earth he would ever let me be involved." She takes a deep breath. "And to tell the truth . . ."

"To tell the truth, you're afraid."

Ruby presses her lips together. "I'm afraid of being pulled into *him*. The kidnapper. Those dreams, his thoughts, the attack on Allison — he terrifies me, Sophia. If I went into his mind I might not have the strength to get out. And it's not just that. He could —"

Her cellphone interrupts her. She is about to let the call go to voicemail, but Sophia raises a cautioning hand.

"You should pick it up, Ruby. It's an answer to the question you just asked. 'How can I help?' "

Ruby rolls her eyes. But the call is from Sheila, so she takes it, putting it on speakerphone and placing the cell on the table.

"Detective Connors just left my office." Sheila's voice is flat and uninflected. "He tells me that you identified the location on the trail where Allison Montgomery was abducted. He found a pink cellphone that proves to be hers. Ditto a pair of pink earbuds, over on Harper, where her abductor appears to have parked his vehicle."

"So it *was* her phone!" Ruby says triumphantly, feeling at least partially vindicated. "That's good about the earbuds, too. Did anybody happen to see the van?"

"Connors assigned a couple of uniforms to canvass the Harper neighborhood. They've turned up one positive, so far. Around dark last night, a woman happened to look out of her window and saw a gray van parked across the street from her house

130

— and close to where Connors found the earbuds. Unfortunately, she didn't see the driver or notice the license plate number. Her description is too generic to be very helpful."

"But it's a confirmation!" Ruby says exultantly. Allison isn't going to end up in Connors' no-body file. He'll have to pursue the investigation. Seriously.

"It's a confirmation of the van." Sheila's voice has a hard edge. "But not of the kidnapping."

Sophia nods as if she has been expecting this. Ruby frowns and leans closer to the phone. "I don't understand."

"Nobody witnessed a man putting an unconscious woman into that van, Ruby. All we have is a gray van. No victim, no driver, no tags. Just a van."

Ruby swallows hard. "But I *know* what happened, Sheila. I'm *sure* of it. He —"

"Wait." Sheila stops her. "What I am about to tell you is completely off the record, Ruby. Connors has come up with his own theory of this case. He has decided that you and Allison Montgomery cooked up this stunt between the two of you. Montgomery needed to get out of town for some reason we don't yet know about, and you were looking to earn some psychic credentials. So the two of you put your heads together and came up with this little psychodrama."

"Psychodrama!" Ruby exclaims. "What does he say we did, exactly?"

"Last night, you parked the van on Harper and waited there for Allison. She left her Trax in the lot, ran up the trail, planted her cellphone, came through the woods, planted the earbuds, and got into the van. You drove her off to a motel or a friend's house — someplace she can hide out for a while. This morning, the housemate reported her missing. You came to my office, claiming there'd been a kidnapping. You showed Connors where to find the evidence Allison planted. Plus, you staged some sort of psychic incident on the trail. Woo-woo, he calls it. Psychic claptrap."

She pauses, and her voice becomes genuinely regretful. "I'm sorry, Ruby. But it's the only way he can explain what happened."

"Well, he can go fly a kite," Ruby says heatedly. "None of that is true, Sheila. Not one single word. And you know it. Don't you?"

There is a long silence. Then, instead of answering, Sheila says, "He's talked to Allison's ex-boyfriend and her sister, Nadine.

Neither of them were helpful — except that the sister remarked she might be a little more concerned if Allison hadn't disappeared for two weeks last year without letting anybody know."

"Uh-oh," Ruby mutters.

"Right. Connors has latched onto that. It gives him a reason to believe that what's happened is just another instance of Allison deciding to disappear — and that you're involved, as an accomplice. He's serious about this, Ruby. He wants to charge you."

"Charge me?" Ruby exclaims, feeling like she's just been punched in the stomach. Sophia raises both eyebrows. "But that's ridiculous, Sheila! He can't —"

"I know it's ridiculous." Sheila sounds tired, and Ruby pictures her rubbing her forehead. "But I know that because I know *you,* Ruby. Connors doesn't. As a detective, he's trained to question everything he sees and hears. Disbelieving is his job. And what he's seen and heard today makes no sense at all to him — unless you and Allison conspired to fake her disappearance. If I allowed it, he would charge you with filing a false police report, right now. Right this minute."

"A false report? But I didn't —"

"And that's just for starters. He's out

there right now, looking for evidence of a conspiracy. And I can't tell him to drop his investigation. That would look like I'm trying to protect a personal friend — and open *me* to a charge of obstruction. In fact," she adds wearily, "my telling you this can be construed as obstruction. Which is why it has to be off the record. Nobody can know that we've talked."

"But he's *wrong,* Sheila!" Ruby protests. "I have never even met Allison Montgomery, as far as I know. There is no conspiracy. I swear!"

"I understand." Sheila sighs. "But look at it from his point of view, Ruby. You knew where Montgomery's car was parked. You showed him where the so-called abduction happened and where he would find the cellphone. You nailed it on the earbuds, and on the van. Connors doesn't believe in psychic stuff, so what else is he going to think? Conspiracy is the only possible conclusion. The only *logical* conclusion."

Ruby pulls in a deep breath. "I see that, Sheila, but —"

"But he's not going to charge you, because I've said no. At least for now."

Ruby lets her breath out. "Well, that's a relief. I was thinking I might have to get China to come and bail me out of jail."

"For *now.*"

Ruby swallows. "What does that mean?"

"It means that I'm out of my depth here, Ruby. I don't know what to believe — or who. The facts appear to support conspiracy. Connors is locked and loaded. I may have to let him go ahead and charge you." Sheila's voice is thin and reedy. "At the same time, I'd be a damned fool not to admit that what you've already given us is helpful. If it's real. If there really was an abduction, and not a conspiracy." She pauses. "And I do mean *if.*"

Ruby makes a face at the phone. "So I'm supposed to say thank you for not charging me for being helpful?"

Sheila's laugh sounds hollow, forced. "No. You're supposed to say you'll keep on helping. We need to find this victim before her kidnapper . . ." Her voice trails off.

There's a silence.

"Before he kills her," Ruby mutters, finally.

"If he hasn't already. You know a lot. I'm hoping you can find out more. I want to know who this man is and where he took her."

"Your detective says I'm a fraud," Ruby reminds her. "He told me to stay the hell out of his investigation. 'No more woo-woo.'

His exact words."

"I outrank him." There is another silence. "You got us into this, Ruby. You have to get us out. You need to find Allison."

Ruby's skin prickles. "You're serious?" She looks across the table at Sophia, who is listening intently. "But I don't know how to do that, except by . . ." She swallows. "By getting in touch with the kidnapper." Her skin feels suddenly cold, and there are goosebumps across her shoulders. "In his mind."

"If that's what it takes, yes," Sheila says slowly. "I'm not sure what I'm asking, Ruby. I have no idea how you would go about such a thing."

Ruby shudders, remembering the dreams. How it felt to be inside the attacker, to know — in horribly graphic detail — what he wanted to do to his victim, to Allison. How ugly it was, how unspeakably awful.

If I go in, she thinks, I might never come out.

"Ruby?" Sheila asks. "Are you still there?"

In a very low voice, Ruby says: "You're right, Sheila. You don't know what you're asking. I don't want to do this."

Sheila hears her reluctance. "I don't blame you. But we don't have a lot of time. Connors may be sold on the theory that this is a fake abduction. But I have to assume that we're dealing with a real kidnapper here. And unless we can pick up a lead from the neighborhood canvass or learn something when we dig into Allison's background, we don't have anything to go on. Not one damned thing. To tell the truth, I'm as skeptical as Connors. But at this point, you're all we've got. And your lead is better than no lead at all."

Ruby shakes her head. "Sheila, I really don't want —"

Sheila takes a breath and comes out with the rest of it. "Of course, if you can tell us where the kidnapper has taken Allison, *you* will be off the hook."

"Me?"

"Yes. Identify him, tell us where he's keeping her, and you're in the clear. A real kidnapping, not a conspiracy."

"But that's blackmail!" Ruby wails.

"Whatever. Sorry, but that's the way it is."

Ruby is cornered and she knows it. After a moment, she says, "Maybe I can reach out to Allison. She might be able to tell us something."

But maybe I can't. Maybe she can't tell us anything because she doesn't know anything.

She doesn't know where she is.

137

Or who he is.

Or she's already dead.

"Whatever works," Sheila says. In a mutter, she adds, "I can't believe I'm asking this. And whatever you do, don't tell Connors. He'd go ballistic. Don't tell *anybody.*"

Sophia is watching Ruby closely. In the silence that follows Sheila's words, Ruby can hear what she's thinking.

If you're serious about wanting to help Allison, this is your chance. But you'll need something to work with, something you can touch and hold. Ask.

Ruby knows that Sophia is right. There is only one way to do this. She squares her shoulders.

"I'll need something that belongs to Allison. A shirt or a blouse — something she's worn but hasn't washed. A shoe would do. The kind of thing you'd give Rambo to start him off on a scent trail." Rambo is Sheila's K-9 tracking dog. A Rottweiler.

"That can be arranged," Sheila says quickly. "I'll send somebody over to Allison's condo to see what we can come up with. It shouldn't take long."

Ruby checks the time on her phone. It's just after four. "Her housemate works, doesn't she? It could be six-thirty or seven before she gets home."

"I'll get a search warrant. That way we won't have to wait." But Sheila doesn't sound enthusiastic, and Ruby knows she is thinking about what the magistrate will say when she tells him that the warrant is for clothing to be used in a psychic's research. And if she gets a warrant, Connors will find out — and want to know why.

Unbidden, an image slips into Ruby's mind. "There's another possibility. Has Allison's car been moved?"

"From the parking area by the river? Yes. It was towed to the impound lot so the crime scene team can go over it. Why?"

"There's a blue nylon gear bag in the back. Allison was planning to go to work at the breast cancer hot line when she finished her run. She probably intended to change. There might be a piece of clothing in the bag — maybe something she's already worn but hasn't washed."

Sheila clears her throat. "If you don't mind my asking, how do you know there's a gear bag in the car? It came to you in that dream?"

"Nope. No woo-woo." Ruby chuckles. "I saw it in her SUV this morning. I'm telling you what I remember."

"Ah," Sheila says, clearly relieved. "Okay, we'll take a look." She pauses. "If we find

139

something, shall I have it brought to your house?"

"Yes, please. I'm not at home right now, but I can be there in half an hour."

"Great. I'll get somebody to bring it over." There is a moment's silence. "I know this is a long shot, Ruby, but we're pretty much at a dead end right now. And if this is what you say it is, time may be running out. I'm not expecting anything. But if you turn up something, I'll be grateful."

"Yeah, well, thanks for the vote of confidence," Ruby says dryly. "Makes a girl feel good."

"Sorry," Sheila says, then adds, "Remember. Not a word to Connors. And please, watch out for Jessica Nelson. She's been hanging around the office all afternoon, trying to sniff out the story. If she gets the idea we're using a psychic to investigate —"

"I am *not* a psychic," Ruby says, out of habit. Sophia, exasperated, rolls her eyes.

"Good to know," Sheila says brightly. "That takes care of that little problem. But call me as soon as your woo-woo kicks in and you come up with something, will you? I really don't want Connors to put you in jail."

CHAPTER THIRTEEN

The rain is still pounding down as Ruby begins the drive home, and it's almost impossible for the wipers to keep the windshield clear. The tourists have disappeared from Wimberley's streets, but five bicyclists in helmets and orange jerseys, drenched, are stubbornly pedaling on through the downpour.

Once you're that wet, Ruby thinks, more isn't going to matter. She smiles crookedly. Once you're a little psychic, does more matter?

The highway, a twisting, two-lane challenge in good weather, is tricky to drive when the pavement is wet. Spook Hollow Road, the main downhill into Pecan Springs, is even trickier. As Ruby approaches the sharp dogleg just past the old Spook Hollow cemetery, a gruesomely vivid image of mangled automobile wreckage flashes into her mind, as clearly as if she is

141

seeing it in front of her. She gasps, clenches the wheel, and brakes, hard. Her car skates around the bend and skids to a stop.

Ten yards ahead, her lane is completely blocked by the twisted wreckage of a car and a pickup truck, crushed together. A man, spread-eagled and bleeding, lies on the pavement, unmoving. The only cop on the scene is frantically hurrying to put down emergency flares and begin flagging traffic. If the warning image, as vivid as the scene itself, hadn't flashed into her mind just before she came around that dogleg, Ruby would have plowed head-on into the wreckage.

Impatiently, the cop waves her around, and she knows there is nothing she can do to help. Clutching the wheel, she skirts the collision and drives on. Her heart is pounding against her ribs, her breath catches in her throat, and she knows beyond certainty that if she hadn't braked, she would be as dead as that man on the pavement.

But I'm not dead. I was warned.

Sophia had said that what happened that morning was a "turning point" and that she should watch for evidence that her abilities were growing stronger. Was she right?

Ruby doesn't know the answer, but she has to wonder. And she is hugely, breathessly, tremblingly grateful to be alive.

But she is also working herself into something of a panic about her phone conversation with Sheila. The chief said that Connors was "locked and loaded" and ready to charge her. She could clear herself by showing him that Allison's kidnapping is a genuine kidnapping and not a combination of conspiracy, hoax, and psychic babble.

But there is a problem, a big one. If Ruby does what Sheila has asked her to do and Connors finds out that she violated his order to stop practicing woo-woo, won't that give him even more ammunition to use against her?

If she tells him she's following the chief's instructions, will that protect her?

But Sheila has told her that their conversation is off the record. Can Sheila *really* get into legal hot water just for talking to her?

Ruby can think of only one person who can answer these questions, and by the time she pulls into the driveway at home, she knows what she needs to do. She phones China at Thyme and Seasons, catching her a few moments before closing time.

"Remember that dream we were talking about this morning?"

"You bet," China says. "What did Sheila say when you told her about it? Is she going to beef up the patrol? Oops, excuse me a sec."

To a customer, China says, "Tea tree oil? It's on the back shelf, about halfway down, on the right." There's a silence, then, "No, on the *right*. Between the cinnamon and oregano oil — the three best antifungal oils. Sorry, Ruby," she says, coming back to the phone. "What did Sheila say about your dream?"

"It isn't a dream," Ruby says. "It's a kidnapping."

"Whaat?" There is a moment's silence. At last, China says, "I sincerely hope you are kidding."

"Would I kid about something like that?" Ruby gets out of the car and ducks through the rain to her back door. "It happened on the trail last night, at the place I saw in my dream. The victim's name is Allison Montgomery. The attacker grabbed her, knocked her out, and got her into his van."

Very softly, China says, "Oh. My. God." Another silence. Then: "How do you know all this? There was an eyewitness?"

"Me." Ruby unlocks the door and lets herself into her kitchen. "*I* am the eyewitness."

"You can't be an eyewitness," China says flatly. "You weren't there. An eyewitness is somebody who actually sees an event and can give a first-hand description."

"I was there." Ruby shivers as she remembers the attacker's massive hand covering her nose and mouth, his fingers pressing her neck. "I can give a first-hand description. Big hands. Hard fingers. I have the bruises to prove it."

Opening the door, she flicks on the kitchen light. There, in the middle of the table, is a lovely vase of yellow roses. Beside it is a note.

For my Psychic Sister, from her Psychic Sister. Yellow roses symbolize wisdom, joy, and power — exactly what we share. Looking forward to our profitable partnership!

At the bottom, in smaller letters: *Just wait until you see my marketing plan!!!*

Ruby shakes her head despairingly. On top of everything else, she'll have to deal with Ramona. But China is saying something and she has missed it.

"Sorry," she says, dropping her bag on a chair. "I didn't catch that."

"What I said was, unless you were *there* — physically, in the flesh, at the moment the abduction happened — you can't be an eyewitness."

"Whatever." Ruby sighs. Pagan, purring, rubs against her ankle and she scoops him up. "Long story short, the detective assigned to the case — Connors, his name is — doesn't believe that there was a kidnapping. He thinks that Allison and I have conspired to manufacture a fake crime because she wanted to run away from home and I was looking for some psychic creds. He wants to charge me with filing a false police report. Or maybe conspiracy. Whatever, it doesn't sound good."

"It isn't," China says. "Cops aren't predisposed to buy wackadoodle stories that don't fit their frame of reference."

"It's not wackadoodle." Ruby rubs her cheek against Pagan's black fur. "It really happened."

"Connors apparently thinks it's wackadoodle. His opinion rules. And if he thinks he can get the DA to prosecute, he'll arrest you. Unless Sheila puts her foot down. Which is a little bit dangerous for her."

Ruby swallows a whimper. "I helped him locate Allison's cellphone and her earbuds, but Sheila says he thinks I planted them. Or Allison planted them. Or something." She puts Pagan on the floor, goes to the pantry, and takes a bag of dry kitty food off the shelf. "But there's more. Worse."

"Worse than getting arrested?"

"Maybe." Ruby tells her what Sheila has asked her to do. "She's sending over a piece of Allison's clothing, so I can try to use it to connect with her. But I'm afraid that if I do, I might get even deeper into trouble with Connors. So deep that Sheila won't be able to bail me out."

She doesn't add, *And I might get into him. Into the kidnapper. Which would be worst of all.*

"Damn." China is suddenly very serious. "I'm sorry, Ruby. I should have foreseen this. My bad. My very bad."

"Foreseen what? You're not the one who's psychic." Ruby fills Pagan's kitty bowl and sets it on the floor. His rumbling purr is ecstatic.

"I sent you to talk to the cops without considering that what you saw in your dream might turn out to be an actual crime. Worse yet, one that had already taken place."

"Well, if it's any comfort, that didn't occur to me either, you know. And I'm supposed to be psychic." She stifles a half-hysterical giggle.

China clears her throat. "I hate to say this, Ruby, but it sounds like you might need a lawyer."

"I might." Ruby puts the kitty food back on the pantry shelf. "As it turns out, I happen to know a good one."

"Oh, really?" China chuckles wryly. "Has she kept many crooks out of jail? Has she had experience in plea-bargaining? Does she work cheap?"

"We may have to negotiate. Can you come over and discuss your fee?"

"I can do that," China says, without hesitation. "McQuaid is out of town on an investigation and Caitie is sleeping over at Chelsea's house tonight. There's food left from the Friends of the Library lunch. How about if I bring supper? We can eat while we talk about how I'm going to keep you out of jail."

Ruby thinks that China, bless her, is exactly the kind of friend you need in a situation like this.

"You have read my mind," she says gratefully.

"Please, no!" China gives a melodramatic moan. "Not *that*."

CHAPTER FOURTEEN

Ruby has just clicked off the phone when there's a knock at the front door. She opens it to Sheila, draped in an olive-drab poncho against the rain. She is holding a brown paper bag sealed with yellow plastic tape printed with the word EVIDENCE in big black letters.

"Thought I'd better give you this myself," she says, handing Ruby the bag. "It's Allison's shirt, out of the gear bag in her car. I'm breaking the chain-of-custody evidence rules here. I didn't want to compromise any of my officers by asking them to bring it."

"Thank you," Ruby says, taking the bag. "I don't know how this is going to work, so I can't promise I'll come up with anything."

"I don't really expect you to," Sheila says, sounding resigned. "But call me, whatever you find. Be sure I get that shirt back. And don't spill anything on it."

"I can do that," Ruby says. When Sheila

has gone, she drops the bag on the hallway table. "Sorry, not now," she mutters to the bag. "You have to wait until I've talked to China about you."

True to her word, China arrives twenty minutes later, with a basket of food and raindrops glittering in her hair. "I hope you're hungry." She puts the basket on the table.

"I'm anxious to hear your plan for keeping me out of jail," Ruby says. "But let's eat first. I'm starved."

"You won't get any argument from me about that." China takes containers out of the basket and puts them on the counter. "Cucumber-tomato soup, sausage quiche, deviled eggs with rosemary." She looks around. "Where's Pagan?"

"Out and about on kitty business," Ruby says. "The food looks totally wonderful. I have some rosé. Want a glass of that?"

"Perfect," China says, putting out the deviled eggs.

As Ruby takes a chilled bottle out of the fridge, she asks, "How was business today? Was there a lot of traffic in the shops?" It feels like a century since she left the Cave that morning.

"About average for the last week of August," China says. "Lots of people are out of town. But the Friends' lunch brought in some customers and we had several calls about next month's classes. We need to get our newsletter out next week. Lori wants us to help publicize her weaving classes. Are you teaching astrology again?"

"Tuesday mornings. And a class on divination on Thursday afternoons." Ruby takes two wineglasses out of the cupboard, feeling relieved to talk — and think — about something other than Allison's abduction. "I'm curious. Why was that customer looking for tea tree oil?"

China grins. "Nail fungus. My suggestion: mix tea tree oil with equal amounts of oregano and cinnamon oil. Powerful antifungal."

"I thought that was it," Ruby says. "Somebody was asking me about that the other day. Maybe you should bottle up a blend and sell it."

"Now, there's a thought," China says. She glances at the vase of yellow roses in the middle of the table. "A secret admirer?"

"Ramona," Ruby says, pouring the wine. "She thinks we should start a psychic consulting service together."

"Oh, no!" China says, her eyes widening. "You wouldn't go into business with your evil twin, would you?"

"Absolutely not." Ruby puts out the plates and tableware. "I've already declined, but Ramona doesn't take no for an answer. When she was telling me about it, she got so excited that every electrical gadget in this kitchen went bonkers. Even the old grandmother clock in the hall started chiming."

Ruby's recitation is interrupted when her cellphone rings, and she sees that it's Jessica Nelson. She debates whether to take the call and decides that if she doesn't, Jessie will just keep phoning. "Persistence" is her middle name — which is a useful personality characteristic to have if you're a reporter. When she gets her teeth into a story, she won't let it go. And Ruby certainly doesn't want her to get her teeth into *this* one. She holds up a finger to China and rolls her eyes dramatically. *Jessica,* she mouths, and China nods.

"Hey, Jessica," Ruby says brightly. "What's up?"

"That's what I'd like to know," Jessica says. "What's going on with this missing person report on Allison Montgomery?"

"Missing person report?" Ruby asks, with as much innocence as she can muster. "Why in the world are you asking *me* a question like that?"

"Come on, Ruby, give me a break," Jessica pleads. "I've seen the crime log for today. And my source tells me that you visited the PSPD this morning, talked to the lead investigator, and made a formal written statement in the case. Are you a friend of Allison Montgomery's? How long have you known her?"

"I *don't* know her," Ruby protests. "It's the truth, Jess. So far as I know, I've never met her."

Jessica plows on. "I understand that Allison is a breast cancer survivor. Is that your connection with her? And if this is a routine no-body incident, why isn't your statement available? I've got a deadline, Ruby. What's the story?"

"Have you asked Detective Connors?" Ruby says. "If he's not reachable, you could try Chief Dawson."

"Connors?" Jessica chuckles sourly. "That man won't give me the time of day, let alone give me something to work with. The chief won't talk to me. I even tried Connie Page, her assistant — I couldn't get a peep out of her, either." Her voice takes on an edge. "Come on, Ruby. Why is everybody buttoned up? I *know* there's a story here. What is it?"

"I'm sorry," Ruby begins. "I wish I could —"

At the sink, China takes an empty pan out of the dish drainer and flings it on the floor with a metallic crash. "Oh, no!" she cries. "Ruby, *help*!"

"Oops," Ruby says into the phone. "Gotta go, Jess. China's just dropped a pan of boiling water on her foot. Talk to you later. Bye." She clicks the phone off. "Good thinking," she says to China.

"Jessica isn't going to quit, you know," China says, as they sit down at the table.

"I know," Ruby says. "I would help her if I could. But she's a reporter. Give her two words, and she'll turn them into a two-page story. With photographs."

Outside the kitchen window, the rain has slacked off, but the early evening sky is still heavily covered with clouds. While they eat, Ruby relates the events of the morning, her conversation with Sophia, the phone call from Sheila, and Connors' theory of the case.

"Good Lord," China says, shaking her head. "You *are* in all kinds of trouble, aren't you." It isn't a question.

Trying not to sound anxious, Ruby asks, "Do you think Connors is going to arrest me?"

"No, but I certainly see his point." China finishes eating and pushes the plate away.

"And I am definitely PO'd at myself. I should have thought of this from the police point of view."

Ruby frowns. "I don't understand."

"What the detective has to work with — *all* he has — are Allison's car, her cell, her earbuds, and that gray van. That's all we know about, anyway. And since your explanation is totally off his radar, the only logical narrative he can come up with is that you fabricated the crime and planted the evidence. You and Allison. Together."

"But a neighbor told the police she actually *saw* the van," Ruby reminds her.

"Doesn't matter," China says. "You or Allison or both of you could have planted the van at the same time you planted the cell and the earbuds. Connors is working through a standard no-body incident checklist, trying to establish the facts of the case. He's probably concentrating on the victim's vehicle, which is going to tell him a lot."

Ruby remembers putting her hand on the hood and hearing nothing but a dull, metallic silence. "That SUV didn't tell me anything," she says. "What's it going to tell *him*?"

"For starters, he's looking for an indication that she meant to return to the vehicle. If there's a purse in the car —"

"There is. I saw it."

"Does the purse contain her driver's license? Credit cards? Money? Glasses, contact lenses? If all that stuff is there, it's probably safe to assume that she intended to return to the car. But not necessarily. Connors will remember that there have been staged kidnappings when the so-called victim left all those items behind, to reinforce the illusion of the kidnap. I had a case like that once."

"Really?" China has had all kinds of cases in her life as a criminal defense attorney, but this one surprises Ruby. "Why would somebody want to *do* that?"

China shrugs. "Because the 'victim' owed a whale of a lot of money to a mob guy who refused to take 'I'm broke' for an answer. She was scared."

"Well, that's not true here," Ruby says firmly. "Allison really *was* kidnapped."

"So you say," China replies. Before Ruby can respond, she goes on. "But if you *did* stage her kidnapping, you can be charged with giving false information to the police. Under the Texas Penal Code, that's obstruction."

"Uh-oh," Ruby said. "That's what Sheila was talking about."

China nodded. "And if the chief of police

attempts to protect a friend from a charge of obstruction, *she* is obstructing."

"Jeez," Ruby says. "It's a lose-lose situation, isn't it?" They have finished eating, so she gets up and starts taking their dishes to the sink.

"It can be," China says, "especially where a psychic is concerned. A couple of years ago, a sheriff over in East Texas got a call from a woman who claimed that there was a mass grave on a nearby ranch. She said she had seen it in a vision. The sheriff felt he had to treat her claim as a legitimate tip, so he got a search warrant and he and his deputies started digging. After a while, they decided the job was too big for them, so they called in the regional FBI office, the Texas Rangers, and a pack of cadaver dogs."

"Sounds like a major production," Ruby says, coming back to the table.

"It was a circus, and it went on for several weeks. It got even bigger when somebody in the sheriff's office leaked the story to the media. Reporters flocked in, along with camera crews, sound trucks, and TV helicopters. In a couple of days, it was all over the newspapers and the cable channels. The ranch owner was never charged — but that didn't stop the media from dogging him and his wife."

"Ah," Ruby says ruefully. "I see where this is going."

"Right. There was no mass grave, no corpses, not a single body. The ranch owner sued the psychic and won a multimillion-dollar award for defamation. God only knows how much the sheriff's office spent on the search, not to mention the FBI and the Rangers. The psychic was charged with obstruction of justice for filing a false police report." China picks up her wineglass and drains it. "I wouldn't be surprised if your detective had this case in mind when he heard your story about the kidnapping, Ruby."

Ruby sits back in her chair and lets out her breath. There is a long silence. Finally, she says, "Well, I'm afraid there's more." She gets up, fetches the evidence bag, and puts it on the table. "Allison's shirt. Sheila took it out of the gear bag in her car."

"Let me get this straight," China says, frowning at the brown bag with its bright yellow EVIDENCE tape. "Sheila specifically *asked* you to use this to get in touch with the victim?"

Ruby nods. "She also asked me not to mention it to Connors — who explicitly told me to stay out of the investigation. 'No more woo-woo,' is what he said, quote unquote. When I reminded her about that, all she said was, 'I outrank him.' "

"Which is true," China agrees. "But you're a civilian. Giving you this piece of evidence is a serious breach of police procedure. Let's hope it doesn't cause a problem for her."

"You mean, if Connors wants to get nasty with *her*?"

"Right. As you say, he's fairly new in the department, which is a plus. He may not know his way around yet. But Sheila is a woman in a man's world. A pregnant woman, at that. She's especially vulnerable to other people's maneuverings right now. A wrong move or two, and she could lose her job." She frowns. "And this could be a wrong move."

"I hate this kind of stuff," Ruby says unhappily. "People playing power games." She thinks of Connors. "Especially *men* playing power games."

"That's life in a bureaucracy, I'm afraid." China regards her. "But if you can locate Allison, you'll be taking Sheila off the hook. And Allison, of course. And yourself." She's still frowning. "Can you do it?"

She doesn't say *This is a real test of your psychic skills.* But Ruby can hear her thinking it, as clearly as if she had said it out loud.

"Honestly, I don't know," Ruby says "Most of the time, when I go into someone': mind, it's unintentional. It isn't something I deliberately try to do. Working with Allison will be a lot harder, because I've never met her. What's more, she isn't here, where I could see her and touch her. This isn't as easy as picking up your phone and making a call, you know. Or turning on your GPS and telling it to locate an address." She knows she sounds whiny, but she can't help it.

"I think you should give it a try," China says. "Do you remember what happened a couple of summers ago, when we were at your friend Claire's house? With Rachel Blackwood's ghost? You helped us under-stand all the weird stuff that was going on in that house. Claire was scared and ready to move out. You made it possible for her to stay."*

Ruby shivers. No. She *doesn't* remember what happened, for Rachel's ghost had invaded her. Or rather, she had willingly yielded, so that Rachel could tell her long-untold story. Whatever Rachel had said had helped Claire, who was still living quite hap-pily in the house. And it had helped *her*

* *Widow's Tears*

160

too. The experience — an important one — had connected her with her own lineage, with her grandmother and her great-grandmother. And with her gift.

China clears her throat. "Is it Sarah?" she says quietly. "Or Ellen Hunt? Is that why you don't want to do this?"

"Please," Ruby says. "Let's not talk about . . . them."

She closes her eyes. She barely knew Ellen Hunt, but she has been trying to forget about Sarah for years, without a great deal of success. Her friend's disappearance is an old hurt, a long-ago wound that refuses to be healed. It is still fresh and raw.

"I think we should," China says. "There are some interesting similarities, you know."

Ruby fights back the sudden tears. Sarah, beautiful Sarah, had been her best friend. When she disappeared halfway through their junior year, people said she had run away — an explanation that seemed to fit her bold, rebellious nature. Sarah was always looking for another adventure.

But even though there was no concrete evidence, Ruby had known with a dreadful certainty that Sarah had been abducted. She couldn't identify the kidnapper — a man whose face she could never quite see — but she had believed she knew where her friend was being held. She had seen the place, an abandoned house at the end of a narrow, tree-lined lane, in her dreams. And not just once, but over and over again, *before* Sarah had disappeared and long afterward.

But when she finally mustered the courage to tell the police where to look, they found only evidence that Sarah had been in the house, perhaps held against her will. She was gone. She had never come back. Was she alive? Nobody knew.

Ever since, Ruby had been living with the belief that this was all her fault. She might have prevented Sarah's kidnapping. Or if she had trusted herself to go to the cops sooner, Sarah might have been found. But she was too late, too late. Either way, both ways, she was responsible.

With a compassionate look, China continues. "If you're able to locate Allison, the cops can send in a rescue team. She's safe, you're off the hook, and so is Sheila. Nobody is going to care how you did it. Except for maybe Detective Connors, although his opinion won't count for much, if you succeed."

Ruby takes a breath, steadying herself against the fear. *Sarah and Allison. Allison and Sarah.* "And if I don't? If I . . . fail?"

"You can always return the evidence bag

to Sheila and tell her that you struck out. I doubt that the chief will let her detective know that she gave you the green light to practice some serious woo-woo behind his back. Of course, Allison may be dead by then." China gives Ruby a hard, straight look. "I guess it depends on how much you want to help her — and how afraid you are."

Afraid? Ruby can feel fear like an icy tide rising inside her, freezing her chest so that it is hard to take a breath. Her mouth is dry and her tongue seems to be stuck to the roof of her mouth.

But China is right. Allison may be dead by then.

No. Allison may be dead by now.

CHAPTER FIFTEEN

The shirt is a dark blue boatneck T-shirt, size medium. Ruby holds it up. On the front is a black logo and the words *Body Matters Fitness Center*. On the back, *Take Care of Your Body. It's the Only One You'll Ever Have.*

"Hey, look!" Ruby is surprised. "Body Matters is *my* gym, China. On Houston Street, across from the library. Allison must go there, too."

China frowns. "I thought you went to the gym on the other side of I-35."

"It closed a few months ago — financial difficulties, I heard. Some of the trainers moved over to Body Matters, so that's where I'm working out now — or I plan to. So far, I've only been there a couple of times."

"Is it possible that you saw Allison there?"

"If I did, I don't remember her."

China looks from Ruby to the T-shirt and back again. "When you described the guy who attacked Allison on the trail, didn't you say he was big — and very strong?"

"Yes." Ruby shivers, remembering. "He was big enough to stop her in her tracks, almost effortlessly. When he knocked her out and she went down, he picked her up and carried her to the van as easily as if she were a child."

"Think about it, Ruby." China is frowning. "Is it possible that —"

Wide-eyed now, Ruby finishes the sentence. "That the attacker works out at Body Matters, too?" Why hadn't she thought of this? "Yes, it's entirely possible, China!"

China taps her fingers on the table. "When was the last time you went to the gym?"

"Friday night." Ruby narrows her eyes. "No, Saturday night. The place was more than half empty, so I figured it was a good time to try out the machines."

"Which were?"

"Well, let's see." Ruby ticks them off on her fingers. "I tried out a treadmill, a bicycle, an incline trainer, and an elliptical. I even got on a humongous whiz-bang Rube Goldberg thing called a combo weight machine." She frowns. "But I was concentrating too hard to notice who was around me. I wanted to see which machines I liked best. I don't remember being aware of *any-body.*"

"Yes, but." China purses her lips. "Didn't Sophia suggest that you might have come into contact with something the attacker had been touching while he was thinking about his plans for Allison? So maybe you used a piece of equipment that he had been using just before you."

"Yes!" The realization jolts her, and Ruby snaps her fingers. "In fact, it could have happened on that combo weight machine. It's exactly the kind of equipment a weight-lifter would use for training. I set the resistance pretty light, but it can be set so it requires a *lot* of muscle. If he was thinking about Allison while he was using it, the physical energy he generated with that machine might have amplified the energies of his thoughts. His desires."

"And maybe he was on steroids," China says. "Maybe he was trying to bulk up. Which amplified his energies even more."

"And then I picked them up when I got on the equipment. Like a virus." Ruby shudders. She hates the idea of being infected by the man's awful thoughts.

And then something else occurs to her. "I wonder if Allison might have been working out at the same time he was. The Body Mat-

166

ters equipment room isn't all that big. He could have been watching her. And thinking about his plan to snatch her the next time she went running."

"Okay." China nods. "Now that you have a possible fix on where you might have connected with him, maybe it will be easier to connect with *her* — and find out where she is right now. That's what we need to know. That's what Sheila needs to know."

Hearing her friend's *we,* Ruby is momentarily heartened. China may be a skeptic, but she's always supportive. If she doesn't believe, she's at least willing to suspend her disbelief, and offer whatever help she can.

Faced with the task, though, Ruby is even more afraid — afraid of failure *and* of success. She has no idea what she's doing with this psychic stuff. It's like stumbling blindfolded through a landscape pocked with bottomless sinkholes and littered with landmines. Stumble into a hole, she could fall forever. Trip over a landmine, she could blow up the whole world. She could get herself — or Allison, or both of them — into some really serious trouble. She might get stuck inside Allison's consciousness and not be able to get out. And if she's stuck inside Allison and the kidnapper decides to kill her, what happens then?

The more she thinks about it, the more frightening it seems. Her stomach is twisted into a knot and her hands are clammy. This is a terrifying nightmare, almost worse than the dreams themselves. There are no options, no alternatives, no escape. She wants to say *I'm sorry, but I can't do this. It's too dangerous. I'm too afraid.*

But China keeps prodding her. "Do you want to do it here, in the kitchen? Or would you prefer somewhere else?" When Ruby hesitates, she says, "You've come this far, Ruby. If you back down now, you're both victims. You and Allison. If she winds up dead, you'll blame yourself for the rest of your life."

Like Sarah, Ruby thinks. Like Sarah.

"The living room, I guess," she says, resigning herself. A few moments later, she is seated in her favorite chair, with Allison's shirt on her lap and China on the sofa nearby.

"What can I do to help?" China asks.

Ruby tries to focus on the task in front of her. If this is going to work, she has to find out who Allison's captor is and where he's imprisoned her. "Maybe you can talk me through?"

"Talk you through?" China's eyebrows go up. "How? What do I do?"

168

"I'm not sure. But if I'm able to connect with her, I'll be Allison. You can help by questioning me — questioning *her,* I mean — about her surroundings. I'll try — or she'll try, we'll both try — to answer."

"Okay. I can handle that." China smiles. "I used to be pretty good at getting clients to tell me stuff."

"But it might not work," Ruby says cautiously. "If Allison is locked in a closet, for instance, or blindfolded, she probably can't tell us where she is. She might not even know what she knows, if that makes any sense."

"Actually, that makes a lot of sense," China says with an ironic laugh. "Back in the day, I had plenty of clients who didn't know what they knew. Or didn't want *me* to know what they knew. If I was going to defend them, it was my job to find out — before we got to the courtroom."

Which makes Ruby very glad that China is with her. She has watched her question people. China almost always gets the information she's after.

But Ruby is still uncertain and deeply, almost nauseatingly apprehensive. She hadn't invited the dreams, and she hadn't intended what happened to her on the trail. She's mostly been a passive receptor of other people's psychic energies. Using her psychic ability deliberately, with her own intention and purpose, is a whole different thing. She can't do this. She opens her mouth to back out.

But China isn't giving her the chance. "Want me to take notes? Or how about if we record it?" She pulls out her cellphone.

Resigned, Ruby says, "Better record it, I guess. I may not remember much." *And it might be a road map for getting me out if I get stuck,* she thinks.

China dims the living room lights and Ruby relaxes in the way she does for meditation, clearing and centering her mind, opening herself to anything, everything that arises. She doesn't know what she's doing, but in a way, maybe that's better.

At least, she thinks, it means that I'm open and ready for whatever happens. More or less, anyway. She knows she has no expectations. Only fears.

In the half dark, Ruby picks up Allison's shirt, noticing that it hasn't been washed since the last time it was worn. She holds it up to her face for a few moments, inhaling Allison's scent, then drops it onto her lap. And with the fabric of the shirt under her fingers she closes her eyes and focuses on Allison, deliberately returning to the spot on the trail where the attacker seized her.

Dusk is falling. Off to her right, the river glints like hammered silver through the trees. She is on her way back to the parking lot, jogging slowly, cooling down, when she hears the loud crack of a branch and the rustle of underbrush. Grasped from behind in a powerful grip, she tries to scream but a thick, sweaty hand clamps her mouth shut and fingers press against her neck. Her ears roar. Her vision blurs and darkens. Her bones are jelly.

Sound disappears. She can't breathe, can't move. She sags, sucked into a silent, swirling blackness. Black, blacker, blackest.

Then a blank space and time — how long, she has no idea — and then darkness and light in chaotic, whirling waves, and she is there, where Allison is.

Wherever there *is.*

CHAPTER SIXTEEN

But no, it's not there. It's *here,* and Ruby is with Allison.

She whispers to her, gently, *Allison, Allison.* She can feel her yielding and opening, and Ruby slips into her mind as easily as a sleeper slips into a dream.

For Allison, there is a flickering instant of surprise, a *who-are-you* moment, and Ruby has the feeling that if this situation were anything else, Allison would resist. But she is stunned and dazed. She is huddled within herself, profoundly bewildered and hurting and utterly terrified. The attacker's brutality has made her vulnerable, and she doesn't have the strength to resist Ruby's gentle intrusion.

Ruby: I'm a friend, Allison, I wouldn't be here if you didn't need me, and I'm here to help get you out of here. You can't see me, but you can feel me, as near to you as your own thoughts. I am your thoughts, really.

The two of us are thinking together, feeling together . . .

Then even that small separation fades and the two of them are in the same space, the same moment, the same mind. The first thing Ruby is aware of is Allison's physical pain, the raw, throbbing ache that is the result of sustained, repeated, ruthless assaults. It's excruciating, and she cringes.

Then, as if across a great, dark void, she hears a calm voice. *Where are you, Allison? Can you tell me where you are?*

The voice. China's voice, and Ruby reaches for it as if it were a rope dangling over a cliff. She seizes it.

Where are you? The voice repeats. *Where are you, Allison?*

She is stretched out on her back, on a surface that gives a little. There is something over her. Something wooly, scratchy.

"On a bed," she whispers. "Under a . . . a blanket." She's whispering because her throat hurts, because she was screaming and screaming and screaming. He likes to hear her scream but then he got scared that the neighbors might hear her so he stuffed a rag in her mouth and tied a gag over it. The gag is gone, but she can still feel it.

Thank you, the voice says quietly, and there's a smile in it. *Are you free? Can you*

173

move? How do you feel?

Ruby raises her arms, one at a time. She flexes her legs and is vaguely surprised that she can move them. As Allison, she remembers being tightly bound, her wrists lashed to the head of the bed, her ankles to the foot, her legs spread apart, while he —

"I'm free," she says aloud, pushing the awful memory away. "I can move." Her mouth is dry as straw, her lips bruised and sore, and she can barely manage the words.

Are you okay? The voice is sympathetic. *How do you feel?*

"Don't ask," Ruby whispers. "I don't want to remember." The horror rises in her and she takes a breath, wishing the voice would go away and let her slide back down into the blackness. He's going to kill her, she knows, and knowing is like the hard, cold steel of a blade pressing against her throat.

The voice becomes stronger, more insistent. *You don't have to remember. I don't want you to remember, not now. Just open your eyes. Look around. Are you alone? Where are you? What do you see?*

Open her eyes? But her eyelids are heavy and gritty, stuck shut. It takes a great effort, but finally, she manages to open them into a gray, silent gloom. On her right is a wall, unpainted plasterboard, dirty white. She turns her head to the left, wakening a whirling dizziness. Her vision blurs and she blinks to clear it. And begins, after a moment, to make sense of the gloom.

Look around. The voice is louder now, and sharper. *What do you see? Tell me.*

She moves her head, fighting vertigo, and whispers a description of what her eyes tell her. Bruises the color of ripe eggplant on her arms. Angry red welts on her wrists and ankles, where he knotted the ropes around them. The narrow bed with a white-painted iron headboard and footboard, where he tied her, spread-eagled. Her bra and panties on the floor — the rest of her clothes, her pink T-shirt, her white shorts, nowhere to be seen. Yes, she's alone. And beside the bed, there's a wooden crate for a table, and a pitcher of orange juice and a half-full glass. She's terribly thirsty and the juice is tempting.

But there's a pill bottle on the crate and a scattering of small white pills. Roofies? Which may be why her wrists and ankles are free now and the gag is gone and there are deep black holes in her memory — for which, she supposes, she should be grateful. She wants to drink the juice but she doesn't dare. In case she's tempted beyond resistance, she swings her arm and knocks the glass on the floor. It shatters.

What else do you see? Tell me, the voice commands, and she responds.

The bed is pushed against one wall in a space about the size of a garage. It *is* a garage, for the floor is concrete and one wall is an overhead door, pulled down and chained. The air is stuffy and very warm, and its general mustiness is laced with the odors of dirty tennis shoes, Chinese takeout, and the sharper fragrance of a pine-scented air freshener. There are no windows in any of the walls, but a pearly gray light filters through a dirty overhead skylight, and when she looks up, she can see a noiseless rain falling in transparent sheets down the slanting pane. The silent movement is hypnotizing, and she stares at it until the heaviness closes her eyelids again and she is falling, too, pulled down and down and —

What else, Allison? What else do you see? It's the voice again, impatient, as if the speaker has asked this question more than once. And then: *Sit up and look around. What else can you see? For instance, tell me what you are wearing.*

What is she wearing? She looks down her length and sees a gray T-shirt, several sizes too large, like a sack that covers her elbows and knees.

"A T-shirt." She lifts it to check. "No underwear."

Well, hey. At least you're not naked. The questioner chuckles, and the chuckle is somehow heartening because it sounds so normal. But then the voice sharpens. *It's getting late. What else can you see? I need to know more before he gets back. He may be on his way.*

On his way. The thought of it makes her want to throw up. She turns onto her left side and pushes herself up, swinging her legs over the edge of the bed. The concrete floor is startlingly cold under her bare feet, as if she has just stepped onto a frozen puddle. The effort makes the room whirl and spin as if she's on a carnival Tilt-A-Whirl. She sits on the edge of the bed for a few moments until the spinning slows and she can describe what she's looking at, whispering, because her throat is so sore.

There's an overhead light in the ceiling, a fluorescent fixture. It is turned off, but in the light from the skylight, she can see that this small garage has been turned into a small gym. A black rubber mat covers the center of the floor. There's a treadmill and a rowing machine and a metal rack of weight sets and a piece of weight-training equipment that looks like a smaller version of the combo unit at Body Matters. Pull-up bars and rings hanging from the ceiling. On the end wall, high up, a window air conditioner, but it's not turned on. The dirty gray-white walls are papered with fitness posters and life-size pictures of bodybuilders and weightlifters, mostly male, a few female. There is a closed door in the wall opposite the bed, presumably locked. Beside the door hangs a cork bulletin board, thickly plastered with signs and notices and papers, lots of pieces of paper. Above the bulletin board is a large clock.

Good, the voice says approvingly. *All good.* And then, *What time is it?*

Time? She squints at the clock. "Six forty-five," she says, and thinks: Six forty-five. She has been here almost twenty-four hours. Or is it twelve hours, or thirty-six or forty-eight? Is it hours or days? How long *has* she been here? How long?

Her head is a pounding drum. She is chilled to the bone in spite of the warmth of the air and beginning to feel annoyed. Who is asking her these silly questions? Why is she sitting here? She could lie down and pull up the blanket and be warm again. She eyes the pitcher of juice. She's smashed the glass but she is so thirsty. A sip or two surely wouldn't hurt. Anyway, what if it did? A few

178

Roofies, and she won't know what comes next. He could kill her and she wouldn't care.

But the voice won't leave her alone. *Hurry,* it prods. *Time is running out. That corkboard on the wall. I want you to take a closer look at it. All those papers and things — there may be a name. Walk over to it and tell me what you see.*

Walk? That's ridiculous. She can't walk. Her bones are rubber. After a moment, she discovers that she has only thought this thought and hasn't said it aloud. She tries again.

"I hurt all over," she says, whimpering a little. "I can't walk. I want to lie down."

No. Get up. The voice is flat, insistent. *I need you to tell me what's on that board.* And then, a little softer, coaching, coaxing: *Come on, sweetie. You can do it. Don't be such a wuss.*

Don't be such a wuss. The annoyance mounts. She pushes herself up and stands, one hand on the table to steady her. There's a dizzy moment, a whirling sensation, and everything blurs. This is the first time she's been on her feet since she was drugged, and the blackness welcomes her. She's about to faint. She sits down on the bed again and puts her head between her knees. In a few moments, the roaring lessens and she manages to stand, feeling stronger.

"I'm not a wuss," she says.

Good girl, the voice replies warmly. *Let's see what's on that corkboard.*

With that encouragement, she sets out. Taking small steps, she shuffles barefoot across the dim room, making her unsteady way around the treadmill and the rowing machine and the weight rack, all the way to the corkboard over the table, against the opposite wall. She puts her hands on the table and leans on it, grateful for the support. She doesn't know what's so special about the corkboard that she has to go to all this trouble to look at it, but she's doing what she's told.

"I'm here," she says. "At the board. What do you want to know?"

I want to know what you see.

He has organized the board neatly, and she names the items. At the top is a large laminated red-and-white poster, "Fitness and Strength," picturing a hunky male performing a dozen exercises that show off his bulging muscles. Under it is a paper headed Daily Workout, listing the things somebody is supposed to do every day: Bench Press, Superset, Parallel Dips, Cable Crossovers, Hanging Leg Raises. Beside that is a calendar from Matt's Construction Company, with August displayed.

The voice says, *We're looking for the name of the person who owns this garage. Do you see any names on the board, anywhere?*

Briefly, she wonders who *we* are and why anybody cares about names. But she scans the board anyway.

"No," she says slowly. "I don't see any names. But there's a photo."

She is staring at a glossy nine-by-twelve black-and-white photograph of a heavyset, thick-necked muscular man in a sleeveless, tight-fitting black weightlifter's costume, knees wrapped in black compression bandages. He's crouching, bulging arms stretched in a wide V above his head, supporting a massive barbell. He has a thick, brush-like black moustache and a jagged scar on his left cheek. His features are squeezed in a fiercely contorted grimace of concentration and effort.

Her eyes are fixed on the man's face. It is the face that loomed over her in the night. The face behind the horrors of the last long hours. She shivers. Her legs are trembling.

Name, the voice says. *Is there a name on the photo?*

She pulls her eyes away from the face and licks her parched lips. "Yes," she says. She reads the caption aloud, her voice trembling. "Roger Conklin of Pecan Springs receives USA Weightlifting Federation Award in the Men's Holiday Open."

The voice is very quiet. *Roger Conklin — is he the man who assaulted you?*

She swallows. "Yes, it's him." Fear rises up in her like a cold, black fountain. She closes her eyes and braces herself against its chill. "Roger Conklin."

Brave girl, the voice says approvingly. *Hang on while I check for his address.* A moment later: *Roger Conklin, 321 Lampasas.* The voice is quietly jubilant. *Now go back to the bed and lie down. We're coming to get you.*

The darkness welcomes her like an open grave. *We're coming to get you* is a dying whisper in her mind.

We're coming to get you get you get you

CHAPTER SEVENTEEN

When he gets the call, Ethan Connors is at his desk in the Criminal Investigations Division bullpen he shares with four other detectives and a Property and Evidence technician.

The Pecan Springs CID is much smaller than his unit with the Bexar County DA's office, where he worked until a few months ago. But then the town of Pecan Springs is considerably smaller than the city of San Antonio. Which means that there's less crime and the cases they work on don't often involve high-powered gang crimes or high-dollar drug deals.

But there's still enough to keep them busy. The other detectives — three men, one woman — are all married, with families, so they try to work eight-to-five as much as possible. Ethan long ago got into the habit of starting early and working late, six days a week, sometimes seven, depending on the load. And since he now goes home to an empty house — well, empty unless you count Einstein, who sleeps all day anyway — he's logging even more hours.

So he is often alone in an otherwise empty CID bullpen, as he is now. He is staring into his computer monitor, scrolling through the posts on Allison Montgomery's Facebook page, looking for clues to her disappearance. He's especially alert to possible places where she might go to hide out or people who might know where she is. Late in the afternoon, the neighborhood canvass turned up one more person who claimed to have seen the gray van, but that doesn't persuade Ethan that there was a *real* abduction, especially because none of the witnesses could identify the driver. He's convinced himself that Wilcox was behind the wheel, that she picked up Montgomery on Harper Lane, and that both the kidnapper and the kidnapping are fake.

But if Montgomery has left a clue to her disappearance on social media, Ethan can't find it. She doesn't appear to have a Twitter account and there's nothing useful on Instagram or Snapchat, so he logs off and shuts the computer down. He's got paperwork to do before he can call it quits for the day. When that's done, he's decided he'll stop at

Gino's and pick up a pizza, which he can reheat when he and Einstein get back from their evening run. That and a couple of glasses of Chianti, and he'll be fine. Just fine.

The little frame house he rented when he moved from San Antonio a few months before isn't far from the river trail where the fake Montgomery/Wilcox kidnapping occurred. It's nothing special, furnished mostly from flea markets and garage sales. But Connors is handy with tools and a paint brush, and he's made the place comfortable for himself and Einstein, an eclectic mix of three or four breeds and a very smart dog. Ethan likes having little projects to do, like the bookcase he's building in his garage workshop. If things go right this weekend, he might even get it finished.

But there's another side to Connors, a second career as an outdoor writer/photographer, and a fairly successful one. The photo-essay assignment he's currently working on for *Lone Star Fishing & Hunting* is about managing whitetail deer on the Texas high plains and will include some pretty damned good photos of hefty bucks with giant (for whitetails, that is) racks of antlers — photos he took himself last year. If he can get some time this weekend, maybe he'll take his camera to Devil's Backbone and hike a couple of trails. It's wild out there. You never know what you might see.

But before he leaves the station this evening, he wants to wrap up his report on the afternoon's developments in the Montgomery case. Based on what the sister said about Montgomery "disappearing" for two weeks the previous year, he has already told the chief that what they've got is a conspiracy. He's wasted a full day on the investigation, so he's recommending that Wilcox be charged with obstruction and making a false police report. They can deal with Montgomery when she surfaces, as of course she will, eventually. The chief hasn't yet agreed, but he's planning to include both recommendations in his wrap-up report. After that, it's up to her.

He pulls up the file and gets started. He is still typing when his cellphone vibrates. He takes it out of his pocket, automatically checking the time: 6:59. It's the chief.

"Meet me in the parking lot in five minutes," she says, and rattles off the explanation.

He listens in mounting disbelief. When she's done, he swallows, hard. "You've called up the hostage rescue squad?"

"That's procedure, isn't it?" the chief snaps. "Five minutes."

Connors stands up, reaching for his jacket. "If this is another goddamned stunt," he grits between his teeth, "I am throwing both their asses in jail. Tonight."

"I'll help," the chief says.

At 7:05, Ruby and China are pulling up a half-block away from the small frame house at 321 Lampasas Street. According to China, Ruby has been sitting in her living room chair for the past half hour or so, unmoving, her eyes closed, answering China's questions in a dull, uninflected monotone. If it weren't for the cell phone recording, Ruby isn't sure that even *she* would believe what actually happened. She doesn't blame Sheila for being skeptical.

Ruby herself is drained and nearly exhausted by the effort to learn where Allison is being held. She wants nothing more than to collapse with a good, stiff drink and forget all the ugliness she has just seen and heard. And felt. Feeling Allison's pain, that was the worst of it — the agony of brutal physical violation, the trauma of psychological invasion, the spiraling sense of helplessness. Ruby is still trembling.

But when China telephones Sheila with

the name Roger Conklin, his street address, and a thirty-second recap of the past half hour's activities, the chief says she wants Ruby on the scene, pronto. She doesn't sound entirely happy about what they've done or convinced that Ruby's intervention with Allison has turned up a solid lead to the place where she's being held. But at least she's willing to check it out — with backup.

"Brave lady," China says, ending the call. "She's bringing backup. If this doesn't work, she'll be out there falling on her face in front of her whole team."

Ruby is in no shape to get behind the wheel, so China drives. Lampasas Street bisects a small subdivision built some forty years before and showing its age. Most of the frame two-bedroom, one-bath houses need a new coat of paint or roof and window repair or just general cleanup. There are no sidewalks, and the grass in the small front yards is sun-fried and littered with toys. The garages are mostly detached, and several of the driveways are blocked with motorcycles and derelict autos.

China parks her white Toyota at the end of the three-hundred block, and she and Ruby get out to watch. The scene is one of orderly chaos. Ruby counts five police cars:

two plus the chief's car parked in front of Conklin's house and one car parked cross-wise on the street at each end of the block, closing off traffic.

The afternoon rain has moved off to the east, but the evening sky is filled with low clouds and the humidity is so high that the August air feels like a sauna. A black PSPD van with heavily tinted windows pulls to a stop and four uniformed men armed with assault rifles and wearing helmets and ballistic vests pile out — a SWAT team. Moving swiftly, they station themselves at the corners of Conklin's house. Seconds later, an EMS ambulance arrives, jockeys around the patrol car blocking the north end of the street, and pulls up across from 321.

"This isn't a job for an army," Ruby protests, as a pair of officers behind black ballistic shields venture cautiously up to the front door of Conklin's house. "And Allison is in the *garage,* for crying out loud, not the house." She can see the chief, standing beside her police car in front of the house. Ethan Connors stands beside her, shoulders slouched, hands in his pockets. "Why don't they just break down the garage door and go in and get her?"

China takes out her cell and phones Sheila to let her know that Ruby is available if she's needed. Sheila turns and waves. Ruby and China wave back. Ethan Connors doesn't look in their direction.

Pushing her phone into the back pocket of her jeans, China answers Ruby's question. "Sheila says they're treating this as a hostage situation. They're starting with the assumption that the kidnapper could be in the garage with her, and armed. Or he might have gone into the house and taken her with him. They're calling the landline number for the house, but nobody's answering. Sheila has also put out an alert for the vehicle registered to him. It's that gray panel van he parked on Harper. An older model Ford."

"But he's not *in* the garage," Ruby protests. "I don't know where he is, but he's not there. They could get her out of the garage right now, without a problem."

"According to you," China says with a crooked smile. "But you're just the psychic, remember?"

"I am not a —" Ruby starts to protest, and then stops.

She *is* a psychic. They are watching a half-dozen or more cops preparing to storm a house and rescue a kidnap victim because she is a psychic. She might as well own up to it, for better or worse.

"I still think they should just go in and get her," she says stubbornly.

China folds her arms and leans against the car. "Look at it from Sheila's point of view, Ruby. She's got a tip — which she's treating as anonymous — that a kidnap victim is being held in that garage. That gives them the 'exigent circumstances' they need to break into the place without a warrant. But what if the tipster is wrong? What if you misidentified the photo you saw on that bulletin board? What if this is the wrong address, wrong garage, and there's no Allison?" She gestures at the cop cars and waiting hostage rescue team. "Sheila's on the spot in a big, big way. So are you. And so is Allison. If she's not here, that's the end of it. Sheila won't be able to call up the hostage squad again."

China is right and Ruby knows it. Her mistake could mean the end of Allison's life and the end of Sheila's career. She watches nervously. A kid on a bicycle attempts to ride around the squad car at the end of the block, and the cop stops him. A mom with twin toddlers in a double stroller stands at the corner for a moment, hesitating, then turns and pushes the stroller in the opposite direction, fast. A small knot of neighbors has gathered across the street from 321 —

men and women, kids and dogs. They're quietly apprehensive, watching the hostage rescue team, armed with their shields, bang on the front door and shout, "Police! Open up!"

And then, quite suddenly, Ruby feels a tingle across her shoulders and down her arms, and at the back of her mind, a rising darkness. Eyes closed, she turns away from China and leans her forehead against the car. Through Allison's eyes, she had seen Roger Conklin's face in the photograph in the garage. She is seeing his face again.

But this time, she is seeing it as a *reflection,* as Conklin glances into the mirror-like sliding window at a fast-food drive-through. She sees his brush-like black mustache and the jagged scar on his left cheek. She sees the window slide open and his beefy left arm reach out and take a cardboard tray holding a large white bag and two lidded drink containers. *Sam's Best Burgers* is printed in red letters on the bag and the drink containers. He puts his order on the passenger seat, drops his change into a cup in the center console, and begins to pull out of the lot.

Ruby turns back to China and clutches her arm. "Call Sheila," she says urgently. "Tell her that Conklin just picked up a double order of burgers at Sam's. He's on his way here, right now. Hurry! Sam's is less than a mile away!"

For the space of several heartbeats, China stares at her, then makes the call. Sheila puts her cell to her ear, turns and stares at China and Ruby as China repeats what Ruby has said. Then she lowers the phone and turns to Connors with an order.

A moment later, the two squad cars that were blocking the street peel off and disappear. At the same time, there is a rush of activity on the driveway. Three cops, guns drawn, run up to the garage. More shouts — "Police, open up!" — and a loud banging, and the sound of a door being kicked open. Pushing a gurney, a pair of emergency medical responders hurry up the driveway.

Ruby and China wait in tense silence for what seems like a very long time. Ethan Connors is on his phone, then he says something to Sheila. Then, with her cell phone at her ear, Sheila faces China and points. China's phone rings and she clicks on and listens, then turns to Ruby.

"Great news!" she exclaims. "They got Conklin. They stopped him three blocks from here, with his takeout order from Sam's. They have him cuffed, in custody."

And then the garage door opens and the

EMS team runs down the driveway, with a woman strapped to the gurney. They hustle her into the ambulance and are gone, siren wailing, lights flashing.

Standing beside the chief's car, Sheila sends Ruby and China a big thumbs-up. Beside her, Ethan Connors turns. He shakes his head and raises his hands to shoulder level, palms out.

Ruby doesn't need to be psychic to read that gesture. It is surrender.

A mock surrender, but surrender just the same.

CHAPTER EIGHTEEN

"Tell me," Sophia says. "I want to hear all about it."

It is the week after Allison was released from the hospital. Conklin has been arraigned and is still in jail, waiting for a bond hearing — although China says he will likely be denied bail. Sophia and Ruby are sitting with glasses of lemonade on Sophia's front porch, looking across a field of sunflowers and goldenrod to the darker trees along Cypress Creek. Evening is falling and the hummingbird feeder at the far end of the porch is hosting a bevy of brilliant little birds, winged jewels hovering in the early September air under the watchful eye of Pyewacket, stretched to his full length on the porch railing. At the other end of the porch, a sweet autumn clematis vine attracts a cloud of diligent bees. A light breeze lifts Sophia's gray hair.

Ruby has the feeling that Sophia already

knows the story, even though only the bare bones of it appeared in the newspaper — without the word "psychic" or a single mention of her name. But she tells Sophia the whole thing anyway. When she is finished, Sophia asks just one question.

"Does Allison remember anything of the time you spent with her?"

Ruby shakes her head. "I haven't talked to her myself, but I understand that she doesn't. Sheila won't accept China's cellphone recording. The story is that the cops were acting on an anonymous tip when they showed up at Conklin's house. And that they caught up with Conklin when an officer spotted his vehicle coming out of Sam's drive-through."

"That's best." Sophia's voice is soft. "Allison will have a hard enough time dealing with the trauma of the kidnapping and the assault — and then there will be the trial. It will be good if she's able to put the whole thing past her and get on with her life." She waves away a curious bee. "Do the police know why Conklin targeted her?"

"He told Ethan Connors that he first saw her at Body Matters, where he was doing weightlifting training. He asked her out — not just once, but repeatedly. At first she said no nicely, but when he kept pestering her, she told him to stop bothering her. The rejection infuriated him, he said."

"Ethan Connors." Sophia smiles. "The detective who refused to believe you when you first reported the kidnapping."

"That's the guy." Ruby sips her lemonade. "Apparently, what really threw him was when they picked Conklin up with those takeout burgers. He had to admit that I couldn't have known where the man was, not by any ordinary means. As to whether or not Connors actually *believes* me — well, the jury's still out on that."

Pyewacket leaps lightly from the railing into his mistress' lap. Sophia regards Ruby for a moment, absently stroking the cat. At last she says, "There's more to come, you know."

"More to come?" Ruby is surprised. "Not on *this* case, I hope."

"Not on this matter," Sophia agrees, "at least as far as you're concerned. But you can't stop here, Ruby. You know who you are now. You have a better sense of what you can do." Her eyes are warm. "And you can already do more than you know."

Ruby shivers. "That sounds mysterious enough."

"It's not meant to be mysterious. I just mean that your resources are already much broader and stronger than you understand. And the more you use them, the better they will serve you."

The more you use them. Ruby sighs. "I should have read the fine print."

That brings a chuckle. "There are some things we don't get to choose in our lives, you know. Our genetic makeup is one of those things. You inherited a very strong intuition, coupled with clairvoyance and a profound empathy."

Ruby starts to say something, but Sophia holds up her hand. "And we don't always get to choose how we use that inheritance. Fate or chance or luck, whatever you want to call it, opens up new possibilities. You've used this experience to reach a new level of competence and understanding. Other opportunities will come — opportunities you won't be able to turn down."

"I hope you're not encouraging me to become one of the Psychic Sisters," Ruby says. Ramona had dropped in for breakfast that morning with more of her plans for their big project. Ruby reminded her that she had already declined, but as usual, Ramona wasn't listening.

Sophia's smile is amused. "There are more and better ways for you to use your gift. And to help you come to terms with what happened with Sarah."

"You know about . . . her?" Ruby bites her lip.

"Just watch," Sophia says gently. "And wait. The opportunities will come."

A mourning dove calls from a tree along the creek, its plaintive call echoing through the evening air. Two scissor-tailed swallows dance and pirouette high in the sky, while a persistent woodpecker drums industriously on a nearby tree.

Ruby looks out over the green landscape. The world seems just as it should, with Nature going about its usual end-of-summer business. She is glad she was able to help Allison. Her guilt about Sarah has lightened — a little, anyway. She and China have grown even closer, Sheila is a little more convinced, and Ethan Connors is a lot less sure of himself.

But she can't help feeling an uneasy nudge of apprehension. Important things in her life — essential things, fundamental things — seem about to change.

She just wishes she knew *how.*

■ ■ ■ ■

SOMEBODY ELSE

BOOK 2

■ ■ ■ ■

If your happiness depends on somebody else, I guess you do have a problem.
Richard Bach,
Illusions: The Adventures of a Reluctant Messiah

I don't want your body, but I hate to think about you with somebody else.
"Somebody Else," The 1975
(a British rock group)

CHAPTER ONE

China Bayles pushes the last cardboard carton into the van and steps back. "Are you sure you've got everything, Ruby?"

"I think so," Ruby Wilcox closes Big Red Mama's rear hatch and gives her nicely curved backside an affectionate pat. "I topped off her oil and checked her tires. Mama and I are ready to roll."

China and Ruby bought the used van several years ago so they could haul things for their shops — China's Thyme and Seasons herb shop and Ruby's Crystal Cave — and Party Thyme, their catering service. They were totally smitten by the rainbow of mystical symbols the van's former owner painted on her, probably under the influence of a certain hallucinatory herb. To Ruby, Mama looks like a cross between a large Crayola box scampering down the highway and a Sweet Potato Queen float on the way to a Mardi Gras parade. In other words, Big Red Mama is picture-perfect.

It is a sunshiny Friday morning in October. The temperature is expected to top out in the upper seventies — cool, after a summer of everyday nineties — and there's not a single cloud in the crystalline blue Texas sky. Ruby is on her way to the Mystic Creek Harvest Festival, where she will have a vendor's booth. So she's dressed for a working weekend in bright purple leggings, red rope sandals, a fire-engine red tank, and a gauzy orange overblouse — a great complement to her frizzy carrot-red hair.

The festival is a popular folk music and arts and crafts weekend that is held every autumn near the Lost Maples State Natural Area, about 150 miles west of Pecan Springs. The annual two-day festival takes place at the Mystic Creek Guest Ranch in Bandera County, always at its most beautiful in mid-October. The Arts and Crafts Marketplace is juried, so it's considered an honor to be invited to exhibit and sell your wares.

China puts her arms around Ruby and gives her a goodbye hug. "They're forecasting showers and thunderstorms on Sunday afternoon, but tomorrow looks great." She steps back. "I hope you and Laurel sell tons of our stuff and Mama comes home completely empty."

Ruby gives her a regretful look. "I just wish you could go. It won't be nearly as much fun without you."

For the past two years, China's Thyme and Seasons and Ruby's Crystal Cave have shared a booth at Mystic Creek. Both times, they did very well, selling almost everything they took — always a mark of a show's success, if you're a vendor. This year, however, there are a couple of big weekend events scheduled at Thyme for Tea, the tea room that adjoins the shops. On Saturday, there's a luncheon for the Hospital Ladies Guild, and on Sunday afternoon, a bridal shower. China has elected to stay behind and see that everything goes perfectly.

But even though China can't be at the festival, she is sending along several boxes of herb products from Thyme and Seasons (soaps, oils, seasonings) and trays of favorite perennials — rosemary, lavender, St. John's wort, thyme, sage, and garlic. These are growing in four-inch pots and ready for fall planting.

From the Crystal Cave (still the only New Age shop in Pecan Springs), Ruby is taking a large assortment of unusual and hard-to-find items: crystals and gemstones, divination tools and talismans, handcrafted runestones, incense and fragrance oils, tarot and angel card decks, candles, dream catchers, and a couple of cartons of books on magic, astrology, feng shui, and meditation. She has also packed the canopy tent, signs, and the portable display racks and tables that she and China always take when they're doing a show. Oh, and the credit card reader, the portable cash register, and change. Big Red Mama is loaded to the gills.

China nods. "I'm sorry, too, babe. It would be great to get out of town for a weekend. But Laurel will be a big help." She grins. "That girl knows our merchandise. Plus, she has some serious muscles." Laurel Wiley, a long-time helper at the shops, eagerly volunteered to help with the festival.

"Laurel's muscles will definitely come in handy," Ruby says, climbing into the driver's seat. "There'll be a lot of toting and hauling."

China shuts Mama's door. "Safe travel," she says, stepping back. "Hope you and Laurel have fun!"

Ruby waves goodbye, backs Mama out into the alley, and drives off. She is picking Laurel up at her apartment on the west side of town, so that's the direction she takes — past the Orpheum Opera House, the offices of the *Pecan Springs Enterprise,* and the old Adams County Courthouse, which looks like a wedding cake carved out of frosted pink granite. The courthouse square also offers plenty of attractive shopping: a Ben Franklin five-and-dime, a couple of antique shops, the Thrift Shop Boutique, a quilt shop, and several small restaurants. Typical small-town Texas.

A dozen blocks farther on, Ruby pulls up in front of the Gatewood apartment complex, and Laurel appears. She slings her small weekend bag onto the floor of the front seat — there isn't room in the back — and climbs in.

"Hey, Ruby," she says cheerfully. "Have we picked a great weekend, or what? The weather is gorgeous, and I am so excited about this festival. I *love* folk music."

A slim woman in her thirties, Laurel is dark-eyed and demure, with a dimple in her left cheek. She looks like a cowgirl in her checked cotton shirt with jeans and a tooled leather belt, and she wears her dark hair in twin braids laced with rawhide strips. Over several years, she has proved herself one of the most reliable helpers at the shops — somebody who can always be counted on when she's needed.

"It's going to be fun," Ruby agrees, putting Mama in gear and pulling out onto the highway. She is heading west for the cutoff to Route 27 — not the fastest way to get where they are going, but the prettiest.

"And there's good news," she adds. "I got a phone call from the ranch yesterday evening. A lot of the vendors will be camping in their own RVs, but since we don't have one, I asked Marianne — who makes the arrangements — to put us in a cabin. At first, she didn't think there would be one available. But somebody canceled, and we were next on the list. No kitchen, but there's a bathroom, a teensy shower, and bunk beds. We'll have a couple of cabin mates."

"I'm sure we won't miss the kitchen," Laurel says comfortably. "If it's like other festivals, there'll be dozens of food vendors. I'll probably end up eating twice as much as I should." She gives Ruby a narrow look. "I was gone for a good part of the summer and missed all the excitement. China told me about the bike accident. You're okay?"

"It was just a *little* accident." Ruby says with a crooked smile. "If that tree hadn't jumped out in front of me, I never would have ridden into it." She chuckles. "Nothing serious — just a few headaches, that's all."

"That isn't what China tells me," Laurel

replies. "You were knocked out, weren't you? China said it was a concussion. And after that, headaches, dizziness, even a blackout or two."

"Something like that, I guess," Ruby concedes. There is also a healing scar above her right temple, which sometimes throbs uncomfortably.

"And then," Laurel says in a meaningful tone, "China said that your psychic abilities seemed to grow stronger, maybe as a result of the accident." Ruby, Laurel, and China have worked together for a long time, and Laurel has already witnessed several instances of Ruby's very genuine psychic gifts — gifts that Ruby herself has always tried to downplay.

"That's what Sophia says," Ruby replies hesitantly.

Sophia D'Angelo is a teacher who offers classes on enhancing intuition at the Cave and has helped Ruby understand more about what she can do — and what it might mean. Research suggests (Sophia said) that even slight brain injuries can boost psychic power in substantial ways, making people more sensitive to the energies around them.

"If you were a radio," she added, "it would be as if your receptive capabilities had been amplified exponentially. You can receive and process signals — both positive and negative — that you couldn't before."

Ruby wasn't eager to hear this, but she has to admit that she's noticed several changes in herself, such as increased dreaming and more frequent déjà vu experiences. She has always been able to see auras, but since the accident, the auras that used to be dim and diffuse are now clearer and more radiant. Her sense of smell is sharper, and her acoustic senses seem to be more acute, to the point where she is able to hear sounds that are inaudible to others.

"Well, if Sophia says it's true, it must be true," Laurel replies in a practical tone. "China also mentioned the Montgomery kidnapping. She said that you got involved because of a dream. Sounds like a great story. Fill me in on the details?"

"Are you sure you want to hear?" Ruby asks. "It's not exactly thriller material. No chase scenes, I mean. No shooting, no blood on the floor. It'll never become a movie."

Laurel laughs. "Maybe not, but China thought it was quite exciting — especially the part where the two of you watched the SWAT team close in on the place where the kidnap victim was being held."

So Ruby finds herself telling Laurel about

212

the abduction of Allison Montgomery. She had been pulled into it by a recurrent dream, in which she saw a young woman kidnapped on the hike-and-bike trail. At China's urging, she had taken her story to Sheila Dawson, the Pecan Springs chief of police, and a friend. It was a tough thing to do, reporting a crime that she had only *dreamed* about. But it was even tougher to hear that the kidnapping had actually happened. Before she knew it, Ruby found herself involved in the investigation — and not in a good way.

As things turned out, the event required Ruby to acknowledge her psychic abilities, which are substantial. But for her, the term "psychic" is colored by an awkward and embarrassed self-consciousness, as if she has an extra pair of hands or a bizarre third eye in the middle of her forehead. She can listen to people's thoughts and feel their feelings, which (if she's not careful) causes all sorts of problems. She can sometimes (but not always) pick up information from people's belongings or things they have touched. She can occasionally see things that are happening someplace else, and she can even move things around, although she isn't as good at poltergeisty things as her ditzy sister, Ramona, who is also psychic

213

and normally *very* weird.

The trouble is that Ruby has spent most of her life trying to hide her paranormal abilities. No little girl wants to be different from her friends, so as a child she pretended that she had no clue about what people were thinking. Or that she didn't already know it was Grandma Gifford when the telephone rang or that the Little League game would be rained out on Saturday and they'd have to reschedule.

She never liked to share her predictions, either. She was right most of the time, but she could be wrong, too. Being wrong was embarrassing — and might be difficult, or even dangerous. What if she told a friend that something good was going to happen, and he counted on it, but then it didn't happen?

Or what if she saw something terribly dark in somebody's life — should she let her know? If she saw it coming, did that mean it was going to come regardless, no matter how hard somebody tried to avoid it? And if she saw something about to happen, did that mean she was *making it happen*?

Which was worse? Being wrong about something bad or making it happen?

Having told her story, Ruby falls silent. After a moment, Laurel says, "I know how uneasy you are about your abilities. And yet you've created the Crystal Cave. Isn't that a bit of a contradiction? I'd think you might want to stay away from that sort of thing. Astrology and the tarot and stuff like that, I mean."

Ruby has seen the contradiction, too, and has to laugh. "Actually, my life got a lot easier after I opened the Cave. Yes, I'm dealing with a lot of different psychic traditions. And with people who think that a shop that specializes in crystal balls and magic wands and books of spells is just totally *awesome,* sort of like the Pecan Springs campus of Hogwarts School of Witchcraft and Wizardry. But the Cave is where I can be me — or maybe it's more like a little bit of me, without going the whole way. The Cave is sort of a protected space, somewhere between normal life and the totally weird. If that makes any sense," she adds.

"It does, actually," Laurel says, considering "Like a play space, maybe. Where you can explore the supernatural without getting sucked into it."

Ruby nods, pleased that Laurel understands. "That's it exactly. I can teach classes in astrology, which isn't especially frightening because it's mostly a matter of reading what's spelled out in the birth chart. In the same way, I enjoy doing card readings, or using the I Ching or runestones or the Ouija board. The cards or the stones or the board tell me what to say. I don't need to tap into any special abilities."

Laurel thinks about that for a moment. "That makes sense, too," she says finally. "All the attention is focused on the tool, and not on you, as a psychic."

"That's it," Ruby says, agreeing. "When I'm using the tools, all I have to do is read what the cards say, or the stars, or the Ouija board. It's like a performance. There's a script, and I can play it over the top or underplay it. Either way, I can do it without getting involved in it."

Laurel raises a skeptical eyebrow. "All the time?"

"Well, no," Ruby concedes reluctantly. "Even a safe reading can turn risky — risky for me, I mean. Sometimes something serious emerges and I can't help getting pulled into it."

Like a therapist who has to keep her walls up and her personal boundaries secure, Ruby tries very hard not to get sucked into somebody else's trauma. But sometimes it's impossible to resist the pull. That's when being psychic can turn into your worst nightmare.

Which is what happened when Allison Montgomery was abducted, and Ruby found herself trying to convince Detective Ethan Connors that a crime had been committed. But he was a man who prided himself on gathering and using facts. Anything psychic was not factual. Anything psychic was irrational, unscientific, and unprofessional. It couldn't be defended in court. It was all woo-woo.

"There is way too much woo-woo going on here," he had told her sternly. "You are going to stay the hell out of my investigation. You got that? No. More. Woo-woo."

And then he had surprised her by showing up at the shop just a few days ago. "I gave you a hard time on the Montgomery case," he said with a crooked grin, "and you turned out to be right. I owe you an apology. I was thinking about dinner. Like, maybe this weekend?"

Ethan Connors was an attractive man — well-built, dark-haired, with ice-blue eyes and a self-confident air. And here he was, actually apologizing. Or at least that's what it sounded like.

So Ruby had a pretty good reason to sound regretful when she told him she had other plans for the weekend.

"I'm signed up to be a vendor at the big

Harvest Festival out near Lost Maples. Folk music and an arts and crafts show. I'm driving out there on Friday and won't be back until Sunday."

"Lost Maples, huh?" There was a moment's silence while he considered that. "I've heard a lot about that festival, but I've never been there. Maybe I'll drive out and see what it's all about. Might be kind of fun. If I do, maybe I'll see you there." He paused, gave it a little more thought, and said, "Matter of fact, I started my police work as a Bandera County deputy. I happen to know of a great little café in Utopia. If I'm able to make it, maybe we could drive over on Saturday evening and get some supper."

"Let's see what happens," Ruby said, with only half a smile. She had counted three *maybes,* a *might,* and an *if,* which told her she shouldn't get too excited about the possibility of dinner with Ethan. Still, he really *was* attractive. Sexy, even. And interesting.

"Okay," he said. "I'll call you. Let you know what's up."

But there was more.

As a cop, Ethan had obviously learned to keep his walls up — to resist any effort to read his thoughts and feelings. But as he was leaving the shop, he dropped his guard just long enough to let Ruby hear what he was thinking. He wasn't apologizing, and he still didn't believe her explanation for what had happened with Allison in that garage. He had asked her out because he wanted to learn how she had managed to pull it off.

Bottom line: he was willing to drive all the way out to Bandera County to find out just how psychic she was. Or wasn't.

So that was that.

He didn't call, of course. Ruby felt a brief disappointment, but she had let it go. After a divorce and any number of romances that went nowhere, she has to admit that she has a lousy track record where men are concerned. Being psychic doesn't mean that she understands what's going on in a relationship. In fact, when it comes to love and romance, she can barely see past the end of her nose. She always wants too much, hopes for too much, and is disappointed every time.

And in this case, she understands all too well what's going on. Ethan Connors isn't interested in getting to know her as a whole person. He is only interested in the part of her that is different.

And Ruby has spent most of her life trying *not* to be different.

More than anything else, it is Ethan Connors' curiosity as a law enforcement officer that has prodded him to drop in at the Crystal Cave.

Before he moved to Pecan Springs, Connors had worked in the Criminal Investigations Division of the Bexar County DA's office, in San Antonio. There, he had come across several cases that involved psychics of one variety or another — all of whom turned out to be hoaxes and frauds.

There was the woman who coaxed her victims into bizarre psychic rituals involving rose petals, magnets, "magical" candles, and clear potions that turned blood red when applied to the skin. Another who convinced her trusting targets to withdraw cash from their banks, then "loan" it to her to be placed on an altar in her "church" — and (of course) to enrich the fraudster's bank account. And still another who had come to the police with a tip about a girl who had disappeared five years before. She had dreamed that the victim's remains were buried under a live oak tree at a crossroads in a nearby state park. Bones were found, right where she said they'd be. Deer bones.

So when Ruby Wilcox popped up with a dream-inspired tip about a kidnapping *before* anybody knew that a kidnapping had taken place, Connors' experience with psychics told him exactly what to expect. She and Allison Montgomery, the so-called victim, had cooked up a conspiracy together. There would be ransom demands, threatening messages from the "kidnapper," and media appearances by Ms. Wilcox. In other words, this was complete and total psychic bullshit. And though the financial motive wasn't immediately apparent, it would reveal itself soon enough.

But it didn't. There were no ransom demands, no messages from the kidnapper, no media appearances.

And as things developed, Connors had to admit that Ruby Wilcox was . . . well, *different* from those other psychics. What she told him about the abduction was supported by the physical evidence he found at the scene. She had discovered where Allison was being held by some sort of bizarre psychic prowling in the victim's mind, and had even told the cops where to find the man who had abducted her. Equally weird, in Connors' experience, was that Ruby Wilcox insisted that the PSPD take all the credit (which of course they did) for rescuing Allison Montgomery and capturing her kidnapper. She wanted none of it.

All of this was beyond anything that Connors had ever experienced. But there are more things in heaven and earth, Horatio, than are dreamt of in your philosophy, he told himself. And when they found and rescued Allison and took her kidnapper into custody, he was very nearly convinced that Ruby Wilcox might be that rare thing: the genuine article. The only authentic psychic he had ever met. The only one who is *different*.

Very nearly convinced. But not quite.

For Connors is a born skeptic who believes in disbelieving everything until he substantiates it to his own personal satisfaction. And over the past few weeks, he has found himself beset by curiosity, unable to answer several deeply puzzling questions.

How on God's little green earth had Ruby Wilcox pulled off such a mind-boggling trick?

Was there some kind of fakery he hasn't

yet uncovered?

What else could she do, if she put her energy and her creative imagination to work?

If she did, would this be a good thing — or a bad thing?

So Connors attempts to build a case. First off, he does some reading about psychics who work with cops. It's all pretty controversial, of course, and the results he finds online aren't very clear cut. But he has friends in other police departments, and after he's talked to a few people and listened to a few stories, he begins to understand that most cops aren't very anxious to admit to the public that they have collaborated with a psychic. It's too creepy. Too weird. Too out-of-the-box.

But privately, it's a different story. He hears about successful psychic crime solvers, all the way from the usual tip that pans out to the more unusual "special extended collaboration." He even uncovers an online report from the federal Department of Justice detailing eight cases in which psychics offered significant information — three of them involving the locations of dead bodies — and suggesting guidelines for the use of psychics in police work. The DOJ guide asserts that *selecting* a psychic is often the most important and difficult step. There are no criteria for this, although the author of the report concedes that a "bad choice might be more of a hindrance than a help."

Bottom line: using a psychic is unconventional. It is also controversial.

But it isn't unheard of.

And one of Connors' friends — a lieutenant on the San Francisco police force — finally tells him, "I've pretty much decided that if telepathy, clairvoyance, or ESP can give us an edge on the bad guys, who am I to say we shouldn't use them? Hell, I'd listen to Al Capone's ghost, if he'd tell me who killed that delivery boy on Lombard Street last week."

This doesn't convince Connors, but it does give him something to think about.

He also looks into Ruby Wilcox's background, learning that she is divorced, with two daughters in their twenties and a four-year-old granddaughter. She lives in a Painted Lady Victorian in a quiet neighborhood, belongs to a Wiccan group in Pecan Springs (he has to learn what *that* is), and teaches popular classes in astrology, tarot, and various wacky forms of fortune telling at her New Age shop, the Crystal Cave. She's also a partner in several related enterprises and has a reputation as a savvy businesswoman.

And a few other, more personal things. Ruby is tall enough to stand eye-to-eye with him (which enhances her *differentness* in Connors' mind). She has an unusual way of paying attention as he speaks (which might just mean that she is peering into his private thoughts). And she wears a citrusy perfume that reminds him too much of Carole (who is no longer in his life).

The perfume is definitely a problem, for it also reminds him of a desire that he would rather forget. He had stayed with Carole much longer than had been healthy for either one of them, hating her dependence on opioids but loving her. He knows that this was part of the problem, for she might have found the strength to pull out of it on her own if she hadn't depended on him to save her — which she did because he was there, and because depending on him was a long and powerful habit.

Still, he's smart enough to know that what happened would have happened whether he'd stayed or whether he'd gone, and that there is nothing he can do now to change things. At least there aren't any kids, which would have multiplied the heartbreak.

But kids or no kids, the end result is that he does not want another woman in his life

— not now, maybe never. He doesn't need one, right? Between his work at the PSPD and his other interests, there isn't time for people, period. He and Einstein, his mixed-breed mutt, live in a comfortable two-bedroom frame house with a fenced yard for Einstein to dig in and a good-size garage workshop for him. He likes doing little projects, like the bookcase he's just finished and the front porch planter box that's next on his list.

He's also cultivating a second career, as a wildlife photographer and outdoor writer. Not that he plans to leave police work anytime soon, of course. He got his first job in policing as a deputy, working alongside his high school buddy, Larry Donahue, who is now the Bandera County sheriff. After several years, he was recruited by the Bexar County district attorney to work as a detective in the Criminal Investigations Division in San Antonio. That's when he and Carole got married. Things were great until the accident. After that, the very good years began to turn very bad.

And about that time, Connors met a guy who introduced him to wildlife photography, which quickly became a passion — a passion that has stuck with him through all the difficulties He likes taking pictures and writing about what he sees, and it turns out that he's good enough at both to sell most of what he produces. Currently, he has a photo-essay assignment for *Lone Star Fishing & Hunting,* about managing whitetail deer in the Texas Hill Country.

He's not sure he can get to the festival — he's working a narcotics investigation that may continue into the weekend. But if he does, he'll take his latest camera, a Canon 5D Mark IV with a 100–400 mm f/4.5–5.6 lens. He grew up in that part of the Hill Country and spent summers cowboying on his uncle's ranch near Vanderpool. He knows that there are plenty of whitetails along the Sabinal River. He'd like to pick up another good shot or two for his article.

But what he would really like to do is pick Ruby Wilcox's brain, to see what's going on in there.

To see if she is as psychic as she seems.

To see if she is *really* different, or just more of the same.

CHAPTER THREE

The Mystic Creek Guest Ranch is just a few miles from the 2,200-acre Lost Maples State Natural Area, one of the few places in Texas where you can find wild stands of native maple trees. These are bigtooth maples, a distant cousin of the eastern sugar maple from which maple syrup is produced. During the Ice Age, when the weather was cooler and wetter than it is now, they grew across all of Texas. As the ice receded and the climate changed, most died out. But a few stubborn stands, relics of a time and a climate long gone, still survive in shaded canyons and along the clear, cool streams of Bandera County, fed by the underground aquifers of the Edwards Plateau.

When they turn off Route 187 at the Mystic Creek road, Ruby and Laurel can see the maples glowing in vivid reds, oranges, and yellows. There's a big sign announcing Harvest Festival Weekend, with an orange arrow that points in the direction of the ranch. They drive across a wooden bridge and down a narrow gravel lane that winds for a mile through woods and open meadows toward the main ranch house and guest complex.

Mystic Creek Ranch is owned by Jason and Marianne Harrison, escapees from fast-track careers in Dallas. They bought it ten years ago and began advertising it as a summer guest ranch for families with kids and a year-round venue for large gatherings like the midsummer Renaissance Faire and the October Harvest Festival. It's still a working ranch, with cattle, sheep, and horses, although Ruby suspects that the animals are mainly for the guests' entertainment. It used to be a game ranch, and visitors are likely to see antelope, Texas Dall sheep, and red deer, as well as native whitetail deer. For people who want to stay over for a night or two during a big event, there are plenty of RV and tent spaces. There's also a bunkhouse for groups and a dozen rustic cabins scattered through the woods.

Ahead, past the ranch house and cabins at the end of the lane, Ruby can see the performance area — a grassy, five-acre field called the Green — where the bands will be playing on Saturday and Sunday. The Arts and Crafts Marketplace is in an adjacent field.

"That's where we're going?" Laurel asks, pointing to the field. It looks like some of the vendors are already there, setting up the display tents and canopies that are necessary for protection from both the sun and rain. Try to do a craft show in Texas without some kind of shade (an umbrella at the very least) and you won't do it again.

"That's it," Ruby says, with the happy anticipation she always feels when they start setting up for a weekend show. "But we have to pick up our space assignment first."

She pulls up at the end of a line of several trucks and RVs leading to the admissions booth, where Marianne Harrison is managing the vendor check-in. In the distance, Ruby catches a glimpse of Marianne's husband Jason, a heavyset, balding man in his late forties, driving the golf cart he uses to scoot around the ranch when he has to get somewhere in a hurry. Jason is an impulsive, abrasive guy with a famously short fuse. The year before, Ruby remembers, he lost his temper and pummeled a food vendor who had violated one of the rules. The vendor ended up with a broken nose. The ranch ended up with his medical bills.

On the surface, the guest ranch seems to be a success. Marianne and Jason have been operating it long enough to know what they're doing, but Ruby is aware that it must cost a bundle — and a huge investment in time and energy — to keep all their balls in the air. They can't do everything themselves, of course. They pay a couple of cowboys who handle the animals and provide riding and roping lessons to the guests, as well as several local women who come in every day to do the cooking and housekeeping. And they aren't solely responsible for the festival. They get a lot of help from volunteers from nearby small communities like Vanderpool and Leakey and Utopia, whose merchants benefit from the outflow of visitors attracted by ranch events. Still, even with all the help, Ruby wonders how Jason and Marianne manage to keep it together on a big weekend like this one.

Marianne is deeply tanned from long hours in the Texas sun, and she wears her blond hair skinned back in a bouncy ponytail that makes her look like a teenager. She's short, not quite five-foot-four in her cowgirl boots, and slender, which is quite a contrast to her husband's bulk. For fun, she raises quarter horses and competes in calf-roping and barrel racing, and she can be as tough as a bull's toenails when the occasion arises. She has managed the vendor part of the festival for five or six years and knows how to deal with the flocks of problems that always fly up like belligerent crows during the weekend.

The truck ahead of them pulls away. Ruby drives up to the booth and rolls down Mama's window. "Hi, Marianne," she says. "Ruby Wilcox, from the Crystal Cave in Pecan Springs. Looks like you've got a full house this year."

"Oh, sure, Ruby. Glad you're back," Marianne replies with an easy smile. "Yeah, big crowd. Nineteen food vendors, twenty-three arts, crafts, and retail. And we're still counting the bands. Ten or eleven, we think, maybe twelve. That's always a problem — we never know exactly which bands are coming until they actually show up. Makes the scheduling a little stressful for Jason." She peers into her computer screen and hits a few keys. Then she reaches into a box, takes out a manila envelope, and goes into her usual rapid-fire spiel.

"You're on Willow Lane, in booth twelve. In the packet you'll find your vendor vehicle pass, info about electrical outlets, a map, and the usual list of rules. My cell number's there if you need it, but unless you want to piss me off, don't call except in an emergency — a lost kid, a fire, somebody gets murdered. There'll be an armed security guard on site from ten p.m. to eight a.m. tonight and Saturday. His name is Luke, and he's a mean six-foot-plus son-of-a-gun who bull-wrestles for a hobby, so nobody's going to mess with him. But we're letting vendors sleep in their booths, if they feel like they need to keep an eye on things. Food vendors are setting up right now, so you don't have to go off site for supper. We've beefed up the Wi-Fi for the festival and credit cards should run better than they did last year. The gospel song service is Sunday morning at seven. Remember that you can't start packing up until four o'clock on Sunday, when the afternoon session is over. You and China have two bunks in Annie Oakley. It's marked on the map. Your cabin mates have already checked in." She looks past Ruby and sees Laurel. "Oops, sorry, hon. China didn't come with you?"

"Not this year. We have a couple of big events lined up this weekend, so somebody had to stay home and take care of business." Ruby gestures. "This is my helper, Laurel, who works with us at the shops. China says to tell you that the next time you and Jason get over to Pecan Springs, be sure to drop in. We'll treat you to lunch in the tea room." Ruby includes Jason to be polite. She and China enjoy Marianne. Jason, not so much. He's a bully.

Marianne grins, her even white teeth startling in her tanned face. "Hey, it's a deal. Hope it'll be a good weekend for you. There's a Western swing band in the barn tonight — the Cactus Junction Boys. Come around seven. Gonna be a big crowd tomorrow, lots of sunshine, but maybe some rain Sunday afternoon. Whatever, it'll be great. Y'all have fun!"

She hands Ruby the manila envelope, glances at the big black pickup in the line behind Mama, and briskly motions the driver forward. "Next!"

But something unexpected has happened. The instant Marianne's fingers touch hers, Ruby feels a jolt, like a static electrical spark, flash up her arm and across her shoulders. Instantly, she's aware that beneath her smiling, in-charge façade, Marianne is very afraid of something. Something big, something scary, something connected with Jason. And Ruby has picked up on it.

"You okay, Ruby?" Laurel is looking at her oddly, and Ruby wonders just how much she has noticed.

"Yeah, sure," she says, although her fingers

are still tingling. She tosses Laurel the envelope, puts Mama in gear, and drives off. Ever since the Allison episode, she has been having more and more unsettling experiences like this, quick glimpses into people's expectations, anxieties, fears, excitements. She hopes this one doesn't mean anything — anything bad, that is. She likes Marianne and admires her persistence in sticking with the ranch, and with Jason, through challenging times.

And right now, Ruby could do without the interruption. It's going to be a busy weekend, and she has better things to do than get stuck in somebody else's fears.

CHAPTER FOUR

The booth space that Ruby and Laurel are looking for is located along a wide grassy strip signposted as Willow Lane, between a stained glass artist and a trio of spinners and weavers from Wimberley.

"Gosh, what a great location," Laurel says excitedly, and Ruby agrees. Down the way, she can see a potter putting up a display of hand-thrown, hand-glazed pots, and nearby is a leather crafter, a candle maker costumed in an old-fashioned long dress and a sun-bonnet, a collector of vintage kitchen items, and several jewelry makers — interesting artisans who will attract a lot of traffic and increase everyone's sales.

Less happily, Ruby notices that Bonnie Lawrence, an artist from nearby Utopia, is back with her hand-painted silk scarves. Last year, Ruby bought a luscious red-and-purple infinity scarf from Bonnie, who is an attractive, voluptuous brunette. Bonnie shortchanged her by a whole twenty dollars, which Ruby didn't notice until she left the booth. When she took the scarf back to get the mistake corrected, Bonnie insisted that she'd given her the right change and actually accused Ruby of trying to steal the money. Now, when Ruby waves, Bonnie scowls, then pointedly turns away. It doesn't look like they'll be mending fences any time soon.

More to Ruby's liking, the food vendor directly across from their booth is from New Braunfels. He is steaming sauerkraut and grilling bratwurst, a blend of fragrances that is topped by the spicy scent of mustard. Ruby doesn't need to be clairvoyant to know what she's having for supper. And she won't have to walk far to get it.

Several years before, Ruby and China decided that they needed something a little more classy for fairs, fiestas, and outdoor markets than a couple of rickety card tables and an umbrella for shade. So they invested in a pop-up tent with a canopy top, a zippered front, and side and back panels for protection against the rain. It's ten by ten, so it fits the vendor spaces at most shows. The white tent has the shops' names printed across the front in large green letters, so it's good advertising for both Thyme and Seasons and the Crystal Cave. The lightweight steel frame goes up in a hurry, and the fabric is waterproof. The tent is fairly wind-resistant, too, anchored with weights on the four corners.

Ruby and Laurel make quick work of erecting the tent, staking it firmly, and setting up the tables and portable display racks. Then they haul the trays of plants and boxes of books and retail items from Mama to the tent. Laurel begins unloading boxes while Ruby covers the tables and starts putting stuff on the racks.

Within an hour, the interior of their tent has the look of an attractive shop. The racks of green plants are set against the back wall of the tent, flanked by colorful bookshelves and shelves of tarot and angel cards, candles, and incense, with delicate dream catchers suspended from the tent struts overhead. The magical items — divination tools, magic wands, and ritual knives (called athames) — are attractively displayed on shelves covered with dark blue velvet. The previous year, Ruby had sold quite a few wands and athames to members of a Wiccan group who drove over from nearby Kerrville. This year, she's brought more.

They have barely finished setting things up when curious vendors start dropping in to see what they're selling and take advantage of the usual early-bird vendor discount. A plump, round-faced woman named Yvonne exclaims, "I've been looking everywhere for this!" and pounces on a copy of *China Bayles' Book of Days,* which Laurel has just put on the book rack. Somebody buys two pots of rosemary and one of sage, and somebody else buys several scented candles. The leather crafter comes in, browses for several moments, and chooses a feathered and beaded dream catcher for his little granddaughter.

"It'll look pretty on the wall over Becky's bed," he says. "But what kind of dreams is it supposed to catch?"

"In some Native American legends," Ruby says, "the Spider Grandmother protects infants and children. So mothers crafted 'spider webs' out of twisted plant fibers and hung them on the hoop of the cradle board. The holes in the web allowed Spider Grandmother's blessings to come through in the form of good dreams, while the web trapped the nightmares — and any bad luck that happened to be floating around."

"Great story," the leather crafter says enthusiastically. "Becky will love it."

When he has gone, Ruby turns to a couple of young women lingering over the shelf of divination tools. "Can I answer any questions?" she asks.

One of the women, who has a tattoo of a snake on one arm, picks up a magic wand. "This is lovely. Rosewood, is it? What's the stone on the tip?"

"Yes, rosewood," Ruby says. "The tip is amethyst." She smiles. "If you're a vendor, the price is twenty-five."

"Thanks" the woman says. "Yes, I'm a vendor. I make wire jewelry. My booth is just a couple of spaces down — I have some things I think you'd like." She puts the wand back on the shelf. "Maybe we can make a trade."

"Sure," Ruby says. "Sounds like a plan."

The other woman looks like a college student in her Central Texas State T-shirt and cutoffs, her blond hair worn in purple-tipped spikes. She holds up a polished bloodstone — dark green jasper with splotches of blood red — dangling from a silvery chain.

"Is this for fortune telling?" she asks. "Or is it a piece of jewelry?"

"It's a pendulum," Ruby says. "But you can wear it as a pendant, too. In fact, people who use pendulums like to keep them in contact with their skin. They're used to answer questions."

"Oh, yeah?" The girl frowns. "So how does that work?"

Ruby picks up another pendulum from the display, this one made of glistening green jadeite. "Some people say it connects us with our unconscious mind — that part of us that knows more than we think. And perhaps with the collective unconscious, as well."

"Oh, really?" The girl sounds interested. "The collective unconscious. That's Carl Jung, isn't it? We studied him in Psych." She cocks her head. "So how do you use this thing?"

"Like this." Ruby demonstrates how to hold the pendulum. "You decide — or let the pendulum tell you — what its movements mean to you. For instance, a front-to-back swing might mean 'no' while a side-to-side movement could mean 'yes' and a circular movement could mean 'maybe' or 'unclear.' And you need to clear your mind, confirm your intention, and focus on the question you want to ask. Focus is important, because if your question is unclear or ambiguous, the response you get is likely to be confusing." She holds out the pendulum. "Here. You try it."

Obediently, the girl grasps the chain, and Ruby takes her hand, to help her loop it over her outstretched finger. As she does, an image of a steaming plate of grilled bratwurst flashes into her mind, along with the unmistakably pungent tang of sauerkraut.

Without thinking, she says, "You must work with the sausage-and-sauerkraut vendor."

"That's right," the girl replies with a smile. "I'm Janice, and the sausage guy is my dad, Herman. We're parked right across from you. How did you know?"

"Oh, just a lucky guess," Ruby says lightly.

Janice giggles. "I'll bet you're psychic," she says. "I'd like to buy the pendulum. But I'll have to run over to the sausage truck to get my purse."

"That's okay," Ruby tells her. "No need for an extra trip. Take the pendulum now. You can pay me later."

"Thank you!" The girl gives her a brilliant smile and waves goodbye.

"You've made a friend," Laurel says when she's gone. "And you gave her the best explanation of the pendulum that I've ever heard. The collective unconscious? Really?"

"Yes, really," Ruby replies, "although the pendulum is limited. Even if you get creative with your questions, all it can tell you is yes, no, or maybe. Tarot cards, on the other and, can answer all kinds of —" She breaks off as Marianne comes into the tent.

"Hey, guys," Marianne says. "Just checking to see how everything's going. Getting settled okay?"

"We're almost all set up," Ruby says.

"And we've already made a couple of sales," Laurel adds with a grin.

"Sounds like you're off to a great start," Marianne says. She pauses beside the velvet-covered shelf displaying the magical tools. "These are fabulous," she says, picking up one of the ritual knives. "And so unique." She studies it thoughtfully for a moment, then puts it down and picks up a wand with a carved ebony shaft and a rose crystal tip. She turns it in her fingers, then puts it down.

"We have lots of craftspeople and artists," she says, "but you two are the only vendors who have anything even remotely like this. You'll probably sell out."

Ruby picks up the wand and taps the rose crystal tip lightly against the cash box. "Let it be so," she commands.

"The more we sell, the less we have to haul home," Laurel agrees.

"And put back on the shelf when we get there," Ruby adds, making a face.

"You two are a *hoot*," Marianne says.

"Good luck!"

When she has gone, Ruby says, "How about if I stay with the booth while you take a shopping break? When you come back, I'll go. Tomorrow will be insanely busy and by Sunday, all the best items will be gone. If we see something we want, we'd better get it now."

"Great idea!" Laurel says, and leaves. Fifteen minutes later, she's back with a birdhouse that looks like a Hansel-and-Gretel cottage and a gorgeous skein of oatmeal-colored thick-and-thin handspun yarn from the yarn booth next door. She holds up the birdhouse. "For my patio," she says. "And I'm going to use the yarn to knit a cap for my sister. You should have a look, Ruby."

"On my way," Ruby says, and goes next door to linger over the baskets of hand-dyed batts and roving; rolls of sheep, llama, and alpaca fleece; and luscious dyed wool locks. Ruby loves to spin, so she yields to temptation and buys a half-pound of gorgeous variegated garnet roving that reminds her of berries and cream. If she ever has time to spin it into yarn, she'll have enough for a knitted scarf.

Leaving the yarn booth, she steps out onto Willow Lane, turns to the right, and finds herself at the booth that belongs to the snake-tattoo woman who makes hand-crafted wire jewelry. Remembering her comment about a trade, Ruby browses through the earrings and finds a pair of Taurus earrings made of polished silver.

"They're gorgeous," Ruby says, fingering them. "Taurus is my Sun sign. My Moon is in Cancer."

"Really?" the woman smiles. "I'm a Cancer myself." She takes some Cancer earrings from the rack, the wires twisted in a pair of graceful arcs. "How about earrings for your Moon sign as well? You could wear either pair, depending on your mood, or wear one of each. I'll be glad to trade both pairs for that rosewood-and-amethyst wand I was looking at a little while ago."

"Perfect," Ruby says happily, putting the earrings into her purse. "Come and get the wand anytime."

The vendors' tents and booths are all attractive, and there's a wide range of tempting shopping, from scarves and vintage clothing to books and antiques. But Ruby knows what she's looking for. She turns and heads for the stained glass booth on the other side of the Cave's tent.

The artist's name is Finn Cassidy, and his work is absolutely stunning. His tent is full of large stained glass panels (lovely but expensive), smaller suncatchers to hang in a window, lampshades and sconce covers, and small pieces like coasters and Christmas decorations — all attractively displayed, with backlighting that makes the colors shimmer. The sign on his booth includes the name and address of his studio: Finn Cassidy Glassworks, Utopia, Texas.

Ruby's eye has been caught by an iridescent blue and green dragon with red flames curling around his head. Her sister Ramona has a birthday coming up, and the dragon, a suncatcher, is a perfect choice. She points to it. "How much for that fabulous creature?"

The artist cocks his head on one side, considering. "I've got thirty-five on it, but let's call it thirty, including the vendor discount and sales tax." He turns the piece in his long, sensitive fingers and his shy smile softens his craggy face. "Sound okay?"

Finn is Irish, Ruby judges from his name and from his slight brogue, green eyes, sandy-red hair, and close-trimmed red beard. Tall and of slender build, with long, delicate fingers, he is wearing a black T-shirt, black jeans, and one silver filigree earring. His longish hair is pulled back into a little ponytail.

"Sounds good to me," Ruby says, putting three tens on the table beside his cash box. "My sister is hard to please, but I know she'll love your piece. Dragons are her totem creature."

Ramona is a bit of a fire-breather herself, with so much psychic energy that she has a hard time controlling it. Actually, the dragon is a *let's-kiss-and-make-up* offering, as well as a birthday present. Recently, Ruby nixed her idea for joining forces in a readings-by-telephone business called the Psychic Sisters, and Mona hasn't yet forgiven her. She hasn't given up, either. She raises the subject every time they're together, and Ruby's repeated *no* doesn't seem to get through to her. As far as Ramona is concerned, it's just a matter of time before Ruby gives in.

Finn begins wrapping the dragon in tissue. "My first sale of the weekend," he says. "Thanks for getting me off to a good start." Frowning a little, he reaches for some tape to secure the tissue. "Have you been a vendor at this festival before?"

"Twice," Ruby says. "The traffic was good both times. The music is always terrific, and things usually run pretty smoothly. Marianne and Jason do a good job organizing the event. It's one of my favorite festivals."

"Jason?" Finn's frown becomes a disgusted scowl. "If you ask me, that guy has an anger management problem. I parked in the wrong place — the signs in the parking lot were turned around — and he nearly bit my head off. I tried to tell him about the signs, but that made him even madder. I thought he was going to slug me, but the security guard who was with him grabbed his arm."

"Yeah, well, he's done that, too," Ruby says ruefully. "Slugged somebody, I mean. Marianne is a really sweet person and very helpful, so most of us try to make things easy for her. We just stay out of her husband's way when he's in one of his moods." She looks around, admiring Finn's work and thinking of the number of hours he has invested in his art. Stained glass requires a great deal of skill, as well as a creative imagination. "Sounds like you're new to this festival."

She tilts her head, catching the plaintive strains of a pair of fiddles and a woman vocalist, coming from the direction of the Green. They're playing "Red-Haired Boy," a melody she recognizes immediately from a CD of Irish folksongs she has at home. But the fiddles are playing slowly and in a minor key, with strangely dissonant chords.

And instead of the ballad lyrics she remembers, the vocalist is singing words she hears
quite clearly but doesn't recognize.

> Red-haired boy, I don't want nobody but
>   you, but you're giving your body
>   to somebody else.
> Irish boy, I'm still true to you, but you've
>   promised your heart
>   to somebody else.

"I'm a first-timer here," Finn says. He
bags the tissue-wrapped dragon and hands
it to Ruby. "I mostly stick to my studio. I
probably wouldn't be here if my ex-
girlfriend hadn't pushed me into applying. I
didn't want to let Marianne down, or I
would have backed out."

As Ruby takes the bag, she wonders
briefly why he might want to back out. But
she is distracted by the music, which has
suddenly grown louder. She turns and cocks
her head, listening as the melody sings
across the meadow.

> I don't want nobody but you, but you but
>   you
> but you're giving your body to somebody
>   else
>   somebody else somebody else

249

"Do you know that old Irish ballad?" Ruby asks. "It's lovely, isn't it?"

Finn lifts an eyebrow. "Irish ballad?"

"The music. A couple of fiddles playing 'Red-Haired Boy,' and a woman singing. But the melody is a lot slower and the words are different. I don't recognize them. Do you?"

"You must have better ears than I do," Finn says with an odd look. " 'Red-Haired Boy' is a great old Irish song. I've always loved it. But all I can hear is somebody hammering."

Ruby hears that, too. And suddenly, as if somebody has flipped a switch, the music stops. She strains, listening for the haunting old melody, but all she can hear is the hammering.

"Here you go." Finn takes a business card out of a cardholder. "I hope your sister enjoys her dragon. If you get over to Utopia, come by the studio and see what else I've done. Here's my card."

"I'll do that," Ruby says, wondering where the music went. Odd that it cut off so quickly, just as they were talking about it. She tucks the business card into her purse. "Well, there'll be plenty of music at the dance tonight. Will you be there?"

He shrugs. "Not sure whether I will or

not. I'm sleeping in the tent." He gestures at one of the larger pieces, a stained glass panel of a cascade of orchids in various shades of purple, blue, and deep red. "I'd hate for somebody to make off with that. It represents hundreds of hours of work." He sighs. "Maybe I shouldn't have brought it. I don't expect to sell it — far as I'm concerned, it's priceless. But I wanted people to see a sample of my best work. I'm hoping I might be able to pick up a commission or two."

"It's gorgeous," Ruby says. She sneaks a peek at the price tag. Eleven hundred dollars — not exactly priceless, but close enough, as far as her credit card is concerned. It's a large piece, probably four feet by four feet, and not the kind of thing somebody would make off with in the dead of night. Still, she understands why Finn is nervous about it. And Marianne has made a point of saying that vendors can sleep in their tents if they want to.

She says goodbye and walks back to the tent to close up for the evening. She's never had anything stolen at a show, and Marianne has said that there'd be a security guard on duty both nights. But there's no point in taking chances, so she plans to put the more expensive crystals and gemstones into the cashbox and lock it up in Big Red Mama overnight. Of course, that's not perfectly safe, either, but it seems safer than leaving it in the booth or taking it with her, especially since she intends to go to the dance.

She and Laurel unroll the tent's side flaps and front panels and zip everything shut, fastening the zippers at the bottom with the usual plastic security seals and pulling them tight. They carry the cashbox out to Big Red Mama, parked behind the tent. Then they grab their duffle bags and go looking for Annie Oakley, the cabin where they'll be sleeping.

And as they walk, Ruby hears the music again. The two fiddles, with the soprano singing those haunting lyrics.

Red-haired boy, I don't want nobody but
    you, but you're giving your body
                to somebody else.
Irish boy, I'm still true to you, but you've
    promised your heart
                to somebody else.

But Ruby doesn't bother to ask Laurel if she hears it, too. This time, it's different. She knows that the music isn't in her ears, but in her mind. It's stuck in her head — an *earworm,* it's sometimes called. One of those melodies that will play and play and play in an endless loop until it nearly drives you crazy.

Ruby sighs. The music is lovely, but she's wondering if she'll have to listen to it for the rest of the weekend.

CHAPTER FIVE

The cabins at Mystic Ranch bear the names of legendary Western figures: Judge Roy Bean, the Sundance Kid, Buffalo Bill, Jesse James. Ruby and Laurel are staying in the cabin named for the famous exhibition sharpshooter, Annie Oakley, who performed for royalty, heads of state, and huge crowds in Europe and America. She shot a cigarette out of the hand of the German crown prince who became Kaiser Wilhelm. Some wags remarked later that, had she shot Wilhelm instead of his cigarette, she could have prevented World War I.

The wood-frame cabin is only a few yards from Mystic Creek, under a sycamore tree with bark the color of old bones and leaves like burnished gold. The cabin is small, with a green metal roof and a narrow porch across the front. Inside, there are two pairs of bunks on opposite walls, a woodstove for heating, a square table and four chairs in the middle of the wood floor, and a door — probably to the bathroom — in the back wall. It's charmingly rustic, but there is electricity and the bunks are already made up with sheets, blankets, and pillows. There's even a blue china vase of wild sunflowers and autumn leaves on the table.

"Ah," Ruby says happily, glancing around. "All the comforts of home." It feels homey, too, with cheerful blue calico curtains at the windows, a braided rug on the floor, and those fresh flowers on the table. It would be even lovelier if that melody would stop playing in her head.

"Looks like our cabin mates have already moved in," Laurel says, nodding to the small suitcase and duffle bag on two of the bunks. She turns toward the unclaimed bunks. "I'll be glad to sleep on top."

"Fine by me," Ruby says, and Laurel slings her duffle bag up on the top bunk. Ruby puts hers on the lower, and pulls out her cell to check the time. "Gosh, it's nearly six. I'm ready for supper. I was thinking bratwurst for me. What about you?"

"I saw a vendor advertising chicken-fried bacon with onion rings," Laurel says with a straight face. "And another one had fried Frito pie."

"Chicken-fried *bacon*?" Ruby is aghast.

"And I've had Frito pie, but what under the sun is *fried* Frito pie?"

"I didn't know, either," Laurel confesses. "Had to ask. Turns out that it's chili con carne mixed with Fritos corn chips, cheese, pinto beans, and onions. Shaped into balls, dipped in batter, and deep-fried."

Ruby rolls her eyes, thinking of the fat calories. But Laurel is just getting warmed up.

"Or we could get some deep-fried salsa," she says enthusiastically. "Jalapeños, garlic, onion, and tomato, shaped into logs about the size of your finger, rolled in cornmeal and crushed tortilla chips, fried and served with cheese dip." She chuckles. "That's got some veggies in it, Ruby. Might be the healthiest thing out there."

But before Ruby can tell her what she thinks of deep-fried salsa, the bathroom door opens and a woman pads out, barefoot and dressed in a pink tank top and denim cutoffs. She is toweling her short, dark hair.

"Hi," she says. "If you're wanting a shower, you may have to wait a little while to let the water heater catch up." Her voice is low and husky. In her late twenties, she is painfully thin, with a pale ivory complexion. A blue and red tattoo of a snake crawls down her right arm, its coils emphasizing

256

the thinness. When she sees the snake, Ruby recognizes her — the vendor who traded the gorgeous Taurus and Cancer earrings for the rosewood wand.

"The water's no problem," Laurel says cheerfully. "We were just saying that it's about time for supper. And then there's the dance, which I personally plan to attend." She grins. "We didn't get to names earlier. I'm Laurel Wiley, from Pecan Springs."

There is a pair of tortoise-shell frame glasses on the table. The woman puts them on. "Erica Dreyer," she says. "From Utopia." To Ruby, she says, "Hope you'll enjoy wearing the earrings."

"I'm sure I will," Ruby says, putting out her hand. "I'm Ruby Wilcox, also from Pecan Springs."

Taking Erica's hand is like grasping a fistful of frozen twigs, and the snake tattoo seems to come alive, crawling down the thin arm toward Ruby's hand. Pulling back, she tries to cover the awkward action by saying, "Stop by any time and pick up that wand."

Erica doesn't appear to notice Ruby's discomfort. "I'll come tomorrow morning, before things get hectic. You have some books that look really interesting. There aren't any bookstores in my little town." She grins crookedly. "Even if there were, they probably wouldn't carry books on tarot. I'm looking for a tarot deck, too."

"Glad to show you what we have," Ruby says, tempted to blow on her fingers to warm them. "I also brought a list of titles I carry in the shop — card decks, too. You can order anything we don't have here, and I'll be glad to put it in the mail. If you want to do that, your vendor discount will still be good."

"Great," Erica says, smiling. "Thanks!" She lifts her arms and wraps the towel around her head, turban-style.

There is a squeaky *meow,* and everyone turns toward the open front door. A pretty gray tabby cat is crossing the threshold, tail in the air, one dainty paw lifted.

Erica steps back. "Is that your cat?" she asks, alarmed. "Get it out of here, please! I'm allergic!"

"Oh, too bad," Laurel says. "No, it's not ours. Shoo, kitty." She herds the cat out and closes the door.

"I apologize," Erica mutters. "I'd love to have a cat of my own, but they make me break out in hives."

Laurel is looking around. "Didn't I hear that we have another cabin mate?"

"Right." Erica goes to her bunk and begins searching for something in a plastic cosmetic case. "Her name is Yvonne. She's selling vintage clothing in the booth next to mine. She's out getting some supper with a friend."

"I'm pretty hungry, too," Ruby says, taking a breath. Her fingers are still tingling, as if they have been frostbitten and are thawing out.

"Well, come on then," Laurel says. "I think I hear that fried Frito pie calling to me. Erica, you want to have supper with us before the dance?"

Erica shakes her head. "Thanks but I think I'll pass on supper. The dance, too, probably. I need to go back to the booth and get a few things sorted out for tomorrow. I'm planning to turn in early. It's been a long day."

Ruby finds Janice minding the sausage vendor's truck when she arrives. Janice pays for the pendulum, which she is wearing. "Thanks for showing me how to use it," she says. She begins putting Ruby's order together. "Dad says it's all just superstition, so I told him about the collective unconscious."

"What did he say to that?" Ruby asks.

But Janice only rolls her eyes and giggles. Ruby's plate of bratwurst and sauerkraut comes with a generous helping of butter-drenched, parsley-flecked spaetzle. Ruby devours everything hungrily while Laurel chows down on her deep-fried Frito pie, pronouncing it delicious. After they've finished they head for the dance, a Friday-night tradition. It's a good place for vendors, volunteers, and musicians to get acquainted and enjoy a relaxing evening before the festival swings into action.

The barn features a large wooden dance floor with tables and chairs around the perimeter and a large strobe light in the center, scattering a rainbow of sparkles over everyone. A popcorn machine occupies one corner and a wine, beer, and soft-drink cash bar the other. Marianne and Jason circulate among the crowd, saying hello to old friends and getting acquainted with new ones. They're togged out in Western shirts, jeans, and cowboy boots. Marianne looks espe-cially attractive, Ruby thinks, her bouncy ponytail fastened with a gorgeous silver hair barrette inlaid with chips of colored glass.

But Jason seems almost too jovial and Marianne's smile is painfully strained. Ruby can't help but remember the jolt she got when their fingers touched, and her aware-ness that Marianne was very afraid of something — something connected with her husband. What was that about?

Tonight's music is provided by the Cactus Junction Boys, a local group of five gray-bearded men who play a fiddle, a five-string banjo, a guitar, a mandolin, and an upright bass. The banjo and the mandolin players are their lead vocalists, one a baritone, the other a tenor, and the others sing backup. Tomorrow, they will play mostly folk and bluegrass, but tonight they are playing Western swing, which the Texas Legislature named the "official Texas State music" a few years ago.

The Cactus Junction Boys put their hearts into their music, and for the next hour, the crowd two-steps and waltzes and polkas to a dozen old dance-hall favorites, songs like "San Antonio Rose," "Stay a Little Longer," "Corrine, Corrina," and "Faded Love," which Patsy Cline sang at her last recording session before she was killed in a plane crash. Ruby is grateful for the loud, toe-tapping music, which overrides the replays of *You're giving your body to somebody else* in her brain.

As the evening wears on, the crowd gets bigger and noisier. The weaver and spinners from Wimberley are there, as well as the leather crafter, the potter, the candle maker (still in her long dress and sunbonnet), the

261

Frito-pie guy, and a dozen other vendors and musicians. Even Erica, who had told them she wasn't coming. She doesn't seem to be having as good a time as the others, however. She stands alone in a corner, watching, her arms folded, an unreadable expression on her face.

But Ruby is enjoying herself. She dances with a couple of the ranch cowboys, a bald man in khaki shorts and a blue polo shirt, Laurel (who likes to lead and is good at it), the leather crafter, and the fried-salsa guy, who is an absolute hunk. She even dances, once, with Jason.

Which turns into quite an experience. If Jason shares any of the apprehension Ruby has sensed from Marianne, Ruby doesn't get a whiff of it, although he clutches her close enough to guarantee an embarrassingly intimate contact as they two-step around the dance floor. Ruby can't escape his testosterone-powered grip without making a scene, but she promises herself not to do it again. Not. Ever.

When Jason releases Ruby, he dances next with Bonnie, who is togged out in skintight jeans, girly boots, and a silky blouse that clings to her ample curves. From the glare Bonnie fires at her, Ruby guesses that she is still carrying a grudge about that twenty dollars. But when Laurel whispers some titillating gossip about an illicit something-or-other going on between Jason and Bonnie, Ruby decides that maybe Bonnie's glare is less grudge than jealousy. She wasn't thrilled by the sight of Jason dancing belt-buckle-to-belly-button with somebody else.

Somebody else, somebody else,
you're giving your body to somebody
    else.

But whatever is (or isn't) going on between Jason and Bonnie, Marianne doesn't seem at all concerned. She is slow-dancing with Finn and obviously enjoying it, resting her fingers on the back of his neck and smiling dreamily into his face. Jason notices the pair of them, too, and judging from his dark expression, he isn't pleased. In fact, the next time Ruby sees them, Jason is crushing his wife against that silver belt buckle of his and shoving her around the floor with a possessive, take-no-prisoners energy.

But Ruby is glad to see that Finn decided to come to the dance, and a few moments later, when the band begins to play "Tennessee Waltz," she looks around, thinking she'll ask him to dance. But she can't find him and ends up instead in the arms of the

pigtailed chicken-fried-bacon guy, who —
in spite of the fact that he must weigh well
over two hundred pounds — proves to be
almost as nimble as Baryshnikov. Not for
the first time that day, Ruby thinks of Ethan
Connors and wonders if he is a good dancer.
She rather thinks not, although she has to
admit that it would be nice if she were
wrong.

For the traditional last dance of the
evening, they all line up across the floor,
start clapping and shouting, and dance a
raucous, foot-stomping "Cotton-Eyed Joe"
that goes on for a good twenty minutes,
until everyone is drenched in sweat and
gasping for breath.

"A great way to end the evening!" Ruby
says, when she and Laurel meet at the door,
fanning themselves. She is happy to step
out of the hot barn with its heavy odors of
beer, popcorn, and cigarette smoke, and
into the fresh, cool evening air.

"I am ready for Annie Oakley and bed,"
Laurel declares. She gazes up at the sky.
"Gosh, just look at all those stars. I never
see that many in town. But it's dark as the
pit out here. We should have brought a
flashlight."

"We did." Ruby pulls a small LED flashlight out of her pocket. She has been here

before and knows that while the marketplace and parking areas have some night lighting, the campground and cabin areas are unlit.

With the aid of the flashlight she and Laurel pick their way along the uneven path to Annie Oakley. The air is rich with the fragrance of cedar and mesquite smoke from the campfires along Mystic Creek, and filled with the laughter and conversation of people leaving the barn. Somebody is whistling the refrain of "Cotton-Eyed Joe," and somewhere in the distance, in the direction of the creek, a fiddle is playing.

Suddenly alert, Ruby raises her head. It is that haunting Irish melody again, "The Red-Haired Boy," with the dissonant chords and the unfamiliar words.

I don't want nobody but you, but you're giving your body
to somebody else.
I'm still true to you, but you've promised your heart
to somebody else.

She stops and puts her hand on Laurel's arm. "Hear that?"

"That guy whistling?" Laurel flips a braid over her shoulder. "Yeah, sure. What of it?"

"No, not him," Ruby says. "The fiddle

Over there, near the creek. It's an Irish folk-song." As she speaks, the melody rises sharply, sounding much closer.

"Nope," Laurel says decidedly. "No fiddle, no folksong. Just whistling. You're hearing things, Ruby."

The melody stops.

"I'm afraid you're right about that," Ruby mutters apprehensively. "It's an earworm." But it had been so *real*.

"Earworm?"

"A sticky song. A melody that won't go away."

"Oh, that," Laurel says. "When I was a kid, I got the Beatles stuck in my head. 'We all live in a yellow submarine, yellow submarine, yellow submarine.' It just wouldn't quit."

"How did you get rid of it?" Ruby asks.

Laurel laughs. "I didn't. I still hear it every now and then." She makes a face. "And now that I've thought of it, of course, I'll hear it all weekend."

When they get to Annie Oakley, their two cabin mates are asleep in their bunks, faces turned to the wall. There's a nightlight in the bathroom, though, so the cabin isn't entirely dark. As quietly as they can, Ruby and Laurel brush their teeth and climb into their bunks.

As she falls asleep, Ruby wonders whether Ethan Connors might be coming to the Harvest Festival, or if he has given up the idea entirely. She knows he was married once, and divorced. Maybe he has a girlfriend.

Somebody else, maybe . . .
somebody else . . .

CHAPTER SIX

Sometime before dawn, Ruby wakes from an uneasy dream so stunningly real that it leaves her gasping and breathless. In the dream, she is wrapping Ramona's birthday present, Finn's stained glass dragon, but it slips out of her hands and smashes on the floor. When she tries to pick up the pieces, one of them slashes her right forefinger to the bone. She can't stop the bleeding.

Half-awake, she peers through the semi-darkness at her hand, expecting to see blood running down her arm.

But of course it isn't. Thinking that she should have hung one of the dream catchers over her bunk to fend off nightmares like this one, she pulls her blanket up around her ears and tries to go back to sleep.

The sun has risen above the eastern horizon and their cabin mates have already left by the time Ruby and Laurel climb out of their bunks. They take turns showering and dress quickly, Laurel pulling on jeans and one of China's green Thyme and Seasons T-shirts and Ruby putting on a rainbow tie-dyed halter top, a flouncy blue skirt with big pockets, and leather sandals. She fastens a blue headband around her frizzy red hair, adds a dab of lipstick and the silver Taurus earrings she got from Erica, and calls it done.

"I know where to get breakfast," Laurel tells her, and leads them to a vendor who is selling scrumptious sticky buns and fragrant coffee — a perfect breakfast-to-go on a fabulous Texas morning. The sky is cloudless, the air is cool, and Ruby can smell bacon frying and hear somebody playing "You Are My Sunshine" on a banjo — a cheerful contrast to "Somebody Else". When they finish eating, she asks the vendor to fill her Thermos with coffee, and they head for the tent to open for business, stopping first to get the cash box and other valuables out of Big Red Mama.

It is just eight o'clock when they get to their spot on Willow Lane. But when Ruby bends down to unzip the front section of their tent, she sees that the security seal that locked the zipper at the bottom has been snipped.

"Damn," she mutters, setting her Thermos on the ground. "Looks like somebody decided to poke around in our booth during the night." She slips the snipped seal into her skirt pocket and unzips the panels all the way to the top.

"Oh, good grief," Laurel says, disgusted. "I hope they didn't steal anything!"

Ruby pulls the panels back to open the tent across the front and takes a moment to glance around. "Not that I notice right off," she says. She points to some leaves that have been tracked onto the rug inside the tent. "But he — or she — definitely came in. We'd better have a good look."

"I thought there was supposed to be a security guard on patrol last night," Laurel mutters.

"This is a big place," Ruby replies. "The guard couldn't be everywhere at once."

"I just wish he'd been *here*," Laurel remarks, and Ruby can't disagree.

A few moments later, they are still looking for evidence of thievery. "I guess whoever it was just wanted a sneak peek," Laurel says, sounding relieved. "Or maybe it was dark and he got into the wrong tent by mistake."

But a moment after that, Ruby discovers what has been stolen. Her best Wiccan knife — an athame with a black hilt inlaid with a silver scroll, a sweeping crossguard with matching scrollwork, and a sharp, double-edged ten-inch blade with a tapered point. Also missing: the knife's decorated leather sheath. Both had been displayed on the velvet-covered shelf that held the other magical tools.

Laurel comes to stand beside her. "The thief took an athame?" she says incredulously. "What a jerk! Do you think it was a Wiccan?"

"It can't be a Wiccan," Ruby replies. "No Wiccan worth her salt would touch a *stolen* athame. Or a stolen wand, either. The magic would be ruined." She pauses. "I wonder if anybody else got broken into. If you'll keep an eye on things here, I'll ask around."

"Sure thing," Laurel says. "Take your time."

The vendors are opening up and getting ready for Saturday's crowds. Catty-cornered across the narrow lane, the candle maker, wearing a long gingham dress, white apron, and sunbonnet, is hanging pairs of hand-dipped candles on a wooden rack. At the yarn booth next door, the spinners and weaver have set up a three-legged Saxony spinning wheel, a carding machine, and a rigid heddle loom on a floor stand — the equipment they are using for their demonstrations. A little farther along, the leather crafter has set up a small workbench and a rack of hand-tooled belts in front of his booth, so he can custom-fit the belts. Next to the leather crafter is Erica, Ruby's and Laurel's cabin mate, with her silver wire jewelry. And next to her is Yvonne, the other woman sharing their cabin. Yvonne, a round-faced, brown-haired, plumpish woman with a blond bouffant beehive straight out of the sixties, has a booth full of really luscious vintage clothing items.

Ruby goes from vendor to vendor, asking them about a possible break-in. She draws a blank everywhere — except for Erica. She is shaking her head over a tray of small items. When Ruby tells her about the stolen athame, she says, "Oh, gosh! So *that's* what happened!" Her eyes are wide. "I'm missing a couple of pairs of earrings and a bracelet. Must have been the same person!"

"Did you see how the thief got in?" Ruby asks.

"I'm afraid I didn't notice," Erica says ruefully. "The side panels on this tent are clamped, so getting in would be easy. I lock up my best pieces," she adds, pointing to a glass display case. "But these were smaller and cheaper. I was in a hurry when I closed up yesterday, so I didn't bother to put them away. My bad." She sighs. "I guess I was depending too much on the security guard Marianne promised."

"It wasn't just us," Ruby tells Laurel, back at their tent. "Erica lost three pieces of jewelry. But she's the only one. Nobody else reports any losses."

Laurel is unfolding a pair of striped canvas lawn chairs so she and Ruby will have someplace to sit when they aren't busy with customers. "What about the stained glass guy next door? Did you check with him?"

"Finn? He's not open yet," Ruby says. "I'll ask him later. But I suppose there's no point in worrying about the theft. After all, we lost just one item, and Erica said her jewelry wasn't very expensive. I'll let Marianne know. Maybe the security guard can make an extra loop or two through the market-place tonight. We don't want it to happen again."

By nine, one of the bluegrass bands is on the stage on the Green, tuning up for the first set of the day. The food vendors have cranked up, and the air is filled with wonderful festival smells — popcorn, barbecue, coffee, fried onions, hot garlic bread. Cars are pouring into the lot and all the booths along Willow Lane are now open — except for Finn's. Shoppers are already strolling from booth to booth, but his tent is still zipped shut.

"That's a little odd, isn't it?" Laurel says. "I wonder why he hasn't opened up. Does he live nearby, or is he camping here?"

"He has a studio in Utopia," Ruby replies. "But he told me he planned to sleep in the tent. Some of his pieces are pricey, and he said he was worried about security. He must have overslept."

Laurel frowns. "Well, maybe it's time somebody woke him up. He knows you. Why don't you do it?"

"I'll take him some coffee." Ruby picks up the Thermos and fills a plastic cup. "That'll get him going."

Coffee cup in hand, she goes to the front of Finn's tent and calls. No answer. She calls again, and leans closer, listening. But all she can hear is a band over on the Green, which has swung into the baleful old ballad "Jealous Lover."

The tent is zipped up tight. Ruby calls again, and then bends over and pulls up the zipper. That's when she is confronted by the smell, the cloying coppery odor of blood mixed with the scent of wet earth. And as she steps inside, she sees Finn. He is zipped into a blue sleeping bag, facedown and unmoving. There is a wet, black-red stain on the bag, about the size of a dinner plate.

Ruby gasps and drops the coffee cup. In the middle of the stain, buried to the hilt in Finn's back, is her stolen athame.

CHAPTER SEVEN

After that, things happen fast. Ruby dashes back to her tent, her heart in her mouth. Her hands are shaking so hard that it takes three tries to punch in Marianne's cell number. Not to be used unless somebody got murdered, she had said.

Well, somebody *has* been murdered, and Ruby blurts that news into the phone.

There is a moment's stunned silence. Then, "Dead?" Marianne cries incredulously. "Finn . . . is *dead*? Oh, no! Please, no!"

Ruby bites her lip, remembering what she had seen at the dance the night before. Finn and Marianne dancing together, Marianne's fingers on Finn's neck, her eyes on his face. Her response just now gives that recollection a sharp significance.

But even if the two of them were just friends, this would be a terrible situation for Marianne — and for Jason, too. This is their ranch and their festival. Murder isn't the best kind of advertisement for your events.

Shocked into a disbelieving silence, Laurel listens while Ruby tells Marianne that the killer used a stolen knife — stolen from *their* display of magical tools. Then Ruby goes behind the tent and throws up her breakfast on the grass.

When she gets back, Laurel says, concerned, "Are you okay, Ruby?"

"No," Ruby says, finding a tissue to wipe her mouth. "It's too awful, Laurel! Who could have done such a horrible thing? *Who?*"

Then Marianne comes running, ashen-faced and breathless, her long blond hair flying loose, as if she was caught in the act of braiding it. She vanishes into Finn's tent. A minute or two after this, Jason drives up in his golf cart and scrambles into the tent after her.

"Bad idea," Ruby mutters.

Standing outside, watching, she wraps her arms around herself. She had barely known Finn, but now he is dead, and the knife he was killed with was taken from the Crystal Cave — from her tent, from *her.* She feels . . . implicated. Accountable. Responsible. Even though she knows she isn't.

"What's a bad idea?" Laurel asks, coming

to stand beside her.

"Jason," Ruby says. "There, in the tent. With Marianne. And Finn." With a shudder, she corrects herself. "With Finn's body." Surely they — both Jason and Marianne — would have the sense not to touch anything — especially the knife.

"Why is that bad?" Laurel asks, not understanding.

"Because —" Ruby swallows hard, hoping she's not going to throw up again. "Because Finn told me that he and Jason got into a big argument yesterday, about parking. Jason shouldn't be anywhere near Finn's body right now. He might tamper with the evidence. Or the cops might think he did."

"You're saying that Jason might have killed Finn?" Laurel asks, blinking. "Over a little thing like *parking*?" She shakes her head. "I can see how that might happen on the spur of the moment, with tempers flaring. But not . . . not hours later, in cold blood. Can you? Really?"

"Not really, I guess." But Ruby remembers the fiercely possessive way Jason had pushed his wife around the dance floor and thinks that Jason might have had other reasons.

She adds, "Jason has a nasty temper and a reputation for losing it in a big way. Finn said the security guard was there when the parking thing came up. He'll probably tell the cops about it." But maybe not — Jason is his boss. That guard might want to keep his job.

"Speaking of the police," Laurel says, "maybe you'd better call them?"

Ruby takes out her phone and is about to punch in 9-1-1 when Jason comes barreling out of Finn's tent, his expression as dark and twisted as a tornado cloud. He climbs onto his golf cart and drives off like the devil himself is on his tail. Marianne stands in the open doorway of the tent, talking on her cellphone — calling the sheriff, Ruby hopes.

As Marianne finishes her call and pockets her phone, a tall, well-muscled man wearing a black Mystic Ranch T-shirt and black jeans and boots strides up, his face carefully impassive. Luke, Ruby guesses. The security guard who was supposed to have been on the job last night but who had been someplace else when Finn was murdered. He and Marianne engage in a brief conversation. The guard ducks inside and comes back out again, his face set in grim lines.

Marianne leaves Luke stationed in front of Finn's tent and comes over to Ruby and Laurel. Her cheeks are wet, her mascara is smudged, and her loose hair gives her a wild look.

"Thank you for calling me, Ruby." Her voice is strained and taut, as if she is barely holding off the panic. "I just talked to Sheriff Donahue. He's dispatched the nearest deputy and will be here himself in a little while. Since you found the body — and especially since it's your knife — he'll want to talk to you, so please stay close. Also, he's asked me to tell all the vendors in this section of the Marketplace that this is a crime scene. The area will be cordoned off and they won't be able to open right away. But they need to stay where they are, so the police can talk to them."

"You told the sheriff that the knife was *stolen,* I hope," Ruby says.

"Of course." Marianne pushes the hair out of her eyes. Her hand is shaking, there is a twitch at the corner of her eye, and she is blinking back tears.

"I'm so sorry about Finn," Ruby says sympathetically. "It's hard to lose a close friend — especially like this."

Marianne's eyes widen briefly and she pulls away, battening down the emotions. "Oh, no, Finn wasn't a friend," she says, speaking very fast. "I mean, well, yes, of course I knew him. I thought he was a talented artist, for sure. But I wouldn't call us *friends.*"

280

Ruby remembers the look on Marianne's face when she and Finn were dancing the night before, and a shiver crosses her shoulders. She knows with a deep certainty that Marianne is lying about her relationship to Finn. She wants to ask, but it isn't an appropriate question. Anyway, she knows that Marianne won't answer, or won't answer truthfully.

Marianne sees Ruby staring at her and drops her eyes. She gulps a quick breath and holds out her hand. "I . . . I guess I'd better get going. I have to tell people about not being able to open right away. I hope they won't be too disappointed."

And then, touching her hand, Ruby is suddenly pulled into Marianne's mind. It is filled with a torrent of frantic feelings, tumbling over and over like debris in a raging flood. A deep grief over Finn's death, an even deeper, panicked anxiety about Jason, and something else. Guilt, was it? Yes, a deep, pervasive guilt, darkened by remorse and self-reproach.

But guilt about what? Not murder, surely. Ruby struggles for clarity, but Marianne's thoughts are such a hysterical scramble that it's difficult to make any sense of them.

Still, there is one image. Out of the maelstrom of everything else, Ruby sees that

Marianne is thinking of the barrette she was wearing the night before, set with chips of bright-colored glass.

Ruby is taken aback. A hair clip? What's *that* about?

And behind and under and through all these questions, there's that song, murmuring in Ruby's ear like a plaintive ghost.

You've promised your heart to somebody else,
somebody else, somebody else,
somebody else . . .

A few minutes later, a uniformed deputy shows up and exchanges a few words with Luke, who nods and walks purposefully away. The deputy goes into Finn's tent, comes out again a few moments later, and begins stringing yellow crime scene tape in a big square around Finn's vendor space and out into Willow Lane. Sheriff Donahue — a short, stocky man wearing a khaki uniform and a duty belt, a dark vest that says *Sheriff* on the back, and a black cowboy hat — arrives and goes into the tent. Then two more deputies appear, and a blue-and-white EMS ambulance pulls into the area just behind Willow Lane.

The parking lot is filling up, festival-goers

are beginning to arrive, and the first band is getting started — Ruby can hear the fast-waltz strains of "Blue Moon of Kentucky." Apart from their corner of the marketplace, the festival is going ahead as if nothing has happened. Somebody has set up sawhorses closing off both ends of Willow Lane. It's empty now, except for the stunned-looking vendors standing around, watching the cops coming and going. They don't seem to know exactly what's happened, and Ruby doesn't tell them.

The candle maker, a young woman with long brown braids and freckles, takes off her sunbonnet. "I suppose this means that we won't have *any* customers today," she says mournfully. "And I spent the whole week making candles just for this show. I wonder if we can get a refund of our vendor fee. It's not fair, really — closing us down because somebody died."

"Don't panic, honey," the leather crafter tells her. A heavyset man in his fifties he wears a brown canvas apron over a blue chambray shirt and jeans. "They're just do-ing their job. They'll get the body out of there and let us open in another hour or so."

The man who made Laurel's Hansel-and-Gretel birdhouse folds his brawny arms.

283

"Think so, buddy? Five gets you ten we'll be closed all day." Glumly, he twists his mouth. "What a thing. Anybody know how the guy died? Heart attack, maybe?"

"Murdered," the sauerkraut-and-sausage vendor says starkly.

"Murdered!" several people exclaim. The candle maker gives a little shriek.

"Shot?" the potter asks. He's wearing a red T-shirt that says "Keep calm and open the kiln" on the front, and "Keep calm and throw something" on the back.

"Stabbed," the sausage-and-sauerkraut guy says. He nods at Ruby. "*She* found him."

Yvonne, the vintage clothing vendor and their cabin mate, stares at Ruby. "*You* found him?" Her hand flies to her heart. "Oh, you poor, poor thing. It must have been a terrible shock. Was he really stabbed?" She takes an apprehensive breath. "Do you suppose he was killed by the same robber who broke into your tent?"

"I found him, yes," Ruby says reluctantly. She's not sure she should be talking about it before she talks to the police. "Yes, it was a shock. And yes, he was stabbed. But I have no idea who did it."

This is one of those moments when she doubts her psychic abilities. If she were *seri-*

ously psychic, she would know who killed Finn, wouldn't she? But she doesn't. Like everybody else, she can only guess.

Erica, their other cabin mate, is standing beside Yvonne. "What's his name?" she asks curiously. "The man who got stabbed, I mean."

"Finn Cassidy," Ruby says. "He's a stained glass artist." Remembering that Erica lives in Utopia, she adds, "He said he had a studio in Utopia. Maybe you happen to know him?"

Erica shakes her head.

"He bought a pair of sake cups from me," the potter says gloomily. "Said he loves sake."

"He bought his supper from me," the sauerkraut-and-sausage guy reports in a matter-of-fact tone. "A smoked jalapeño dog and a side of spaetzle with bacon and onions. He said it was real good."

"Not bad for a last meal," the birdhouse maker remarks judiciously.

One of the spinners from Wimberley says, "I bought a tulip suncatcher from him yesterday afternoon. I saw a rooster I liked, but I didn't have enough money with me. I told him I'd be back to get it this morning." She shudders. "You never imagine a murder happening at a fun event like *this,* do you?"

Yvonne wraps her arms around herself. "Should we be afraid?" she wonders anxiously. "I mean, this isn't a *serial* killer, is it?"

"The Butcher of Willow Lane?" The birdhouse vendor chuckles like Count Dracula. "I hardly think so, m'dear. But I'd advise you to be on the alert, just the same."

"Most likely a drug deal gone wrong," the leather crafter says authoritatively. "Happens all the time. Drugs and money. That's what's behind ninety percent of the murders these days."

"Drugs, *sex,* and money," the birdhouse vendor corrects him. "Don't forget sex. But I agree. Probably drugs. He was a hippie type — you could tell by that ponytail."

"Well, I'm sorry the poor man got himself killed," the weaver from Wimberley announces briskly, "but I can't stand around all morning and gossip. I've got a rug on the loom and I want to get back to it."

It's a signal for the vendor group to break up. Erica collects the wand she traded for, and the others begin to drift back to their booths. Over on the Green, the band has started playing a John Denver song, "Thank God I'm a Country Boy."

"Maybe I could go and listen to the music," Laurel says. "You could call my cell when the police say we can open and I'll come right back."

"Maybe you ought to stick around," Ruby says. "The cops will likely want to talk to both of us. After all, the knife came from our booth. You might have to back up my story about finding it missing."

She pulls the chairs out and sets them up under the canopy. It's still early, but the sky is clear and the sun is already bright — and warm. As the day goes on, she knows they will be glad for the shade.

"You're probably right," Laurel says. "But you don't really think the police will suspect *you,* do you?" She gets her bag and pulls out a half-finished sock, knitting needles, and a ball of blue yarn flecked with brown. She takes one of the chairs, picks up her sock and studies it for a moment, then begins to knit.

"I certainly hope not," Ruby says. "But if they do, you can vouch for me. I mean, we were together the whole evening."

There's always some downtime at a show, and Ruby has come prepared, too. Her project is a pink crocheted romper and bonnet for Grace's baby doll, Sugar. Grace is her granddaughter, her daughter Amy's little girl.

Laurel looks up from her sock. "The

whole evening?" Her needles flash. "But we weren't together during the dance."

"Well, no," Ruby concedes. "But you know I was *there*. And we went to bed at the same time. We were together all night."

"I . . . think so," Laurel says, teasing, perhaps — but not quite.

Ruby stares at her. "You *think*?"

"Sometime in the night, I heard somebody tiptoeing across the floor," Laurel says reluctantly. "Thought I heard the door, too."

"It must have been Erica or Yvonne, going to the bathroom," Ruby says. "It wasn't me." She hooks a loop of pink cotton yarn. "After all the work we did setting up the booth — not to mention the dancing — I was dead tired. I had a bad dream that woke me up, but I went back to sleep." She picks up another loop and pauses in mid-stitch, thinking about that bad dream. The stained glass dragon, shattered. *Finn's* dragon. And now Finn is dead.

Laurel glances at Ruby's project. "What's that?"

"An outfit for Grace's baby doll. This is what it'll look like when it's done." Ruby is showing Laurel the photograph on the instruction sheet when a shadow falls across the page. She looks up and does a double-take.

Ethan Connors is looking down at her. "Ruby?" he growls. He isn't pleased.

CHAPTER EIGHT

Connors wasn't sure until late Friday that he would be able to make it to the festival. A narcotics investigation had kept him working late every night that week — so late that he and Einstein hadn't been able to take their regular run until long after dark.

And it was almost eleven Friday night when his team took their last suspect into custody, a tricky bit of business that had required some last-minute coordination with the San Antonio police. There wasn't time to call Ruby Wilcox and let her know he was coming, so he figured he'd catch a few hours' sleep, then jump in the truck and head out to Bandera County and the Mystic Creek Ranch. After his strenuous week, the festival would be relaxing, with nothing to do but listen to music, soak up the autumn sunshine, and maybe satisfy some of his curiosity about Ruby.

His *professional* curiosity, that is. As a cop,

he would simply like to get a better understanding of this psychic ability of hers, which interests him. Nothing personal, of course, although he has to admit that she is an attractive woman.

In fact, he has Ruby on his mind when he arrives at the ranch, pays his entry fee, and pulls into the parking lot behind the big marketplace. He's been handed a map with vendor locations, so he figures he'll find Ruby's booth first thing and they can make arrangements for supper. Then he can go off and listen to music.

But as he parks and gets out of his truck, he notices several official vehicles, and his longtime friend, Larry Donahue, the Bandera County sheriff standing beside a squad car. Larry is uniformed and armed, and the deputy he is talking to is cradling a long gun.

"Hey, Donahue," Connors calls. "What's going on?"

"Hey, Connors." A big grin splits Larry Donahue's face. They shake hands, then share a quick brother-to-brother hug. They both grew up in nearby Kerrville, where they were high school buddies. They split up for college, Larry going to Texas A&M and Connors to the University of Texas at San Antonio. But they teamed up again

291

when they both took deputies' jobs in Bandera County, where they partnered for the next several years. They both dated a girl named Marge — Connors pretty seriously. But she ended up marrying Larry, and shortly after, Connors met Carole. Then Larry ran for sheriff and Connors moved on to San Antonio, to the Bexar County CID. But they stay in touch and get together when they can.

"Good to see you, man," Larry says, stepping back. "You're a long way from home."

"Just a couple of hours," Connors says. Apologetically, he adds, "I intended to give you a heads-up, but I was working a narcotics case and the weekend sorta snuck up on me."

"I know how that goes," Larry replies. "Hey, now that you're here, how about staying over with us? The guest room is always available, and Marge would love to see you. Come for supper, too. We can always put another plate on the table."

Connors hesitates. "I may have supper plans, but they're iffy. How about if I say yes to the offer of a bed but check back with you later about supper." He glances toward the deputies' vehicles. "Something going on here, looks like. What's up?"

"Report of a fatal stabbing," Larry says

He reaches into his squad car for his Stetson and puts it on. "One of the vendors."

"A fight?" Briefly, he wonders about Ruby, who seems to be a magnet for trouble. But surely she wouldn't —

"Nope. Not a fight. A vendor knifed in the back while he was sleeping in his tent." He frowns. "Say, now that you're here, maybe you wouldn't mind giving us a hand. I'm a couple of deputies short this weekend, and from what I've just been told, looks like this might be a complicated investigation."

Connors doesn't hesitate. "Glad to, as long as I can stay within earshot of the music." He grins. "And if you'll tell Marge to bake us a batch of her biscuits for breakfast tomorrow morning. You know, I would have married her just for those biscuits."

"Yeah, but I'm the one who got her." Larry claps him on the back. "Come on, Ethan. Let's go see what we've got here."

What they have is a dead man in a tent, facedown in a sleeping bag, a knife plunged into the middle of his back. The front flap of the tent is closed, and the cloying scent of blood hangs in the air.

Connors tightens his jaw. "Knifed in his sleep, looks like."

"Fancy knife," Larry says, squatting down.

"Decorative hilt. Unusual. Might tell us something."

Connors can see that the hilt is polished black, inlaid with a silver scroll and with matching scrollwork on the elaborate cross-guard. He can't get a good look at the face without moving the victim's body, but he appears to be young, in his early thirties — a talented artist, if he was the one who crafted the dozens of pieces of stained glass on display in the tent.

Connors feels, as he always does, a sharp sense of sadness for the life lost, the hopes and dreams unrealized, the relationships shattered. Why? What had he done that might have provoked the attack? Who hated him enough — and was cowardly enough — to plunge a knife into his back?

Larry gets to his feet. "Our forensics guys will be here in a few minutes. The ranch owner told Peterson — the deputy who was first on the scene — that the knife was stolen from the vendor next door." Dryly, he adds, "Who also just happens to have discovered the body."

"Okay," Connors says slowly, understanding the implications. "Wonder how the two of them are connected. The vendor and the victim, I mean. Friends? Lovers? Competitors, maybe?"

"Right." Larry nods. "I'll leave that question to you. One of the ranch owners — Marianne Harrison — is waiting outside now. I know both her and her husband Jason, so I'll do those two interviews. You can talk to the woman who discovered the body. And also supplied the knife."

"On it," Connors says. He is glad to get out of the tent, away from the smell of blood, from the body on the floor.

But he can't escape the sadness. From experience, he knows it will stay with him until they learn who did this thing, and bring him — or her — to justice.

CHAPTER NINE

Ruby raises her head and gasps. Ethan Connors is looking down at her, scowling.

"Good Lord, it's *you,*" he says, with exasperated surprise.

He is broad-shouldered and slim-hipped, with a face that isn't handsome but is nevertheless attractive. His dark hair is cut short and he is wearing neatly pressed chinos, a red plaid shirt, and a black Astros baseball cap. He looks good, and Ruby is actually quite glad to see him.

Until he shakes his head and says, "I am *not* believing this, Ruby. Can't you stay out of trouble for one single day?"

"Wait . . . what?" Ruby frowns. "I'm not in any trouble."

"Oh, is that right?" he asks acidly. "I understand that it's *your* knife that killed the guy in the tent next to yours." He jerks his thumb in the direction of Finn's tent. "Do I have that right? *Your* knife? Buried to the hilt in the victim's back?"

Ruby drops her crocheting into her lap. "Yes, it's our knife. I mean," she corrects herself hastily, "it's a knife from our booth. But actually, it's not a knife, it's an athame."

"It's not a knife," Ethan repeats sarcastically. "Well, it sure looks like a knife to me."

"Plus, it was stolen. Last night. The killer came into our tent and took it."

"How very convenient," Ethan says dryly. "For the killer, that is. Who didn't have to look very far for a weapon."

"Not very convenient for poor Finn," Ruby retorts. She turns to Laurel. "Laurel, this is Ethan Connors. He's a detective. Tell him that the knife was stolen. Last night. From our booth. Although I don't know why *he* wants to know," she adds, feeling very cross. "This isn't his case. He's from Pecan Springs. He's a hundred and fifty miles from home."

Laurel flutters her eyelashes at Ethan. "Ruby's right," she says, smiling prettily. "The knife was stolen. Last night. From our booth."

"Show me," Ethan commands.

Ruby gets out of her chair and points to the velvet-covered shelf. "It was part of that display. With the other magical tools."

He goes to the display, bends over the two

remaining athames, and turns back to Ruby. "I thought you sold incense and crystals and tarot cards. Weird stuff but basically harmless. What's with these *knives*?"

"I told you." Ruby folds her arms. "They're not knives. They're athames."

"Oh, yeah? These things have blades, like a knife. The blades are sharp and come to a point, like a knife. Pretty damn lethal, if you ask me." He gives Ruby a glance that just misses being a dirty look. "Have you touched these knives since you discovered the theft?"

"I guess so," Ruby says slowly. "I rearranged the display so it wouldn't look like something was missing. Why are you asking?"

He shrugs. "Oh, just thinking that the thief might have left fingerprints. Cops like to look for fingerprints, you know. It's kind of a habit with us. Helps us find thieves, killers, people like that."

"You don't need to be sarcastic," Ruby says, but she feels foolish. She should have thought of the possibility of fingerprints — although when she'd discovered the knife missing, she had believed it was just a simple theft. She couldn't have guessed that the thief had used it to *kill* somebody.

Ethan glances at Laurel, then back at

Ruby. "Mind stepping outside? I've got a couple of other questions."

In a whisper, Laurel says, "Don't let him push you around, Ruby."

"You bet I won't," Ruby says, not bothering to whisper. She follows Ethan out of the tent. "I'm surprised to see you here," she says.

"I told you I was coming, didn't I?"

"No," she replies, lifting her chin. "Actually, you said that *maybe* you *might* come. You'd let me know. And since I didn't hear from you, I totally forgot about it."

This isn't true, but she isn't going to give him the satisfaction of knowing that she might have thought about him once or twice. Maybe even three times.

"Look." He sighs. "I had a hellish week with a narcotics investigation that started out big and got bigger by the day. I figured I'd get my head out of police work, enjoy the drive out here, check in with you, listen to some music, soak up some sunshine." He pauses, eyeing her. "And maybe tonight, take you out to supper at that café in Utopia I mentioned. They make a mean fudge pecan pie."

"Fudge pecan," she says thoughtfully. "I like fudge pecan."

"I do, too. I was looking forward to it."

His expression tightens. "So what happens? I drive into the parking lot, and the first person I see is my buddy Larry Donahue. Turns out he's here to investigate a murder and he wants —"

"Excuse me." Ruby puts up her hand, stopping him. "Sheriff Donahue is your *buddy*?"

"Yeah. We worked together as deputies here in Bandera County. Then he ran for sheriff and I moved to San Antonio. But we get together and go hunting three, four times a year, sometimes more."

"I get it," Ruby says. She can't be *very* psychic, or she would have seen this coming. The detective and the sheriff, just a pair of good old boys. The detective's decision to come to the festival has nothing to do with her and everything to do with seeing his buddy. "So you ran into your friend the sheriff in the parking lot and he told you that . . ."

Ethan finishes her sentence. "That one of the vendors was fatally stabbed while he was sleeping in his booth last night. A couple of his deputies are out this weekend, so he asked if I'd be willing to give him a hand."

"You said yes, of course."

"Of course I said yes. What's so surprising about that?" He frowns. "When Larry was bringing me up to speed, he said that the knife —"

"Came from the vendor next door."

"Right." He fixes her with a dark look. "And now I find out that *you* are the vendor next door."

"Well, yes. But that's hardly my fault," Ruby says. "I didn't choose this spot, it was assigned to me. And it's not my fault that the athame was stolen, either. Or that somebody used it to kill that poor man. Or that —"

"Wait." Abruptly, Ethan stops her. "What about that thing you do?"

She stares at him. "What thing?"

"You know what thing, Ruby." He is trying to sound offhand, but his voice — and his narrowed eyes — betray his intensity. "The thing you did back in Pecan Springs, when Allison Montgomery was abducted."

Ruby gave a vague gesture. "I don't —"

"Yes, you do. You get inside people's heads. You got inside *my* head. You knew what I was thinking. It was . . . unnerving."

"Oh, that thing." Ruby looks away. "Well, I really don't like to —"

"What I want to know is whether you've done it in this case." He pulls in a breath and speaks rapidly, as if he's not at all happy with what he's saying and is trying to spit it

301

out fast and get it over with. "Whether you might have come across anything you should tell me about. Tell us." He clears his throat. "Tell the sheriff. And me."

Ruby is mildly incredulous. "You mean, you are asking *me* to help you and your buddy with this investigation? *Really?*"

But why is she surprised? She already knows that Ethan's interest in her is purely professional. That — as a cop — he wants to figure out how she manages to get inside people's heads. Or rather (since he still doesn't quite believe it), how she makes it *appear* that this is what she's doing. And now, quite coincidentally, he has come across a situation that gives him the perfect opportunity to test her. A field trial, as it were. She would be the subject of his experiment with things that go bump in the night.

He frowns. "If you have any information that would lead us to the person who killed Mr. Cassidy, it's your duty as a citizen to help."

Her duty. "Even if it's woo-woo?" She chuckles dryly. "You've already made it pretty clear how you feel about that."

"Yeah." His jaw tightens. "I guess." He pauses, thrusts his hands into his pockets and says, "Hell's bells, Ruby, you know how

302

much it costs me to say this." He is obviously irritated with himself. "In fact, I'll bet you're digging around in my mind right this minute, seeing just how abysmally stupid I feel."

"I am *not* digging around in your mind," she says sharply, offended. "I wouldn't do that." And then she thinks, well, maybe he has a right to that opinion. He's seen me do it. But he can't know how hard I try *not* to do it.

"Look, Ethan." She takes a deep breath and tries to make herself sound like a reasonable person. "I truly want to respect everybody's privacy. I don't want to know stuff I'm not supposed to know, so I stay out of people's minds as much as I can. But I don't have to get inside your head to see that you're feeling abysmally stupid about this. It's written all over you. Any halfway observant person could see it."

He is silent for a moment. "Right again," he says finally. "Messing around with psychic stuff is — or has been — at the top of the list of things I don't want anything to do with, as a cop." He meets her eyes. "Until you came along, the only psychics I'd ever seen were frauds and con artists. Or just plain crazy."

"So which one am I?" She folds her arms.

"A kook? A fraud? Crazy? All three, rolled into one."

"None of the above." His tone is almost (but not quite) apologetic. "Sure, I was skeptical. Who wouldn't be? But I have to admit that you gave us something on the Montgomery kidnapping that we couldn't get by ourselves. So I've been doing some reading about psychics who work with cops."

"Uh-oh," Ruby mutters darkly.

"Yes. Controversial, and the results are open to all kinds of criticism, from all different directions. But if telepathy, clairvoyance, ESP, whatever — if tools like that can give us an edge on the bad guys, we ought to be using them. So if you've got something on this case, I'll be glad to hear it." He pauses. "Woo-woo or not. Woo-woo or whatever."

Ruby feels gratified. It's a nice speech, and she is almost persuaded. "Okay. I get that you're willing to suspend your disbelief." She hesitates, frowning. "But what about your buddy the sheriff? This is *his* investigation, isn't it? Where does he come down on this?"

"I don't know," he says. "It's never come up before. But Larry is a damned smart cop. I think he's pragmatic enough to take whatever information he can get, wherever he can get it."

Ruby is still hesitant. She is thinking, of course, of what had occurred with Marianne that morning, when she had witnessed her frantic, mixed-up tumble of thoughts and feelings. Grief about Finn, anxiety for Jason, and guilt and self-reproach. But guilt about what? And what if she is wrong? What if she implicates Marianne and she's totally mistaken?

"There is something," she says slowly. "But it's woo-woo. And I'm not sure . . ."

"Tell me." Ethan says. "Please."

"I don't really think I should," Ruby says. "It's all very vague and —"

"Wait." Ethan looks over her shoulder. "Put a pin in this, Ruby. We'll talk later."

CHAPTER TEN

Ruby turns to see the sheriff coming out of Finn's tent with Marianne, who hurries off in the other direction. The sheriff says something to a deputy standing nearby. The deputy goes around Finn's booth and waves at the EMS team. Two guys in blue scrubs come up with a gurney. Leaving it in front of the tent, they disappear inside.

"Want those sawhorses moved, Sheriff?" the deputy asks. "Couple of vendors have been asking if they're going to be able to open up this morning. They're kinda upset."

"It'll be another fifteen or twenty minutes before the victim's out of here," the sheriff says. He looks at his watch. "If folks ask, tell them they can count on opening by ten-thirty, ten-forty-five at the latest. But keep this tent closed up and taped off. Better put Abbott on guard, too."

The deputy goes off. Out on the Green, a band is playing a loud, fast version of

"Foggy Mountain Breakdown." The sheriff glances at Ruby and then gives Ethan a quizzical look. "Who's this, Detective?"

"Ruby Wilcox, Sheriff," Ethan said. "It was her booth that the knife was stolen from — and she's the one who found the body."

To Ruby, he says, "Ms. Wilcox, this is Sheriff Donahue. It's his case. As I told you, I'm just assisting."

To the sheriff, he adds, "Full disclosure, Larry. Ms. Wilcox was involved in a case I worked on a couple of months ago in Pecan Springs. She helped us locate a kidnap victim and apprehend the kidnapper."

The sheriff raises an eyebrow. "That right?" he asks, with an appraising glance at Ruby.

Ruby tries to smile. "Actually, I —"

"Interesting case," Ethan says hurriedly. He gives Ruby a significant look.

"Nice to meet you, Ms. Wilcox," the sheriff says, inclining his head. In his mid-forties, he's clean-shaven, with, deep-set blue eyes, sun-browned skin, and a laconic manner. "Maybe you can fill me in. You knew Mr. Cassidy, did you?"

So while Ethan looks on, Ruby explains what she knows, start to finish. She tells them about meeting Finn, buying the dragon suncatcher for her sister, hearing

307

that Finn would be sleeping in his tent that night, seeing him at the dance later — and finding him dead that morning, in his sleeping bag.

She takes them into her tent and introduces Laurel, then shows the sheriff the display of magical tools from which the athame had been taken.

"Athame?" The sheriff cocks a puzzled eyebrow. "Hang on a minute. I thought we were talking about a knife. The knife that killed Cassidy."

"An athame is a special kind of knife," Ruby says. "Wiccans use it in rituals, usually to cast a circle and draw the quarters — the four corners of the compass. Or to bless the chalice, in the same way that a priest uses a cross. In the darker traditions of the craft, it can also be used to curse."

"Curse?" Ethan asks. He looks interested. "Is that the same as a hex?"

"Not quite," Ruby says. "A hex is any spell, while a curse is designed to cause harm. Wicca is a goddess religion and most Wiccans are against what's called baneful magic. Words are powerful, and a curse has deep significance. It might be tempting to use it. But a curse has a way of boomeranging on the one who curses."

He nods shortly and Ruby gestures to the

display. "These are the two smaller athames. The larger one — the one that killed Finn — was here when Laurel and I closed up last night, before we went to supper. It was gone this morning."

A uniformed EMS attendant comes to the front of the tent. "Sheriff, we're ready to take the body to Kerrville. The medical examiner's office has been notified. He'll meet us at the hospital."

The sheriff nods. "Tell the ME to let me know when he fixes a time of death — I need it as soon as he can get it. Sooner, if possible."

"Yessir." The attendant disappears.

The sheriff swivels back to Ruby. "You were talking about Wiccans. What's a Wiccan?"

Ruby takes a breath. Explaining Wicca to a nonbeliever is sort of like explaining Catholicism to a Martian. "Wicca is a contemporary pagan religion. Wiccans believe in both a female and a male deity and have a special reverence for nature."

"Pagan, huh. That figures." He doesn't seem especially perturbed, just curious. "I assume that you brought the athames and wands and other things because you expect to sell them. We've got some pretty bad actors in this county, but I can't think right off of any pagans. Who do you reckon is gonna buy stuff like this out here?"

Ruby smiles. Out here on the Texas range, he means, in cattle country. "There's a coven in Kerrville," she says. "Last year, their members bought quite a few magical items from me. Wands, athames, pendulums, divining tools."

The sheriff does a double-take. "In *Kerrville*? I might expect that in a big city like Austin, which everybody knows is weird. But you're sayin' there are *witches* in Kerrville?"

Ruby nods, hoping she isn't getting anybody into trouble. "They're green witches," she adds helpfully. "They're deeply involved with environmental issues. *Local* issues. They volunteer a lot."

"Green witches in Kerrville," the sheriff says, stopping just short of rolling his eyes. "You're telling me something I don't know." He turns to Ethan. "You know anything about this sorta stuff, Ethan?"

"Some," Ethan acknowledges. "I looked into it a little deeper after I met Ms. Wilcox this summer."

He *did*? Now, Ruby is the one who is surprised.

He goes on, speaking to the sheriff in a lawman-to-lawman tone. "Last count, there

310

are sixty-some groups — covens, they call themselves — in Texas. About a dozen are located in the Austin area, three or four in San Antonio, and a couple in Pecan Springs and Wimberley. The rest are mostly up around Dallas or over in Houston." He pauses and adds, deliberately, "They may seem to be on the radical fringe, but Wicca has been recognized by the courts as a legitimate religion. They're peaceable. In fact, they're pacifists. The trouble generally comes from folks who want to give them a hard time."

Ruby stares at him. She had no idea that this man knew so much about Wicca — or cared enough to dig out the information. Was it just another part of his job?

"Well, maybe," the sheriff says. "But in this case, looks like maybe they're not all that peaceable. Finn Cassidy could have been killed with a hunting knife or whacked with a machete. Even a Swiss Army knife would have done the trick. Instead, somebody went to some extra trouble to break in here and steal a Wiccan ritual knife. Gotta be a reason, seems to me. Most likely, we're looking for somebody who's involved with this Wicca thing. Somebody who wants to make a statement — religious, political, whatever."

"The killer couldn't have been a Wiccan," Ruby protests quickly, wanting to nip this idea in the bud. "Detective Connors is right, sheriff. Wiccans are peacemakers. Killing is *not* —" She shudders, thinking of the Wiccans in her group. "Well, we just wouldn't *do* it, that's all. We couldn't."

The sheriff shrugs. "Christians are supposed to be pacifists, but they kill folks, too. Why, just last week we arrested a preacher from the First Temple of Jesus God. He got into a fuss with his neighbor and ran him over with his riding lawn mower." He pulls out his phone and takes a couple of photos of the magical tools display. To Ethan, he says, "Let's see if we can pull any prints off the knives here."

"I put them out," Ruby says. "And I moved them around after we saw that one had been stolen. You'll find my fingerprints on them."

The sheriff takes off his cowboy hat, runs his hand through his thick, dark hair, and puts his hat back on again. "How well did you know the victim, Ms. Wilcox?"

Ruby thought she had already explained this, but she does it again. "I met him for the first time yesterday afternoon. I bought a piece of stained glass from him. A suncatcher. It's a birthday present for my sister."

"That's when he told you he was planning to sleep in his tent?" Ethan asks.

"That's right. There was a security guard, but Finn said he had some expensive pieces and didn't want to risk any losses."

"Is that a usual thing at these shows?" the sheriff asks. "Vendors sleeping in their booths, I mean."

"Not so much," Ruby says. "Some shows don't permit it. Liability, maybe." As she says this, it occurs to her that Finn might have had another reason to sleep in his tent. But what?

"Did he know many people here?" Ethan asks.

"I don't think so," Ruby says slowly. "It was his first time at the festival. Marianne knew him — she said she had a couple of pieces of his work." She considers saying more, but Ethan had cautioned her to wait, so she would talk it over with him first. But there is something else the sheriff needs to know.

"When I bought my sister's birthday present, Finn told me that he and Jason got into a disagreement in the parking lot yesterday," she says.

"Jason?" Ethan asks.

"Jason Harrison," the sheriff says. "Ranch owner. Marianne's husband." He adds, "I know the guy slightly — he's got a short fuse."

From the tone of his voice, Ruby guesses that the sheriff knows rather more than that about Jason Harrison. Domestic violence, maybe? She wouldn't be surprised. Marianne might put up with it for the sake of the ranch. It's hard to leave an abusive husband when your livelihood — and a place you love — depends on making a go of a marriage. But she doesn't ask, and neither does Ethan.

Instead, she relates Finn's story about the argument. "Finn said he thought Jason was going to slug him. He mentioned that the security guard — Luke, I guess — was on the scene and saw what happened. You might ask him."

"Thanks," the sheriff says. "I will." He pauses. "Did you see Cassidy at any other time — other than yesterday afternoon, I mean?"

Ruby considers how much she should say before she talks to Ethan about what she had glimpsed in Marianne's mind. "There was a dance last night. He was there."

"Did he dance with anybody?"

Ruby takes a breath. "With Marianne."

"Who else?"

"Nobody that I saw," Ruby replies. "But I don't think he was there long. When I looked around for him, he was gone."

The sheriff's eyes flicker but he turns away quickly. "Questions, Connors?"

"Yes," Ethan says. He pulls out a pen and a small notebook. "Back to the knives, Ms. Wilcox." He gestures toward the display. "Who knew they were here? Besides you and your helper, that is."

A good question, Ruby thinks. She frowns. "It's a little hard to remember. We weren't actually open for business yesterday, but quite a few vendors dropped in to see what we had. Somebody bought a book about herbs —"

"That was Yvonne," Laurel puts in.

"She's a vendor?" Ethan asks, making a note.

Ruby nods. "Yes. She sells vintage clothing. Janice, the daughter of the sausage-and-sauerkraut vendor, bought a pendulum. The guy who does leather bought a dream catcher like that one." She points to a hoop decorated with beads and feathers, hanging from a tent strut. "Another person bought a couple of plants, and somebody else — I don't remember who — bought candles."

Somebody else. As if on cue, the refrain

315

pops into her head again. *Somebody else* *somebody else . . . you're giving your body to* *somebody else . . .*

"Marianne was here, too, wasn't she?" Laurel prompts.

Ruby shakes her head, trying to get rid of the lyrics. "That's right, she was. There's always a lot of browsing and early buying while people are setting up. Vendors give a discount to other vendors. It's kind of a friendly, getting-acquainted thing to do."

Ethan purses his lips. "So what you're saying is that a half-dozen people were here and saw the knives —"

"Oh, more than that," Laurel says. "Although only a few paid any attention to the athames."

Ethan nods. "Maybe a dozen, then. Including the two of you."

Ruby and Laurel exchange exasperated glances. "But if either of us wanted to kill him," Ruby says, "we wouldn't have been stupid enough to do it with a knife from our booth." Surreptitiously, Laurel gives Ruby a thumbs-up.

"Yes," Ethan says, still scribbling, "there's that."

"But I'm back to my question," the sheriff says. "If a Wiccan didn't do it, why would the killer want to use a Wiccan knife —

especially a *stolen* Wiccan knife?"

"To cast suspicion on a Wiccan?" Laurel says tentatively.

"To cast suspicion on *us,*" Ruby says.

Ethan looks up from his notebook. "Can you think of anybody who might want to do that? Anybody who might have a grudge against you?"

Ruby hesitates. It's a sobering thought. "Well, there's Bonnie Lawrence," she says reluctantly. "She still seems to be upset over a twenty-dollar disagreement we had last year. I know it sounds petty, but . . ."

She lets her voice trail away. Actually, after seeing the glare Bonnie aimed at her at the dance, she could imagine the woman breaking into her booth. And it was possible that Bonnie had a relationship of some kind with Finn. They were both from Utopia, weren't they?

"Bonnie Lawrence?" Ethan asked. "Who's she?"

"The silk-scarf woman, across the way." Ruby turns and points toward Bonnie's booth. "She and I had a little dust-up last year. She made a twenty-dollar mistake and she wouldn't own up to it. There's a rumor —" She breaks off. "But that's not relevant. To Finn's murder, I mean."

"How do you know?" Ethan is making

notes. "We need to hear it."

Laurel speaks up. "Some people are saying that she and Jason are having a thing. But you know how people talk. That may not be true."

"And anyway," Ruby says, "it has nothing to do with *Finn*. Especially when Finn and Marianne were —" She pulls a breath.

The sheriff is watching her closely. When she doesn't finish the sentence, he says, "Come on, Ms. Wilcox. We need to hear that, too. Whatever it is."

She lets her breath out in a whoosh. "Marianne and Finn were dancing together last night — close-dancing, I mean."

"How close?"

"Pretty close. Jason didn't seem happy about it."

"What else?"

She shakes her head. There's more, but later.

Ethan pockets his pen and closes his notebook. "If something else comes to mind, let us know."

"Don't you mean 'somebody else'?" Ruby asks wryly.

"Yeah. That too," he says.

The sheriff looks from Ruby to Laurel. "Since you two may have handled the murder knife, one of my deputies will be

318

around to get your fingerprints. And I have something to show you." He reaches into his jacket pocket and takes out a small plastic evidence bag. He holds it up to Laurel. "Have you seen this before?"

Laurel leans forward, peering at the object in the bag. "Maybe." She straightens, with a puzzled frown. "But I can't remember where."

Ruby can. "It looks like the barrette Marianne was wearing at the dance last night," she says. It was decorated with chips of — yes — stained glass. "Where did you find it?"

"Thank you, Ms. Wilcox." Impassively, the sheriff puts the evidence bag back into his pocket. He's not going to answer her question.

But nobody has told him that Ruby is psychic and that she can tune into his thoughts, if he isn't careful. And at this moment, he lets his habitual guard drop just far enough for her to learn that he found Marianne's barrette in Finn's tent, inside the dead man's sleeping bag. Which, to the sheriff's orderly, disciplined mind, makes Marianne a prime suspect in Finn's murder.

But the barrette leads Ruby down a different path, to a different conclusion: that Marianne and Finn were lovers, and the

319

barrette was his gift to her. It also explains the fear that Ruby glimpsed in Marianne's mind. She knows she lost the barrette when she was with Finn, in his tent, both of them in his sleeping bag. She is afraid the cops will find it.

This means that the sheriff is most likely wrong when he concludes that Marianne killed Finn — although Ruby isn't sure how to tell him this, or whether he would believe her if she did. Probably not, since she would have to tell him how she learned it. Which would no doubt sound like an entirely cockamamie explanation. He would put her at the top of his psycho list, right up there with newspaper astrologers and the guys on TV who claim to bend spoons.

Ruby is quite sure that Marianne didn't kill Finn. She has somebody else in mind.

Somebody else. Marianne's husband. Jason.

Jason saw his wife dancing with Finn. He knew — perhaps he had known for some time — that they were lovers. He could have stood outside Finn's tent, listening as Finn made love to his wife, as they talked about Jason's attack on Finn in the parking lot, and perhaps about the possibility of her divorce and their remarriage. He could have crept into the Crystal Cave tent and stolen the knife, waited until Marianne had left, and then gone into Finn's tent to kill him while he slept. And Marianne knows all this — and fears that her husband has killed her lover.

Ruby hesitates. It's her responsibility as a citizen to report this. Whether the sheriff believes her or not is *his* business, of course. Hers is simply to tell the truth.

But she is saved by the bell. She has just opened her mouth to speak when Sheriff Donahue's cellphone rings.

He listens for a moment, growls "On my way," and turns to Ethan. "I've got to go. You with me, Detective?"

"Sure thing," Ethan says easily. He looks at Ruby, cocks his head, and quite deliberately, intentionally allows her into his mind.

Supper tonight. Sixish. Things we need to talk about.

Ruby nods. She has things to talk to him about, too, for she understands not only who killed Finn, but why. As well, she now understands the lyric that has lodged in her mind, repeating itself over and over in an endless loop.

Jealousy. For Jason, it was all about jealousy, perhaps the most powerful and deadliest of human emotions. It can simmer beneath the surface, silently and invisibly, then erupt in a volcanic explosion of rage and vengeful fury.

I don't want nobody but you, but you're
  giving your body
                    to somebody else . . .

CHAPTER ELEVEN

"Want to talk about it now?" Ethan asks.

"Give me a few minutes to decompress," Ruby says, stretching her legs and leaning back in the seat. "It's been a wild day."

It is nearly six-thirty on Saturday evening and she is riding in Ethan's silver F-150 crew cab. They are on Route 187, on their way to the Lost Maples Café in Utopia, about ten miles south of the Mystic Ranch.

Route 187 is a narrow scenic two-lane highway that winds through the Texas hills beside the beautiful Sabinal River, along an ancient track the Spanish called Comanche Trail. Bruised-blue storm clouds are piling up above the southern horizon, promising rain before the night grows much older. To the west, the sun is slipping behind the juniper-covered hills, spilling a shimmer of magical light across the landscape. It isn't hard for Ruby to conjure up a Comanche band — warriors, women, and children, with their dogs and patient ponies — settling into their camp on the banks of the shallow, spring-fed river, fathers pitching the night's shelters, mothers sending the children to catch fish for the evening meal or fill woven reed baskets with the pecans that have fallen from the October trees.

After the morning's tragic beginning, the day was crazy-busy, and Ruby is glad to unwind. She and Laurel were finally able to open their booth at eleven, when the sheriff's investigation was finished, the crime scene tapes were removed, and customer traffic began to flow. She and Laurel worked without taking a break until five-thirty, when the marketplace closed. They would have to get to the booth early the next morning to restock — and they had already sold out of quite a few things. The dream catchers were all gone, for instance. They'd sold almost all of China's potted herbs. And the book rack was nearly empty.

Ruby feels pretty empty, too. She had taken a few minutes to grab a quick shower and change into denim leggings and a loose white cotton roll-sleeved shirt over a blue tank top. All she'd had to eat all day was a corn dog, two chocolate-chip cookies, and a bag of cold curly fries. She is ready for supper.

But supper will have to wait just a little longer. "Whoa," Ethan says, braking to a quick stop and pulling off the road. "Just look at *that.*"

"Look at what?" Ruby asks.

He turns off the ignition. "Whitetail buck with a massive rack, down there by the river. Perfect shot. Stay here while I do this." He gets out of the truck and reaches behind the seat — for his deer rifle, Ruby thinks.

In dismay, she looks toward the river and sees the buck, head down, drinking at the water's edge. The falling sun turns his tawny coat to shining gold. He is stunning.

"You're not going to kill that beautiful animal!" she protests.

"Are you kidding?" Ethan is hauling out his camera, which has a long lens. "Of course not. Stay put and stay quiet." He steps around the rear of the truck, uses the bed rail to steady the camera, and begins shooting.

A few moments later, he's back. He leans over, holds the camera so Ruby can see, and flicks on the display. "Isn't he amazing?" he says, sounding awed.

"Yes," Ruby breathes, rapidly revising her estimate of Ethan Connors. The photo looks like something out of a magazine. "You do this for fun? Take pictures, I mean."

"Yeah — for fun, and a few extra bucks." He turns the camera off and puts it back behind the seat, in its bag. "I write for outdoor magazines. Editors are more likely to buy articles that come with professional-looking photos."

"I'm sure," Ruby murmurs. He's a *writer*? This is a side of the man she hadn't suspected. "Do you get many stories published?"

"Some." He starts the truck and pulls back onto the highway. "I had a piece on Texas raptors — hawks and bald eagles — in last month's *Texas Highways*."

"Eagles?" Ruby frowns. "In Texas?"

"Sure. They're mostly in East Texas, but there's a nesting pair on the Llano River every year, about ninety miles north of here. Same pair, same nest, same tree — at least until it collapsed last spring and the eagles had to relocate. And there's a winter population of a dozen or so along the Colorado River, where it feeds into Lake Buchanan. They come south to fish in the lake when their hunting waters in the northern US and Canada freeze over." He smiles. "I enjoyed doing the article — got some good photos, too."

Ruby thinks that Ethan is trying to be offhand about this, as if it were just a weird sort of weekend hobby, but she can hear the pride in his voice. And once started, he seems to feel like talking. He had told her that he grew up in this area — in Kerrville, it turned out, forty-some miles away — and as they drive, he tells her more about himself. He has three younger sisters. His mother was an elementary school teacher, his father (who died when he was in high school) a lawyer. Summers, he worked on an uncle's ranch just a few miles from nearby Vanderpool, where he "learned to like riding horses and roping cattle," as he puts it.

"But not enough to make it my career," he adds. "If you want to be a serious cowboy, you have to love being bucked off your horse into a patch of prickly pear. You're gonna get stomped on by a bull every so often, too. I figured there was more to life than that, so I went to the university, banged around in a couple of jobs I didn't like, then went back to Kerrville to work as a deputy — and discovered what I wanted to do with my life."

"Isn't being a cop just as dangerous as getting bucked off your horse and stomped on by a bull?" Ruby asks.

"Maybe." He chuckles mirthlessly. "But a cop can stomp back. Metaphorically speaking, of course. Stomping is against the rules."

After several years in Kerrville, he was recruited by the Bexar County district attorney to work as an investigator in the county's Criminal Investigations Division in San Antonio. He was there for some time, getting more investigative experience under his belt, and then became a detective with the PSPD.

And along the way he'd been married to somebody he'd known since high school. "We were both still kids," he says, adding gruffly, "Old enough for sex but not grown up enough to be married." He doesn't say what happened to the marriage, and Ruby doesn't want to pry. She would also like to know if he's seeing anyone, but he isn't inviting her into his mind to find out.

As he finishes his narrative, they reach Utopia's Main Street, driving past the vet clinic, the post office, the First State Bank of Uvalde, the Five Points Market, and the Ranch Outpost Hardware & Feed. Ruby wonders where Finn Cassidy had his stained glass studio — and Erica and Bonnie both live in Utopia, too, don't they? But she wonders only briefly, because supper is just a block ahead.

Utopia is a village of about 225 residents

on the eastern bank of the Sabinal River. It's one of those blink-and-you-miss-it towns — most of the time. But sometimes, and suddenly, it becomes a "destination," springing to life like the legendary village of Brigadoon, which is said to rise out of the mysterious Scottish mists once every hundred years.

In the summer, it's the Open Pro Rodeo that brings Utopia to life, attracting bronc busters, bull riders, calf wrestlers, and barrel racers from all over Texas. In the fall, during deer season, camo-clad weekend hunters flock like lemmings into town to pick up beer, steaks, and other necessities at the General Store before they head out to their deer leases.

There's also a nine-hole golf course, the setting for a novel and then a movie, *Seven Days in Utopia,* which brought a film crew and three big Hollywood stars (Robert Duvall, Lucas Black, and Melissa Leo) to town and paid dozens of Utopians to work for an intoxicating few weeks as extras, doing for the movie cameras what they would normally be doing in their jobs at the General Store or the Pico convenience store and gas station or the Lost Maples Café.

That's where Ethan is taking Ruby this evening — the Lost Maples Café. It's located in an old building that, over the course of its century-plus history, has served as a Masonic Lodge, a doctor's office, a drug store, a post office, and a school. Parked in front is a motley collection of battered ranch trucks, spiffy new luxury vans, a lipstick-red Hummer, and a quartet of mud-spattered Harleys flying Confederate flags. Ethan parks, and he and Ruby get out.

There's a crowd inside the café, and most of the booths and tables — 1950s Formica-topped tables surrounded by wildly mismatched kitchen chairs — are occupied. A short wait gives Ruby time to appreciate the funky chic décor: rusty corrugated-tin walls studded with vintage signs, farm tools, sepia photos of pioneer folk, trophy deer heads, and posters and photos of the movie crew. A jukebox — an antique Wurlitzer, outlined in red and orange blinking neon — is playing classic country: Hank Williams singing "Your Cheatin' Heart," which (Ruby thinks) is remarkably appropriate. She feels a sharp and sudden sadness as she thinks of Finn.

A cheerful, dark-haired young woman named Angie leads them to a booth, equips them with menus, asks if they want their iced tea sweetened, and dashes off. When she returns with large glass mugs of tea, they order jalapeño poppers to start with.

330

Ruby chooses her favorite Texas roadhouse comfort food: chicken-fried steak, mashed potatoes, sweet corn, and fried onion rings. Ethan orders a taco plate called "The Kitchen Sink" which has everything — eggs, potatoes, cheese, onions, ham, sausage, bacon, and jalapeños — cradled in a flour tortilla about as big as a trash can lid and blanketed with salsa that's hot enough to set your hair on fire. A laminated legend on the napkin holder announces that "Pie Fixes Everything," but they agree to consider dessert when they get that far.

The poppers arrive first: jalapeño peppers stuffed with cheddar and cream cheese, wrapped in bacon, breaded, and deep fried. Ruby inhales one long, deep breath, sighs happily, and settles back for some serious Texas eating. She is on her second popper when Ethan asks, "Are you ready to talk *now*?" There is a focused intensity in his blue eyes.

She licks her fingers. "Does the sheriff think Marianne did it?" It's the question that's been on her mind all day.

"He'd be a fool not to," Ethan says dryly, "given that her hair clip was found in the victim's sleeping bag. He interviewed her for an hour this afternoon."

Ruby's eyes widen. A whole hour. "Did

she admit that she was with him?"

Ethan frowns, and she hears him thinking that there are things he shouldn't talk over with her. She waves her hand, letting him know that he doesn't have to answer the question.

"I know she was *there*," she says, "But I also know that she didn't kill him. For one thing, she was absolutely thunderstruck when I phoned this morning to tell her that Finn was dead. For another, when she came to our booth while she was waiting for the sheriff to arrive, I slipped into her mind and —"

"*Slipped?*" Ethan fixes his eyes on her face. "You *slipped*?"

"I'm just telling you what happened," she says defensively. "You can believe or not, but maybe you ought to hear it before you decide."

"Okay, okay," he says. "So you were inside Marianne's head. What did you see there?"

"She was really shaken up — grief for Finn, a lot of anxiety for Jason, and fear. I caught an image of that barrette, which I'm sure Finn must have given to her. She missed it and realized that she had lost it in his tent when she was . . . when they were making love. That's why she was afraid."

"When they were making love?"

Ruby frowns. "Did somebody go over his sleeping bag? Did you find . . . maybe her hair? And what about the knife? Were there fingerprints? Semen?" She's seen enough episodes of *CSI* to know that the sheriff has probably already asked these questions — and answered them.

"The forensics isn't finished, but we found hair, yes. Long blond hair, probably hers, as well as his shorter red hair, both of which are going to the DNA lab in Austin. The knife was wiped clean, but the killer over-looked a partial thumbprint under the crossguard. It doesn't seem to match Marianne's — or yours or Laurel's, for that matter. It'll be run through AFIS as soon as possible, though."

"AFIS?"

"The FBI's automated fingerprint data-base. But it only works when somebody's prints are already in the system." He grins bleakly. "There's more. Marianne admits that she was with Finn last night, but only from ten until about eleven-thirty. Her claim is backed up by Luke, the security guard, who says he saw her leaving the Willow Lane area at that time. He walked past Cassidy's tent five minutes later, saw a light and checked it out. He and Cassidy exchanged good nights and he went on.

When he came back again an hour or so later, the light was off."

"So that settles it," Ruby says, with satisfaction. "Finn was still alive when Marianne left."

"Unless she came back and killed him later."

Ruby sighs.

"Well, she *could* have." Ethan picks up another popper. "You said that when you slipped into Marianne's mind, you saw a 'lot of anxiety for Jason.' Any idea what that means?"

Ruby hesitated. She couldn't quite tell whether his question was serious or snarky. After all, this is the man who had such difficulty believing her report of Allison Montgomery's kidnapping. But she decided to treat it as serious.

"It means that she thinks *he* killed Finn. Jason, I mean. She knows what kind of a temper he has. When he was at the dance last night, I saw him watching Marianne and Finn dancing. He looked . . . stormy."

She licks the cheese off her fingers, wondering how much she should tell him. And then decides to heck with it. He might as well know it all, all at once. He can decide what to believe — or not.

She pushes her plate away and folds her

334

arms on the table. "You know how the words to a song get stuck in your mind? Well, all weekend, I've been hearing lyrics running through my head. I first heard them when I was talking to Finn yesterday afternoon. At the time, I thought I was actually hearing music — a band playing out on the Green. But I realized that the music, and the words, were only in my mind. They keep coming back, and they have a message."

"A message?" Ethan raises both eyebrows, managing to look simultaneously curious and incredulous. "What message?"

"The tune is an old Irish folksong, 'Red-Haired Boy.' The words go, I don't want nobody but you, but you're giving your body to somebody else. I'm still true to you, but you've promised your heart to somebody else."

"To somebody else." Ethan swigs his iced tea thoughtfully. "You're saying that jealousy is the motive."

"Yes," she says. "I bought a dragon suncatcher from Finn, and our fingers touched. That's when I heard the music for the first time. He must have been aware of Jason's jealousy. I heard his concern, in the form of the song. In those lyrics, over and over. And he had red hair, of course. Finn, I mean. He was Irish. The folksong is Irish."

"It fits, I guess." Ethan picks up the last popper and puts it in his mouth. After chewing for a moment, he says, "You think Jason did it?"

She nods. "Last year at the festival, he got mad and beat up a food vendor — a young guy half his weight. He broke the guy's nose, and the ranch had to pick up the medical bills. And then there was that argument in the parking lot. Jason is a jealous man with an uncontrollable temper." She pauses, listening. The jukebox has swung into Loretta Lynn's "You Ain't Woman Enough to Take My Man." Another song about jealousy — a jealous woman, this time.

"Jason is definitely a bad actor," Ethan agrees. He pauses, and a grin flickers at the corners of his mouth. "But you're wrong, Ruby. He didn't kill Finn."

"Wrong?" Ruby is feeling very sure of herself — and just slightly miffed. "I'm not saying you have to believe me, Ethan. But that doesn't make me *wrong.*"

Ethan licks his fingers. "Gotta agree with you on major points. Jason has a hair-trigger temper, and he's eaten up by jealousy — not to mention some guilt over that thing with Bonnie. Yep. Your explanation makes perfect sense." He smiles in a kindly way.

"Except for the little matter of the time of death, that is."

"The time of death?" Ruby rubs the scar over her right temple, which is throbbing.

"The medical examiner puts it at midnight to two a.m. Three at the outside. And while Jason has a pretty strong motive, he didn't have the opportunity. He has an alibi."

"An alibi?" Ruby stares at him, non-plussed. "That can't be right. He must be lying." Alibis can be manufactured, she knows. "Where does he *say* he was? With Bonnie?" Her mouth tightens. Of course. Bonnie would lie for him. She'd love to. That way, he would be in her debt forever.

"Nope, not Bonnie." Ethan shakes his head. "Right after the dance, Jason sat down in the ranch dining hall with a couple of the ranch cowboys, the sausage guy from New Braunfels, and three of the Cactus Junction Boys. They were playing Texas Hold 'em, and Jason was winning, big-time. The band members quit and went to bed about midnight, but the guy who makes those leather belts and the corn dog vendor took their seats. Everybody else stayed to the bitter end. I've talked to all five of them, and they tell the same story. The game ended about four-fifteen. Jason was there the entire time, without a break. He walked away from the table with three hundred seventeen bucks — and a solid alibi."

There is a hard, heavy lump in Ruby's throat and she can't swallow past it. Jason has an *alibi*? No. Ethan can't be right.

But if he is, she is wrong.

"Here you go, folks," Angie says cheerily, putting down their plates. "Enjoy your grub. Holler when you're ready for pie."

For another little while, neither of them have anything to say. The jukebox is playing Patsy Cline's "She's Got You," the classic lament of a young woman who's lost the love of her life to another woman. Ethan digs eagerly into his food.

And Ruby, suddenly not as hungry as she was, picks at hers.

CHAPTER TWELVE

Ruby's chicken-fried steak is so tender she could cut it with a fork, the onion rings are hot and crunchy, and everything else on the plate is perfectly delicious. But she barely tastes the food. She is wracking her brain, trying to think how she could have been so freakin' *wrong.*

Jason was playing cards all night. He couldn't have killed Finn. She had been reckless and irresponsible to accuse him of murder when he was blameless. Well, not blameless, maybe. But not guilty, either.

Get used to it, Ruby. Jason didn't do it. Somebody else killed Finn.

You were wrong. Just. Plain. Wrong.

Again.

When they have finished their food, Ethan points to the sign on the napkin holder. "Pie fixes everything," he says. "I recommend the fudge pecan."

Ruby sighs. "A fix would do me good. But

I'm not sure I can eat a full piece."

"Me, either. Want to share?"

She nods. When Angie appears, he says, "Two coffees, one fudge pecan pie, and two forks." When she has gone, he leans forward. "You haven't said a word for fifteen minutes. Want to tell me what's wrong, Ruby?"

"*I am*," she says. The jukebox is playing "She's Got You" for the third or fourth time, and she wishes whoever is feeding it would choose a different song. She raises her voice over the music. "I'm wrong. I've accused an innocent person. It . . . bothers me."

He regards her thoughtfully, his head to one side. "Wrong about Jason?" If he's amused by her awkward confession, he doesn't show it.

"Yes." His gaze is penetrating, and she looks away. "I was lucky with Allison. But I can't count on being right. That's why I try not to use my so-called gift, you know."

"No, Ruby, I don't know," he says, and there is a deep — and unexpected — compassion in his voice. "Why don't you tell me?"

Ruby hesitates. This is the most closely held secret in her life, perhaps because of the brutal pain, or perhaps because there has been no closure. It happened so long ago, and yet it's still raw, fresh, unfinished.

340

She has shared the story only with China and her mentor, Sophia. Can she tell this man, whom she barely knows? If she does, he'll understand how imperfect her gift is, how erratic, how unreliable. The truth is a hard thing, and painful.

Still, there is something in his face and in his eyes that gives her a strange kind of confidence. And he is a lawman, after all. There are parts of the story that he might understand. She takes a deep breath and blurts it out.

"When I was a teenager, I had a friend named Sarah, my best friend. She was the prettiest, smartest girl in our class. We shared everything — boys we liked, teachers we had a crush on, family secrets. But halfway through our junior year, Sarah disappeared. I was sure she'd been kidnapped. I didn't know who did it, but I knew where she was being held — knew *psychically,* I mean. I saw it in a dream, not just once but several times. It was a real house, a place I knew, outside of Pecan Springs." She closes her eyes, remembering the abandoned house set deep in trees at the end of a gravel lane. "This went on for days, for a week, longer. I finally told our high school counselor about the dreams. She made me go to the police and tell them about the house."

Ethan raises a questioning eyebrow. "Did they believe you?"

"The counselor might have, but not the cops." She makes a face. "They questioned me — grilled me, really — for what seemed like hours. I'm sure they suspected that I had some inside information. Like, maybe I'd been part of the kidnapping plot and got cold feet or something."

"Cops have to cover all the bases," Ethan says.

"I suppose." Ruby sighs. "Finally, in the end, they told me to take them to the house. But Sarah wasn't there. She'd never been there, they said. And she was never found." The old pain still hurts, and her voice breaks against the jagged edge of remembering.

"Hundreds of thousands of children are reported missing every year." Ethan's voice is gentle. "It's a national tragedy, Ruby. You're not the only person who's lost somebody she loves."

"I know," she says, sighing again. "But knowing doesn't help. If I'd gone to the police earlier, they might have found her. However you look at it, I was wrong." These are twin facts she can never escape, burdens she can never lay down.

Ethan's eyes are intent on hers. "My guess

is that the cops didn't have any other leads to follow — at least, not any promising ones. You shouldn't beat yourself up about —"

"Please." She holds up her hand to stop him. She has to say this, get it out, *all* of it. "Some people say that certain things have to happen the way they happen, and there's nothing we can do to change that. Maybe I was a necessary part of something bigger, something I don't understand and probably never will. Maybe I was a punch line in a cosmic joke. I *get* that, and it's okay. But —"

"Hang on. Certain things *have* to happen? What does that mean?"

"Just what it says." She isn't sure she can make him understand because she's not sure she understands it herself. She would like to believe that people are able to make decisions that change the course of their lives. But she's remembering something Sophia has said to her, more than once: *There are things in the future that you can change, and things that are going to happen, whatever you do.* Certain events are already laid out, and the best you can do is to move along that path, trying to stay on your feet, trying to stay self-aware.

Aloud, as if in explanation, she says, "I tell myself that I couldn't find Sarah because

343

I wasn't *supposed* to find Sarah. I don't know if I actually believe that, but in the grand scheme of things, it probably doesn't matter what I believe, one way or another. What matters is what happened, and there's no changing *that*. She's gone, and I wasn't brave enough or wise enough to find her."

"Every cop has a case like that somewhere in his files," Ethan says quietly. "*I* do. More than one. Some of them keep me awake at night."

She sucks in her breath and blows it out again. She knows that Ethan made the trip out to Bandera County because he wants to find out just how psychic she is — or isn't. It's nice of him to want to make her feel better. But he needs to hear what she has to say, not dismiss it.

"After Sarah, I couldn't trust myself. That's why I was reluctant to get involved with Allison. And why I was so surprised when things worked out okay — when I could actually point the police to where she was. But now I'm wrong again. I was sure that jealousy was the killer's motive for Finn's death, which meant that Jason was the killer."

Ethan is quiet for a moment, thinking. Then he says, "What was it that made you sure?"

That's easy. "The lyrics that keep going through my mind. *I don't want nobody but you, but you're giving your body to somebody else.*" She looks at him across the table. "You know how a song gets stuck in your head after you've heard it a time or two — or three or four? Like those darned songs that jukebox has been playing ever since we got here. I'll probably be hearing them in my sleep. I'll bet you will, too."

"Songs?" He glances up, surprised. "What songs?"

She waves her hand. "Why, Loretta Lynn, of course. Can't you hear it? Somebody is playing 'You Ain't Woman Enough to Take My Man' for the fourth or fifth time. A little while ago, it was Patsy Cline, unhappy because all she has left is a picture, because somebody else has stolen her lover." *Somebody else . . . somebody else.*

Ethan leans forward and puts his hand over hers. "Ruby," he says, very low and very seriously. "Nobody has played the jukebox since we came into this restaurant."

She gapes at him. "Are you *deaf*? You can't hear Loretta Lynn? Or Patsy Cline?"

"No. Not one damned note." He points over her shoulder, in the direction of the jukebox. "In fact, I've been in this place dozens of times. I have never once heard it

345

play. It's an antique."

"But it was working when we came in," she protests. "The neon lights were blinking, and it was playing that old Hank Williams song, 'Your Cheatin' Heart.' I remember, because it seemed so fitting."

He is staring at her.

"Ethan," she wails, "I *swear* it was!"

"I believe you, Ruby," he says softly. "But it *isn't* working. Take a look. See for yourself."

She leans out of the booth and turns to look back at the jukebox. He's right. The Wurlitzer is standing there, dark and silent against the wall.

"But I can still hear Loretta Lynn. Or I could, until . . ." She takes an unsteady breath, listening as the song fades eerily away, as if into some immense distance. Shaken, she says, "If the jukebox isn't playing, then the music must be —"

"In your mind. In your psychic imagination." Ethan's voice is intense. "And you're right when you say that those songs are about jealousy. But while it's probably accurate to say that Jason is jealous of his wife, we know he didn't kill Finn. So who did?"

"Here's your pie and coffee, folks," Angie says, setting down mugs, a plate with a gigantic piece of chocolatey pie, and two forks. "Sorry it took so long. The kitchen is super busy tonight."

The pie is definitely to die for, warm and fragrant, tasting something like the batter you whip up for brownies (but eat half of before it gets to the oven) and a dark, slightly bitter fudge sauce laced with lots of crunchy nuts. Topped with two frosty scoops of vanilla ice cream, it is remarkably delicious.

Not only that, but Ruby discovers that there is something surprisingly intimate about sharing a piece of pie, two heads bent over a single plate, each person plying a fork, both people intent on the same thing. She finds herself distracted — pleasantly distracted — by Ethan's nearness. But not distracted enough to forget about his question.

"So who did?" she repeats. If Jason isn't the murderer, it's somebody else. *Somebody else. Somebody . . .*

She looks at him, suddenly understanding. "Ethan, these songs I'm hearing — they're all about a woman who has stolen some other woman's man. Maybe 'somebody else' is a *woman.*"

"A woman?" Ethan licks his fork, frowning. "But how does that fit into the situation we've got here? In our previous scenario, it's Finn who is trying to steal Marianne from her husband. And it's Finn who's dead."

Ruby is silent for a moment, then, "I wonder," she says, forking up another bite of pie. "I wonder about Finn. Is there a *woman* who might be jealous of his affair with Marianne?"

"There's an idea." Ethan puts his fork down. "So maybe we need to do a lot more of what we usually do in a case like this. Dig into Finn's personal life. Find out how he spent his time, where he traveled, who he knew. Friends, girlfriends, neighbors, people he worked with. Did somebody owe him money? Was he suing anybody? See if any of it links to people who were at the ranch last night. Finn lived here in Utopia, didn't he? Maybe we should drive by his place and see if —"

His cellphone rings. He fishes it out of his pocket and looks at it, frowning.

"Sorry. It's Larry. I promised to check in with him this evening, so I've gotta take this. Back in a couple of minutes." He pushes what's left of the pie toward her and slides out of the booth. "Help yourself to the rest." He grins.

"Pie fixes everything, you know."

CHAPTER THIRTEEN

Outside, the air is cleaner and cooler, and Ethan sucks in a fresh breath. "Hey, Larry," he says into the phone. "Got any new developments?"

"A few," the sheriff says. "That partial we picked up on the knife? We got the AFIS report back. No match, unfortunately."

"That would have been too easy."

"Yeah," Larry says with a sigh. "Where's the fun in that, huh? We've also got formal statements from Jason Harrison's alibi witnesses. They all say that he spent the whole damn night in that poker game, so he's definitely off our list."

Ethan thinks about what Ruby has just said, that the songs she keeps hearing in her head are about a woman who has stolen some other woman's man. Tentatively, he says, "How about Harrison's wife — Marianne. The ranch boss lady."

"Mmm. You think she might have done

it?" Larry sounds doubtful.

"She had the opportunity, didn't she? Say they quarreled, she went next door and picked up the knife, waited until he was asleep, and stabbed him. She doesn't have an alibi, does she?"

"Correct," Larry says slowly. "But the partial on the knife doesn't match."

"The partial is under the crossguard," Ethan reminds him. "It could have been there for weeks, and the killer just missed it when he — or *she* — wiped the knife. There's plenty of evidence that Ms. Harrison was with the victim before he died. They were intimate."

"True," Larry says. "I've known her for a long time, though, and I just don't . . ." He takes a deep breath, and Ethan hears both the regret and resolve in his friend's voice. "You're right, damn it. Marianne stays on the list. I'll get Peterson to interview her first thing tomorrow. He's tough. He can probably get more out of her than I can."

"Good deal. I'm over here in Utopia right now. Cassidy had a shop here, didn't he? I can check it out, if you want."

"I sent Jamison over to secure the place. But since you're there, sure, go take a look. Jamison says it's both a studio and a residence, but he only glanced around and said here was nothing out of order. That is, it doesn't appear to have been broken into." There was the sound of papers rustling. "Got a pencil? Here's the address."

Ethan pulls out his notebook and takes it down. "There's a lockbox on the door?"

"There is, but I'll have to get the code from Jamison. Check with me when you get there."

"I'll do it," Ethan says. He pauses. "I think we need to do more of what we usually do in a case like this, Larry. Dig into Cassidy's personal life. Talk to his neighbors, see if we can find out who he was dating, get a look at his finances, credit card statements, stuff like that."

"Right." Ethan hears Larry's chair squeak and pictures him leaning back, running a hand through his hair. "This is our first murder in a couple of years, you know. Most of our crime is straight-up drugs, assault, burglary. Hell, the last vehicle theft we had was Charlie Simpson's tractor — a Massey Ferguson with a front-end loader — and that was early in the summer. We don't get a lot of practice in serious detective work." He pauses. "What about the Wiccan lady that owned the knife. The murder weapon. You talked to her any more about this?"

"Some," Ethan says. He's tempted to tell

Larry that he and the Wiccan lady are sharing a piece of fudge pecan pie at the Lost Maples Café. That she's been listening to Loretta Lynn and Patsy Cline on a long-silent jukebox. And that this music has given her an idea or two about the motive for Cassidy's murder.

But he doesn't. He has the feeling that his friend the sheriff isn't quite ready for woo-woo.

When Ethan leaves, Ruby is alone with her coffee and the rest of the pie.

And that damned jukebox again, and Patsy Cline, who is lamenting that all she has left of the romance is a photograph, while somebody else has the guy she loves.

Ruby eats the last few bites of pie and has a sip of coffee. Then she turns around for one more look. She can still hear the music, but the neon lights are off, and the jukebox is definitely *not* playing. The song, now a mash-up of lyrics, is in her head. *I've got your picture, she's got you. Somebody else . . . somebody else.*

Well, she doesn't have a picture of Finn, but she has something else, doesn't she? She has his business card. Ethan was suggesting they might drive by his studio, so they would need an address. It should be on the card. Now, where did she —

She picks up her purse and begins rummaging through it. This takes a few moments, because as usual, her purse is pretty much a mess. But she finally finds the card in a side pocket, along with a couple of old grocery lists, a gas station receipt, and the drycleaner's ticket for her blue jacket, which she was sure she'd lost. Well, good, she thinks. At least I can retrieve my jacket without a hassle.

She takes the card out and turns it in her fingers. Handsome and really quite unusual, it is printed on translucent plastic with a rectangular border of what looks like colored chips of glass. In the center, in an elegant script, is the name of his studio — Finn Cassidy Glassworks — at 109 Vine Street in Utopia. Plus his phone number, his website, and the address of his Facebook page.

Ah, his Facebook page. Maybe . . .

She takes out her cellphone, clicks on the Facebook app, keys Finn's name into the search box, and watches as his page comes up.

Finn's Facebook page has an attractive, eye-catching header that pictures a collection of his glass pieces. She scrolls down, looking through dozens of colorful photos of his stained glass work, some taken in his shop, others in homes, churches, galleries — all of it very beautiful.

There are also several photos taken in his workroom, with artwork under construction, laid out on a worktable and on a light box. Behind the table are shelves along the wall, with large sheets of colored glass stacked upright on edge in narrow vertical cubbies, and pegboards neatly hung with tools. Finn's Facebook page is telling her that he is a methodical, meticulous artist who took pride in keeping his workroom neat.

But who was he when he *wasn't* being an artist?

She waits for the page to load more photos. Mostly, she is seeing pictures of his glassworks, lovely, but just glass. Finally, though, she is looking at snapshots of a party at Finn's studio — an open house, probably, with art pieces on display and tables of party food. The nicely dressed partygoers, drinks in hand, are milling through the rooms and spilling onto a wooden deck framed in flowering vines.

And there's a photo of Finn with a young, dark-haired woman in a sleeveless, figure-hugging red dress. She is pencil-thin, with large dark eyes behind tortoiseshell-rimmed glasses. Finn's arm is around her shoulders, his head is bent toward hers, and he is about to kiss her. Eager to be kissed, she raises her right hand to his shoulder. A tattoo of a blue and red snake curls around her arm.

Ruby shivers. The hair rises on the back of her neck. In the photo, the snake tattoo seems suddenly alive, coiling itself around the woman's arm just as it had when she shook the woman's hand the day before. When those fingers had felt like frozen twigs.

The dark-haired woman is Erica, Ruby's cabin mate at the festival.

Erica Dreyer. She is tagged in the photo, so she must be on Facebook, too. Ruby clicks on her name and her account comes up. And there, in the gallery of featured photos, are numerous selfies of Erica and Finn, together. Fishing from a boat on a Hill Country lake. Enjoying the view from the top of Enchanted Rock, near Fredericksburg. Sitting close together at a table on the Riverwalk in San Antonio, drinking glasses of wine. Sharing a pizza, curled up on a sofa watching television, bathing a dog. Laughing, holding hands, embracing, kissing. Erica and Finn. Finn and Erica. Clearly a couple. In love.

Ruby clicks through the gallery, noticing

the dates of Erica's posts. The photos of her and Finn span at least a year, perhaps more. A year of hiking, biking, traveling together. A year of being friends, being a couple, being (undoubtedly) lovers. A relationship that is now finished. Finally. Fatally.

Ruby puts her phone down and sits for a moment, thinking. The photos testify to a *past* relationship. They say nothing about what happened in Finn's tent the night before and whether Erica had anything to do with it.

But Ruby can think of other evidence. When she was waiting with the other vendors for the police to arrive and begin their investigation of Finn's murder, Erica had asked her the victim's name.

"Finn Cassidy," Ruby remembers saying. "He's a stained glass artist. He had a studio in Utopia. Maybe you happen to know him?"

Erica had shaken her head — and yet they had spent a year of their lives together. Anybody else, even a casual acquaintance, would surely have cried, "Oh, my God! Not *Finn*!"

Another thing. Erica had known about the knives. She had come into the booth the previous afternoon and lingered over the shelf of magical tools. She had traded two

pairs of earrings for one of the wands —
and the athames were on the very same
shelf.

And something else. Laurel had said that
she had been awakened in the night by
someone getting out of bed, tiptoeing across
the cabin, opening and closing a door. It
could have been the bathroom door. It
could have been the outside door. It could
have been Yvonne.

It could have been Erica.

It could have been Erica.

But Ruby has already made one mistake,
when she was convinced that Jason had
killed Finn. How can she be sure she isn't
making another? The truth is that she knows
almost nothing about Erica, beyond what
she has just seen on her Facebook page and
what little Erica has said about herself. She
has met her only briefly and has actually
had a sudden but intense negative reaction
(those icy twigs of fingers) when their hands
touched.

Was that significant? What does it mean?
She doesn't know.

What's more, her psychic gift, which is
notoriously *unreliable,* won't be of much
help here. She doesn't have any of Erica's
possessions that she could use to pick up
information — a shirt or a scarf, for in-

stance, a piece of Erica's clothing. She doesn't have the athame that was used to murder Finn. As a murder weapon, the knife may still be charged with some of the frightening energies of the person — Erica? — who plunged it into Finn's back. The sheriff has the knife, although Ethan might be able to arrange for her to have access to it, later.

But later is *later,* and Ruby is beginning to feel urgent. Her heart is racing, her breath is coming faster, her skin is prickling. She doesn't understand why, but it seems to her that for some reason, she needs to know more about Erica now. Right now. Tonight.

Then it occurs to her that she actually does have something that's available at this moment. She puts her fingers to her ear. In fact, it's right . . . *here.* The Taurus earrings Erica made.

But what might be even better, she has another pair in her purse — a pair that she hasn't worn or charged with her *own* energies. She takes the small plastic bag containing the Cancer earrings from her purse and slips them out of the bag, into the palm of her hand. Erica hasn't worn these, but she handcrafted them, so they must contain at least some of her energies. Plus, they're made of silver wire, coiled into shape. Made of *silver,* which (she remembers reading somewhere) is an excellent conductive metal. If it can conduct electricity, what else can it conduct?

And maybe just as importantly, Erica said that Cancer is her Sun sign, also — and Cancer is deeply empathetic. Could her Cancer Moon connect with Erica's Cancer Sun? Maybe, maybe not. But she won't know unless she tries.

Ruby leans back in the booth, her hands in her lap. She closes her eyes and folds her fingers over the tiny earrings, feeling them grow warm in her palm, imagining the silver as a conductor of feeling, of thought, of sensation, of memory. She clears her mind of everything else and begins to breathe steadily, evenly, relaxing muscle by muscle, feet, legs, shoulders, arms, neck, face. Letting herself go boneless, limp. Relaxing into her seat and focusing on the earrings she holds in her hand.

For a moment she's warm, as if the warmth of the silver is warming the bones of her hand, her arm, her shoulders, her spine. Then the warmth fades, and she begins to shiver. Cold, cold, colder, a chill wind blowing through her as through the bare branches of a winter tree. The sounds of the restaurant are indistinct, ebbing and flowing around her like waves breaking on a beach. And then she is falling straight down, down down *down* into a bottomless well of infinite darkness, the slender silver wire she holds in her hand her only connection to the world above, her only means of return.

But it is also her only connection to Erica, to the woman who made the earrings. At that instant, the silver is charged with a jolting surge of energy, and in the next, the well is not a well but Erica's endlessly tortured darkness, and Ruby is inside the fierce black memory of what happened in Finn's tent. She is seeing the images as Erica relives them in her mind, turning them over and over, recalling, remembering, reexperiencing the moments that led up to the plunging of that knife into Finn's sleeping body, at once horrified by what she has done and savagely glad she has done it. And laced through it all, the words of the song.

Giving your body to somebody else . . .
                    somebody else . . .

CHAPTER FOURTEEN

With a disconcerting jolt, Ruby comes to herself. Her fingers are clenched around the silver earrings, still hot in her hand, and she slowly, painfully flexes them. The sounds of the café become distinct again, and the colors are returning to their original sharpness. A couple walks past the booth, talking and laughing. The woman is wearing a sultry perfume, the man smells of cigarettes and beer. Somewhere in the room a child giggles, a chair scrapes, dishes clatter. Limp and drained of energy, Ruby is back in the world of places and people, the *real* world.

She has learned what she needs to know from Erica — most importantly, she knows she's not *wrong.* She takes a deep breath, shaken by what she has glimpsed and feeling a profound relief to be out of the deep, dark well that is Erica's heart. She knows she has to tell Ethan what she has learned.

But will he believe her? *Can* he believe

her, after hearing about both Sarah and Jason and knowing how wrong she had been on both counts?

And here's Ethan now. "Sorry about that," he says, sliding back into the booth. "It took longer than I thought. Larry wants me to take a look at Cassidy's place while we're here. If you've finished your coffee, we need to go."

"Not yet, please." Ruby turns on her cellphone, clicks a couple of times, and hands it to him. "You need to check this out first."

"What's this?" Ethan peers at the screen. "A Facebook page? Whose? Who are these people?"

"It's Finn Cassidy's page." Ruby points to the photo at the bottom of the screen. "You don't recognize him? That's Finn, with his girlfriend. That is, she *was* his girlfriend, at the time the photo was taken. His ex-girlfriend now, apparently."

His ex-girlfriend because Finn was in love with Marianne. He had been making love to her, the two of them together in his sleeping bag, while outside his tent, Erica listened and imagined and smoldered, until finally, she burst into a murderous rage.

"I didn't get a very good look at his face," Ethan says matter-of-factly. "And dead people don't always look like they did when they were alive." He frowns. "But yeah, that's him. So who's the girl?"

"Her name is Erica Dreyer. She's a vendor at the festival, selling silver wire jewelry. She made my earrings." Ruby lifted her finger and touched one. "She's also my cabin mate in Annie Oakley."

He raises an inquisitive eyebrow. "Annie Oakley?"

"The cabin where Laurel and I are staying. We're sharing it with this woman. Erica. She told us she lives here in Utopia."

Ethan enlarges the image of Erica and Finn, studying it. "How did you get to this page?"

"Finn gave me his business card when I bought the suncatcher from him yesterday." She slides the card across the table. "I noticed his Facebook address on it and went to that page first. When I recognized Erica, I looked up *her* page. Let me show you."

She takes the phone, clicks over to Erica's page, and hands it back to him. "Scroll down through the posts. You'll see plenty of photos of the two of them. They seem to have been a couple for at least a year."

"Wow." He glances quickly through the photos. "Great job, Ruby. We may make an investigator out of you yet. You say this woman —" He looks down at the screen. "You say Erica Dreyer is a vendor at the festival? I'll let the sheriff know." He reaches for his cellphone. "He'll want to get somebody to check her out and —"

"Ethan." Ruby puts her hand on his wrist. "Here's the thing. Erica was in my booth yesterday afternoon. She was looking at a wand in the display of magical tools — right beside the athame. She had to have noticed that knife, so she knew where it was. What's more, during the night, Laurel heard somebody in our cabin get up and go outside. It wasn't me and it wasn't Laurel. It could have been our other cabin mate, Yvonne. Or it could have been Erica."

He's staring at her. "During the night? *Last* night?"

She nods. "I think it *was* Erica, Ethan. She and Finn had broken up, and she wanted to get him back. She went to his tent to plead her case and heard him and Marianne, talking. Making love. She went to my tent, took the knife, and waited until Marianne left. She might have even waited until he was asleep. Then she killed him." Starkly, she adds, "And this morning, when I told her who had died, she pretended not to know him."

Ethan doesn't take his eyes off her face.

"And how do you know all this? Is it woo-woo?"

Ruby understands that there's no point in telling him about the earrings. He either believes her or he doesn't. "I just *know,*" she says simply.

After a moment, Ethan puts her cellphone on the table. "You say this woman lives here in Utopia?"

"That's what she told Laurel and me. She makes jewelry. Maybe she has a website." Ruby picks up the phone and types Erica's name into the browser search bar, along with the words "jewelry" and "Utopia." In a moment, there it is, an attractive page with Erica's photo and examples of her work. Ruby goes to her contact page, but there's only one of those get-in-touch forms.

"No street address," she says. She wasn't expecting one. It's not terribly bright to put your physical address online.

"What's her last name?" Ethan asks, taking his phone out of a pocket. "I'll get Dispatch to look up her address on the state's database."

"Dreyer." Reading off her web page, Ruby says, "Erica J. Dreyer."

He speed dials a number. "Hey, Madge, Ethan Connors here. See if you can pull up a residence address for Erica J. Dreyer,

Utopia, Texas." He takes out a pen and small spiral-bound notebook and flips a page, waiting. A few moments later, he says, "Vine Street, one-eleven. Got it, thanks." He jots down the address in the notebook.

"One-eleven Vine? Oh, my gosh." Startled, Ruby points to the business card on the table. "Finn's studio address is one-oh-nine. So he and Erica were next-door neighbors!"

And that would make a breakup especially difficult and painful. Erica would see Finn every day. She would be constantly mindful — with the heightened hyperawareness of a rejected lover — that he was right next door. In a small town like Utopia, she would run into him anywhere, everywhere. Picking up mail at the post office, buying a loaf of bread at the General Store, eating lunch at the café, filling the gas tank at the Pico station. It could be very hard, almost impossible, for her to let him go.

"Next-door neighbors," Ethan says, and puts the address into his phone. A moment later, he holds up a map on his screen. "Just a couple of blocks away. I need to connect with Larry on this, but since we're here, it makes sense for me to talk to her, if she's home. I can check out Finn's studio at the same time."

"Erica may still be at the festival," Ruby

says. "She was planning to stay at the cabin tonight."

"Well, we're here in Utopia," Ethan says. "So let's find out."

CHAPTER FIFTEEN

Full dark has fallen while they were eating. It hasn't yet rained in Utopia, but the air is heavy with the fresh scent of wet rangeland, mingled with the sharper, more resinous tang of juniper and sage.

The breeze from the south has a chilly edge to it, and Ruby wishes she'd brought a sweater. Storm clouds scud across the full moon and flickering shadows race over the silvery landscape. There is a quick jab of lightning to the east and a distant growl of thunder, punctuated by the staccato chirping of late-season crickets. A pair of motorcycles pulls away from the café, their engines a diminishing metallic roar as they head north out of town, racing to beat the storm home. On the other side of Main Street, the lights are on at the Gospel Tabernacle and Ruby can hear voices raised in an old hymn: "Oh, they tell me of a home where no storm clouds rise."

Ruby wonders if someone has chosen the hymn deliberately — and then wonders if the music is real, or just in her mind. Either way, it's a change from *somebody else . . . somebody else.*

Ethan is on the phone to Sheriff Donahue as they leave the café. "Got something interesting, Larry. Turns out that a woman named Erica Dreyer was involved with Finn for a while —"

"For at least a year," Ruby puts in, "judging from the photos on her Facebook page."

"There's online photo evidence of at least a year of involvement," Ethan says. "She's a vendor at the festival. She definitely knew where the knife was in the Crystal Cave booth, and she stayed in one of the ranch cabins last night instead of coming back here to Utopia, where she lives — next door to Cassidy's studio. In fact, one of her cabin mates heard her get up and go out sometime in the night."

He is walking fast and Ruby has to hurry to keep up with his long strides. At the truck, he opens the passenger door for her and she climbs in. Still on the phone, he gets into the driver's seat.

"Hell, no, not me. It was Ruby — Ms. Wilcox, I mean — who thought of it. She took a look at Cassidy's Facebook page and noticed a photo that included the Dreyer woman. When she checked out *her* page, she found a number of photos of Dreyer and Cassidy. Looks like they spent a lot of time together, in a lot of different places. However, this morning, at the scene, Dreyer pretended not to know Cassidy."

Still talking, he puts the key into the ignition. "Dreyer. D-r-e-y-e-r. Erica J. One-eleven Vine. I'm just leaving the café. How about if I swing by her place? If she's there, I'll have a little chat with her."

He turns the key and the motor starts with a deep-throated roar. Into the phone, he says, "Yeah, right. Maybe something useful. Never can tell. Say, you got that lockbox code yet?" He listens, then pulls out his notebook and jots something down. "Thanks." He clicks off and pockets the phone.

"Lockbox?" Ruby asks.

With one hand, he shifts into reverse, swings the wheel, and backs away from the curb. "Cassidy's place hasn't yet been fully searched. It's good practice to lock the place and string crime scene tape until you can get somebody to go in and have a good look, pick up the computer, check for contraband, et cetera. There's a door key in a lockbox, which opens with a code."

Ruby's cellphone rings while Ethan is telling her this, and she sees that the call is from Laurel. They are heading south on Main Street and coming up on Houston Street, which crosses Main at the south end of town. Beyond Houston Street, there's nothing but country — open, hilly range-and, with patches of woods.

Ruby takes the call as Ethan turns right at the intersection and heads toward the village park and the river. "What's up?" she asks.

"It's about Erica," Laurel says, sounding excited. "I came out of the shower in our cabin a while ago to find her throwing her stuff in her bag. She was in a big hurry, and she didn't answer when I asked why she was leaving. I thought it was kind of weird. Then just now, I was on my way to the Green to listen to that bluegrass band from Bandera, and I saw her red Kia SUV pulling out of the parking lot. She has taken her booth down, too, even though vendors aren't supposed to leave until tomorrow afternoon. I had a hunch —" She hesitates again. "Well, I thought I ought to let you know. It just seemed a bit bizarre to me, given everything that's happened this weekend."

"Good hunch," Ruby says. "Thanks. What time did you see her leave?"

"A few minutes ago. Maybe three, four?"

"Got it. Thanks, Laurel. Talk to you later." Ruby clicks off and turns to Ethan. "Erica has packed up and left the festival. She drove off three or four minutes ago. I wonder if she's on her way here."

He glances at his watch. "If so, it'll take her about twenty, twenty-five minutes. Gives us a little time." He frowns. "But maybe she's not headed home. Any idea what she's driving?"

"A red Kia SUV, according to Laurel."

"Tell Laurel I love her." Ethan is on his phone again. "Larry, Ms. Wilcox just heard from a friend that the Dreyer woman has packed up and left the festival. She may be making a run for it. Let's put out a BOLO on her red Kia SUV." He turns to Ruby. "Her description?"

"Late twenties," Ruby says. "Short dark hair, about five-seven, very thin. Tortoise-shell glasses. Oh, and a snake tattoo on her right arm."

Ethan repeats that and adds, "I'll cover this end, in case she shows up here. You might send some backup this way, if you've got anybody you can spare." He chuckles. "Yeah. You said it, buddy."

He clicks off with a grin, his face pale in the light from the dash. "Sheriff says it was a lucky break."

"What's a lucky break?"

"You getting the report from your friend that Dreyer left."

Ruby grins back. "Hey, that was no lucky break. No woo-woo, either. That was the old girls' network. It's what we do."

He makes another right, onto Vine. The Utopia village park stretches out to their left, with its rodeo arena, baseball field, and campground laid out between Vine Street and the Sabinal River. There are no streetlights, and since the houses are set back from the road and only a few have porch lights, the block ahead is dark. Ethan cruises slowly down the street, checking the house numbers displayed on mailboxes at the curb — although there isn't a curb. No sidewalks, either.

Finn's place is marked with a small wooden sign announcing Cassidy's Glassworks. The street number is 109, so Erica's house is just ahead, next door at 111. Ethan pulls onto the grass on the opposite side of the street and turns off the truck's headlights. He unlocks the console between the seats and takes out a flashlight, latex gloves, a pair of plastic handcuffs, and a handgun.

"A gun?" Ruby asks nervously.

"Just a precaution. I don't like to go into

unknown territory unarmed. Especially after dark." He begins pulling the gloves on "You stay in the truck. Lock yourself in Okay?"

"But I want to go with you."

"No way." He checks the gun to be sure it's loaded and tucks it into the waistband of his khakis, at the small of his back. "A crime scene is no place for a civilian."

"It's not a crime scene. Finn was killed at the festival."

"It's a crime scene. It's already been secured. You're staying put. Period. Paragraph. End of story."

Ruby sighs. "Well, at least you didn't say 'No place for a woman.' "

"That too." He grins, then says, quickly. "Sorry. Being a woman has nothing to do with it."

Ruby doesn't believe that, but there's no point in arguing with him. "I need your cell number," she says. "In case."

He scowls. "In case of what?"

"What do you think?" She rolls her eyes. "In case of a bear attack. In case of an invasion of little green men from Mars."

"I sincerely doubt that . . ."

"You're leaving me here as a lookout, aren't you?" She is making this up. "How am I going to let you know there are tanks olling down the street if I can't reach you? left my carrier pigeons at home."

"Carrier pigeons? I thought witches used ravens."

"I left them at home, too. Overtime gets expensive."

He half-smiles. But he gives her the number.

"Thank you." As she puts it into her phone, he opens the door and gets out of the truck.

"Stay here," he says again. Then adds, with a half-suppressed chuckle, "And see if you can stay out of trouble, Wilcox. *This* time."

CHAPTER SIXTEEN

The moon has slipped behind a thick blanket of clouds. The darkness outside the truck is absolute, except when the landscape — the park on her left, the street and houses on her right — is illuminated by the brief and intermittent lightning flashes.

There isn't much to look at inside Ethan's truck, either, except for a brown plush toy dog on the floor at Ruby's feet. He'd said that he was divorced, with no children. Who does the dog belong to? A girlfriend's child? None of her business, Ruby reminds herself. She frowns at that, but doesn't ask herself why. And she refuses to ask the toy dog.

Three minutes after Ethan leaves, she is bored. She takes out her cellphone. There's an email from China: "All well in the shops. Decent day but not spectacular. Hope you've sold everything already and plan to listen to music for the rest of the weekend."

Ruby is tempted to tell her that she's

investigating the murder of a stained glass artist by a jealous ex-girlfriend who stole a Wiccan athame to do the job. But the plot sounds too incredible, so she refrains. She'll wait until she gets back to Pecan Springs and can look China in the eye while she tells the whole story.

There's an email from her sister, Ramona: 'Got another wonderful idea for our Psychic Sisters business. Can't wait to tell you. You'll love it — guaranteed!" Ruby wrinkles her nose distastefully, wishing Ramona would find something else to get excited about.

There's also one from her Wiccan planning group, reminding her of their meeting on Wednesday evening. It's at Sophia's house, in Wimberley, where Ruby is supposed to talk about using tarot in rituals. There are also several junk emails and a notice from the Pecan Springs library, saying that the book she requested is available for pickup.

She clicks over to her Facebook page. Nothing very earthshaking there, either, unless you count a request for friendship from two guys she doesn't know and doesn't want to. They're probably fake, anyway.

But she has a book to read. *Y Is for Yesterday* is in her phone's ebook reader. Sadly, *Z Is for Zero* will never be written, for Sue

Grafton has died and all of Kinsey Mill-
hone's fans and friends are still in deepes
mourning. Ruby opens the book and settle
into the mystery, thinking that if she were
Kinsey, Ethan would have no problem
admitting her to his crime scenes. And she
could help, she's sure of it. Like Kinsey, she
would notice some small, vital clue that he
had overlooked. She would solve the mystery and he would be glad she was there.

She has read only a couple of pages when
a startling bolt of lightning flashes close by
followed by the loud rattle of thunder. She
looks up from her phone. It is beginning to
rain, lightly at first, just a smattering o
drops on the dusty windshield. Then harder
and harder, the rain sheeting down the
windshield, the blue-white lightning turning
the trees into wind-whipped silvery ghosts
She thinks of the tent at the festival and
hopes it is zipped tight against the rain and
anchored against the wind. She looks toward
Finn's house but it is dark. If Ethan is stil
there, he must be using his flashlight. He's
going to get soaked coming back to the
truck. Or maybe he'll wait until the storm
passes.

She is about to go back to *Y Is for Yesterday* when she sees a vehicle coming down
the street toward her. At first, she thinks

378

that it might be the backup Ethan asked for. But it isn't. As she watches, it slows, turns, and pulls into Erica's driveway. The headlights go out. In the brief glare of a lightning flash, she sees that the car is a compact SUV — Erica's red Kia. The driver's door opens. Erica gets out and runs toward the house, ducking through the rain.

Hurriedly, Ruby taps Ethan's number. It rings just once.

"What's up?" he asks in a low voice.

"Erica's home," Ruby says. "She just drove up and parked in her drive." As she watches, a light comes on in the front window. "She's in the house."

"Got it," he says curtly. "On my way."

She starts to say, "Do you want me to —" But he has clicked off.

A moment later, she sees his flashlight, bobbing between the two houses. A moment after that, he is on the porch, knocking at Erica's front door. The porchlight comes on and there is a brief exchange. After he goes in, the front door remains open behind the screen door, the light falling onto the porch in a golden door-shaped block.

Ruby looks up and down the street, but there is no sign of the backup that might or might not be on its way. She hesitates, but only for a moment. She opens the truck door and jumps out.

The rain is so cold and hard that it takes her breath away. Grateful that she is wearing flat sandals, she runs as fast as she can across the wet grass and the puddled street, but she is soaked to the skin before she reaches the shelter of Erica's porch. At the front window, the drapes are open. There is a large flowerpot under the window and she moves it aside so she can peer in, trying to stay out of sight.

Erica and Ethan are standing toward the rear of the room, near the open door to the kitchen. Ethan's back is to the window. Erica is facing him. Her hands are clenched at her sides and her voice is flat and hard.

"I had nothing to do with it!" she says. "I don't know what you're talking about, and I don't give a damn *who* you are." She stamps her foot. "I want you out of my house. Get out — now!"

"I'm sorry, Ms. Dreyer," Ethan says patiently "That's not going to work. Sheriff Donahue wants to interview you about the death of your friend Finn Cassidy. I'm taking you to the sheriff's office over in Bandera."

She folds her arms. "I'm not going anywhere with you."

"Let's not make this so hard, okay?" Ruby

380

can't see his face, but she can tell from the sound of his voice that he is giving Erica that engaging smile of his. He adds, "Look, it's not that far. The sooner we're on our way, the sooner you'll be back home and can go about your business. I'm sure you want to get this cleared up just as much as we do. Isn't that right?"

There is a silence. Ruby thinks that perhaps the smile has won her compliance.

"That's right," Erica says. "I really would like to get it cleared up. I wouldn't want you to think . . ." Her voice trails away and she hesitates. "But I have to feed my cat before I go. In the kitchen. Is that okay?"

"Sure," Ethan says, and his stance eases a little. "Go ahead. Feed your cat. Then we'll go."

Erica turns and leaves the room.

Ruby hesitates. Feed your *cat*? The hair prickles on the back of her neck. No. Wait. That's wrong. Erica doesn't have a — she couldn't — she's allergic to cats!

An instant later, Erica is standing in the kitchen doorway, a mean-looking shotgun in her hand, leveled at Ethan. Her voice is controlled and businesslike. "I'm not going anywhere with you. With you, or anybody else." She gestures toward a chair. "Sit down."

Ruby doesn't think twice. "Police!" she yells at the top of her lungs. "Drop that gun *Now!*"

And she picks up the flowerpot and heaves it through the window, shattering the glass with a loud crash.

Distracted, Erica looks past Ethan toward the window. Ethan steps forward, grabs the barrel of the shotgun and twists it out of Erica's hands. He drops it on the floor, kicks it into the corner, and in one fluid motion whirls her around and clasps her wrists behind her back. Whipping a pair of plastic cuffs out of his pocket, he has her cuffed before Ruby can draw a breath. In another motion, she is on the floor, facedown.

"Wow," Ruby says admiringly, through the broken window. "That was *amazing.*"

Ethan whirls around. "Wilcox, is that *you*?"

"It's me," she says, and goes to the open front door.

He faces her, his mouth a hard, flat line. "I thought I told you to stay in the truck."

"If I had stayed in the truck," she says reasonably, "she could have shot you. You might be dead right now. You could at least say thanks."

On the floor, Erica is writhing. "I loved Finn," she whimpers. "I loved him, I loved

382

him. But he loved somebody else. And I couldn't let her have him." Her voice rises, grows harsh and strident. "I couldn't, can't you see? I just couldn't let her have him!"

Ethan glances at Erica and at her shotgun in the corner. "Yeah," he says. "I guess you're right. Thanks for not staying in the truck."

Ruby folds her arms, indignant. "You guess I'm right? You *guess*?"

He comes toward her. "Okay," he says. "I'm not guessing. You're right. She could have shot me if you hadn't lobbed that flowerpot through the window." He smiles, his blue eyes searching her face. "I mean, *really.* Thank you, Ruby."

"You're welcome." Over the sound of the storm, she hears the wail of a siren. It stops with a loud chirp in the street out front. "There's your backup," she says unnecessarily.

"My backup is already here," Ethan says. He puts a hand on her shoulder and with the other, smooths the damp hair off her forehead. "Your hair is wet." His gaze drops, and she is suddenly conscious that her wet white shirt, loose-weave and now nearly transparent, is clinging tightly to her.

"You are all wet," he says in a husky voice, leaning toward her.

"That's what happens when you go out in the rain without an umbrella," Ruby says. Her voice is trembling. She clears her throat.

Outside, a vehicle door slams, and then a second, and Ruby can hear male voices.

"Right." Ethan straightens, drops his hands, and steps back. "I owe you. Big-time. Rain check?"

Ruby nods. "Rain check."

There are lots of things she doesn't yet know about herself, and many things left to learn about herself and Ethan.

But she doesn't have to be psychic to figure that one out.

■ ■ ■ ■

OUT OF BODY

BOOK 3

■ ■ ■ ■

She was a stranger in her own life, a tourist in her own body.
Melissa de la Cruz

If I ever had an out-of-body experience, I'd try to come back to a different one.
Tom Wilson

PROLOGUE

Adrienne Mitchell had the feeling that this might be Edith Bernard's final week on this earth.

When Mrs. Bernard's daughter hired her as her mother's private duty night nurse, Adrienne took one look at the medical chart (Parkinson's, stage five) and at the patient, who'd been refusing food for several weeks, and thought to herself, *I'd better leave my posting up on LinkedIn. I'll be looking for another job pretty darn quick.*

Adrienne had been on deathwatch before and knew what to expect, more or less, although she'd learned that unexpected things could happen. There was the time a woman asked her to fetch a jewelry case from her dresser, told her to open it and pick anything she wanted. (What she thought was cheap costume jewelry turned out to be a real diamond necklace by a noted Art Nouveau designer — or so the guy on *Antiques Roadshow* told her when he appraised it for an unexpected $4,000. And there was the middle-aged gentleman who asked her to kiss him on the lips as he died — he wanted, he said, to feel passion one last time. Adrienne kissed him gently and held his hand, and when he was gone she cried a little, also unexpected.

But old Mrs. Bernard had been comatose for a week, and Adrienne wasn't anticipating any oddball deathbed requests. In fact, this was one of the easiest assignments she'd had in several months. She usually spent the night in a small room next door to her patient's first-floor bedroom, with the door between the rooms slightly ajar. She could relax in a comfortable chair with her knitting (a pair of Norwegian boot stockings with a corrugated rib and a tricky checkerboard heel, for her daughter-in-law) and Turner Classic Movies on the small television, just barely audible, so she could keep an ear tuned to her patient.

But while Mrs. Bernard was occasionally restless and her bedding needed adjustment, she rarely uttered a sound. And since she wasn't eating, she didn't have to be fed. The only thing that Adrienne had to do was change her diaper occasionally. That was this week. Next week, it would be time for a catheter.

Something weird did happen, however. Something that had never happened before — and Adrienne fervently hoped would never happen again.

It was her third night on the job, just after two a.m. She was watching the 1939 Brontë film *Wuthering Heights* (with Merle Oberon as the spoiled, selfish Cathy and a young and hunky Laurence Olivier as a smoldering, about-to-burst-into-flame Heathcliff), and beginning to turn the heel of the second sock. She was trying to figure out why she had only thirty-four stitches on her needle, instead of the requisite thirty-six, when she heard a strange noise in her patient's bedroom. It was the sound — the *distinct* sound — of a heel on the wooden floor.

Startled, she dropped her knitting, pushed herself out of the chair, and went to the door. In the dim greenish light of the nightlight, she saw a tall figure, like a medieval monk in a hooded cape. He was bending over Mrs. Bernard.

Adrienne screamed. The caped figure straightened, strode to the open window, and hoisted a leg over the sill. In an instant, he was gone.

But on his way out, he dropped something.

A syringe.

CHAPTER ONE

A soul! a soul! a soul-cake!
Please good Missis, a soul-cake!
An apple, a pear, a plum, or a cherry,
Any good thing to make us all merry.
One for Peter, two for Paul
Three for Him who made us all.
Traditional children's "a-souling" song

"Hey, Ruby — is this what you're looking for?"

China Bayles comes through the door between Thyme and Seasons and the Crystal Cave, brandishing two dried cornstalks like a pair of trophies. "From my garden," she says.

"They're perfect, thanks!" Ruby Wilcox says happily, taking the stalks. "Did you see my big jack-o'-lantern? I carved it last night. It's out front with the bale of hay. With these stalks, some stretchy cobwebs, and a couple of brooms and a witch's hat, that ought to about do it, don't you think?"

Halloween is always a big event at the Crystal Cave, where Ruby tries to balance the gaudy commercial trick-or-treat holiday with the more serious celebrations that take place at the same time: Samhain, All Souls' Day, and the Día de los Muertos, Day of the Dead.

Samhain, celebrated by Ruby's Wiccan and Pagan friends, is an ancient Celtic festival that begins on the night of October 31 and continues through the next day. Occurring halfway between the autumn equinox and the winter solstice, this pagan celebration of the dead takes place at the end of the harvest season and the beginning of the dark days of winter. For those who honor it, Samhain is the beginning of the spiritual new year.

All Souls' Day, on the other hand, is a Christian tradition, observed on November 2 by placing lighted candles on the graves of loved ones and offering prayers for their eternal souls. "Soul cakes" (cookie-like flat cakes made with raisins and allspice, nutmeg, cinnamon, and ginger and marked with a cross) were traditionally set out with glasses of wine the night before — All Hallows' Eve, or Halloween. They were also given to those who came to the door "a-souling." In return, the "soulers" prayed for the souls of dead relatives of the generous person who had given them the cakes. (If you're thinking that this is the origin of our contemporary trick-or-treat, you're probably right.)

And there's one other way to celebrate. Día de los Muertos is a contemporary three-day Mexican festivity that begins on October 31 and ends on November 2. During this time, the souls of the dead are believed to revisit their earthly homes in search of the food, drink, and fellowship they enjoyed when they lived in their bodies. Home altars welcome these disembodied spirits with candles, incense, flowers, a pitcher of hibiscus tea, and favorite festive foods, especially moles, tamales, and the sweet, egg-rich *pan de muerto* (bread of the dead).

All three of these celebrations are held at a time when the boundary between the worlds of the living and the dead — the world of the body and the world of the soul — is said to be paper-thin and easily crossed. At the Crystal Cave, it's one of the most important holidays of the year, for the Cave's customers generally have an interest in spirits, the underworld, and ghosts. Today is Thursday, October 30. So this year, the three-part holiday is taking place over the weekend.

Taking China's cornstalks, Ruby opens the front door of the shop and adds them to the display of hay bales, pumpkins, cobwebs, and witches' stuff. "That takes care of that," she says, dusting her hands. "Thank you."

"Glad to help," China says. "Are you all set for the party tonight?"

Held in the last week of October, China's annual Halloween party is always a lot of fun. The whole gang will be there. China's husband, McQuaid, of course, and their kids, Brian and Caitlin. Their friends Sheila Dawson (Pecan Springs' police chief) and her husband Blackie Blackwell (McQuaid's partner in the PI business). Tom and Sylvia Banner, their neighbors just up the road. Ruby's daughter Amy, Amy's partner, Kate, and their little girl, Grace. Plus a dozen other friends, most of them in costume.

"All set," Ruby replies with a smile. "What are you wearing?"

"It's a secret," China says. "I want you to be surprised. What about you?"

"No secret. I'm a gypsy fortune-teller. Again."

"Ooh-la-la," China says, and rolls her eyes. "Ethan is coming with you?"

Ruby makes a face. "He was planning to,

out he just called. Something came up — a drug deal gone wrong. He doesn't think he'll make it."

She and Ethan Connors, a detective on the Pecan Springs police force, had met in late summer, after Ruby had had several terrifying dreams about a kidnapping. Since this was a criminal matter, China urged her to tell Sheila. That was bad enough, but the dreams turned into a nightmare when Ruby learned that the kidnapping had actually occurred just the night before, when Allison Montgomery was grabbed while she was running on the hike-and-bike trail. And when Sheila assigned Connors to the case, things only got worse.*

It was an uncomfortable beginning. A disbeliever by nature and a skeptic by training, Ethan was suspicious of Ruby's psychic abilities, while Ruby was naturally defensive. But in the end, Connors had to acknowledge that the cops wouldn't have solved the case without the information she provided, even if it was "woo-woo": irrational, nonfactual, and totally unscientific. His suspicions were tempered even further a few weeks later, when the two of them found themselves thrown together at a Hill Coun-

* NoBODY

try harvest festival and Ruby had helped Connors and the sheriff solve a brutal murder.*

After that, it looked like the relationship might be going somewhere — until Ethan's workload ramped up and things stalled out. Ruby was pleased when he'd said yes to China's party and disappointed when he called just now to tell her he couldn't make it.

"I'm sorry he can't come," China says. "I want to meet him, and I know McQuaid does, too." China's husband is a former Houston homicide detective who now has his own private investigations firm, so she understands about the unpredictable demands of a law enforcement career. But right now, she is watching Ruby with concern.

"You're feeling okay, Ruby?" she asks. "Have you recovered from all that psychic stuff that went on at the Harvest Festival? Coming so soon after the Montgomery kidnapping, it must have been a harrowing experience."

"It was," Ruby confesses. "I wish I had an off button. Or a road map to tell me where I'm going with this. Or where I've been."

* *SomeBODY Else*

They both laugh, but China knows Ruby's story. And neither of them think it is funny.

A natural psychic, Ruby has spent most of her life trying to pretend that she *isn't*. This began when she was a girl and wanted desperately to be like all her friends. If she understood what somebody was thinking, she pretended she didn't have a clue. If she had an intuition about something that was going to happen, she hid it. She didn't want anybody to know that she was different, that she possessed skills and abilities that her friends lacked.

But recently, her psychic abilities seemed to have strengthened to the point where she could no longer hide them, and she found herself in situations where she had to put them to use. Overwhelmed by all this and feeling totally inadequate, she sought help from a friend and teacher, Sophia D'Angelo, who lives near the artists' community of Wimberley. Sophia suggested that Ruby's enhanced capabilities might be related to the mild concussion she had experienced in a bicycling accident that summer.

"You were already exceptionally empathic," she said. "Even as a child, you had a high degree of telepathic awareness and clairvoyance. A slight brain injury could have boosted that power in substantial ways, making you even more sensitive to all kinds of energies, positive and negative."

"If that's what's happened, why can't I handle it better?" Ruby had asked. She told Sophia about the ugly events at the Harvest Festival. About the murder of one of the artists, and the antique jukebox — unplugged and inoperative — that had had a message for her. She knew the thing about the jukebox sounded weird, and it was. It was uncanny. It was scary. What happened afterward, when Ethan confronted a killer with a shotgun, was even more frightening.

But what worried Ruby the most was how *wrong* her initial intuition had been.

"I accused an innocent person," she wailed to Sophia. "If I am as psychic as you say, why do I keep getting things wrong?"

Sophia had counseled patience. And practice.

"You've spent a whole lifetime downplaying your abilities, Ruby. Recognizing your power and learning how best to integrate it into your life — that's going to take patience. If you're serious about using your abilities in a positive way, you'll need to practice, deliberately. And pay attention." She smiled. "The Universe will offer plenty of real-world invitations to explore this part of yourself — to learn and grow, psychically.

Start watching for them."

"Practice?" Ruby said, dubious. "What kind of practice?"

"It's something like dancing," Sophia said. "Anybody can whirl around the floor and enjoy herself. She can even look good when she's doing it. But somebody who wants to do classical ballet or modern jazz dance needs to be willing to put in weeks and months and years of practice, a lifetime, really. It's a matter of mastering the body. Of knowing how exactly to use the arms, the legs, the trunk, and all the muscles. Just because somebody can jump doesn't mean that she can do a grand jeté."

Ruby nodded. "I can see that."

"Well, the same is true of our psychic abilities. A strong but unskilled psychic can make a few intuitive guesses and be seventy or eighty percent more accurate than 'normal' people. But developing our capabilities to the point where we can use them to seek accurate answers to particular puzzles — that takes serious work. It takes practice."

She gave Ruby an enigmatic glance. "And sometimes it takes us where we don't want to go. Difficult places. Dangerous places."

Ruby shivered, not liking the sound of that.

"But we have to be willing to go there,"
Sophia said quietly. "That's why we're given
this gift, you know. Everything that challenges you makes you more, Ruby. But it's
not free. It comes at a cost."

"What cost?" Ruby had asked, suddenly
half-frightened.

"It's a devil's bargain." Sophia gave her a
steady look. "You won't know until you're
asked to pay it. And then you'll have to
decide."

Now, China takes Ruby's hand. "An off
button or a road map," she says, repeating
Ruby's wish. "I understand." She smiles
ruefully. "Well, if it'll help to talk, I'm available. Anytime, day or night. I worry about
you, you know."

She doesn't have to tell Ruby that. Ruby
can *hear* China worrying. She can hear her
thinking that Ruby hasn't fully recovered
from her bicycle accident that summer or
from the psychic events of the past weeks.
She can also hear her thinking that it would
be nice if that detective could come to the
party, because Ruby hasn't had a serious
romantic interest for far too long. And
without a spicy helping of romance every
now and then, life is like a plain old meat-
and-potatoes diet.

Which makes Ruby smile, because *she*

happens to think so, too. A spicy helping of romance — especially shared with Ethan, who manages to be sexy without even trying — would be quite, quite tasty.

But all she says is "I know you worry," and actively pushes herself out of China's mind. She doesn't like to invade other people's privacy, especially that of her friends. She gives China's hand a quick squeeze.

"And I appreciate it. But seriously, I have completely gotten over that silly little accident. Good as new, even better, maybe. Don't give it another thought."

China hugs her, hard. "If you say so, sweetie," she says, and goes back to her shop.

A little while later, Ruby's cellphone rings — the Exorcist theme, which she likes because it is amusingly spooky and makes her customers smile. As she picks up the call, a face flashes into her mind, the image startlingly distinct. She doesn't have to glance at the caller ID to know that it's Jessica Nelson, a reporter at the *Pecan Springs Enterprise* and a longtime friend.

A few years ago, Jessie was abducted. She kept her cool, made her escape in a rather spectacular fashion,* and got a great deal of

* *Mourning Gloria*

national media attention. Some months later, she turned the experience into a true crime book that earned her even more attention, as well as a couple of awards for investigative journalism. She is lively, energetic, and always positive. Hark Hibler, the *Enterprise*'s editor and publisher, says she is his best reporter, especially when it comes to digging deep for a story.

"Hey, Jess," Ruby says. "I haven't heard from you for a while. What's up with you these days?"

A shadow falls across the room, and with it comes a chill and a shiver of apprehension. Whatever is up with Jessica, Ruby already knows that there's a problem — a *big* problem.

"Oh, just the usual," Jessica says, in a studiedly offhand tone. "You know what they say — nothing exciting ever happens in Pecan Springs. But it occurred to me this morning that we haven't seen each other in way too long. I really need to catch up on . . . well, you know. Guys, clothes, family, all that good girl stuff. How about supper? Like, maybe tonight?"

Ruby knows there is more to Jessica's phone call than this, but she only says, "I can't tonight. How about lunch on Monday? The shop is closed and I won't be so ushed."

Jessica doesn't hesitate. "How about lunch oday? Or is it too short notice?"

Ruby's uneasiness ratchets up a notch. Whatever is on Jessica's mind, she is obvi-ously feeling urgent about it.

"Lunch today sounds good," she says. "Why don't you come over here? Easier for me and it's on the house. Thursday is soup-and-salad day." *Here* is Thyme for Tea, the tea room that Ruby and China own and manage, adjacent to their shops.

"Hey. Free lunch." Jessica chuckles. "An offer I can't refuse. What's a good time for you?"

Ruby checks the tea room schedule and sees that one of the local clubs is coming. "Late would be better. The Quilt Guild will be here for lunch. We'll be crowded and I'll be busy."

A good busy, of course. Group bookings are a blessing for the bottom line — not that the bottom line is in danger. While the tea room menu is simple, people like its emphasis on organic locally grown and healthy foods. It has been far more success-ful than Ruby or China expected. Plus, it brings customers into their shops. A winner for everybody.

"Late works better for me, too," Jessica

says. "Save us a table for one-thirty?"

"I'll do that," Ruby agrees. "I'm looking forward to seeing you, Jess."

But as she clicks off the call, she knows she hasn't imagined her friend's anxiety. They aren't getting together because Jessica misses her and wants to chat about guys, clothes, and girl stuff.

She wants to persuade Ruby to *do* something. Something difficult and disagreeable. No, more than that: something dark and threatening.

Something dangerous.

And whatever it is, Ruby already knows she doesn't want to do it.

CHAPTER TWO

Jessica is late for lunch, and as the minutes tick past, Ruby wonders whether she has decided to cancel and has forgotten to call. She is clearing off a table in the tea room when she turns and sees her friend at the door, strikingly professional in a khaki blazer, a silky red blouse, dark slacks, and gorgeous red heels.

"Hi, Ruby," Jessica says. "Sorry I'm late. I had to do an interview in Austin this morning, and the traffic on I-35 was even worse than usual."

"No problem at all." Ruby points to a table in the corner. "That's ours. Let me check a few things out and get our plates. I'll join you in a minute."

She steps back and surveys the room. A couple of tables are still occupied, but the people are getting ready to leave. China is at the cash register just inside the door, and they won't be seating any more diners.

Jamie Reynolds, their midday helper, wil
clear the rest of the tables and then head to
the kitchen to help Cassandra Wilde with
cleanup and prep for tomorrow. By the time
Ruby and Jessica sit down, they will have
the place to themselves.

The Crystal Cave and Thyme and Seasons
occupy the side-by-side front rooms of an
old stone building on Crockett Street, a
couple of blocks east of Pecan Springs
courthouse square. The larger room behind
the shops is the home of Thyme for Tea,
which is open daily from eleven to one for
lunch and from three to five for tea, with a
three-course English Tea (savory tea sand-
wiches, scones, and sweets and fruit) on
Saturday afternoon, by reservation. The
room holds ten tables and forty diners when
it's completely occupied. Behind it is the
fully equipped kitchen where Cass prepares
the luncheon menus, tea items, and the dinners she sells via The Thymely Gourmet,
her meal-delivery service.

Guests often say how much they enjoy
dining in the tea room. The beaded wain-
scoting is painted hunter green, wreaths and
bundles of dried herbs hang on the old
limestone walls, and pottery planters filled
with ferns are fitted into the sills of the tall,
narrow windows. The tables are dressed in

dark green cotton and set with pretty plates, floral chintz napkins, terracotta pots of herbs, and scented candles. French doors open out onto a wooden deck where another dozen people can enjoy the surrounding gardens when the weather is nice enough to eat outside.

It isn't especially nice today. The blustery late-October wind has brought chilly morning showers down from the Panhandle. The tree branches are bare against a dark sky, and the deck is littered with wet leaves from the nearby weeping willow.

But today's luncheon menu features clam and corn chowder, a salad, and hot herb bread — a perfect meal for a chilly day. And in the kitchen, Jamie is stacking plates and cups in the big commercial dishwasher, while Cass — white-aproned, smiling, and amazingly unflustered after cooking lunch for thirty-five — is about to start assembling today's home-delivery dinners. When Cass first joined the team, she was blond, beautiful, and wore a bountiful size extra-extra-large. "All curves and nothing to lose," she liked to say about herself. (Cass is not shy.) She's still blond, beautiful, and curvy, but she's down to a modest size large and still losing.

"Help yourself," Cass says, when Ruby

tells her she has a guest for a late lunch. So Ruby snags a couple of plates of salad, ladles chowder into two bowls, and filches a mini-loaf of fresh herb bread. She arranges the food on a tray and carries it to the table where Jessica is checking her cellphone.

When she sees the food, Jessica smiles and drops the phone into her leather shoulder bag. "Ruby, that looks *delicious*!" She leans over her bowl of chowder and inhales deeply. "Smells wonderful, too."

"Cass is a terrific cook," Ruby says. "We'd be lost without her." She puts the empty tray on the service shelf and comes back to the table with mugs and a pot of Earl Grey tea.

"Cass is still doing the personal chef thing?" Jessica asks, unfolding her napkin.

"Yes, and her customer base is still growing. People work for eight hours in Austin or San Antonio, commute for an hour each way, and are glad to come home to her heat-and-eat meals. Cheaper than going out. Healthier, too. And delicious."

"You three — you, China, Cass — certainly have it all together," Jessica says. "You're wonderful role models for women who want to go into business for themselves. The *Enterprise* should do a feature story on you."

"That would be great," said Ruby, pouring their tea. "We can always use the publicity. If you decide to do it, though, you might include Lori Lowry, the weaver who rents the loft for her yarn shop and studio. She's looking for more students."

"Sure thing," Jessica says. "I'll talk to Hark about it this afternoon."

Ruby met Jessica Nelson several years ago, when Jess was still a journalism student at Central Texas State and an intern at the *Enterprise.* Jessica doesn't talk about it easily, but Ruby knows that there was a terrible tragedy in her life. When she was a girl, her mother and father and twin sister died in a fire that was eventually ruled as arson, although nobody was ever charged with the crime.

Jessica is in her late twenties now, a lively young woman with golden boy-cut hair, a quick smile, and a favorite fragrance — Clinique's Happy — that matches her sprightly, vibrant style. But her easygoing manner is at odds with the watchful intensity in her brown eyes. She is a skilled reporter: intelligent, probing, and fiercely competitive. Hark says that once she sinks her teeth into a story, she's ruthless.

She especially thrives on crime stories, like the book she wrote after her abduction and escape. And last year, her detailed, in-depth series on Medicare fraud in the Pecan Springs Community Hospice won the Molly, a major award for investigative journalism sponsored by the *Texas Observer* and named for Molly Ivins, a Texas journalist and well-known political commentator. Hark always says he feels fortunate to have Jessica on the staff, but he knows that someday, she'll announce that she's moving to a bigger newspaper in a city where there's more crime. Pecan Springs, he says with a grimace, doesn't have enough criminals to suit her.

Jessie and Ruby haven't talked for a couple of months. But it doesn't take them long to catch up, and by the time they finish their salads, they've nearly exhausted the usual girl-gossip. Ruby has told her about what's been going on at the Crystal Cave and the workshops that she and China are planning for the rest of the year.

But Ruby doesn't mention the Allison Montgomery kidnapping or what had happened at the Harvest Festival a couple of weekends before. Ruby trusts Jessica, but she is a journalist, after all. Ruby isn't about to bring up her psychic adventures, which Jessica would be tempted to turn into a front-page story. Or about her sister Ranona's idiotic idea for partnering as the Psychic Sisters, which Jessica might think was a joke.

Jessica tells her about her recent trip to Cozumel, but not about breaking up with her latest boyfriend, Kelly, an assistant professor in the English Department at CTSU. Ruby picks up that little bit of news when Jessica gives a sad, involuntary sigh. She hasn't intended to listen in on her friend's thoughts, so she retreats immediately and doesn't let Jessie know that she knows about Kelly.

But there is something else, and it has nothing to do with broken romances. Ruby picks up her soup spoon, dips it into her chowder, and says, "So what's behind this lunch date, Jess? It's good to get together, but I have the feeling that there's more."

Not looking up, Jessica begins buttering a piece of herb bread. "Yes, there's more."

"I'm all ears," Ruby says.

"I had a talk with an informant in the Pecan Springs Police Department yesterday." Jessica takes a bite of bread. "He gave me some background on a recent case that he was involved in." She pauses, then adds, very deliberately, "I was a little surprised to hear how deeply *you* were involved in it, Ruby."

Ruby dives back into her chowder. "Me? Sorry. Drawing a blank here. I don't remember —"

"Yes, of course you do. The Montgomery kidnapping. Allison Montgomery. The jogger who was abducted from the hike-and-bike trail this summer." Jessica puts her bread down and leans forward. "I've just learned that there are several fascinating elements of that case that didn't make it into the story I bylined in the *Enterprise.* They didn't show up in the police report, either."

Ruby frowns. "And how do you know this?"

But she doesn't need to ask. Jessica is picturing her informant, and to Ruby's huge relief, he is *not* Ethan Connors. This guy is much younger, in his twenties, with hair so blond it's almost white. His name — his first name? his last? — is Mason. He seems to have been on the SWAT team that rescued Allison.

"I'm not going to reveal my sources and methods," Jessica says firmly. "A crime reporter has to have a few friends who are willing to let her in on what's *really* going on, you know."

"I see," Ruby says. "Well, I doubt that your guy can tell you —"

Jessica puts a warning hand on Ruby's arm. In a comically spooky voice, she says, "Don't try to weasel out on me, Wilcox. I know what you did."

Ruby laughs nervously. "What I did? Well, it wasn't much, really. I just —"

Jessica withdraws her hand and goes back to her chowder. "It took some convincing to get my informant to talk about what happened. He wasn't what you might call eager. He kept saying that he was just repeating what he'd heard from guys on the force."

With a sigh, Ruby gives in. "What exactly had he heard?"

Jessica leans forward again, lowering her voice. "He said you used some sort of weird psychic trick to get into the victim's mind so you could find out where she was being held."

"It wasn't a *weird* trick," Ruby says defensively. "It was —"

She stops, realizing that she's giving herself away.

"Well, it wasn't," she mutters. "You can't play tricks with stuff like this. Not when somebody's life is on the line."

Jessica reaches out and pats Ruby's hand. "I didn't think it was weird," she says quietly. "You did what you had to do. Plus, my informant isn't the sort of guy who would make something up for the sake of a story. Still, I always try to get confirmation. Thank you for confirming."

"You're welcome." Ruby narrows her eyes. "Now that you've got it, what are you going to do with it? You're not going to put it in the *Enterprise,* I hope."

Jessica goes on as if she hadn't spoken. "I was impressed by what I heard, but I wasn't terribly surprised, you know. Everybody says you're psychic."

"I can't help what everybody says," Ruby replies, half under her breath.

Jessica nods sympathetically. "Of course, everybody expects the owner of a shop like the Crystal Cave to be psychic, don't they? If you ask me, you've done a really good job, hiding your real abilities behind all those fun things — the tarot and rune stones and crystal balls. You've got everybody thinking that the magic is in the Ouija board and the tarot cards and all that other stuff. If people want to be 'psychic,' all they have to do is buy the board or the cards. Or whatever." She shakes her head admiringly. "I don't mean to sound cynical, but what a great sales gimmick!"

"Now, you wait just a darn minute," Ruby says crossly. "That is *not* what I —"

"Just kidding." Jessica holds up her hand.

palm out, like a traffic cop. "I have always had the impression that there was something serious and important behind those parlor games. I'm glad to know I was right. You *are* psychic. Seriously."

"Well, so what?" Ruby sits back in her chair, feeling irritated. "So maybe I was able to offer the police a little help when it came to —"

"According to my informant, it was more than a 'little help.' If it hadn't been for you, Allison Montgomery would be dead by now, and her killer would be on the prowl, looking for his next victim." Jessica finished her herb bread and licked her fingers. "Look, Ruby. I fully understand why your contribution had to be kept out of the newspaper, and why the police report has to say that the cops were acting on an 'anonymous tip' when they showed up at that garage. They couldn't very well say that a psychic told them where to go and what they would find when they got there." She arches her eyebrows. "Which pisses me off, speaking as a reporter. Readers deserve to know the *facts,* whatever they are."

"Okay, Jess, I give up," Ruby says. "We have established that I gave the PSPD a helping hand in a kidnapping case. So are you going to tell me why we are talking about this? And if you're thinking tha you're going to put this stuff into a story you are absolutely one hundred percen *wrong.* Think whatever you like about wha your informant told you. But I know for a fact that the chief of police will disavow every word. It wasn't in the police report, i wasn't in the original newspaper story, and you are not going to publish it." She clenches her jaw. "Not. One. Word."

"Publish it?" Jessica's eyes widen. "Oh jeez. Oh, no! That's not what I had in mind I'm sorry you . . . I didn't mean to imply . . . No, honestly, Ruby!"

"Well, then, what is it?" Ruby demands "I mean, I treasure your friendship, Jess And you are always fun to talk to. But please tell me why we are having this conversation."

Jessica takes a deep breath. "It's about something else entirely. An investigation I've been working on for the past six month now." She glances around, then lowers her voice. "I am investigating a serial killer. I know what I'm looking for, but I've gone as far as I can go on my own. I need some rather . . . specialized help. I need *you.*"

"A serial killer?" Ruby is startled, ther skeptical, then half-amused. "Here in Pecar Springs? What are you smoking, Jess? I read

:he newspaper every day. One of my friends
s the chief of police, and I know a few
people on the force. I haven't heard of a
single unsolved murder."

"That's because I'm the only one who
knows about him," Jessica said reasonably.
'But yes, there *is* a serial killer. And yes,
one of the deaths took place in Pecan
Springs. But it happened several years ago.
And at the time, it wasn't recognized as a
murder."

"Then what . . . how —"

Jessica holds up her hand again. "I have
identified seven other similar deaths that
have taken place over the past three years in
nearby small towns. In fact, that's one of
the reasons these deaths haven't been fully
investigated. They have occurred in seven
different police jurisdictions, miles apart.
Nobody has spotted them because nobody
has looked at the big picture."

"What about the Texas Rangers?" Ruby
asks. "Isn't that their job?"

Jessica nods. "The Rangers can be called
in when there are crimes that span several
jurisdictions. But they can't just show up
and launch an investigation. They have to
be asked first. And the problem is that these
deaths don't *look* like murders. The victims
have all been terminally ill, so they appear

to have died from natural causes. In addition to that, at the time the deaths occurred they would not have appeared to be related to one another. There was no reason for somebody looking at them to think that there was any possible connection between an old man who died in Seguin and a teenager who died thirty miles away and eight months later."

"Hey, wait." Ruby pulls her brows together. "Go back a sentence or two, Jessie. Did you say these people were *terminally ill*?"

"Yes. Some of the victims have even been in hospice care. That's the brilliance of this scheme, you see." Jessica leans forward, her voice earnest. "Even if he was suspicious, a small-town justice of the peace would have a hard time justifying an investigation into what looked like a heart attack. Or the final throes of Parkinson's."

Ruby rolls her eyes. "Well, gosh, Jess. I don't mean to sound callous about it, but people die all the time — especially people who are terminally ill. If it looks like these folks are dying from natural causes, what makes you so sure they were murdered? You couldn't be . . . well, imagining it, could you?" *Or so eager to find material for your next true crime book that you've let a fiction run away with the facts?*

Jessica waves away Ruby's question and plows on, solemnly and with conviction. "But that's the beauty of it, Ruby. Don't you see? Nobody has said, 'Oh, gosh, look — we've got a whole string of unsolved serial killings, happening all over Central Texas! We have to find out who's behind these crimes! We have to stop this killer before he kills somebody else!' "

Ruby tries again. "Well, if these deaths don't *look* like murders and cops don't think they are murders and there are no obvious connections between them, what makes you think they are —"

"But there *are* connections!" Jessica says emphatically. "There *is* a pattern. And once you know what it is, it's totally obvious that the murderer isn't choosing his victims at random. This is a deliberate, well-organized, master killer who has a method for choosing his targets." She gives Ruby an imploring look.

"And if you'll help me the way you helped the police with the Montgomery kidnapping, I'm sure we can find out who's behind this — and stop him."

CHAPTER THREE

The way you helped the police with the Mont gomery kidnapping.

Ruby stares at Jessica. She is remembering the advice Sophia had given her about developing her psychic gift. "If you're serious about learning to use your skills, it's going to take lots of deliberate practice.' With an enigmatic smile, her friend had added, "The Universe will offer plenty of real-world opportunities to explore this part of yourself — to learn and grow, psychically. Some will be simply invitations. Others will be assignments. Start watching for them."

Is Jessica's investigation an assignmen from the Universe?

Well, if that's what it is, Ruby thinks, the Universe can find somebody else to do its dirty work.

"This is not my thing, Jessica," she says very firmly. "Talk to Ethan Connors. He's a detective with the PSPD and has had years of investigative experience. Or if you don't want to involve the police, talk to China. Didn't you do a story fairly recently on that marijuana-growing operation she discovered when she went looking for her daughter's missing rooster?" The rooster had been nabbed from his cage in the poultry tent at the Adams County fairgrounds. China and her neighbor, Tom Banner, not only caught the thief but made one of the largest pot busts in Adams County history.*

"Nothing doing." Jessica shakes her head. 'The police will ultimately have to be involved, but I need more information before I'm ready to share this story — especially with Connors. He's a just-the-facts-ma'am kind of cop. He wouldn't be interested in my speculations. And while I respect China's intelligence and experience, she doesn't have your . . . well, your resources. Your *psychic* resources. She can't help me the way you can." She frowns doubtfully. "At least, the way I think you can. Based on what Mason told me."

"Which is what?" Ruby isn't entirely sure that she wants to know what a cop has said about her. On the other hand, she probably *ought* to know.

* *Queen Anne's Lace*

Jessica lowers her voice. "Which is getting inside the mind of the victim, as you did in the Montgomery case." She sits back in her chair. "I've been doing some reading and I think it's what's called an 'out-of-body experience.' Is that right?"

Ruby hesitates, then nods. "It's called that sometimes, yes."

But just thinking about Allison Montgomery's kidnapping makes her shudder. She is not going to do anything like that ever again. At the same time, though, she can't help but be curious about what Jessica has discovered.

Jessica leans forward. "Well, that's what I need you to do. If you can get inside the mind of this killer, maybe we can find out who he is and what he's planning." She gives Ruby a direct look. "Full disclosure. I can't say that I actually believe what Mason told me, you understand. But I've followed every lead I've turned up and I have gotten exactly *nowhere* on this serial killer story. If this out-of-body thing works, you could stop the murderer before he strikes again. You could bring this guy to justice. Who knows how many lives you'll save?"

Ruby shakes her head. "I really don't want to —"

"Please. Don't say no now."

"Honestly, Jessica, this is not the kind of thing I —"

Jessica puts her hand on Ruby's arm. "At least let me tell you what I've found. The evidence, I mean. And the sooner the better. Tonight?"

Evidence? Ruby puffs out her breath. "Tonight won't work for me. I'm going to a Halloween party."

"China's party?" Jessica asks eagerly. When Ruby nods, she says, "I'm invited, too. How about if we get together for an hour or so afterward?" She gives Ruby a beseeching look. "*Please,* Ruby. This is important."

Ruby considers. "Well, I suppose," she says finally, reluctantly. "We could find a quiet corner at China's house and —"

"No, let's not do that. There are things I want to show you on my computer. How about *after* the party? It won't take any more than an hour, I promise. And I'll be glad to come to your house."

With a sigh, Ruby gives in.

China and her husband, Mike McQuaid, live in a big Victorian house that is perfect for a party, with plenty of room for guests to gather around the table in the dining room or in the kitchen or the living room.

Or, on mild evenings, walk in the garden or sit on the front porch and watch twilight fall over the Texas Hill Country.

On this late-October night, Cass and China have arranged the serve-yourself party food — dips, chips, savory meatballs, snack mix, chicken wings, pepper poppers, and a variety of desserts — on the dining room table, with a Halloween centerpiece of pumpkins, black and orange candles, a black plastic skull and a clutter of realistic-looking spiders. In the kitchen, there are sodas, beer, wine, and a sangria punch bowl.

The guests all know each other, of course. China and Mike's kids are there: Caitie, now a pretty, petite fourteen; and Brian, a sophomore at UT, and his girlfriend, Casey. Blackie, McQuaid's business partner and fishing buddy, and Blackie's very pregnant wife Sheila. (Sheila keeps insisting that she is *not* carrying twins.) Neighbors Tom and Sylvia Banner: Tom volunteers as a ride-along deputy for the sheriff's office; Sylvia raises sheep — Gulf Coast Native sheep bred to tolerate the Hill Country's hot, humid weather — and sells their fleece. Sylvia has been in several of Ruby's tarot classes and is a frequent visitor at the Cave.

Ruby's daughter Amy and her partner Kate are there, too, along with Ruby's little granddaughter Grace, until Grace (who is dressed as a princess with a gold crown) disappears upstairs with Caitie, to play with her stuffed animal collection. Also there, many Pecan Springs friends. Cass, of course, and Lori Lowry, the weaver who rents the loft above the shops. Hark Hibler, the editor of the *Enterprise* and Jessica's boss. Attorney Charlie Lipman, who knows more of Pecan Springs' dirty little secrets than anybody else and somehow manages to keep them all under his hat. Bob Godwin, the owner of Bean's Bar and Grill, and Lila Jennings, from the Nueces Street Diner, who makes the best jelly doughnuts in the world. Oh, and Jessica. And Ruby, of course.

Some people are costumed. Sheila is a very round orange pumpkin, and her husband Blackie is a cowboy. Lori is a pirate, in a black silk blouse with a purple vest, a red sash, and skinny black pants tucked into tall purple boots. A pirate hat and a black eye patch make her look like the real thing. Cass is dressed as a medieval noblewoman in an elegant blue and silver tunic with fur trim. McQuaid is wearing a long-sleeved black T-shirt that says *Trust me, I'm a Ninja,* with black jeans and a Ninja sword at his belt, and China is a Ninja warrioress, in a very short black tunic, black tights, black elbow-length gloves, and wicked high-heeled black boots. Jessica is a bat, and Charlie Lipman, everybody's favorite lawyer, has come as Count Dracula, with a black cape and vampire fangs. ("Fitting," McQuaid says with a chuckle. "Lawyers are bloodsuckers.")

China's old-fashioned kitchen is large and high-ceilinged, with white-painted cabinets, windows onto the garden — invisible now in the October darkness — and a large table in the center of the room. Ruby is at the table, filling a glass with sangria from the punch bowl, when Hark comes up behind her. He is dressed as Nostradamus, in a black and red robe with white ruffled undersleeves, a gold medallion, and a Renaissance hat and gray wig.

He puts his hand on Ruby's shoulder. A quick flare of regret flashes through her, whether Hark's or hers, she can't be sure. Probably a blend of both, although her regret is different from his. Hark is a great guy, warm and generous, with a sharp intelligence she has always admired. The two of them have dated off and on for several years and Ruby has always enjoyed his friendship. But she has never been able to feel about him the way she knows he feels about her.

"Hey, Hark," she says, as lightly as she

can, and turns away from his hand.

"Hey, Ruby. Haven't seen you for a while." He regards her nearsightedly, since he isn't wearing his usual dark-rimmed glasses. He is taking in her gypsy costume: white off-the-shoulder blouse, a tiered multicolored cotton skirt with knee-high black boots, a couple of red and orange silk sashes, and a red silk scarf tied around her head. "As always, superlatively gorgeous. What's going on with you these days?"

In spite of herself, Ruby is pleased at the compliment. "Oh, just the usual," she says carelessly, although life hasn't seemed at all *usual* lately. "Everything going well at the newspaper?"

Hark bought the *Enterprise* from its local owners several years ago and has been working hard to keep the small-town paper alive and relevant in an era of online news. The job is made even more challenging because he insists on covering *all* the news, both good and bad. This is a seismic shift in editorial policy, for the previous publisher sanitized every story before the paper went to print, which made Pecan Springs look like the cleanest, coziest little town in Texas. "Cozy is comforting," Hark says, "but not when it's a lie."

So he prints stories that reveal the town's

gritty underside. The recent pot bust tha China and her neighbor Tom were involved in, for instance, or Jessica's series on Medicare fraud, or the story behind the death of a student documentary filmmaker. As a friend, Hark is gentle and easygoing. Bu journalistically speaking, he's fierce. He hates fake news. He tells it like it *really* is in Pecan Springs, which does not always go over very well with members of the Chamber of Commerce. The chamber, and many of the older residents of Pecan Springs prefer cozy.

Hark reaches down to snag a cold Lone Star longneck out of the beer cooler under the kitchen table. Over his shoulder, he says "You and Jessica had lunch today, I understand." Straightening, he slides Ruby a narrow-eyed glance. "Did she tell you about the story she's working on?"

"Maybe." Ruby is hedging. She doesn't want to rat Jessica out. "Which story is that?"

"The one about all those terminally il people who just keep dying." He twists the cap off his beer. "More accurately, who are being done in by some mysterious killer in some hitherto unexplained way, just because." He glugs his beer. "According to Jessica."

430

Smiling in spite of herself, Ruby raises her glass and takes a sip of sangria. "She might have mentioned something about it, yes."

"Well, you can forget it. She's obsessing, Ruby. She's desperate to find a subject for her next true crime book. But it's all nonsense, what she's doing. And it's dragging her away from her work. The work she gets paid to do. For *me*." His face is drawn into stern lines. "And if she doesn't stop, I predict that she's going to get herself into some serious trouble." Another glug. "As in getting herself fired."

"Fired?" Ruby is startled. "It's that bad?"

"It's that bad," Hark says grimly, wiping his mouth with Nostradamus' sleeve. "There's another young woman in the editorial room who could handle the cops-and-courts beat just as well as Jessica, and without all the drama. I am just about ready to let Heather take —"

"Pardon me, Ruby," says Sylvia Banner. "Let me step in here for just a moment."

Distracted from her conversation with Hark, Ruby moves away from the table to let Sylvia have her turn at the punch bowl. "Hey, Sylvia," she says. "Did Lori Lowry talk to you about getting another fleece?" Lori likes to use uncombed, untreated fleeces to demonstrate wool prep to the

431

students in her fiber classes. Sylvia's sheep produce a very fine, much-prized wool every bit as good as Merino.

"No, I haven't seen her," Sylvia says. "Is she here?"

Blond and sturdily built, with the broad forehead and Nordic coloring of her ancestry, Sylvia is a talented spinner and weaver who teaches workshops on natural plant dyes. She has also given several presentations on Scandinavian weaving to Ruby's weaving guild.

"I sheared in August and I have only a couple of fleeces left," she adds, filling her glass and putting the ladle back in the punch bowl. "If Lori wants one, she should let me know right away."

"She's here tonight," Ruby says. "She's a pirate. I saw her in the living room a few minutes ago, talking to China." She frowns. She is picking something up — a deep, deep sadness, rising from Sylvia like a chilly mist. Impulsively, she says, "Is everything okay, Sylvia?"

Sylvia shakes her head ruefully. "Thank you for asking, Ruby, but no, it's not. I lost my sister a few days ago. I can't seem to . . ." She bites her lip. "Well, you know. Things are pretty hard right now."

"Oh, dear!" Ruby is jolted. Sylvia's sister

Gretchen suffered from ALS — Lou Gehrig's disease, a progressive neurodegenerative disease that affects nerve cells in the brain and the spinal cord. She had taken a couple of classes in astrology at the Cave, and she had always had intelligent, thoughtful questions. "I'm sorry, Sylvia. So sorry! I suppose, though, it must have been expected. I don't remember seeing her at the shop recently."

Sylvia shook her head again, more emphatically. "Actually, it was a surprise. Of course, with ALS, nothing is really predictable. But she was only in the middle stage of the disease, and lately, she's seemed better. Then all of a sudden, *boom.* A heart attack, and she's gone. Completely unexpected."

Sylvia's grief is still fresh and raw, and Ruby can feel it. "Of course," she says, thinking that losing a sister would be terrible, no matter the circumstances. And Gretchen was a lovely woman. "I'm sure you'll miss her."

"I already do." Sylvia smiles sadly. "She was always amazingly cheerful. In spite of her illness — or maybe because of it — she was able to show the rest of us how to be grateful for the little things in life. Things we don't always notice, or that don't seem to count for much." She sighs. "Tom and I decided to put off the funeral until my parents can be here. But I need to start cleaning out her apartment tomorrow. I'm not looking forward to it."

"That's always such a sad job," Ruby replies. "I've got to be at the shop tomorrow, but if there's any way I can help, let me know."

Beside Ruby, Hark shifts his weight from one foot to the other, and Sylvia glances at him, suddenly realizing that he is there.

"Oh, sorry," she says, turning away. "I've interrupted your conversation. I'll go look for Lori."

"No problem," Hark says politely. "Sorry to hear about your sister."

"Thanks," Sylvia replies, with a brief smile. When she has gone, Hark clears his throat.

"We were talking about obsession," he says. Somebody laughs loudly, and he raises his voice. "*Jessica's* obsession."

Ruby leans a hip against the kitchen counter. "But isn't that what good reporters do? Obsess about their stories?"

"Of course." He moves closer to make room for Tom Banner, who is adding another six-pack to the beer cooler. "But good reporters have the ability to obsess about more than one story at a time. Jessica is obsessing on this one when she needs to be obsessing on a couple of other important assignments." He scowls. "The *Enterprise* isn't the *Washington Post,* you know. We have only four reporters, and two of them are part-time. While Jessie is off on a wild goose chase, the rest of the gang is putting in extra hours." He drains his beer bottle. "I know that she wants to get you involved, one way or another. I don't know what she has in mind, but I thought I'd mention it to you. In case you have any influence with that young lady."

"Influence, ha," Ruby says with a short laugh, remembering their conversation. "And anyway, you're her boss. You have more influence than I do. Aren't *you* supposed to tell her what you want?"

"I have," Hark says glumly. "Time and time again, in fact. I am just about at the end of my tether with her. If she doesn't pull herself out of this obsession and pay attention to her assignments, I'll find somebody else to take her beat."

"Wow," Ruby says quietly. "You sound serious."

Hark's face is stormy. "I *am* serious. Friends don't let friends drive off a cliff, Ruby. Don't encourage Jessica. She's wasting her time on this wacko serial killer story. It's a dud, a bomb, a big loser. There's nothing to it."

A tall, dark-haired cowboy wearing a black hat, chaps, and a gun belt with a pearl-handled revolver comes around the table — Sheila's husband Blackie. "Hey, Hark," he says genially. "Done any serious fishing lately?"

Hark barks a laugh. "Too busy working. How about you? Caught any crooks lately?"

"Matter of fact, we have," Blackie says with an easy grin. "McQuaid and I chased down a death-row escapee in a salvage yard in south San Antonio not too long ago. But we let the local cops make the arrests. We figured they could use the credit."

"Sometimes works out better that way," Hark agrees. He makes a sour face. "But if you ever get tired of playing cops and robbers, maybe you'd like to sign on as a reporter."

He casts a meaningful glance at Ruby. "I sure could use another one."

CHAPTER FOUR

It is nearly ten when Ruby thanks China for the hospitality and drives home to her Painted Lady, which takes the cake as the gaudiest historic home in a neighborhood of Victorian homes. During the day, the Lady's vibrant colors — purple siding, fuchsia shutters, porches and gingerbread trim painted spring green, smoke gray, and passionate plum — make her a standout among her more conservative neighbors.

Tonight, the lights Ruby has left on give her a warm welcome-home feeling, and as she unlocks the front door and goes in, she is greeted by the familiar scents of lemon oil floor polish and rose and lavender potpourri. She feels as she always does, that her Lady has been waiting for her to arrive and settle in for the rest of the evening. She can almost hear the house contentedly humming the old 1970s song: "Our house is a very, very fine house . . ."

As she hangs up her jacket on the coat tree in the hall, Pagan jumps out of his special corner of the living room sofa and curls around her ankles, politely requesting a small bowl of nice warm milk, *please, if it's not too much trouble.* Pagan is an all-black cat who showed up one stormy night the previous spring. Having decided that Ruby's house was his new home and that Ruby was his new assignment, he moved in and got on with the job.

"No trouble at all, but you'll have to wait until I've changed," she tells him, and goes upstairs to trade her gypsy costume for faded green sweats. Expecting Jessica, she goes back downstairs to the kitchen, put the kettle on for tea, and heats milk for Pagan, who dips his pink tongue into it and rapidly makes it disappear. Then, while she gets out the green china teapot and the peppermint tea, he goes to sit beside the back door, staring at it expectantly.

Ruby's friend Sophia says that all black cats are psychic, but that Pagan got an extra-large dose. Ruby believes it. She often catches him watching her with a look in his eye that makes her suspect that he is reading her mind. And there he sits, parked beside the back door, waiting. Jessica is one of his favorites.

438

When she arrives, she greets him before she speaks to Ruby. "Oh, hello, Pagan!" she exclaims, bending over to pat his head. "Handsome fellow, you are. Bad-ass midnight kitty."

Pagan purrs, naturally, and arches under her hand, showing off his sleek fur and his remarkable black tail. He likes nothing better than to be complimented by a pretty woman.

Ruby pours tea into two squat pottery mugs, watermelon-green on the outside and watermelon-pink with black seeds on the inside — a gift from Amy and Kate. She is remembering what Hark said about obsession earlier that evening. He is a pretty level-headed guy. Plus, he is Jessica's boss. It probably wouldn't be a good idea to encourage Jessica to pursue what he sees as a wild goose chase.

"Fab green eyes," Jessica murmurs, and Pagan cranks up the volume of his purr a notch or two.

"Laser eyes," Ruby says. "If you mess with that cat, he will turn you into particles of dust and send you floating into the ether."

"You're making that up," Jessica says, taking a laptop out of her bag. She is still wearing her bat costume: a fleecy black bat-wing sweatshirt with perky bat ears, black tights

and black stiletto heels, as well as black bat
dangle earrings. She has taken off the black
mask and hood she wore at the party, and
her short straw-colored hair is sticking out
all over her head.

Ruby puts the mugs of tea on the table.
"Let's stay in the kitchen, shall we?"

"Love this space," Jessica says. She glances
around, taking in the watermelon-themed
room: watermelon border and red striped
wallpaper, red kitchen table with chairs
painted green and red, with little black
seeds painted on the seats, and a watermelon rug. "It's so cheerful. And yummy."

"I'm thinking of redoing it," Ruby says,
pulling out a pair of chairs. "Maybe oranges
and lemons instead of watermelons. Wallpaper, paint, a new rug. I love yellow. And
orange. And it's time. It's been watermelon
for a couple of years."

"Yellow suits you," Jessica says. "Lots of
energy in yellow." She puts the computer
on the table, opens it, and presses the power
button. "I want to show you some emails
and interview transcripts. And photos and
document scans."

"Before we get started," Ruby says, "Hark
wanted me to tell you —"

"I know." Jessica sighs. "I saw you talking
to him. He told you I'm obsessing."

Ruby tried for a no-nonsense tone. "You're not only obsessing, you're neglecting to obsess about your boss' obsessions."

"I know that, too. But the thing is —"

"The thing is that you can manage only one obsession at a time. Right?"

"Too true, I'm afraid." Jessica combs her fingers through her hair, tidying it somewhat. "But I understand Hark's issues, honest I do. I'll try to do better. I promise."

Ruby hesitates, wondering how much she should say. "Actually, he told me that there's somebody else on staff who can handle your beat. He even used the F word. As in fired," she adds hurriedly, so there won't be any mistake.

"Heather McNally." Jessica's mouth tightens. "She's been angling for my job for weeks now. She's a good reporter, but she spends too much time sucking up to the boss. And you know Hark. He likes attractive women who pay attention to him." She straightens her shoulders. "But that's not important. Let's sit down, Ruby. What's really important is what I'm about to show you."

Feeling guiltily that she hasn't done justice to Hark's concerns, Ruby sits. Pagan leaps lightly into her lap and settles comfortably, purring. Reaching over him, she spoons

441

honey into her tea and stirs. "Emails and transcripts and scans, huh? Is there a quiz afterward?"

"Could be. So pay attention." Jessica logs on and begins to type. A moment later, an email appears on the screen. "It began seven months ago, when I found this in my inbox. It came last March 14, addressed to me at my *Enterprise* email address. I get a lot of really bizarro emails at the newspaper, but this one stood out."

She reads it aloud. " 'Dear Jessica, Dr. Death is my hero. Like him, I have managed the passings of a number of terminally ill people, and I can tell you that their deaths (involuntary euthanasia) were a release for both the sufferer and the family. Death with dignity! I am passionate about this cause, and I think it would make a good story. You'll be hearing more from me.' It's signed Azrael."

Ruby feels a cold chill in the pit of her stomach. "Wow," she whispers, leaning forward to read the email for herself. " 'Dr. Death.' That's what the newspapers called Jack Kevorkian, wasn't it? Dr. Death. And this guy — Azrael — he's saying that he has actually *killed* people?"

"Right. Jack Kevorkian claimed to have assisted in at least a hundred and thirty deaths. But he practiced what he called *voluntary* euthanasia, where the terminally ill patient says 'I want to die' and pushes the button that administers the medication that does the job. Which is *not* legal in Texas, by the way." Jessica pauses. "And as you can see, that isn't what this guy is claiming. He calls what he's doing 'involuntary euthanasia,' which is —"

"Murder," Ruby says. In her lap, Pagan twitches the tip of his tail.

"Exactly." Jessica's voice is flinty. "Azrael, whoever he is, is confessing to murder."

Pagan decides it's time to go outdoors. He meows, jumps down from Ruby's lap, and heads for his kitty door.

"Maybe Azrael is just blowing smoke," Ruby says. "It's easy to make claims that aren't true, especially in an anonymous email."

"Of course," Jessica says with an emphasis that makes her bat earrings dance. "My first thought was that this came from some unhappy, insecure little guy who was trying to pump up his baby ego by pretending to be somebody important. The *Enterprise* is a magnet," she adds ruefully. "We may be just a small-town newspaper, but we attract crazies by the dozens."

"Everybody's looking for fifteen minutes

of fame, I suppose," Ruby says.

"Thirty, if they can get it. Better yet, an hour." Jessica picks up her mug and sips her tea. "When I asked Hark to take a look at the email, he said he remembered getting a couple from this same guy — Azrael. They started arriving after he ran an opinion piece on assisted suicide. He had already decided that the sender was a kook, so he said I should just block him. If I replied to the jerk, it would encourage him. And this creep is obviously looking for a story. He wants somebody to write about him."

Ruby thinks about what Hark said earlier that evening. She's wasting her time on this wacko serial killer story. It's a dud, a bomb, a big loser. There's nothing to it.

"But you didn't block him," Ruby says. If she knows Jessica, Hark's opinion only fueled her fire.

"Nope. I was curious. And concerned. I mean, what if Azrael *isn't* just some nut job wanting his ego petted?" She takes another sip of tea and sets her mug down.

"So I replied, asking for details. You know, a talk-to-me email, inviting him to tell me more. But my reply bounced, and when I traced his email, I found out that he was using a virtual private network. This guy was hiding his internet service provider's address. In fact, he has used a *different* VPN for all five of the emails he's sent me. He's going to a fair amount of trouble to stay out of touch."

"You've got to give him an A for persistence," Ruby murmurs.

"You bet. After that first one in March, his emails arrived in April, June, August, and last week. Each one announces a new instance of 'involuntary euthanasia.' I've replied to each, and my replies have all bounced. Obviously, Azrael only wants to tell me stuff. He doesn't want to answer my questions."

"Azrael," Ruby says thoughtfully, staring at the email on the screen. She recognizes the name. "Azrael is the name of the Angel of Death."

"That's him," Jessica says. "When I looked him up, I found out that he is the archangel who's assigned to carry the soul away from the body. Sort of like an escort service for the dead." She takes a deep breath. "Sorry," she mutters. "I don't mean to mock. This whole thing is just so . . . over-the-top."

Ruby nods, intrigued in spite of herself. 'But the name Azrael — that fits with 'Dr. Death,' doesn't it? And I seem to remember a serial killer who was called the Angel of Death. Wasn't he a hospital worker who killed his patients?"

"Actually, there have been several, as I learned when I started doing research." Jessica leans back in her chair and crosses her bat-wing arms. "Donald Harvey was a hospital orderly who claimed to have killed eighty-seven patients back in the nineteen-seventies and eighties. He mostly used cyanide and arsenic, to 'end their suffering,' he said. Then there was the VA nurse — a woman — who injected her victims with a heart stimulant. And the doctor — Michael Swango — who was accused of killing sixty people in the US and six in Zimbabwe. There was a best-selling book written about him." She pauses. "But all of these murderers were carrying out their so-called mercy killings in the places where they worked. This guy — Azrael — makes house calls."

Intrigued in spite of herself, Ruby lets out her breath. "So what has he told you?"

"Very little," Jessica says. "He never identifies his victims or where they're located. But he has said he *doesn't* kill in hospitals." She brings up a second email. "This is the one he sent me in April."

Ruby leans forward and reads from the screen, aloud. " 'I've just helped another sufferer and his family escape the anguish of a painful death. I could give you the details, Jessica, but I think you'll appreciate the story more if you dig it out on your own. And to make the challenge even more interesting for that book I know you want to write, I'll tell you that my clients — as I like to think of them — are *not* patients in a hospital. I think you'll agree that this makes the story even more interesting.' "

Ruby frowns. " 'That book I know you want to write.' *Are* you writing a book, Jess? If you are, how does he know?"

"He's reading my blog," Jessica says. "Like lots of journalists, I blog about my projects — stories I'm working on, stories I'm looking for. I invite readers to send me tips, leads, ideas. And they do, lots of them. Most of the time the story they want me to write has already been done, or it's not worth doing. I thank the sender and hit the delete key. But every now and then, a reader's suggestion pans out. Like that article I wrote last month about the funds that disappeared from the Pecan Springs animal shelter. That tip came from a reader, and now the manager is about to be indicted."

Ruby looks at the email again. "It sounds almost as if Azrael is taunting you. Daring you to start investigating him."

"Oh, he can be far more in-your-face than that," Jessica says, going back to the key-

board "Here's what he sent me in June.'
She pulls up a third email and reads it.

" 'What's *wrong* with you, Jessica? Why
aren't you jumping on this story? You can't
be much of a crime reporter if you can't
locate my victims. Do you want me to send
you a list of names?' And here's the latest
one. 'A sufferer has died with dignity right
on your own doorstep. I'm in the process of
selecting another, but you're way behind
me. If you're serious about writing our
book, you'd better get started.' "

"*Our* book?" Ruby is startled.

"Yes. He is now pretending that the two
of us are involved in this creepy collaboration. He knows I'm interested in writing a
book. I know he's committing these murders
because he wants me to write about them."
Jessica's eyes are dark. "The killing and the
writing — in Azrael's mind, they're linked.
He's making me complicit, Ruby. I *hate*
that, and I don't want to think about it. But
I'm half afraid he's right. Media attention
can encourage people to do weird things. I
worry that it gives psychopaths like Azrael
just what they're looking for: a big stage
and a bright spotlight."

"I suppose you've shown these emails to
Hark," Ruby says slowly.

Jessica shakes her head. "He doesn't want

to read them. He still thinks this is just some crazy who gets his jollies by yanking my chain. But he could be saying that because he doesn't want me to spend time on the investigation. We're short on reporters with experience. All of us are overloaded with assignments."

"Maybe Hark is right," Ruby parries, remembering what he'd said to her just a couple of hours before. *Friends don't let friends drive off a cliff.* "What makes you think Azrael isn't just another lonely blog reader looking for attention from an attractive girl crime reporter?"

Jessica turns down the corners of her mouth. "Well, for a while there, I pretty much agreed with Hark. He's had years of experience with people who are willing to make up all kinds of stuff just to get a story." She paused. "But something happened in May — a month after I got the second email — that convinced me that this is the real deal. And scared the livin' bejeebers out of me."

She went back to the keyboard and brought up a photo of a sweet-faced, gray-haired woman in green scrubs with a stethoscope around her neck, bending over a frail elderly woman in a bed. Beside the bed was a table with a vase of yellow roses, framed family photos, and a digital clock.

"This episode took place in San Marcos," Jessica said. "The lady in scrubs is a private duty nurse named Adrienne Mitchell, and that's her patient, Mrs. Bernard. The patient is dead now — she had stage five Parkinson's. Adrienne worked the night shift in Mrs. Bernard's residence. In early May, she heard a strange noise in her patient's bedroom, about two in the morning. When she went to check, she surprised an intruder, dressed in a dark hooded cape, standing beside Mrs. Bernard's bed. She stopped him from doing what he had come to do, and he fled. But as he climbed out the window — the same way he must have come in — he dropped a syringe. It was later found to contain potassium chloride."

Ruby blinked. "Potassium chloride? Isn't that what they use to —"

"Yes. It's one of a three-drug cocktail that is used in executions. Potassium poisoning causes cardiac arrest." Jessica goes back to the keyboard and pulls up an image. "The syringe wasn't all he left behind. Look at this, Ruby."

On the screen is a color photograph of a gilt-edged card: an image of a statuesque, forbidding-looking angel with two pairs of black wings and grasping, skeletal hands.

450

Like a medieval monk, the angel is shrouded in a black cloak with a hood that completely obscures his face. The name *Azrael* appears in blood-red letters across the bottom of the card.

"Amazing," Ruby whispers. She stares at the image on Jessica's laptop. She recognizes the card. It is from a deck of angel oracle cards — cards used for divination and personal guidance — that she once carried in the shop. This particular deck didn't sell very well, probably because most of the images were ominous and unsettling. That had been quite a while ago, though, and she no longer carries it. She doesn't even remember the name of the artist.

"It's a compelling image, isn't it?" Jessica says. "The nurse found it on the floor, next to the window. She got on the phone right away and reported a home invasion. The cops were there within minutes and conducted the usual investigation. The intruder must have worn gloves, for there were no prints on the syringe, the card, or the window. None of the neighbors reported a strange vehicle in the area. There had been no previous threats. Mrs. Bernard had no enemies, and no great fortune to tempt beneficiaries. Everybody was mystified. So that was the end of it, pretty much, until . . ."

She hits a few keys and brings up a scan of a newspaper clipping. "A week or so after this weird break-in, Adrienne — the nurse — was interviewed by my friend Crystal Lessing, who is a reporter for the *San Marcos Daily Record.* During the interview, Adrienne mentioned finding the Azrael card, and Crystal quoted her. She also published that photo of the card. I happened to pick up that issue of the *Record* and saw it."

"The card itself," Ruby says. "Do you have it? Or maybe you know where we could get it?"

Jessica shakes her head. "The San Marcos cops took it, along with the syringe. I suppose it's still locked up in their evidence room. Why?"

"Just wondering," Ruby says. She isn't quite ready to tell Jessica that if she had the card, she might be able to use it to reach out to Azrael. Assuming that her psychic skills are functioning, that is. Which is not necessarily a safe assumption. She clears her throat. "So what happened after that?"

"A couple of days after the interview appeared in the paper and on the *Record*'s Facebook page, Crystal got a phone call from a man in Seguin — Charles Bradbury — and an email from a woman — Sandra Lewis — in New Braunfels. Both of them saw her story. And both of them told her that they had found identical cards in the possession of family members who had just died."

Ruby's skin prickles. "I suppose you talked to them."

"You suppose right," Jessica says. "By this time, I was thinking that there might really be something to Azrael's emails. As it happened, Crystal had just taken maternity leave. She wasn't doing any follow-up on her story, so she gave me the names of the people who contacted her." She types in a command and a Word document comes up on the screen. "You probably won't want to take the time to read this now, but I can send you the file. It's the transcript of the interviews I did with Charles Bradbury and Sandra Lewis."

"I'd rather you just tell me," Ruby says. She picks up the teapot and refills their mugs. "In a nutshell." She glances up at the clock. "It's been a long day."

Jessica smiles faintly. "In a nutshell, their stories are surprisingly similar. Mr. Bradbury was taking care of his brother Buddy, who suffered from muscular dystrophy.

Buddy, who lived in Seguin, was only thirty six. Two years ago, on the day before Christmas, Bradbury went to help his brother dress for breakfast and found him dead. A heart attack, the doctor said. Bradbury discovered a card — similar to the one dropped in the attack on Mrs. Bernard and signed with the name Azrael — propped against the mirror on the dresser in Buddy's room. He noticed it because it seemed so unusual. What's more, he didn't remember seeing it there before his brother died. Crystal's story brought this to mind, so he contacted her."

"And Sandra Lewis?"

"Mrs. Lewis was staying in New Braunfels with her mother, who had stage four breast cancer. The mother died in her sleep on Valentine's Day, about four or five months after the diagnosis. The family couldn't afford nursing care, so Mrs. Lewis and her sister had been taking turns staying with their mom. They were relieved, for her sake and their own, that things hadn't dragged out for months and months. The family doctor issued a death certificate without an autopsy. Mrs. Lewis kept saying that they knew it was only a matter of time, but she couldn't help but feel guilty."

"I get that," Ruby says softly. "Feeling

guilty about feeling relieved, I mean." Her mother had been diagnosed with Alzheimer's several years ago. She is well cared for at the Castle Oaks senior facility in Pecan Springs, but there are many dark days. Ruby understands how death might bring relief.

Jessica is going on. "Mrs. Lewis found the Azrael card under her mother's pillow. Nearly knocked me off my feet,' she said. She couldn't imagine where it came from, especially since it wasn't there the day before, when she made up the bed with fresh linen. There had been no visitors, and her mother hadn't been out of the house for nearly three months. That scary card wasn't the kind of thing her mother would want, according to Mrs. Lewis." Jessica smiles slightly. "She thinks an angel should have a halo and fluffy white wings and wear a white robe, not a scruffy black hoodie and *black* wings."

Ruby thinks that Seguin and New Braunfels are only about fifteen miles apart — and only about twenty miles from San Marcos. She asks, "What became of the cards?"

"Thrown away. When they read Crystal's interview with Adrienne, both were pretty deeply disturbed, because that card — the one Adrienne found — was dropped during a break-in. And because of the syringe, o: course. Charles Bradbury told me he'd ever debated whether he should talk to the Seguin police. But in the end, he decided no to. His brother had died more than two years before, and his body was cremated 'Even if somebody did get into Buddy': room and do something bad to him,' he said, 'it was too damned late to do anything about it.' " Jessica pauses. "When I interviewed them, I asked each of them to sketch the cards, as they remembered them." She keyed in a command. "Here are the sketches."

Two side-by-side pencil drawings of Azrael — both similar to the card dropped during the San Marcos attack — appear or the computer monitor. Both bear the word *Azrael* at the bottom.

Ruby studies the drawings for a moment but they don't tell her anything special. "Sc you've uncovered three instances where Azrael seems to show up," she says. "Deaths ir San Marcos, Seguin, and New Braunfels Were there more?"

"Yes," Jessica says without hesitation "Crystal gave me the photo of the card that appeared in the *Daily Record.* I emailed i to all the police departments and sheriffs offices in a seventy-mile radius — as fa:

north as Austin and as far south as San Antonio. In the email, I asked whether anybody in the department had ever seen such a thing. The card, I mean."

"And?"

"And I got two affirmatives." Jessica takes a deep breath. "An officer in Fredericksburg remembered seeing a card like that when his uncle — who had brain cancer — died the previous spring. He remembered it because it caused quite a bit of family discussion. Nobody recognized it. They couldn't figure out where it came from."

"And the other affirmative?"

Jessica pulled up a hand-drawn sketch of an Azrael card lying at an angle across a solitaire layout. "A sheriff's deputy in Hays County sent me this. At the time — this was several years ago — he was working as an emergency med tech. He had been called to a rural home just outside of Wimberley. The deceased had been ill with lung cancer. Unlike the others, he died during the daytime, while he was sitting in his wheel-chair, playing solitaire on a tray table. The EMT saw the odd card and remembered it. When I asked him if he could recall when this happened, he dug around in his mem-ory and produced the date. Bet you can't guess what it was."

"His birthday?"

Jessica blinks at her, then her face clears "Oh, right. You're psychic."

Ruby chuckles. "Just a good guess. People always remember things that happen on their birthdays."

Jessica shrugs. "Well, anyway, that's wher it was. The officer in Fredericksburg coulc also give me a date, since the guy who diec was his uncle. And on top of those two, I've found two more. These came from ads I placed — a sixteen-year-old girl who hac leukemia and an elderly man suffering from metastasized cancer. Here's the list."

She brings it up on the screen — place, name, sex, and disease, in date order, from earliest to latest. "As you can see, there are eight instances where an Azrael card was found at the scene of the death, including the break-in in San Marcos. So we have seven murders and one attempted murder. The victims all died in residential settings, none of them in a hospital. They were al alone when they died, which happened at night, with the exception of the guy in the wheelchair. Their ages range from sixteen — the girl with leukemia — to sixty-nine the woman with breast cancer. The earliest occurred three years ago in Pecan Springs, the most recent in Marble Falls, early last nonth." She quickly copies the list, pastes it nto an email, and types Ruby's address in he "To" box. "There. Now you'll have the ist, too."

"But you didn't get any cards," Ruby says egretfully.

"No cards, sorry. Is that important?" She rowns. "Do you need a card to get into Azael's mind?"

"I'm not sure," Ruby says. She doesn't want to think about getting into Azrael's nind. It would be like falling into a filthy esspool. "You keep saying 'he.' You think Azrael is a man?"

"I've been assuming he is," Jessica says, "if only because eighty percent of all serial killers are male. But I don't know that for sure, of course. I suspect that the killer njected his — or her — victims with potasium chloride, since that was in the syringe hat was dropped in the San Marcos case, when the killer was interrupted and fled." She pauses. "It doesn't take a lot of strength o give an injection. Nurses do it all the ime. Yes, Azrael could be a woman."

Ruby bites her lip. "Do you think these are the only victims?"

"I'm afraid not. These are just the ones I've found so far. Last week, I placed ads in he personals column of several newspapers in Central Texas." She brings up a few line of text: *If you have found or received a car(picturing Azrael, the Angel of Death, in as sociation with the recent death of a friend o loved one, please contact JessicaNel(PSEnterprise.com.* "I've also put the ad or Craigslist and in the weekly shopper news paper in towns in the Central Texas area.' She sighs. "Yeah, I know. I'm obsessing."

Ruby nods. She gets that, and she can se(why Hark is concerned. But she under stands the reason for Jessica's urgency now and the skepticism she felt earlier is gone Jessica clearly has reason to believe that a killer is out there, targeting the sick and dy ing, the most vulnerable. And if Jessie i right, he will keep on doing it until he i: stopped.

"Why did you pick those cities?" she asks

Jessica shrugs. "It's a needle-in-a-haystacl situation, isn't it? For all I know, this kille may be murdering people down in Browns ville or up in Dallas. If there are othe victims and I can find them, they may holc the key."

"The key to —"

"To his method of selection." Distractedly Jessica runs a hand through her hair, rum pling it. "I've been reading about serial kill ers. Most don't murder at random. The choose their victims according to race or gender or physical characteristics — there's something that links every choice. But the 'something' may be extremely subtle. That's why serial killings may seem haphazard."

"Haphazard?"

"Yes. No connections among them — and even, in some cases, no bodies. Some serial killers have murdered a dozen people before a victim was discovered and an investigation was opened. It's a matter of working backward to try to establish the pattern and fill in the blanks, the way the police tried to do with the Golden State Killer out in California. Have you read about him? He wasn't caught until they traced his DNA through one of those genealogical sites."

Ruby frowns. "But surely there's enough here to interest the police, Jessie. You ought to take this to them. Show them what you have."

"And they would handle it how, exactly?" Jessica turns her hands palms-up in a so-what gesture. "The pattern seems clear enough in hindsight — Azrael is killing people who are about to die here in Central Texas. But how does that help, going forward? What are the cops going to do? Compile a list of everybody who's terminally ill in all the neighboring counties? Patrol

461

their houses? Post a guard? Or maybe they should notify the public, so everybody can panic." She chuckles wryly. "It's not the kind of case the police can solve, Ruby. No, unless they catch this killer in the act. And how likely is *that*?"

Ruby has to agree with Jessica's assessment. She studies the list on the screen, which — laid out in black and white — makes her shiver. So many people. So many innocent people.

From: JessicaNel@PSEnterprise.com
To: RubyWilcox@CrystalCave.com
Subject: Victim List

Pecan Springs: female, 27, ovarian cancer

Seguin: male, 36, ALS (Charles Bradbury's brother)

New Braunfels: female, 69, breast cancer (Sandra Lewis' mother)

Fredericksburg: male, 47, brain cancer (uncle of Fredericksburg officer)

Wimberley: male, 52, lung cancer (EM tech solitaire)

Boerne: male, 63, bladder cancer

Marble Falls: female, 16, leukemia

San Marcos: female, 68, Parkinson's (unsuccessful attempt)

Ruby takes a deep breath. "Okay, Jessica. Let's say you're right and the emails you're getting are related to these deaths. Let's also say that these eight — and maybe others you haven't identified yet — are murders and an attempted murder. And that this killer has created an angel-of-mercy motive to justify what he's doing."

"Exactly," Jessica says. "I don't buy that death-with-dignity bullshit, not for a minute. I believe Azrael enjoys killing for killing's sake. But like other serial killers, he doesn't kill just anybody. He needs a *reason.* So he's decided to do it in a way that minimizes the chance that he'll be discovered. So far, he's chosen terminally ill people who are living at home, most of them with family members as caregivers. All of his victims were alone and all but one of the killings were at night. He must be casing the scenes carefully, choosing situations where he thinks he will be able to get in, do his dirty work, and get out without being spotted."

Ruby nods. "The San Marcos situation, where the nurse interrupted him, was an anomaly, sounds like."

"Yes, and it gives us the first clear clue. Without the syringe and the card, we wouldn't know any of this. We wouldn't even know it was happening." Jessica shakes her head. "That's what makes this so damned frustrating, Ruby. All we can do is wait and watch."

"But watch for *what*?" Ruby says in a wondering tone. "Do we question every obituary?"

"Exactly. We don't even know for sure when he's killed someone, because the deaths aren't recognized as murders. Until, that is, he tells me what he's done. But even then, he doesn't tell me who. Or where or when. He's pretending he wants me to find out — which he surely doesn't. He's just taunting me."

Ruby thinks for a moment. "Have you done any background work on the victims? Do they share the same doctor? Maybe they've been to the same hospital. Or maybe they use the same pharmacy. Somewhere, somehow, Azrael must have access to a database of names, addresses, maybe even diagnoses. There has to be *some* connection among them."

"I've done as much background work as I can," Jessica says, "but it's hard to know the right questions to ask. I can tell you that the victims had different doctors. Two were patients in the same hospital but several years apart. The others had been patients in

lifferent hospitals. The towns they lived in
re too far apart — they couldn't have used
he same pharmacy. There was no common
hospice supervision. And no common home
nursing care connection."

"Well, you're the one who's been working
on this," Ruby says. "If you can't see any
way to link the victims, except through Azael, nobody else can."

Jessica shakes her head and her large bat
earrings dance. "Not true, Ruby. *You* can."

Ruby presses her lips together, feeling
slightly sick.

"Look." Jessica leans closer. "Here's what
I know. In the Montgomery kidnapping, you
had some sort of out-of-body psychic experience that took you into the victim's mind.
You got her to describe her surroundings.
You got her to tell you her kidnapper's
name. With that, it was easy to find where
she was being held. You did it in that
instance. You can do it in this one. You can
tell me who he's planning to kill next."

"Let me get this straight," Ruby says. "You
want me to —"

She breaks off, frowning. "But I can't do
that, Jessie. I was able to intervene with Allison because I was personally involved from
the beginning — from *before* the beginning,
with those dreams. But here, I have no

465

physical connection to anyone or anything. The evidence you have is all in your computer. Can you see? I'm completely out o touch, so to speak."

Jessica pulls her mouth down. "So wha kind of evidence would you need?"

"If you could find an Azrael card that the killer left behind, maybe I could help. O maybe not. I just don't know." Ruby make a face. "One of the things I'm learning about this psychic stuff is that it comes and goes. I mean, I'm *unreliable,* Jessie. I'm wrong at least as often as I'm right, maybe more. Sophia, my teacher, says I'll improve with practice. But she also says that most o the time, the best any psychic can do is oper a door to what's beyond, so to speak. We can never control what comes through, or when, or how much. If I can help, I will But don't count on me." She repeats it slowly. "Don't count on me."

Jessica looks discouraged. "I understand Ruby. But I'm not ready to give up. Can keep you posted on anything more I learr about this? Maybe something will come through."

"I guess so," Ruby says. "Just remember You can't trust me. I —"

The kitty door swings open and Pagar comes in, carrying something in his mouth